FOUND in NIGHT

BEN ALDERSON

OFTOMES PUBLISHING
UNITED KINGDOM

KIRSTY, FOR ALWAYS BEING MY ROCK.

CHAPTER
ONE

THE CORPSE WAS caught in a silent scream.

It was bent, arms and legs pinned awkwardly to the trunk of the giant tree before me. And it wasn't the only body. I stood in the clearing of the forest, Nyah at my side, staring at the many dead nailed to the monstrous trees. I counted twelve. Twelve innocent lives stolen, their bodies hung up like decoration. My stomach twisted and turned. The forest, which only moments before had held me in grand awe, now filled my mind with horror.

Golden blood dripped down the rusty brown bark. The same smeared blood covered each body; deliberate marks across their ashen skin.

Whoever had killed the elves had to have been strong. Disturbed. It had taken time and effort. They were hanging statues, trapped in the pain of their final moments, mouths hanging wide with blood stained teeth. Nesta, the Alorian High Guard, had warned me of bandits and thugs waiting for wandering souls, but these murders were different.

The sun shone upon the many Sigils etched into the forearms of each of the dead. Marks I had seen before.

"Druid marks." Nesta echoed what I was thinking, fiddling with the silver acorn that hung from the chain around her neck. "They're exactly the same on the body of that missing Healer who turned up two days ago."

As Nesta mentioned the elfin woman, we all froze. Meryl was one of many missing elves to turn up covered in marks. Her fragile, broken body was found floating in the riverways below Kandilin, a sigil much like those before us etched into her bronze arm.

"And the wound is fresh..." Nyah whispered, using the tip of her sharpened knife to move the dangling tunic which half-covered it. "Whoever did this made sure they had enough time to mark each of the bodies..."

"You have sharp eyes." Nesta walked towards the closest of the bodies and pulled a short, silver bone dagger from her belt. "I shall take this back to compare. It is clear this mark has importance, or why else would they craft them?"

"Because the Druid knew we would find it. It's a message," Nyah said, low and urgent.

Nesta ran the dagger down the arm. Her face contorted in discomfort as she sliced the skin surrounding the sigil, sinew and blood dripping as she pulled it away. I looked away and kept my gaze on Nyah, who was still watching. The sound almost made my morning's food spill onto the forest bed.

To distract myself, I connected to my air, feeling around the dark belly of the forest that imprisoned us. I reached past the four Alorian guards and Nesta, then Nyah who stood beside me. Spreading my reach as far as my power allowed, I searched for life. Each time I used my power, instinct took over. My awareness swam amongst the sea of trees. I brushed against every sun-kissed leaf, bark and twig. Lost to the group, I gave into my element. I was about to retract when I felt a slight shift in the wind. A warning.

"We're not alone," I whispered, pulling back into my consciousness. The hairs on my arms stood on end, a sure sign my instincts were right.

Nesta spared a glance at me then raised her hand in a signal. Within seconds, the guards were moving. They made no sound as they ran across the forest bed towards the trees closest. One by one they crawled like cats up the rough bark before them until they were concealed in the heavy, thick foliage above. I raised a hand and sent a volley of air across the forest bed. My action moved the leaves in a swirl until all footprints were covered beneath a fresh layer of debris.

They left Nyah and me alone in the clearing of the forest just as we'd planned; although I had hoped this wouldn't have been necessary. Since arriving in Kandilin, the Druid's threat loomed over us. Everyday there was a possibility he would attack. The rush of my blood told me this was what was coming for us.

"How many?" Nyah asked, already crouched with a hand on her sword. She, like Nesta and the guards, was dressed in the silvers and whites, her wild, red hair pinned from her face. The days in Kandilin had changed her appearance. The excess activity every day had carved out her cheekbones and pointed her jaw.

"I couldn't tell. Something didn't feel right when—"

Nyah raised a hand, silencing me. She closed her eyes, her ginger brows knotted. I'd seen this face of concentration back on the Island when she located Gallion and Hadrian during the Druid's ambush.

"I don't feel anyone's emotion, but something is definitely not right." Nyah kept her eyes closed as she relayed what she felt.

"He is relying on us to find it." My mind passed to Hadrian, as it did every day during our expeditions.

"I know he is. And I want nothing more than to see Hadrian back to his normal, sarcastic self. But the moment

I feel like you're in danger, we are getting out of here. Plant or no plant," she said firmly.

I looked back to one of the bodies closest to me. A cold sensation passed up my arms and down my legs, making me heavy beneath the dead's wide stare. "You're taking this 'protector' task serious—"

Before I could finish, figures dressed in black shadow burst through the tree line. Without a sound, they ran forward. Nyah sprang into action.

Their sudden screams lit the clearing, breaking its silence. A flock of birds burst from their tree in fear. Nyah's lip curled, and a powerful growl seeped between her clenched jaw.

My eyes moved quickly to catch up with the blurring bodies.

I fumbled for my sword, pulling it free at the last moment as the attackers flew across the space and greeted us.

A light *whish* sounded above us. Arrows tipped with white feathers rained down from the trees. Lightning fast, they sped towards the attackers. They didn't miss. A handful of the attackers stopped as wood and metal impaled their bodies.

The impaled looked at the arrows piercing their shadowed bodies, and the screams that followed sent my blood alight. The hidden guards shot another volley of arrows from behind them. The arrows hit their mark. For a moment, the attackers halted before picking up their speed again, unfazed. Only one went down and didn't get back up, an arrow pierced from the back of her head through the front of her lifeless face.

Nesta flipped out of the foliage of a pine tree. Mid-spin, she released an arrow, which lodged itself into the neck of one of the attackers just before it reached me.

"RAISE YOUR SWORD!" Nesta screamed, turning quickly as another shadowed figure thrust a rusted blade at her. It missed her by inches. She spun and pulled a dagger free from her belt, slicing it across her attacker's arm.

Paralyzed with fear, I relied on those around me to keep the attackers at bay, trying to get a glance at them while they clawed and screeched at the group. For days, I had fantasied about fighting. I had trained enough for it. But now, in the face of these strange creatures, I was as frozen as the dead that watched from their trees.

Nyah screamed. As if her cry was cold water, I was thrust out of my state of fear. I threw my hands out. A slash of wind raced towards those surrounding her. My magick ripped them from the ground and smashed them into the surrounding pines, raining pine needles down around them.

In every direction, swords sliced into flesh. Where blood should have sprayed, black shadow dripped out. And no one fell; the attackers kept coming.

There was a shift in the wind beside me, and I snapped my head to the left. Time slowed as I caught my reflection in the silver of a blade. A low grumbling vibrated from the attacker's throat, turning my attention to its face.

Inky veins spread across his face, each filled with shadow. His eyes bulged, the whites now blue and red, and the hue of his skin was death. I faltered for a moment, trying to take in the truth right before me.

The attacker grunted and lunged. Stars burst behind my eyes as something heavy collided with my face. I stumbled back, covering my nose. My fingers were wet, warm and red.

"Argh," I cried, fueled by anger. My body flooded with it.

I dropped my hands, palms covered in my own blood. With a flick, my metal gloves clicked, and my claws came free. I dove forward, lunging away from the swing of the blade again, and drove my metal claws into the attacker's stomach.

He leaned forward, mouth slack, and screamed. I cringed as spit splashed onto me. The wretched stench of death battered my senses. Flickering shadow escaped from his throat and reached out of his mouth. Like living tentacles, they tried to touch me, but I pushed him back with all my might. His head cracked against the ground; music to my ears.

"Zacriah, to your left!" Nyah snapped.

My reactions were too slow, and something hit the back of my neck, dragging me down to the ground. I turned briefly and saw the flash of yellowed teeth. But as quickly as my attacker moved, he stopped, eyes rolling into the back of his head. Black shadow dispersing into the air around us. His head began to slip from his shoulders, a clean line separating it from the body. As the head tumbled to the ground, rolling to a stop before my feet, I caught Nyah standing behind him, sword extended.

Nyah nodded, chest rising and falling deeply. Then she joined the fight.

I spun, readying myself. I reached for the sword I dropped when a high-pitched laugh turned my blood to ice.

It was a young girl. In the afternoon light, I could see her disheveled appearance; blood hair frayed around her plump face, the same look of death clinging to her skin and expression.

She moved with great speed. Black smoke seeped from her body as she ducked and dived from my advances. Words mumbled from her cut lips as she brought the bone club down on my shin. The pain was unbearable. I dropped to my knee, bringing up my arms to block another one of her hits. For a small girl, she packed a punch, unearthly strength filling her animated body.

I threw my hands up and sent my air into her body before she brought down another smash of her club. I burst into her lungs, trying to latch onto the air within, but there was none to find. No breath within her small body.

Lashing a whip of air at her legs, she fell, giving me a moment to stumble away from her.

She raised her head and looked up at me. "Master needs you."

Her voice was rough and strained.

"Master needs you," she repeated, rising from the ground.

I knew who she spoke of.

She ran again, but I was quicker this time.

I pulled a short dagger from the leather holder on my belt and thrust the silver metal into her stomach.

She looked at the dagger half buried in her then smiled so widely, it sent a shiver coursing through my spine.

"Master forgives you." She pushed herself closer, making the dagger slip deeper into her.

I dropped my hold on the hilt and stumbled backwards. She showed no sign of pain as she began her prowl towards me.

"He needs you. I need you." Her voice deepened until it registered in my mind. I had heard it before.

"THE HEAD." I could hear Nyah shouting somewhere behind me. "SEVER THE HEAD!"

"Won't you come and ask for forgiveness? Sorry, sorry, sorry," she sang, running a small finger across the dagger's hilt.

"Sorry, sorry, sorry."

With each apology she sang, I felt the bubbling change begin, as if she called it forward.

I'd only connected to my Dragori form once before, and even then, the pain was nothing like it was now. When the coven of empaths successfully unlocked the block Gallion had placed within me all those years ago, it was equally freeing and terrifying.

My body was a hurricane, roaring from the inside out. I felt my bones snap and skin rip, shredding to allow for my inner being to come through. The forest, the attack, the girl melted from my vision.

Time didn't matter during the shift. In my mind, it felt like hours had passed, whereas in truth it occurred within the blink of an eye.

A new rush of power flooded over me, cleansing my mind of panic.

The forest was a wash of new colors, smells and sounds. Everything heightened in my beastly form. I could hear the girl's footsteps, smell the dried copper of blood in her mouth.

My wings moved first. With a mind of their own, they thrust towards the girl and sliced at her neck. The claw on the tip of my wing caught flesh and pulled back with force. A chunk of skin and muscle came away, and the girl's head tilted to its side. There was no blood, but the gash on her neck burst with shadow, snaking and dancing between the severed skin. Still, she smiled.

"What are you…" I growled, wings readying for another slice.

"Master's fa—"

I gasped as her head popped from her shoulders and tumbled to the ground. Nyah stood breathless behind her, black shadow clinging to her sword.

"I said the head!" she spluttered, red-faced.

The rest of the headless body just stood there, immobilized. Behind Nyah, two other bodies stood in the same positions; the rest were laid out on the floor, including one of our guards.

The fight was over, but I felt like it had only just begun.

"What in Volcras are they?" Smoke seeped from the necks of the headless bodies.

I took cautious steps towards the young girl's body.

"I don't know, but we're not staying around any longer to find out." Nyah reached out for my arm and pulled me away. Stepping around me, Nyah pushed the body, and it toppled under her touch. The moment it hit the ground, it burst in a cloud of smoke and stench. We reeled back, coughing.

"The Druid," I said, waving a cloud from my face. "We are standing in his web. He knew we were coming."

It was impossible to believe someone in Kandilin would sell out our plans, but it was the only explanation.

"Apologies for the interruption, but I believe there are more sympathizers nearby. I suggest leaving immediately and returning to Kandilin," Nesta said. She was a sharp looking elf, her long honey hair scraped off her face into a knot. There was a splatter of golden blood on her face, highlighting her sharp cheekbones and pointed chin. "I have never seen this before, the dead alive once again."

She must've caught me looking, as she pulled a laced cloth from beneath her breast plate and cleaned the splatter. "The Druid has his dark grasp on our people now." She gestured to the bodies scattering the floor, a prang of sadness covering her striking eyes.

"Are there records that could help us understand what power or dark magick the Druid has over the dead?" Nyah asked, plucking the cloth from Nesta's hand and rubbing it across her damp forehead.

"Since the Druid's supposed defeat on his ship, news has spread of sympathizers—twisted Alorian elves who've idolized druids since their fall many years ago. And it seems those rumors are true. I don't know what this means, other than it is not wise that we stay a moment longer."

Throughout her speech, I noticed Nesta's constant glance at me and the slight pinch of her brow. Nyah too couldn't keep her eyes off me. For a moment, I'd forgotten about the wings and curled horns on my head, or the fact I stood inches taller than them both.

Conscious under their stares, I called forth my elven form.

The shiver started at my feet and pulsed across my body. I scrunched my eyes against the discomfort that still haunted my mind from the ritual. By the time I opened my eyes, I knew I was back to normal. My uniform was ripped and seems stretched from my Dragori form. The forest was dull once again, all sound and smells lost to me.

"Well, that was… impressive," Nyah muttered, shaking her head.

"I'm still not used to it," I replied, fiddling with my hands. Maybe the dead Alorian guard would still be alive if I had used my power straight away. I couldn't help but add the weight of his death to my shoulders.

Nesta placed two fingers into her mouth. The high-pitched whistle filled the forest around us. A piercing cry responded. We all looked up as three amber griffins passed overhead. Their silver armor reflected light across the forest bed. I raised a hand to block the bright glint of light.

The griffins soon landed, their thick talons tearing up the ground. One raised up on its hind legs as it came to close to the body of one of our attackers. Even they could sense the unnatural power that clung to the dead.

"Never mind dwelling on what we could have done." Nesta and the guards began to walk for the griffins. "Come, quick before we are greeted with another attack."

With my hands raised in cautious greeting, I climbed on the back of the biggest griffin with Nesta in front of me. I wrapped my arms around her thick waist and clung on. A click of approval came from the griffin's beak, and its feathers shook in pleasure. Nyah sat with another guard.

"What about the bodies?" I asked, feeling the movement of the griffin's wings as it prepared for flight.

"It is too late for them. Let us hope the Goddess shows forgiveness for their actions today."

"And our guard?" His body still lay on the forest bed, surrounded by his killers.

"The Goddess works in many ways," Nesta shouted above the roaring winds as we launched into the sky. "Knowing when your life is subject to sacrifice is part of being her child. It is all for the better cause."

CHAPTER
TWO

NEWS SPREAD LIKE Hadrian's wild-fire the moment our griffins passed over Kandilin. From the skies, I watched as a crowd gathered below on the podium, shielding my eyes from the light reflecting off the Alorian Soldiers' white and silver armor.

I clamped my eyes shut and held on tighter to Nesta as we prepared for landing. I still didn't enjoy the final part of a griffin's flight. Even after experiencing it almost every day for the past week, I never got used to the weightless feeling of my stomach that snatched my breath as we descended.

My stomach turned, mirroring my damp forehead and cramping limbs. Flying I loved, but the unruly behavior of a griffin was highlighted as they flew back to the ground. Nesta had explained during my first flight days that the moment a griffin was in the air, they were free of control. When guided to land, they rebelled by making the journey as uncomfortable as possible.

"Think of it as punishment for our commands," she'd told me, a hint of laughter creasing her wise eyes.

"If they are free of control, why do they follow the instruction to land in the first place? Why not just ignore it?"

"Because loyalty is their greatest asset. Griffins are no more than oversized younglings; they push boundaries but always comply in the end."

Just as she finished explaining, she pulled on the leather reins and we pelted towards the ground.

I broke the day dream as it happened in real time. Opening my eyes, I saw her yank hard on the reins.

Our griffin dived towards the ground, its wings pulled tight to its body. I wanted to scream, but if I opened my lips, I risked a mouth full of air and insects. I had learned that lesson during my first flight.

The descent seemed to drag on for a long while. Only when I recognized the familiar click of talons on wooden panels did I open my eyes again. The other griffins from our flock had landed. Nyah and the surviving guards had already dismounted and stood around waiting for Nesta and me to join.

Nesta turned over her shoulder, her pointed ear almost catching me in the face, and smiled. "You almost winded me with that grip. You will get used to them soon."

I smiled weakly back at her. "Why do I have a niggling feeling I've heard that before?"

"Because you have been blessed to have me as a rider." Her laugh was sweet and trill like a bird.

Aware of the crowd of waiting hands and soldiers, I bit my lip and jumped from the griffin's back. I didn't want them to see, nor sense my discomfort, so I pushed my feet into the ground and steadied my dizziness. Three deep breaths and my spinning mind had stilled. I turned back to offer a hand to Nesta, but she was already jumping from its back and landing beside me.

Marium greeted us and quickly escorted us for a debrief. It was part of the routine I'd fallen into over the past seven days, ever since Gallion sent word of the plant that could help Hadrian heal. The day when I finally grasped hope he would get better.

In the morning, after breakfast, we'd be sent out on a search party and return empty-handed. Each time, the silent Marium greeted us. But there was no denying today was different. We'd never returned to Kandilin with one missing party member.

I didn't miss the look Marium gave Nesta, and the slight bow of Nesta's head as she silently confirmed Marium's query.

Marium, although the main waiting hand, never spoke a word. At least not one I had heard. I'd watched from a distance as she commanded with her eyes, not once giving guidance or answering queries of those around her. It was known not to provoke her, yet why, I still had not worked out. She reminded me of Alina. A thought that only turned my stomach. In a certain light, they almost looked the same.

My feet echoed across the paneled flooring as I followed behind Nyah towards the main building in Kandilin. The Council Hall was the heart of the city, a puzzle of wood and glass. It hovered over the central riverway of Eldnol below, balanced perfectly across two giant trees on either side of the waterway. Kandilin was small compared to Olderim, but that didn't take away from its sheer beauty and power. It'd been built at a height to prevent from invasion from below. There was only one way out of the city by foot, and that was down the winding pathway towards the north of the town. I'd still not ventured there, instead opting for griffin flight as my main means of transportation.

I peered over the bridge that connected the west of the city to the Council Hall, welcoming the usual flip of my stomach. Far below, I watched dreamy ships float upstream, heading in the direction of Lilioira.

Nesta had explained that the riverway connected every city, town and village in Eldnol like a stretching vein of life. It was a path for trading, just like a dirt track I would find in Thessolina. Home. The thought knotted my brow and made me fiddle with my hands. I missed home. At least those who were still there. Mam and Fa.

A shadow distracted me from the painful thoughts. I looked up, watching the looming building come into view, blocking out the sun and all around it. The Council Hall was beautiful, a grand structure that dwarfed everything around it. As we closed over the bridge, a haggle of cloaked figures burst from the doors, huddled in conversation. I moved out of their way as they brushed past me, sensing the urgency from their rushed whispers and quick feet.

Unconsciously, my eyes drifted to a window towards the top of the building, hoping to catch a glimpse of *him*. Hadrian. It was easy to conjure the memory of the struggle four days previous as he was moved to his new room. At first, Hadrian refused, his thunderous mood only worsening with every passing day, but soon, he gave into the many hands that carried him to his new dwelling.

He'd not said much to me since, not that I gave him much of a chance. It was hard being around him with the secrets I was forced to keep. Secrets that even now weighed my shoulders down. I was forbidden to speak of the Druid. Still Hadrian believed it was his father who caused all of this. Lying to Hadrian was close to impossible, so I opted to stay away from him, creating more of a distance between us.

"We request an audience with Queen Kathine's council." Nesta's stood tall, hands on her waist.

The two guards stopped their chatter and looked towards the group. Like twins, each was equally tall, broad and rude. Although their grand silver helmets covered their faces, I was sure from their tone that they were scowling.

"You are early. You were not expected back till sundown," the first guard said.

"Just open the doors." Nesta's voice dipped.

When Nesta meant business, her tone was as sharp as the blade around her waist. The guards got the hint, both moving to the large brass door rings and pulling them open. They nodded to Nesta, who thanked them as we passed inside. I felt their shielded eyes follow me every step until the doors closed behind us.

Each time we passed into this historic building, I lost my breath.

The bottom floor was open and large. A rolling space with two sets of wooden stairs disappearing to the second floor on either side. Rows upon rows of benches took up most of the room, a single walkway cut down the middle of the room. Our destination was to the far side of the room where the council sat, waiting.

We passed in single file towards the front where the long desk was placed. The woven carpet of silver and emerald cushioned our heavy footfall as we closed in on the many waiting eyes of the council. Stopping before the desk, the council greeted us with a mixture of stares and emotions.

The council was made up of Queen Kathine's greatest warriors and scholars. They'd been sent in place of her majesty as her mouthpiece until she visited herself. I'd asked Nesta why she'd not just come herself, and she only raised her shoulders and shook her head.

Sitting along the desk were the six that Queen Kathine trusted in her place. Each with their own skills, it was down to them to guide us during the times of tension. Shame they only added to said tension.

"I see you are one short," Kazmir, the elder healer and head of the council, said. Her voice seemed to bounce across the room and envelope us in its high tones. She was the oldest of the council, with a braid of silver and chestnut hair. Her hunched stature only added to her age, but her eyes were bright blue, like the open skies and the ocean on a summers day. Like all Alorian elves, she had a hint of gold that hung beneath her skin.

"We were ambushed," Nesta replied, her voice cold. "I gave the order to abandon the day's search."

"And here I thought *he* simply became lost. I see the Dragori is still unmarked…" Kazmir's judging eyes looked me up and down. "And empty-handed."

I took a careful step forward, trying my best to hold her intimidating gaze. "We couldn't find it. I still believe we're looking in the wrong place."

"Since when do you know more about the lands of Eldnol than its very people?" Penna practically knocked his chair to the floor as he stood abruptly. He was the chief Gazer, an elder who studied the stars and mapped out Eldnol itself. He was short for an Alorian elf; I wondered if he had red swirling within his golden veins.

He was also brash and rude. His face seemed to always be pinched as if he sat on a thistle.

"I meant no disrespect—"

"Then keep your beliefs to yourself." Penna's face turned ruby. "Nesta, what is your verdict?"

"I am with Zacriah. I lost a man today, a good man, in search of a flower that promises to fix the prince. Do I believe it? Well do you want the answer to that?"

Kazmir reached and pulled at Penna's hanging sleeves to seat him. Nesta's responses had Penna choking on a reply.

I caught Nyah shifting on her feet out the corner of my eye, and the raise of her freckled hand as she pressed it to her mouth, stifling her laugh.

I shook my head and looked back up, flicking my tongue across my teeth. I was angry, tired and frustrated, and this old buffoon would soon learn how to speak to me.

"What gives you the right to tell me how to behave when all I've done for the past seven days is follow your commands—which have lead us only into an ambush?" I enjoyed watching Penna's face slack as I shouted back. "If you are the blessed fool that the stars have chosen to speak through, then why can't you locate a measly flower? Instead, you keep sending us on missions with nothing more than dead ends to pluck from imaginary stems."

"Now, Zacriah, that is quite enough." Kazmir's voice was hoarse and stern.

"No. It's not." I waved my hand to silence her. "Until you figure out where it is, don't come asking for me. I am pulling myself out of any further expeditions until we have a genuine lead."

Someone sniggered to my side.

"I suggest you calm down, Zacriah. You forget you are speaking to the very people keeping you safe." Kazmir was calm, but a hint of warning warmed her voice. "We have shown you and Prince Hadrian nothing but kindness. You owe us respect."

"Keeping me safe? From what, a missing Druid? Do we even know his name, his true identity? No. I owe you nothing. You know *we* would rather return to Olderim. It is the council who are keeping us here."

Kazmir nor Penna replied. The six council members shot each other a look, and Kazmir sat back down. I couldn't help the laugh that slipped past my lips. "And Hadrian is locked up in that room, too weak to leave by himself, and still no one has addressed whether his father is even alive. Have you discussed when you are going to tell him that? Or have you been too busy sending us on a wild chase to find some mysterious flower?"

Nyah was standing before me, one hand on my shoulder. "Zac, you need to calm down."

Her voice was like an anchor. It broke through the haze of anger, bringing me back into the room.

I looked at her, stunned. "Are you joking? I finally have the backbone to speak out, and I am in the wrong? I speak only the truth. If *they* don't want to swallow it, that is their trouble."

"I know." Her grip on my shoulder tightened, her eyes flashed and her brows pinched, then my anger melted away like butter over a fire.

No, she didn't!

"Thank you, Nyah. We appreciate your help." Kazmir hands were planted on the desk, each knuckle white from tension.

I tried to pull the anger back, even with the added incentive of Nyah's betrayal, but I couldn't grasp a hold of it.

"I'm sorry," Nyah whispered over the red glow of her hands. I didn't believe it.

"Can we get back to the matter at hand, or are there any more complaints you would like to bring forward. No? Excellent. Nesta, please step forward and share the news of said ambush." Kazmir turned her attention to Nesta, forcing a weak smile.

I detached myself from the debrief. I could hear the faint mummer of Nesta as she described the attack, saw the shock on the faces of the council as she displayed the skin with the sigil and caught the hushed chatter. But I didn't care. I just wanted out.

"It seems that the sympathizers have finally crawled out of the woodwork. And their presence only solidifies what we already knew. The Druid did survive Emaline's burial at sea. Our understanding is he has yet to show himself on the shores of Thessolina, so I can only think that he is biding his time somewhere off the grid." Penna spoke up this time.

"Have your stars not told you were to find him?" I finally spoke up, a small sliver of frustration returning to me. Penna only looked at me but didn't answer. I could tell my comment offended him. His neck blotched with splash of red.

"Whilst we are on topic of Thessolina, we have received news from Vulmar palace. Our soldiers say the city and its people are up in arms. They blame the missing King and Prince on our little friend. We have heard all about the incident between the Druid's commander, Alina, and what you did to her. Your display of magick has rooted fear in Niraen's hearts," Penna said.

Kazmir cleared her throat and shook her finger at me. "And that is what we will allow them to think. The moment news of the Druid spreads to Niraen ears, true panic will set in. Letting them believe a rouge wielder of magick is their only concern is a blessing. Nesta, I ask that you prepare a griffin and send your best soldier with a note. Explain the news about the Druid sympathizers and command that your troops overseas increase their patrols and keep a keen eye out for any sympathizers on their shores. We need to halt this before it gets any worse."

Nesta nodded. "Of course. I shall prepare and have the word out by sundown. But the Niraen people are still hostile towards our soldiers. Since 'King Dalior' so evidently spread his lies about the Alorian people, they still believe we are partially to blame."

I knew what Nesta was referring to. The speech the Druid gave in his perfect disguise had rooted itself in the heart and minds of my people. Hadrian's people.

"Take Hadrian with you. His presence would calm the people." I didn't want Hadrian to leave, but it was the best option.

"Absolutely not. If the Goddess has brought the Dragori together, we must keep it that way. Separating you will only increase the risk that the Druid gets to you. We almost lost you to him once." Kazmir was serious. She hardly took a breath until she had finished talking.

The youngest and most ethereal of the five council members stood up at the end of the table. The folds of her white dress rippled like water when she walked around the desk and stood before it.

She turned to the rest of the council, her raven hair curling down to the bottom of her spine.

"I feel that this is the time to bring up the topic of the fourth Dragori. Word has traveled on the wind of the fourth in my homeland. The Morthi elves talk of an elfin girl who caused the ground to tremble beneath her feet. The last we have heard about her was two moons previous when she was exiled for risking the lives of her people. Since then, she's become little more than a faint memory."

It was the first time I'd heard about the fourth Dragori, or even spent a moment thinking about them. My mind was lost, too busy worrying about Hadrian's health, the missing Druid and the fact Emaline has still shown zero interest in helping us. Now the idea of the fourth only spiked my worry.

"I appreciate your concern, Cristilia, but for the moment that is nothing more than a rumor. I believe our efforts should be spread more on the issue at hand." Kazmir brushed Cristilia's request off like it was nothing more than a flurry of snow on her shoulder. Cristilia only dipped her head, spared me a glance with her onyx eyes and returned to her seat without another word.

I didn't drop her gaze. How did I not notice a Morthi on the Queen's council? Even from the light of the circular window that haloed the council, I noticed the black rush of her blood. Morthi blood. And the double point of her ears that escaped her thick crown of hair.

"We return to the search at dawn," Kazmir announced. "Take the rest of the day to rest, train, eat. Whatever it is that your bodies desire. Penna will consult with the stars and find a more trustworthy lead."

Penna shot a look to Kazmir but would not dare speak against her. Even if her comment was an open offense against him.

That was it for the debrief.

I rolled my eyes when she announced we would still look for this mysterious plant.

Hadrian was not well. That much was clear from his thinning body and colorless skin. But what it was that caused his demise was still as unknown as the plant we searched. I needed to see him.

As I followed our group from the council hall, lost in the thought of Hadrian's frail face, a high scream caused horror to flood through my body. Every fiber of my being was sent into a hurricane of panic, and I ran. Stepping beyond the hall, I looked up.

Billowing clouds of smoke and flames licked across the top of the council hall. The black smoke seeped into the sky, mixed with fire so blue I thought it was water.

A bolder of horror sank in my chest.

The council hall seemed to shudder for a moment.

The hungry blaze crawled up every panel of wood, burning from the origin. Hadrian's room.

CHAPTER

ThREE

ALL SENSE OF control slipped away like sand through my hand.

Without more than a thought, I connected to my air and pulled it towards my body. Thrusting my hands towards the paneled floor, the force propelled me into the sky. I heard the shouts beneath me, but the closer I got to the fire, the quieter they became.

Drowned out by the vicious roaring, I felt every part of my surroundings as the wind kept me aloft. I flew straight into the heat, straight for Hadrian.

The blue fire reached out of what had been Hadrian's window like angry, grasping hands. I wouldn't have been able to enter through it, so I changed my direction with a twist of my hand and thrust myself through the window of a room beneath Hadrian's where the flames had yet to reach.

Glass burst around me as my body slammed into the pane, and I lost my grasp on my magick. I fell to the ground of the smoke-filled room, rolling over broken shards. I felt them nick at my arms and face.

I pushed the pain into a deep prison within me. I had no time to dwell on the blood that warmed my cheeks.

Standing, I ran for the open door and stopped amid an ocean of smoke in the corridor.

My chest racked as I coughed, trying everything to block the thick smoke from infiltrating my body. Panicked, I blindly reached out for the pure air beyond the building, latched onto it and brought it forward. Pushing my hands out in front of me, I sent the torrent towards the corridor and watched it clear the smoke.

I ran down tunnel I'd created, holding my air firm to give me time to pass through. *I need to get to him.*

I didn't stop running until I rounded a corner and caught the blue glow in the distance. I shot towards it, but the entire stairwell ahead was alight in flame.

I recoiled, my face burning from the fast-growing heat.

My scream grew in frustration, and I slashed a hand at the fire, sending a whip of air towards it. The second my magick touched the unnatural blue flames, they exploded in life and raged. I was thrown backwards, pain vibrating up my back.

"Hadrian," I wheezed, looking around me for another way up. "Hadrian!"

Nothing. All I could hear was the crackling of wood and the hissing of hot glass.

In a blink of my eye, the fire had crawled from the stairwell and spread towards me. I scrambled backwards and watched it overtake everything in sight.

My heart sped up as a sound echoed all around me. A loud groaning, as if the building itself screamed in agony. The entire floor shifted, and my stomach flipped from the massive jolt.

"Get up!" Nesta hovered over me. She put her arms beneath mine and hoisted me to standing. "This building is going to crumble. We have to get out."

She tried to pull me back. With a final pull, I yanked myself from her grasp.

"I have to find Hadrian," I screamed over the roars. "I won't leave him."

She shook her head, which shone with sweat. "He's—"

A scream slipped out of her mouth, and we both were sent crashing into the wall. The building had moved again. I was running out of time.

In her daze, I pushed myself from the wall and moved. To my left, a door was hanging open. I left her in the corridor and stumbled through it, closing myself in. I just hoped she got out.

Hadrian.

Just his name captured my attention again.

I searched the room for another way out. Besides the window and the door, I was left with one option.

Looking at the ceiling, I could see smoke dancing through the thin slats.

The fire had spread in the room above, but it didn't matter.

I closed my eyes and begged the Goddess for help. The urgency in my power built around me, the air throbbing with stress. Even with my eyes closed, I heard the glass of the window rattle as my wind danced around it.

I didn't stop reaching for the air until every slip of it in the small room belonged to me.

With a large push, it expanded. Using my arms to direct the pressure, a ball of spinning wind shot above me and smashed its way through the ceiling.

Wood exploded above, raining down around me. Something heavy smashed into my shoulder, urging me to create a shield. I quickly connected to my magick again, spinning a shield of air around my body. I heard the dull thud of wood as it hit my barrier. Yet nothing passed.

Nesta pounded on the door, but the noise of the fire was too loud to hear what she said.

With a large push, I jumped, using the air to propel me to the next floor. I passed through the ripped flooring and landed beyond the hole I'd created.

The room was barren of life. Two beds where on opposite ends of the walls, both dressed in white linen and cream blankets. A thin layer of smoke swirled on the ceiling, but that was it. My heart skipped a beat when I noticed the lack of fire.

I moved to the door and placed my hand on the brass handle. Electrifying agony erupted through my arm. I pulled my hand back and held it to my chest, bubbles of raised blisters now covering my entire palm.

"Volcras!" I hissed, holding my burned hand to my chest. Just moving my fingers an inch caused stabbing pain to race through me.

The tugging in my gut had intensified, telling me Hadrian was close.

Pushed with urgency, I kicked at the door. It took four hard kicks for it to open. The moment it swung wide, all I could see was blue.

The fire had clung to the walls floor, but I couldn't stop. I needed to get through.

I took a step but stumbled as the floor jolted beneath me. Like a symphony, the foundations creaked and the floor beyond the room crumbled, falling into the mouth of flames.

I threw myself backwards. The back of my head smashed into the wall, conjuring stars to dance behind my eyes. I raised a hand to the back of my head, feeling warmth, and my fingers came back sticky.

Something cold splashed the side my face, and I screamed in panic.

"Give me your hand," someone grunted, hands grasping my arms.

Opening my eyes, I was greeted by Emaline.

"Why is it I am here saving your sorry ass again?" Her face was speckled with soot. She pulled herself through the window, her white-feathered wings tight to her back.

"Hadrian..." I spluttered, rubbing the lump on my head as the room jolted again.

"He is safe. Now, hold on." Emaline didn't wait for me to follow. She stood and pulled me up. Just as I remembered from the battle on the ship, Emaline had strength like I had never felt before. With ease, she pulled me into her arms and turned for the window.

"Hadrian… safe…" I managed through coughs. My lungs felt as if they would explode, smoke invading my blood and mind.

My stomach lurched as she threw us beyond the window. Wind screamed past my ears as we fell. All I saw was smoke and fire.

Suddenly, my body was yanked backwards as Emaline opened her wings and stopped our free fall.

I strained my neck to look back just in time to watch the building shudder a final time. A blaring crack sounded around us, and the building, with the surrounding tree, tumbled into the riverway. I watched with tear-blurred eyes as the council hall plunged from view.

Emaline landed on the walkway, and I tumbled out of her grasp.

There was a final loud crack and cries erupted around the town from those standing around watching the Council Hall break beneath the fire and fall from view. The bomb of it crashing into the ground far below was horrific.

Destruction hung all around us.

Where the council hall had stood proud was now a void space. The heart of the city was no more.

I crawled to the edge of the walkway, now broken in shards, and stopped before a sharp drop into the riverway below. I could see the council hall in ruins across the riverway where it lay. Small vessels were crushed beneath its weight and planks of wood floated calmly with the gentle tide of the river. Smoke filled the air, and the burned tang of ash coated my mouth.

The members of the council stood around, their faces ashen with shock. Nesta was there, breathless and soot-stained. Seeing her released a weight from my shoulders. *She made it out.*

I recognized Nyah's face and a group of Alorian elves who I was sure I'd seen before.

But no Hadrian.

"You didn't save him!" I screamed, my fingers cutting into the broken plank.

"His Highness is safe and under guard," Kazmir quickly said before she doubled over with yacking coughs.

I turned to her, eyes wide. "But…"

"Emaline was with him, Zac. She saw it firsthand. Why did you go in? Do you know how serious that was! You risked your life for nothing." Nyah kneeled beside me, tears cutting marks down her dirtied face.

"Who did it? Who tried to kill him?!" I screamed my question, multiple possibilities passing through my mind.

"Hadrian Vulmar is a danger to himself and now our people."

I looked at Penna. If my eyes could kill, he would have been dead where he stood. "He didn't do this. The fire, it wasn't normal. It wasn't his."

I recalled the blue flames and could still see traces of them behind my eyes.

"Heartfire." Cristilia stepped through the growing crowd, her hands clasped in sorrow before her.

"It is not possible. Do not speak such blasphemous words amongst us," Kazmir said. "I expected more from my council members."

Mutterings of distaste spread around her. Heads turned and fingers pointed, as if she'd gone against the very Goddess.

Nyah helped me to stand.

"Heartfire?" someone asked.

"Enough! I will not have these words thrown around so carelessly." Kazmir looked more flustered with each second.

"No, you will tell me! Tell me what this means for Hadrian—WHERE IS HADRIAN?" I said.

Nesta stepped forward and interrupted. "I shall take you to him now."

"You will not. Hadrian has been removed from Kandilin. He is not to be seen until it is safe." Kazmir pushed past Cristilia with her shoulder and turned her back to the barren space. "You see what he has done, after the hospitality we have shown him."

I couldn't stop the tears.

I reached a hand to wipe them away, and they came back black with ash.

Many elves now stood beyond their homes, watching. I heard loud cries and screams as they took in the horror and destruction in the center of the city.

"Nesta, I command you to take them to their room and ensure they do not leave. This will not go unpunished," Kazmir said.

"I respect the council, but this has nothing to do with Zacriah." Nesta was positioned close to Emaline, whose lips were white with tension. Emaline's gaze flickered to Nesta as she spoke up.

I shook my head as Nyah tried to pull me away. "No, please, he couldn't have done this."

My pleading was wasted. Nesta took my other arm and helped Nyah pull me away. All I could do was watch the griffins screech as they dipped in and out of the smoke cloud like it was a game.

CHAPTER
FOUR

"WHAT ARE WE going to do?" I questioned Nyah, who sat with her head buried in her hands. Since we were escorted back to our dwelling, she hadn't moved from her seat at the end of my bed.

I busied myself with looking beyond the room, but the two guards Nesta had reluctantly left with us still stood beyond the door. It was clear Nesta was on our side, but there was only so much so could do in such a situation.

This was not the first time in Kandilin I had felt like a prisoner. I just added this to the ever-growing list of annoyance I had for Gallion leaving us here.

"Wait it out. You can't blame the council. Hadrian has just destroyed one of the oldest buildings in Eldnol," Nyah replied. "Who knows if everyone made it out? He could have killed someone, Zac!"

"I still don't understand how. The fire was blue. We all saw it. It was not natural. What if Hadrian is hurt and they won't tell us?" It was hard to imagine him getting out of there unharmed.

"Do you think she did it, Emaline?" I knew the accusation was misplaced. "She's made it clear she wants nothing to do with us, but she finds the time to visit Hadrian! It doesn't add up."

"Emaline is not one for keeping secrets, nor is she willing to promote those who do." Cristilia materialized before the door of our room. I gasped, surprised by her sudden appearance. "I would have gotten here sooner, but as you can understand, we have been busy calming the city after today's events."

Nyah jumped up from her seat, hand already on the hilt of her dagger. Had Nyah not sensed her arrival?

"I feel you deserve to hear from me before more hateful lies are spread about Prince Hadrian and what he has done. The council will want you to believe he is to blame..."

"How did you—" I said, looking to the closed door she had just passed straight through.

"I am not Alorian. I do not heed their rules."

Nyah's hand still hovered above her weapon. "But you are on the Queen's council. You help set the rules you choose not to follow?"

Cristilia bowed her head and raised her arms towards Nyah. "I am no threat. I am here regarding the Prince, nothing more."

"No bother. I should have realized Morthi elves are not accustomed to knocking before entering..." Nyah jibbed.

"If it pleases you, I can leave now," Cristilia sang, unbothered by Nyah's comment.

I stepped forward. "No. Please stay. Do you know what Emaline did to Hadrian? You said something about Heartfire. What type of Alorian magick has she used against him?"

All my worries and queries that had built up came flooding out. I needed answers, and I wanted them now.

Cristilia walked across the room and stood before me. "I must tell you that Emaline, although the catalyst for what happened, has no ties to her Heart Magick, not like Prince

Hadrian. She was only following my request, which unfortunately resulted in the…"

"What do you mean? You did this?" Nyah shouted, a stormy expression covering her face.

"I did." Cristilia's ethereal face pained. "Although I feel it is only right you listen to what it is I asked of Emaline. I asked her to speak to him, to tell him the truth about his father."

Disbelief coursed through me like liquid metal. "Why now? Why tell him when he is still so unwell?"

"Because it is the truth that sometimes heals the greatest of wounds. And enough time has been wasted pretending the Prince's illness can be cured by a plant or healers. Emaline told him to *heal* him. Hadrian has been bed bound for to long; we need the three Dragori back to full strength."

The sudden weight of guilt bared down on my shoulders. Hadrian would now know that for days I'd kept the truth from him, holding him back from what he deserved to know.

"He is going to hate me." The idea panicked me. I had felt more distant from Hadrian in the past week, but that did not deter the feelings that grew with each day that passed. Everything I had done was for him.

"Prince Hadrian will understand why you kept it from him. Once the sun sets, I shall take you to him," Cristilia said.

"Is he hurt?" I asked, images of his reaction playing out in my head.

"Just as I thought, he has healed. The Heartfire burned away his ailments. But now we must not worry about these things instead of the repercussions of his actions. The Queen is coming."

Nyah gasped. "But she never leaves her kingdom."

"News of his Heartfire has intrigued her."

I shook my head. "It has been only a few hours, and the Queen is days north. How has news reached her so quickly?"

"Queen Kathine is the mother of this land. I suppose news reaches her through the whispers of the very soil she has sworn her life to protect. She arrives at dawn in a few days."

∽

THE WAIT FOR the sun to set was agonizing. Cristilia promised to return to get us and left Nyah and me in the room with the truth of what happened blurring around us. Although we expected her, it didn't stop us from jumping when she stepped through the door like it was no more than air.

"Follow me," Cristilia said.

I walked to the door first with Nyah following behind me.

"Where are the guards?" I whispered to Cristilia as I stepped beyond the room.

"Your guards will not see us. Now come."

"How?" Nyah said.

"You know little of Morthi magick. Stay close. I will create a gleam of shadow around us."

Night had fallen upon the town. Bats danced and screeched above us, cutting before the moon, which hung proudly in the night sky. It seemed we were in a bubble of sorts. I noticed a faint ripple that surrounded the three of us as we walked, blurring whatever was beyond it. Nyah must've seen it too, as she tripped on the back of my boots as she reached out to touch it.

"Do not touch," Cristilia said, black shadow blurring from the palms of her hands, feeding the shield around us. "If you don't want those beyond my shield to see a floating hand with no body, then keep your hands to yourself."

"Got it," Nyah said.

I didn't know much about Morthi and their magick, but as we walked, Cristilia moved her hands in circular motions before us. We passed unnoticed through the western city, following a path in the trees to the north.

"Do you travel like this a lot?" Nyah asked.

"Only when I need to."

We reached the primary pathway of the city and began our descent to the lower level of Kandilin. We walked down the winding walkway that roped around one of the largest trees in this part of the city. Spinning vines wrapped around the railing and pink flowers swayed in the occasional wind. The closer we got to the ground, the thicker the vines seemed to be. We passed many glowing windows of homes etched into the very tree itself, yet still, no one noticed us as we moved passed.

My legs ached by the time we reached the main entrance to the city. The long walk was tiresome. Nyah squeezed my hand as we closed in on it.

Countless guards and soldiers patrolled the gates. This must have been the most guarded part of the town. How would we pass unseen?

Cristilia's hands moved faster in frantic gestures, and she didn't stop walking. She reached the gate first and faded straight through it as if she was nothing more than a shadow. Nyah squeezed my hand tighter as I kept up my pace, and we passed through after her. I closed my eyes, expecting to slam straight into it and ruin our disguise, but I didn't.

A cold rush passed throughout my body, and I came out the other end, Nyah still holding on tightly to my hand.

Cristilia turned to look over her shoulder and smiled, her hands still moving.

The way she bent the night around us was incredible and terrifying.

Once we reached the forest, I looked up. The city was invisible above the dense canopy that covered the entire sky above. The grass came up to my waist, and the many thick trunks meant we had to squeeze through tight gaps to get past. After a few minutes of walking, Cristilia dropped her hands and the faint shadow of night around us disappeared.

"Do not stray. We still have a way to walk."

We finally came to a stop at the side of a small ravine. The water gushed down the narrow stream and carried on with its journey. Silver scales flashed in the dark water, dancing around reeds and rocks that jutted from the water's surface.

"Where is he being kept?" Nyah asked, stepping forward and scanning the area. "I feel no emotion here."

Cristilia just pointed to a cluster of boulders nestled behind hanging vines to the side of the ravine. I didn't notice it before, but as I looked closer, I could see a faint light glowing through the vines. "We will find Prince Hadrian through there."

"I don't like this," I said.

"Please, trust me. Prince Hadrian is there in the baths. He is waiting for you. You sense no emotion, empath, because the crystals block it."

Pushing the vines to the side, she disappeared into the cave's opening.

"If this is an ambush we've been lead into, I am going to be so angry with you," Nyah said.

I raised my hands. "Don't blame me. You were just as keen to follow her."

Nyah went first, moving cautiously towards the cave. "What can I say? I love an adventure. Especially when they're laced with a possibility of danger." She winked and faded into the mouth of the cave.

The entire cave glowed with golden light. Small crystals protruded from the rock walls, lighting the way as we followed the curving walkway inside. Soon, the narrow walkway opened up, and I saw the many pools of water, each reflecting silver ripples onto the ceiling.

Cristilia was standing ahead of us, talking to the two robed figures who both waded in a pool waist deep. Unlike the rest, this particular pool of water was lit with a dancing blue light.

The source of that light was Hadrian, who sat between the figures. He looked straight at me.

"Leave him with us," Cristilia hushed, gesturing for the two figures, who promptly listened. They climbed out of the pool in a daze and left, all without sparing Nyah and me a single glance.

Cristilia waved us forward while she whispered to Hadrian.

I forced a smile, but he did not return it.

It was impossible not to notice the glow that seeped from his naked body. Blue flames burned beneath Hadrian's skin. The same flames that devoured the council hall. The same flames that were imprinted in the back of my mind every time I blinked.

"Does it hurt?" My question echoed across the cave. I silently scolded myself for asking that first before saying anything else.

Hadrian shook his head twice.

"Heartfire doesn't hurt the user." Cristilia's childlike voice echoed across the low-ceiling space. She was equally mesmerized by the flames beneath his skin.

"This is Heartfire?"

She nodded, her eyes closed. "It pains me to say, and I know the council do not like the possibilities that come with this, but yes, Hadrian has connected to his Heartfire."

Hadrian didn't react as she spoke of the Heartfire. His arms moved slowly in the water, keeping him upright.

"What does this mean?"

"It means many things. The Druid's power affected him greatly. However, he is a risk to himself and those around him just as Kazmir said, even if she wants to keep pretending she does not know what this is."

"Hadrian, how are you feeling?" I asked, voice shaking.

Hadrian stood from the pool and took three steps to get out. He was shirtless, his trousers wet and clinging to the curved muscles in his legs. He stepped towards the edge of the cave and picked up a white tunic that hung from a crystal on the wall.

"Better." His voice was cold as he buttoned the tunic up.

"If the Druid is now connected to Hadrian what does this mean?" Nyah questioned. "No offense, but it sounds intense to me."

"You must understand what it means," Cristilia answered. "When the druids created the Dragori, and the Goddess Dalibael took them away as punishment, she missed something important. A final link in the chain that tethers the Dragori to their original masters—Heart Magick. It is a warped power that causes destruction and is activated by an unknown force only the druids retain. Expired histories say it was a linked between the Dragori and the druids themselves. The Goddess missed this imperfection and almost lost the Dragori in the druids final fall. But she was able to cease the power and keep it buried. It saddens me to see it come to life as it once had before."

My mind raced as she spoke. Not once had Gallion nor the book mentioned anything regarding Heart Magick. Why should I believe the words of an outspoken Morthi?

"If this is true, then why has Hadrian been affected by this if the Goddess herself removed this power?" It made no sense. Her power was greater than any, even the Druid's.

Cristilia turned to me with a pained expression, placing two gentle hands on my shoulders. "I do not have all the answers, Zacriah. I only know as much as the council."

Then she turned to Hadrian. "Prince Hadrian, my suggestion for you is to leave your fire alone. I must speak with the council. If we have a chance at finding the cure, then we need them on our side."

A cure?

Hadrian nodded. "May I ask a favor of you?

"Of course, Prince." Cristilia tipped her head.

"Leave me with Zacriah. It has been many days since I have shared a private word, and I must admit, I cannot wait another moment."

His words made the hairs on the back of my neck stand to attention.

"Yes, thanks, Cristilia." Nyah smiled.

"That goes for you too, Nyah," Hadrian said.

"It is good to see you back to your normal... self," Nyah replied. "Cristilia, I guess I'm following you."

"We shall wait for you outside. I must take Zacriah and Nyah back into the town soon, but I will let you have a quick word."

In the excitement of finally having time with Hadrian, I had almost passed it off as nothing important.

"Wait!" I called as Cristilia almost left from view. She stopped with her back to me, not turning around. "You said there is a cure."

Her shoulders relaxed, and she released a long breath. "The Staff of Light. It was a physical replication of the Goddess's power; only it can burn away such power as it once had before."

"Where is it?" I asked. "Is it kept in Lilioira?"

"That is the only problem, Zacriah; it has been many years since the Staff of Light's name has crept up in books and history. Let me speak with the council. Penna may know of its origins."

With her final word she left me with more questions ready on my lips.

"Hadrian..." I whispered, turning back to him.

He stood right before me, blue flame lit beneath his skin. I did not hear him step close to me as I spoke to Cristilia, and seeing him this close stole my breath.

"Hello, Petal," he replied, his hands warm as he cupped my face.

I laughed, a tear slipping from my eyes. Seeing Hadrian awake was more rewarding than anything we'd been through thus far. "Are you sure it doesn't hurt?" I asked, mesmerized by the dancing glow beneath his skin. I ran a finger down his neck.

"I feel nothing but relief for seeing you." Hadrian's voice was rough from the days of not using it.

"You destroyed the Council Hall..." It all came spilling out of me. I told him of the Queen's visit, and the distrust the council had towards us.

"I told you I didn't want to stay there..." He winked, the whites of his eyes slightly yellow.

I choked on a sob. "Can you ever be serious?"

"I know what I've done. I couldn't stop it." He raised his hand before my face, the blue light only increasing beneath his skin.

"Cristilia told me Emaline came to see you."

He nodded, looking down. "She did. And with her visit came a lot of news that I had, until then, not known about. When do you think they would have told me about the Druid's survival? Or that there is a strong possibility my father is still alive?"

I cringed at the mention of his father. "I tried to warn them. I wanted to tell you but the... the council had me swear not to. They said it was best for you."

"I must return to Olderim and take up my place as Prince for my people. They cannot keep me here any longer. Emaline said the Druid is missing, but what does that mean for my father? Is he dead or still out there?" He ran a hand over his shaved head, and over the raised red scars from the gold cage. The healers had tried to fix them, but the stubborn marks would not fade.

"They won't let you leave," I said.

His head cocked to the side. "I trust that you of all people will support my choice in returning home. Once Queen Kathine arrives, I'll inform the council that we are to leave, and that is final. We may be on Eldnol soil, but I am still your Prince. Queen Kathine has no say over the doings of Niraen elves."

He walked past me, and I grabbed hold of his hand, tugging him back. "I want nothing more than to help you, Hadrian, but you still don't know everything. The Druid may be missing, but his presence is still crawling across the land. We cannot just leave; you know what this means for us."

"I don't think you understand just how serious I am." With each word his hand grew hotter in mine. "I will leave with Queen Kathine's permission or not. I just hope you come with me."

As if Hadrian couldn't take another moment, he dropped my hand and left the cave.

CHAPTER

FIVE

I GROWLED INTO my hands, a mix of emotions racing through me. I understood his frustration, but this reaction was uncalled for. Kicking out at the wall closest to me, I released some tension before I chased after him.

Cristilia and Nyah stood beyond the mouth of the cave, but Hadrian was not with them. Nyah pointed towards the forest ahead of us, and my eyes picked up the faint blue glow bobbing in and out of the darkness.

"Go speak to him but stay out of view. Remember, you are not to be here." Cristilia's words of warning echoed in my mind as I followed after Hadrian.

And he knew I was chasing.

He looked back over his shoulder, his golden eyes catching my gaze, but he didn't stop.

I stayed a few paces behind, unsure what to say. It'd been two weeks since the battle of the ship, not enough time to forget what had happened.

My lungs burned as I picked up my pace into a run. I thanked the Goddess for his Heartfire; it was the only way I was able to keep up with him and not lose him in the dark of the forest.

There was this unspoken tension between us and had been since the incident with the Druid. I felt awkward in his presence, pushed away from him by the secrets I was forced to keep. The guilt had burrowed so far into my stomach, it would be hard to weed out.

"Hadrian, we need to talk," I called out. "You can't just run off when you find something difficult."

"I find conversations that start with those five words never end well," Hadrian called back at me, slowing his run to a walk.

"Then is it not best we get it over with?"

Hadrian replied weakly, "Not yet."

"So, are you planning on just walking around all night?" I asked, breathless and frustrated.

"No…" His reply dripped with mischief. "Walking is not as fun as flying."

Hadrian shifted within the blink of an eye. He stood taller before me, his ram-like horns at the sides of his head and bat-like wings curled around him.

"What do you think? Fancy joining me?" Hadrian's voice was deeper than usual and had a slight growl.

He knew the coven of empaths had unblocked the link between my Dragori state but had still not seen me in my secondary form. I'd only shifted twice, once with the coven and today during the ambush. Both times were out of my control.

"I don't think I can."

"Well, if you want to talk to me, you are going to have to learn quickly."

Hadrian bent his legs and was airborne in seconds. He hung before me, his wings beating night air upon me with a devilish smile painted on his face. Black scales reflected the firelight from the closest lit post, which made it look like rough cut diamonds on his skin. For a moment, I was mesmerized. A gust of wind made my eyes water as Hadrian shot up into the air with a great force.

"Ahh." My complaint echoed around me.

I looked up, trying to spot where he was but saw nothing.

"Focus." I closed my eyes and opened my mind to the change. "Come on, come on."

It resisted at first, but the more I focused and pulled, the animalistic feeling within turned in acceptance. It was growling in the pit of my body, waiting for me to take control. Waiting for me to give it release.

It didn't hurt as much as it had this morning. A rippling sensation, as if the air in my lungs burst across every part of my body. I kept my eyes shut until the feeling ceased, and the night air around me relaxed. Flashes of bright silver lit up behind my eyes. I didn't need to open my eyes to know It had worked.

I looked up into the waiting dark towards the last place I saw Hadrian. All it took was a thought, and the muscles in my back followed my command. My wind brushed against my boots as the ground fell away.

There was a flash of blue in the sky above me, a sign from Hadrian who hid within the branches of a nearby tree. I could hear his laughter.

I flew for him, dodging a reaching branch that materialized before me.

"If we get caught—" I began, but Hadrian interrupted.

"I don't think I can be in any more trouble. Now, let's see if you can keep up, Petal."

He jumped from the tree and flew skyward. I followed closely, pushing my wings to new speeds as Hadrian stayed ahead. The ground was far below now, almost invisible through the thick night.

Up, up we flew, closer to the wall of canopy. Hadrian burst through it first. I closed my eyes and raised my hands to shield me from the foliage but came through unmarked.

Hadrian hovered above the crown of trees. There was nothing but night sky around us. I came to his side and kept aloft, stunned by the beauty. Clouds speckled the night sky, moving slowly before the moon, which seemed even more prominent from such a height. There was a chill in the air, but it didn't bother me, not with Hadrian's warm body beside mine.

"This is incredible," I said, my eyes trained to the never-ending sea of treetops beneath us.

"I am glad I get to share this with you," Hadrian said. "Finally."

I turned and faced him, my wings moving in time to keep my balance. "You have been thinking about this?"

"Ever since I first took you flying, I have thirsted for it again."

I remembered that day when he took me to the fields away from Olderim and showed me his beastly form; how he held me close to his chest and explored the skies with me.

"I meant what I said back in there. Returning home is the second most important thing to me at this moment." His comment brought me back to the moment.

"And what is the first?" I asked quietly.

A clawed hand reached for mine and held on. "You."

I squeezed his hand. "I can't tell you how relieved I am to see you... healed."

"Even after I destroyed a building and any relationship with the council?"

"Yes, even after that."

His ability to make light of our situation was both frustrating and endearing. I looked him up and down, my wings skipping a beat for a moment, making me dip midair.

Hadrian reached out, laughing, and held me up.

I could see just how different Hadrian's Dragori form was to mine as we were both bathed in the silver moonlight. Hadrian's wingspan was double the size of mine, and they had a red undertone. My scales were opal and silver, yet his were black. And his body was warmer than mine. Although the heat was most likely due to the Heartfire swirling beneath his skin. His nails were black and pointed, his knuckles dusted with scales like armor. As he flexed his hold on me, the scales reflected the light and came alive when they rippled.

"It's your father—that's why you feel so rushed to leave?"

Hadrian nodded. "If there is a chance he is still alive, I have trust in it." His response had me stumbling over my words. "Either he is dead, alongside my mother, and it is my duty as Prince to take my place and lead my people; or he is alive, and there is no saying what state he will be in, wherever he is. That type of magick, taking the appearance of another is not common. I don't understand how it works, its dark magick. What evil infection the Druid has used against him may have changed him for the worse."

"What if the Druid expects you to go looking?" I said. "He had you once already..."

"Then let him. I can promise our next encounter will not end as it did before."

"The council—"

"I care little of what the council think. It is my father, Zacriah. Family. Would you leave yours if you knew there was a chance they were alive?"

I understood his want to find him, for my parents had been on my mind for days. I'd been informed by the council my parents were safe, but I knew just how quickly that could change from my own experience over the past weeks.

"You must do what you feel is right," I whispered.

"Can we just have a few moments where we do not talk about this? I just want to enjoy the silence up here. I believe it will be the last chance to enjoy it for a long while." Hadrian looked back out at the night as the stars winked into life above us.

We hung there for a while, my hand in his, and spoke no more.

Only when we returned to the ground, my wings tired and body heavy, did we say our goodbyes.

"I will see you in a matter of days." Hadrian held onto my cheeks and leaned in. A warm kiss pressed against my head.

"Will you be okay here?"

"I am sure I will keep myself busy."

That was not what I meant, but Cristilia found us before I could explain more.

∽

CRISTILIA GUIDED NYAH and me back to our room. We had to leave Hadrian in the cave where the two figures stood confused as to where he'd disappeared off to. I knew there was more to Cristilia's abilities, but as we walked up the never-ending walkway, all I could think about was sleep. That and the words Hadrian and I had exchanged.

We passed through the main gate unnoticed and back into the town, shrouded from view within Cristilia's bubble of night.

That night and the two that followed, I dreamt of blue fire, inked Druid marks and creatures of smoke.

I'd not left my room for the few days the town waited for the arrival of Queen Kathine. Nyah kept me company.

We read books, searching for a mention of Heartfire or the Staff of Light, but we found no insight into either.

Cristilia had visited us at night, bringing news of Hadrian's growing boredom. I had asked if she would take me to see Hadrian, but she refused. It seemed she didn't want to put us at risk. Not that it seemed to bother her the first time she snuck us from the town.

The uncertainty of meeting Queen Kathine worried me and kept me up most of those nights. Nyah showed no issue with sleeping as she camped out in my bed. When we gave up on searching books, we opted for physical exercise. Nyah didn't want us to slack and miss any time to train. Especially when news reached our room of another body that was found covered in Druid marks.

On the morning of the Queen's arrival, Nyah woke me with a wooden cup of fresh spring water, which quickly brought my senses awake.

"Better get ready. Today is the big day." She had already dressed. She wore a pair of black pants and a grey tunic. Her ginger hair draped over her shoulders, framing her exhausted face. "I took the liberty in picking out an outfit for you."

"Thanks." I yawned.

Nyah began moving the furniture in my room back into place. We had moved them out of the way as we trained yesterday and had yet to put it back. "That bruise you gave me yesterday is massive; I'm so proud."

I stretched my arms above my head. "What can I say? I have a good teacher."

Nyah waited for me to change into the earthy green robe, which hung loosely around my arms, and a brown belt that matched the boots given to me on my first day in Kandilin. I chose to go with Alorian made garments instead of my ripped Niraen guard outfit I'd arrived wearing.

Anything to appease the council and make today go as smooth as possible.

Once we left our room, Nesta waited beyond it to guide us and fill us in on the coming day. We had not seen her since the fall of the council hall, and she embraced us both.

"Queen Kathine arrived this morning and has requested a public audience with the council and you both." Nesta spoke over her shoulder as we passed Alorian guards and rushed handmaids who danced around us with hands full.

"Where will we be meeting?" I spoke up, dodging one elfin man who almost tumbled into me.

"The heart of the city," Nesta replied, her golden face pinched with concern.

"How is the possible?" Nyah asked. "Hadrian destroyed the entire thing."

"Many hands make for light work. During the past days, we have been able to rectify part of the destruction." Reading the confusion on my face, Nesta added, "You will soon see."

As we walked through the town in the trees, we could see what she was talking about. Paneling connected the west and east side of the town once again. Although the council hall was still absent, the large walkway acted as a stage.

As we got closer, the civilians of Kandilin stepped out of our way. Their distrusting stares caused the hairs on my arms to stand. It would see the entire town was out to watch the audience this morning. Some elves looked our way, but most kept their eyes glued to the woman who stood in the middle of the city.

Queen Kathine.

She stood a foot taller than the guards around her. Dressed in elven chain, Queen Kathine was a statue of silver. The closer we got, the more I sensed her presence and power. Across her shoulders, a design of frosty leaves gave her frame a broad illusion. The same intricate design wrapped around her waist where her white skirt hung over tight trousers. Her braided brown hair and thick brows were striking, and her brown skin glowed. She was the perfect depiction of beauty and power.

She wore no crown, nor did she need to. The air of royalty practically danced around her.

"Both of you go and stand before the council. You will be addressed when the meeting starts," Nesta said, urging us to a place before the table. "And a tip, don't speak to Queen Kathine unless you are spoken to first."

Then Nesta pushed us forward.

I kept my gaze unmoving from the council members as we walked before them. Kazmir, Penna and Cristilia sat with the rest of the council on an oaken desk. Kazmir raised a hand for us to stop, and we both bowed our heads.

Under the gaze of the council and entire town of Kandilin, I felt vulnerable. I was confident that was how the council wanted us to feel. This was nothing more than a show of power.

All heads snapped towards the Queen as her voice rained out. "Where is the third?"

I knew she was talking about Hadrian. He was the only one absent, whereas Emaline could be seen sheltering between guards to my right. Nesta stood beside her.

"He is being retrieved as we speak, my Queen," Kazmir rose from the desk and responded.

"My one request was simple. Have the three here when I arrive." Her gaze narrowed on Kazmir.

Queen Kathine moved towards myself and Nyah. The soldiers around her began to follow, but she raised a firm hand to stop them.

"No need."

When she reached us, she extended a hand. "I am glad to finally meet you both, although I wish it were under different circumstances." She whispered the last part. "Do not let those fools frighten you. They like to believe control comes from fear."

Her handshake was as firm as her tone.

"It is a pleasure to meet you, my Queen," Nyah said, dipping into a curtsy.

Queen Kathine just smiled. "Gallion has told me much about you, young lady."

Nyah blushed, her skin matching the color of her hair. "Only good things I hope."

"Oh, yes, only good things."

I stayed quiet, and that didn't go unnoticed. "Gallion has also talked about you, Zacriah Trovirin. It is a pleasure to meet you."

"And you." I bowed again.

"I must take my seat, so we can get this started," she said.

She turned away from us and moved to the desk, taking her place between Kazmir and Penna in the middle seat. More like a throne. It was made from twisted wood, the tips crowned with crystals like those in the caves we had visited.

Queen Kathine rested both her forearms on the desk and waited. Soon after, there was movement from the bridge connecting the west side of Kandilin that caught everyone's attention, and all heads turned to Hadrian.

Hadrian walked ahead of his escorts. With a head held high and shoulders pinned back, he moved like a King. There was a flush of color back in his skin, but the blue Heartfire still glowed from his body. Those he passed shied away from him.

He wore the deep purple and brown, Thessolina colors, which stood out compared to those dressed in silver around him. His choice to wear these colors was a clear message. Kazmir's face soured as she looked upon him.

"Here comes the boy of fire. The Prince of destruction, wearing his crown of ashes," Penna said, voice louder than it needed to be.

Hadrian walked straight to the desk and extended his hand across to Queen Kathine, ignoring Penna's comment.

"Queen Kathine, I must say it is a pleasure to see you again." His voice carried across the watching crowd.

"You have grown mountains since our last encounter," she replied, shaking his hand twice.

The fact Queen Kathine didn't think twice before touching Hadrian's glowing skin proved he was no threat.

They dropped hands but not their stare. "How is Queen Sallie? I heard you recently welcomed your younglings into the world. I must first offer my congratulations." Hadrian bowed his head.

At the mention of her children, her eyes shone for a moment. "Your blessing is welcomed. My wife is doing well. She would have visited, but we both agreed the twins are so young it was best to keep them away from possible harm."

Hadrian's arms raised. "Ah, that would be me. I must apologize. I am unsure which version of events you have heard." He looked at Penna and Kazmir with intent. "But as I am sure you can understand, that was a mistake."

"Do I now?" she responded, her voice tipped with ice. "All I am aware is that one of the oldest buildings in my land has been destroyed and that accusations have been passed from hand to hand. That is why I am here, to seek the truth and ensure that it does not happen again."

Hadrian's proud smile faltered. "Please, ask whatever you desire. But I too have requests for you."

The tension between Hadrian and Queen Kathine morphed between my very eyes. First, they felt like old friends and now, the greatest of enemies.

"I would like to start this meeting with a blessing from our Goddess." The Queen's voice raised in volume, yet she didn't shout. Magick. Her words seemed to bounce off every tree, leaf and watching elf in Kandilin until everyone bent their heads.

"May the Goddess Dalibael grant us light to uncover the darkness that shrouds the truth. We ask the Her to look down upon us with her great wisdom and clarity and help show us the path of mercy and virtue. May she forever love us and banish the dark."

The town was bathed in silence as Queen Kathine finished her prayer. Even the wind seemed to still.

"Prince Hadrian Vulmar of Thessolina. I welcome you to speak your heart on the destruction of our Council Hall. Please, explain the reasoning for your actions after such gratitude has been shown to you during your stay here." Queen Kathine stood once again, her hands raised to sides as she questioned Hadrian.

There was a low rumble as he cleared his throat, then he looked up with his golden jeweled eyes and shocked the entire crowd. "Heart Magick."

CHAPTER
SIX

QUEEN KATHINE'S EXPRESSION melted into shock. Her hand slammed down on the desk, wood creaking in protest under her force. Her jaw tensed as she bit down hard, muscles in her cheeks rippling.

Hadrian had gone against the one wish that was placed upon us by the council. Not to reveal the truth. Not to mention Heart Magick.

The only person who didn't look shocked was Cristilia, who smiled to herself where she sat.

"Our Goddess is light, life and truth. Since she'd been invoked before this meeting, I feel that it is only fair that I follow her three virtues. In truth, I admit that the news is not a positive one, but it is important that you know before I explain what has happened here." Hadrian was talking to the entire town now, whether they heard him or not. This was an act of defiance against the Queen and her council. If he was in trouble before, it was nothing compared now.

"How dare you spill those lies to my people," Queen Kathine shouted.

"Lies." Hadrian laughed. "Do you swear on your Goddess, our Goddess, that I do not speak the truth?"

The Queen opened her mouth but lacked a response.

"Thank you. I shall continue. The return of the Druid, as I have only recently learned, has brought more than just panic to these lands, but a magick that for centuries has been forgotten by most. Right now, the Druid is hiding in plain sight, abducting our friends, family, allies and threatening our very existence. What happened in the Council Hall was out of my control, something I regret deeply and wish I could change. But I cannot go back and redo my wrongs. What I can do is look to the future and find a way to stop it from happening again. From this morning I will be returning to Olderim and take my place as King until my father is found—"

"You will not be leaving Eldnol, Prince Hadrian," Queen Kathine said quietly. I could see the anger rolling off her in waves of heat that could match Hadrian's fire.

Hadrian seemed stunned, but a small part of me was happy to hear those words. I didn't want him to leave. It was a selfish emotion that flooded my mind, but I couldn't deny it.

"You cannot return when you are still such a threat. Heart Magick is not something you can just control. Until the Druid is destroyed, you cannot return and risk the lives of your people. What happened here may—will happen again. Mark my words."

I stepped forward, taking a breath for confidence.

"Hadrian, Queen Kathine is right. You told me the reason for *our* existence is to put an end to the Druid just as our predecessors once had." I turned to the Queen and bowed, keeping my eyes to the fresh paneled floor as I spoke. "Queen Kathine, I request that we send a party to find the fourth Dragori."

"I already have scouts in Morgatis," she replied, voice stern. "I am searching, but that is not where our efforts should be placed. No matter where Prince Hadrian goes, his power will only bring destruction. He cannot control Heart Magic."

"What of the sympathizers?"

It was all I needed to say to catch her attention. Her icy gaze bore into me and froze me to the core.

"I am aware of the sympathizers, the spineless traitors. From today, I am doubling the soldiers in each city, town and village to cease their attempts."

Nesta stepped forwards and bowed. "My Queen. What of his shadow creatures? Animated dead that run off his power. During the mission two days back, within the border forest of Kandilin, we were attacked by a handful of them."

The Queen stood there for a moment, her eyes locked to a spot on the desk as she focused on her thoughts. She then turned like thunder towards the council, her voice booming across them. "Is this a detail you decided not to pass onto me?"

Penna's scared expression as his queen screamed at him was a vision I would not forget in a hurry. "Not at all, my Queen. With everything that happened with Prince Hadrian, it slipped passed us."

"How dare you insult me. You, as my council, are my eyes and ears beyond Lilioira. What other information have you simply *forgotten* to tell me?"

"That is all, my Queen. My deepest apologies."

"Oh, sit down." She waved a hand at him. "Nesta, as you are the only one to have mentioned it, I will allow you to explain what happened to me, can you do that?"

Nesta bowed, her honey colored hair not moving in its knot. We stood there in silence, and Nesta revealed the little information she knew about the creatures. The Queen stood as still as stone, listening to every word that fell from Nesta's plump lips.

"You say they did not cease their attack until the head was taken from its body?" The Queen asked.

Nesta nodded. "Correct. It was Nyah who figured that part out."

Nyah blushed beside me, pulling a strand of red hair that fell in front of her eyes and tucking it behind her ear.

"Stand forward, brave soldier," Queen Kathine commanded. "Is this true?"

I couldn't help but smile as Nyah got the recognition she deserved, something she'd never be given back in Olderim.

"Yes," Nyah replied, arms pinned to her side as she bowed her head an inch.

Queen Kathine made a sound and raised the corners of her mouth so slightly that it could've been missed. "I must say I am impressed. I have known many brave soldiers from Thessolina. Your prince must be proud of your blood line."

Nyah cleared her throat and looked up. "Thank you, although I must say that my mother was Alorian and my father Niraen."

"Blessed." Queen Kathine smiled a final time and directed her attention to the crowd. "I ask if anyone has news of similar creatures spotted or encountered?"

"I have," I said. "Before Hadrian was captured by the Druid, we were attacked by a cloud of what I thought were birds, but they were not. Much like those in the forest, these seemed to be real creatures created by shadows. Animated dead."

I looked at my arm and still saw the faint claw marks that were etched onto my skin. Just another reminder of that horrific day and the events that followed.

"Then it is clear, more than ever, that the Druid has returned. And if these creatures still linger amongst us, it means his disappearance is not the end of him." Queen Kathine turned to the council again, urging them to rise from their seats. "We must prepare for the worst. It is clear that our efforts need to be put into finding the Druid to stop his warped plans."

"What about my father?" Hadrian spoke up.

"For all we know, King Dalior is lost." The words stung. Hadrian's blue hue intensified as he turned to the person who spoke. Penna.

I bit down hard on my lip, worried for Penna's safety. I didn't want Hadrian acting out. From Penna's cold smirk, that is what he wanted.

"Watch your mouth, Star Reader, or you will not have one for long." Hadrian's threat barred down on him. The entire council, including the Queen, flinched from the heat that rippled from Hadrian as his Heartfire grew.

"Prince Hadrian, I ask that you stand down. This is no place for common arguments."

"You are not my Queen, nor do you hold command over me. Keep your pets in line before I show them why Heart Magick is so feared."

This was not Hadrian speaking. I sensed his dark turn. Nyah flinched, mouth pinched with worry as if she sensed something more. Her gaze kept flickering to Hadrian then back to the Queen.

I moved, standing between him and the council, and placed my hands on his chest. I felt the fast beat of his heart and the large breaths he was taking.

"Stop. Enough," I said.

I moved my head until Hadrian only kept his eye contact with me. The purple shirt he wore began to wilt as the warm blue flame ate away at it. It hissed as it grew, turning material to cinders and creating streams of smoke to crawl into the waiting air.

"You need to control this, Hadrian; otherwise, you know what will happen."

His Heartfire was bubbling beneath him, waiting for an excuse to devour.

"The Staff of Light," someone said, distracting us all.

Cristilia stood from her place on the desk, an ivory dress spilling around her; a waterfall of beads and silk.

Her words were like Emaline's water, cooling Hadrian's fire until the smoke settled and his shirt hung awkwardly off his shoulder. He truly looked like a prince of ash.

"The Staff of Light is the only resolution to Prince Hadrian's affliction."

Queen Kathine face paled at the mention of the Staff.

"Queen Kathine and council, you know this is the only way to prevent the Heartfire from changing the Prince. He must be cleansed if they ever have a chance of stopping the Druid. My heart pains to say this aloud, but we know well enough that the Druid has linked his power with the Prince's. They are soul tied."

I flinched from Hadrian. Soul tied?

"But in the wrong hands," Kazmir said, "it could be catastrophic."

"It is a risk that must be taken in order to help him." Cristilia walked around the table and faced Queen Kathine directly. She was shorter than the Queen, but she held herself proud before her. "My people remember the damage of Heart Magick more than yours, so I urge you to heed my request. It is not a power that should be so simply forgotten."

"There are risks," Queen Kathine replied, her gaze lost as she mulled over the possibilities. "My grandmother hid it away for a reason."

"The risks outweigh the possibility of great destruction, or the Druid using Prince Hadrian against the others… against us."

Queen Kathine looked up then, her eyes cutting into Hadrian.

Hadrian pushed me aside. "What do you mean the Druid could use me?"

A collective gasp from the civilians in the town blossomed.

"Heart Magick is demonic; the only chain left in the link between the Dragori and their original creators. Whatever the Druid did to you during your capture, he has replaced the link that was taken by our Goddess, which has left you connected to the Druid in ways we do not understand. I fear we will never understand."

"Then we must destroy it again," I said, panicked for Hadrian. "We have to find the Staff."

"I appreciate your bravery, Zacriah Trovirin, but it is a dangerous journey. Not even I know where the Staff is located. You must find the Keeper. They will only share the location to a Dragori, not even a Queen." Queen Kathine kept her hands clasped behind her back as she spoke to me.

"Then I will go. Let me find the Keeper and the Staff," I almost shouted my request.

Cristilia answered, "The Dragori should not be separated; they are stronger together."

"Prince Hadrian is in no state to go on a mission such as this," Queen Kathine said.

"Do not speak for me, for I shall go. I am the reason for such a mission."

I looked to Emaline, who stood in silence the entire meeting. I had noticed her during the start, hidden amongst the civilians around her. Now at the mention of her assistance, she tried to slip into the crowd.

"Then all three will go, alone. I cannot spare soldiers during a time like this. Emaline Sowdin, I can see you trying to leave. Step forward and join your brothers."

"They are no brothers of mine," I heard her hiss.

"Not by blood," Queen Kathine said. "By magick, yes."

Emaline stopped her attempt, and the crowd around her separated as the Queen called her out. She stood, looking around at those who moved from her, and released a loud breath before taking her place up amongst us.

"As your Queen, I command that you journey with Prince Hadrian Vulmar and Zacriah Trovirin to find the Keeper who will guide you to the Staff. It is important you stick together. Separating you now will only increase the chance of you getting picked off by the Druid. We cannot risk losing any of you again. One may be lost to Heart Magick."

I had sensed a dark presence when Hadrian spoke, almost saw it reflect behind his eyes, but lost? In my mind, if the Staff was a possibility, he was not lost.

I could see from Emaline's tight, pale lips that she wanted to complain. But she didn't dare, not to her Queen.

"When do we leave?" Hadrian questioned, his Heartfire calm and faint.

Queen Kathine didn't answer but turned to Cristilia for council.

"Sunrise," Cristilia replied.

"And who is the Keeper?" I asked. "Where will we find him?"

No one answered.

A cool breeze wrapped around us all and a low rumble of thunder echoed in the distance. We all looked up to the sky to see it darkening beneath clouds that gathered. A storm was coming.

"It is a short journey," Queen Kathine said, skipping her gaze between the brewing storm. "Weather permitting."

"There is a temple in Thalas, two-day griffin ride north of here. You will start there. Ask the coven who dwells in the temple for guidance. My council here acts as my voice, but the coven in the temple speaks for the divine. It is with them you can find insight into the Staff's location."

"With all due respect, I feel cheated. I do not feel comfortable going on a wild chase for a mystical Staff when my father is out there. I know he is." Hadrian spoke up again.

"I vow that on your return, King Dalior is our next concern. Until then, it is important you find the Keeper and the Staff. Take heed of my words, Prince Hadrian, the presence of your Heartfire is not a Godly one." Cristilia stood tall, the ominous clouds causing a halo around her frame.

He nodded once, eyes closed. "Then I will go."

I stepped forward. "And so will I."

Everyone looked to Emaline, who stood shoulders hunched.

Queen raised one thin brow, and Emaline quickly said, "If I must."

CHAPTER
SEVEN

THE SKY WAS thick with tension.

Clouds descended like angry beasts, coating Kandilin in dull light and hot rain. The sky opened, unleashing an army of droplets the size of fists. I had heard whispers of an Eldnol storm, but nothing prepared me for the weight of the rain that smashed into my exposed skin.

As the first drop of rain splattered against the new podium, it signaled the end of the meeting, and the crowds began to part to take shelter from the storm. We scattered into our rooms and waited for the storm to pass. Even in the hollow chamber within the tree, my hairs stood on end as the lightning clashed alongside thunder. Now and then, a flash of light would illuminate mine and Nyah's face in shocking shadows before settling back into darkness. The torrential downpour of rain sounded as if the Goddess herself was running across the world.

"I'm coming with you," Nyah said, twisting her wet hair and letting it spill onto my floor. "Last time I left you… well, we know how that ended."

"I know." There was no point arguing. I knew Nyah well enough to know the moment we left, she would be following in pursuit. She listened to nothing but her intuition, not even a Queen. In a way, the only Queen Nyah referred to was herself. One thing I loved about her was her ability to follow her instincts without second guessing the consequences.

"Let's hope the storm passes by tomorrow; otherwise, it's going to be one wet journey," she said, gazing beyond the carved window. "Why couldn't the Druid pick a warmer season to turn up? Snow will soon blanket Eldnol, and I hate snow."

I forced a chuckle, but in truth, I couldn't find the energy for laughter, not with a looming quest ahead. My body prickled with warm anticipation for the events to come; rain or snow, I would find it.

"I just hope we find the Staff without wasting time," I said. "You noticed Hadrian's anger. That is not the real him. I know it."

"I sensed it. Like burning flame bubbling within his mind. His emotions are spinning out of control." Nyah nibbled at her nails.

"I should have guessed you would flex your power."

"What can I say? I've got to make sure my boy if safe."

I sat next to her, the feathered bedding soft beneath me. "I'm worried about him, Nyah. He looked normal, but I can still see the pain behind his eyes. He has not healed, far from it."

Nyah took a dramatic breath and placed a hand on her heart. "What? Are you worried about Princey? Shocking. I didn't see that coming."

I nudged her with my shoulder, a small laugh slipping from my mouth, this one authentic. "You just can't help yourself, can you?"

"What do you think?" she answered with a wink.

∽

TIME SLIPPED BY like the lazy flow of clouds beyond the window.

Far from tired, I packed a small sack for the following day, which seemed only to bring up more questions. I had no clue what conditions we would face, where we'd sleep and what we would be eating. So, I just stuffed my metal claws, an oversized robe and the healing salve for my hand. The cold climate of Eldnol had caused my wrist to be stiff in the mornings.

I lost myself in the dark view from the window. Where was Hadrian now? Was he kept in the cave, in a prison of crystals and pools? I wished I could see him, although I knew tomorrow I would finally have the time with him I had been thirsting for.

The storm had passed, but the city was still empty of life. I saw only the occasional glint of silver pass in the night, phantom of Alorian soliders passing in the dark. In the distance, griffins clicked, and the window whispered its light lullaby.

Tiredness made my limbs heavy, as if molten metal was poured in my veins, weighing me down. I clambered into bed, ready to enjoy what could be my last night in comfortable lodgings. As I drifted into the hold of sleep, I saw Hadrian in my mind's eye, blazing blue with his mouth opened in a scream.

The crash of thunder woke me.

I sat up in bed, my body drenched with sweat. I couldn't remember the dream, but its nasty presence hummed in my body and mind. Anxiety made me sluggish; my heart fluttered like the wings of a dying bird.

In my panic, I scanned the room, half-expecting a shadow creature to materialize. I could almost hear the laughter of the Druid in the roaring wind outside.

I wanted Hadrian. I needed him.

The loud noise came again, but this time it followed with a hollow sound. My eyes shot to the door as my mind caught up with what it was. Someone was knocking.

Hadrian?

I slipped from the bed and went for the door. Opening it slowly, I saw Cristilia, not a single drop of water on her.

"May I come in?" she asked.

Dumfounded, I opened the door for her to pass through. A waft of burning coals oozed from her as she passed me.

"Why knock when you could have just come in?" I asked, remembering how we passed through the gate of the city the previous night.

Cristilia gave me a knowing look. "That behavior is not something I condone. I did not want to frighten you."

"That's good to know," I replied, securing the door, not admitting her loud banging *had* frightened me.

"I wanted to see you before you leave tomorrow," Cristilia said. "It is a journey with many risks, and I believe that the Queen plans to bless you each with a gift tomorrow. I wanted to give my own. A story." Cristilia gestured to the bed. "May I?"

"Sit, yes," I replied, rubbing my eyes of sleep.

She perched herself on the end of the bed. I chose to stand.

"I wanted to tell you a story; one that has weighed heavy on my people since the last of Heart Magick. No one but the Morthi elves know the destruction that follows in the footsteps of the magick. Not even the Queen has records of it."

Crossing my arms over my chest, I tried to still the shiver that overwhelmed me. I remembered her mentioning something during the meeting about her people not forgetting Heart Magick as the Alorian elves had.

I nodded, pressing her to carry on.

"You may have wondered why I have helped you so keenly. It is because of what Heart Magick means. To show you how important finding the Staff is. I was as afraid as the rest of the council when I watched Hadrian's azure blaze destroy the council hall. They knew what it was but would never have accepted it. Sometimes brushing something beneath a bed of grass is easier to ignore. I would not let that happen. You and Prince Hadrian had to know what it meant. I may not have been around during the end of the war between darkness and light, but the memory of it lives in the land of my people, Morgatis. Do you know much about the Dragori that came before you?"

"Very little." I wanted to say more but preferred to hear her story.

"I shall explain. The druids were able to capture a Dragori by the name of Tazlim, an air wielder like yourself. Once Tazlim's Heart Magick was unlocked, and the link between the druids and their creations was solidified, havoc and death followed. My people have not always lived below ground in caves and mazes of rock. Across the rolling sand dunes and deserts, we had settlements, large towns and cities made from cloth and sand. That was until Tazlim touched foot on our shores and unleashed magick like we have never seen before."

As she told the story, I could picture it within my mind. Twisting tornados of sand and leveled towns. I knew the Morthi lived below ground and believed that to have always been true. Hearing a Dragori had the power to ruin lives in such a way broke my heart.

"Many lives were lost, stolen by the Heartair that flowed through Tazlim's veins. It was not until the last Druid was believed to be killed did the connection to Heart Magick end."

"What happened to Tazlim?" I asked, mouth dry.

"I am unsure. I know he was never the same. The guilt was too much for him to bear. He disappeared not long after the druids end."

I imaged Hadrian. What would happen if this power finally took a hold of him? Allowing the Druid to control him, it would be catastrophic.

"Is that why your people are afraid? Why they exiled a girl that believed could be a Dragori?"

Something passed behind Cristilia's eyes, an unknown expression that took her from the room and into her own mind. "Yes."

She stood and walked for the door.

"Have I upset you?" I called after her, a sinking feeling in my stomach making me sick. What did I say?

"Remember the story; find the Staff. Only it can save Hadrian and the elves in his way. Once Heart Magick takes over his body, there will be no stopping him."

She pulled at the door, allowing the night to seep inside my room.

"Always follow your instincts, Zacriah. I will not see you in the morning. Please forgive my absence. I am certain we shall see each other again."

"But—"

Cristilia passed through the door, leaving before I could finish my sentence.

She left me with questions in my mouth and confusion in my mind.

CHAPTER
EIGHT

MY YAWN MADE my entire body shiver.

I had not slept after Cristilia left, not with the weight of her story on my mind. Every time I closed my eyes, the horror of wind and death flashed, keeping me awake.

Morning sun dried all remnants of rain from the day before. The warmed wood panels we stood on as Queen Kathine blessed our journey smelled strange. It was hard to ignore as the weather became warmer and the smell intensified.

I stood between Emaline and Hadrian, facing the Queen and her council. As Cristilia promised the night before, she was not with them. Her seat was empty at the end of the desk.

The moment Hadrian saw me, he embraced me in the strongest of holds. He held me with no care that the entire town watched. His confidence lit my insides afire. My cheeks warmed, and I held on. He pulled back, placed a warm kiss on my head and held me at arm's reach.

"I cannot express how ready I am to have time with you," he whispered, looking down at me.

"Everyone is watching," I muttered, overly-aware at the spectacle of the Prince of Olderim and a common born Niraen displaying such open affection. I had never liked public displays of affection. Knowing those watched on as I shared a personal moment caused my forhead to dampen. There was something about the quiet, passion-filled stares that built tension when two elves were alone.

Hadrian's laugh warmed my body. "Let them watch, Petal, we might inspire songs."

I blushed and shied away. Hadrian released me and held my hand as we turned to the council, who watched with a mixture of expressions. Queen Kathine was smiling, and so was Kazmir to my surprise, but Penna looked displeased. I rolled my eyes.

Emaline stood beside us and kept her attention on the council. For a moment, she looked at us both then glanced down to our entwined hands. Her sudden smile was warm and honest as she looked back at each of us.

Her brown skin glowed with the golden blood that flowed beneath it. Her hair was slicked down, raven and short. Unlike myself, Emaline had her weapon of choice with her. Should I have brought something? She stood tall, a trident in her left hand. It was a bronze color with four pointed forks, each thin and sharp, the sun glinting off their points.

"Now it makes sense," she said before looking back at the council. I wanted to ask her what she meant, but her warm smile explained.

"Silver suits you, Zacriah Trovirin," Queen Kathine commented on my appearance.

To show respect, I'd requested an Alorian soldier's uniform when I woke, which I regretted the moment I changed into it. The overlapping silver breastplate was heavy and stiff, and the sharp cut sleeves where too long on my arms. Fitting ivory colored trousers were hidden beneath the thick skirt that wrapped around my middle.

Emaline was dressed the same, but Hadrian was still in Niraen colors as he had been yesterday. He had his hood up, covering his head and ears and the hue of blue flame that still coursed beneath his skin. His golden eyes pierced through the shadow the hood cast across his face.

Queen Kathine stood and addressed the three of us, the crowd watching. She invoked the presence of the Goddess Dalibael as she had yesterday and gave a brief explanation of why we were all there once again.

"The council and I have decided to present the three Dragori with the same gifts. We hope they aid their journey and create a speedy return." She moved around the desk and stood before it. She gestured to the three Alorian soldiers that stood waiting with arms full at her side.

"My first gift, may it help the speed of their journey," Queen Kathine's voice boomed. "Three of our finest griffins. Each griffin has recently passed their training in the aviary and is ready to enter the world as companions to our Dragori. May they become fine riders."

Queen Kathine nodded, and the first guard placed the silver whistle in his mouth. I could feel him blow air into it but heard no noise. Then, in tandem, three griffins descended from the skies and landed before us all. The crowd erupted in claps and cheers. Queen Kathine beamed at the reaction. "One for each of you."

They were all the same size. It was their coloring that set them apart. One was amber with white splotches down its feather spine. I knew it was mine, for it didn't stop looking at me. The other was midnight black with yellowed talons and a sharp beak. The last was speckled black and white, like the fur of a snow leopard.

"Each has been prepared for the journey. Please step forward and greet your companions."

We moved in unison towards the creatures with our hands raised in greeting. Taking slow steps, we reached out and ran our palms down their beaks. Mine chirped in pleasure, and his tail twitched. I turned to Hadrian who greeted his griffin, but he did not mirror my excitement. He had picked the black one and seemed to pay it no mind. I raised a brow at him as he caught my eye contact, but he just shook his head and ignored the griffin.

The moment I looked away, the crowd roared with laughter. I saw them point towards Hadrian, and I quickly looked back. Hadrian was sprawled on the floor, his griffin making what only could be a laughing noise. His talons hit the ground as he danced above the fallen prince.

"He pushed me!" Hadrian stood back up. The soldiers around him offered to help him, but he swatted their attempts away. "Can I request another?"

No one responded to his question.

Queen Kathine was giggling into her sleeve, which she stifled when she caught a glimpse at Hadrian's angered face. "Now you are each introduced, I would like to offer you another gift." She waved her hand and the second soldier stepped forward. In his hands was a rolled parchment. It was stained and the length of my arm, tied in a white ribbon.

It was given to Emaline, who bowed in thanks.

"This is a map scribed by Penna, Stargazer himself. It will show you Eldnol in all its glory and help you navigate. I give this to you, Emaline Sowdin, Dragori of water and ocean, for it is you who know these lands the best. I trust you will use your knowledge to help guide your fellow travelers."

Emaline thanked Queen Kathine but paid no mind to the contents of the map. She placed it, still rolled, under her arm.

"And finally."

We all watched the third soldier step forward. The object in his hands was small. It was given to Queen

Kathine who whispered her thanks. She took steps towards Hadrian, whose face was still speckled with embarrassment from his fall. I almost laughed just seeing his serious expression.

Queen Kathine opened her hand and presented the gift to Hadrian. "I give this to you, Prince Hadrian of Thessolina, as promised. This represents my truth that during your absence I will search for your father. I understand how important family is, and it pains me to see you in this dark grasp of worry."

The tears that wet my lashes surprised me. Although we stood around watching, the conversation between them both was very personal. Hadrian released a breath and bowed his head. "I appreciate your words, I accept them." With that, he plucked the object from her hands, and I noticed it was a frosted flower bud. I almost confused the glittering texture for a diamond until Hadrian held it up before him for the crowd to see, then slipped it into his breastplate.

"It is custom in Eldnol for promises to have a physical representation," Emaline whispered next to me. Could she sense my confusion? "A bud captured in ice is a royal symbol for truth. It is the greatest gift the Queen could give."

Queen Kathine gave him a smile and turned to us all.

"Head for Thalas Temple, seek the coven of Dalibael and ask for their guidance." Her voice was loud once more, washing over us all. "May the Goddess watch over you."

"May the Goddess guide you," the city responded.

We each bowed.

It was time to leave. I only hoped we succeeded before Hadrian finally cracked. Each time I looked upon his blue hue, I pictured the destruction that waited.

CHAPTER

NINƐ

SAYING GOODBYE TO Nyah was not difficult because I knew she would be following close by. I tried to question how she would, but she tapped her freckled finger to her nose and winked. She faded into the crowd and allowed the council to wish us luck. Penna was the only member who seemed lackluster in his farewell.

We each mounted our griffins, Hadrian seeming reluctant to climb his, and waved our goodbyes the crowd. It was more of a performance than the beginning of a journey.

As the wind rushed into my ears, a calm settling of relief washed over me.

Emaline stayed ahead of us from the moment we launched into the Eldnol skies. The view above the town morphed from blue to grey, and as the sun set later that day, it was blushed with pinks and purples.

For the first half of the day's journey, my mind was occupied with the view. Once we left Kandilin town and flew over the forest it was hidden within, all we could see were hills. Beneath us opened to incredible views for as far as I could see. Like a vein, the main riverway was below us, and we didn't deviate from its course. It reflected the sun's light as if it was glass, interrupted only by ships and small vessels of trade.

I loved watching the shadows we created on the land far below.

We ebbed through clouds and created a scene beneath us. It was hard to make out the smaller details, but I was sure we passed over an Alorian or two. I could only imagine their shock when our large shadows moved over them. At one point, I raised my hand to wave, but the wind was too harsh that high up, so I kept my body closer together.

The plan was to fly until sundown. I would have thought we would stop during the day, but we didn't. Emaline just kept up her flight and burst ahead.

I had opted to call my griffin Jerk. I laughed as I tried the name, and Jerk cooed back. It was a perfect name. The entire day so far, Jerk would break his calm flight by flicking his head up and down and sending me shifting over his back. Yes, Jerk was the perfect name.

Hadrian flew beside me most of the day. His griffin was faster than mine, which meant Hadrian had to struggle to slow its pace to stay beside me. It was impossible to talk with the rushing wind between us, and each time Hadrian looked at me, his eyes were wet with tears from the winds force. Whereas I was unbothered by it. I had not felt this close to my element before, not in the protective hold of the air that kept us aloft.

Jerk surprised me when his course suddenly changed. I opened my mouth in surprise as my stomach flipped, only to be rewarded with a mouthful of wind. I squinted and watched Jerk follow Emaline and her griffin, who descended to the ground. Landing was still my least favorite part of flying a griffin. That had not changed.

I clamped my eyes shut as Jerk excitedly shot towards the ground. The last thing I saw was Jerk deviate from the route and fly towards the open expanse of river. I only opened my eyes after I heard the loud splash of water and felt my feet become wet.

Jerk had landed *in* the river. He clicked with pleasure as he waded slowly through the water, dipping his beak in for a refreshment.

"Excuse me!" I said, patting Jerk's neck and pointing to the muddy riverside where Hadrian stood waving beside his griffin. "Mind dropping me off before you go for a swim?" Being around water caused my stomach to turn. I still could not swim, and Jerk was one more frantic movement from throwing me off.

As if Jerk understood my comment, he flicked his head back and coated me with water before swimming to the shore. His wings glided through water, his feathered tail shifting to keep us going in the right direction. Hadrian's laughter carried across the river to me. I couldn't see Emaline. By the time I reached the shore and Hadrian extended a hand for me to climb off Jerk, I saw the outline of her griffin in the distance. But still, she was not to be seen.

"Where is Emaline?"

Hadrian's hand gripped tightly on mine, and with a hard pull, I jumped the gap from Jerk to the muddy ground. "She does not seem to be in a talking mood."

"I don't blame her," I replied, squinting in his direction. "It was clear from the moment we met her she wanted nothing to do with the Druid and us. And now she's been dragged in again. If I were in her position, I would be upset."

The entire journey Emaline hadn't turned back to see if we'd been following, nor paid us any attention. It's not like I attempted to talk to her either. I was overly aware I didn't want to annoy her any more than she already was.

"Did you see where she went?" I asked, trying to catch a glimpse of her.

"By the time I landed, she was already walking off. I am sure she will come back. She left her sack with her griffin." Hadrian pointed out. "And talking about griffins, I think I would rather fly myself than have one. Mine does not seem to like me very much."

"They can join the list of people and creatures that have it out for you." I tried to make light of the situation, but it fell flat.

"You are not wrong, Petal. As long as your name is nowhere on that list, then I do not care."

"We will have to see," I replied, looking to see the lump of Emaline's sack still strapped to her griffin's side. "Fa once told me an adventure would either make or break a couple."

"Good thing I do not count this as an adventure." He wrapped his arm around me, and we left Jerk to his swim.

"We need to try with her if we want this to work." Hadrian knew I was talking about Emaline again. "She is the best fighter out of the three of us, and her magick is powerful. You might not remember it, but I do. She destroyed the golden cage with her water. We need her."

"I can only try so much," Hadrian said. "If she is unwilling to befriend us, then what can we do?"

"Try, try and try again." I stroked Hadrian's griffin as we reached it. "There will be a reason behind the way she is feeling. We just need to find out what it is, and if we can help."

"Since I am the Boy of Fire and Prince of Destruction, as Penna called me, how about I offer to make the fire tonight?" Hadrian said, fumbling in his sack.

I laughed. "Penna was right about something."

"Please, enlighten me to what that strange man has said that makes him right..."

"You are *so* dangerous." I pulled in closer to him, whispering, my lips close to his.

"Just you wait and see," Hadrian said.

I planted a quick kiss on his lips. "Have you ever considered just how dangerous I might be?"

"About as dangerous as a blunt dagger," Hadrian replied.

Flirting with Hadrian was as exhausting as sparring with him. He never gave up on his quick-witted replies.

Opting to change the conversation, I looked around again for any sign of Nyah.

"Nyah was supposed to follow us, but I haven't seen any sign of her," I said.

My mind had passed to Nyah many times since leaving. When we were about to leave Kandilin, she was pulled aside by Nesta. The last I saw of her as we took to the skies, she was in deep conversation.

"She is the most persistent person I know," Hadrian said, rubbing his hands down my arms, "She will turn up when the time is right."

He was right, but I couldn't shake the feeling we wouldn't be seeing her for a long while.

"Look…" Hadrian nodded his head to Emaline, who walked out from the patch of towering pine trees.

I wasted no time in walking over to her. She was fiddling with her pack when I came up behind her. My footsteps were heavy on purpose; I wanted her to know I was coming.

"Such lovely views," I said, opting to start with a broad topic.

"If you like water and wood." Her reply was short.

"I'm sorry you had to come. I know it wasn't something you wanted to do…"

Emaline turned. "You are wrong. I would do anything to protect those I love, and if it means escorting you both, then I will."

"Escorting?" Hadrian's muffled laugh made us both look at him.

"Sorry, did I say escorting? I meant protecting," Emaline said.

Her comment was a jab at the two times she'd had to save us, but I smiled it off and extended my hand. She was right after all.

"I haven't really had the chance to thank you for, well, saving us."

Emaline just stared at my hand but didn't reach for it. "Well, don't. I am sure there will be more opportunities for me to do it. Save your thanks for the next time."

"I shall." This conversation was going nowhere.

"If you wouldn't mind getting your griffin from the river and preparing it, I would like to get back in the skies." She unfolded the map before her. "We still have a while to go before I am happy stopping for the night."

"Absolutely." I nodded and turned to leave, but not before taking a glimpse at the map Penna had produced for the journey. It seemed rushed as if a child drew it.

"And there I was thinking we were setting up camp here…" Hadrian scoffed.

I raised a brow. "Wishful thinking?"

"I suppose," he replied.

I pressed my fingers into my mouth and whistled. The noise penetrated the landscape and caught Jerk's attention. He made a shrill cry, jumped into the air and flew towards me.

I had to stumble out of the way as Jerk came in for the clumsiest of landings.

There was a low chuckle that came from Emaline's direction, but I paid it no mind as I tried to calm Jerk.

"Shh," I cooed, grasping the reins and pulling him towards me. "You're making me look a fool."

Jerk just yanked and pulled until he finally settled when Hadrian pulled some dried meat from his pocket. With a short throw, Jerk plucked the meat from the air and chewed merrily on it.

"Trust me to have the one that chooses not to listen," I said, my arms aching from wrestling him.

"Just like his rider, food is the way to its heart," Hadrian replied.

∼

WE WERE UP in the air once again. Emaline lead on her griffin, leaving Hadrian and me struggling to keep up her pace. We flew on until the skies winked with stars and day light spilled away from us.

From this height, we watched the night come to life and spread over us the moment the sun passed behind the landscape. With the night came the chill in the air. I was finally thankful for the many layers we'd packed, as it was the only thing that kept me warm.

Hadrian didn't seem bothered by the cold breeze, which I put down to the Heartfire that intensified beneath his skin. He even took the position in front of me, which helped with keeping the direction as he glowed like a wry-light.

My eyes were heavy. I tried to fight the sleep but soon gave in. I was shocked back awake as my stomach flipped.

We were heading back for the ground once again. About time, I thought.

In my tired daze, it was hard to see where we'd landed, but I could hear the gentle rush of water close by and the rustle of leaves. I was too tired to work out my surroundings, Jerk dropped to the ground, resting his head across his front legs. The poor beast was exhausted from the flight. Just another example of his young age.

A spark of fire shot out from beside me and crashed into the pile of dried logs and sticks Hadrian had fetched from the surrounding forest. The blue flame roared, coating the pile of wood, which instantly warmed the space. Thanks to the new light, I noticed that Emaline was sat opposite me, her eyes alight by the flames.

I gave her a smile, and she just held my gaze for a moment then directed her attention back to the piece of bread she chewed. For as long as I remembered, I always preferred the company of women. There was no particular reason why, nor was I bothered to work it out. It just the way I was. My burning urge to befriend Emaline was hard to ignore.

Hadrian untied a large pot from the side of his griffin. I noticed a small bag of vegetables that he also picked out. Moving over to the fire, he placed the pot atop the fire and emptied the vegetables into it. He emptied the water pouch he carried into the pot and waited for it to bubble.

"It is your lucky night. You both get to experience my rare soup," Hadrian said.

"I'm honored," I joked back. "And what makes it so rare?"

Hadrian snapped a carrot in his hands and chucked it into the pot. "Well, because I have never attempted to make it before."

Hadrian kept looking to Emaline, waiting for a reaction but was given nothing to play off of.

"Would you like some Emaline?" he asked.

She just shook her head and picked at her bread.

I shrugged at Hadrian, and he carried on preparing his pot in silence.

"Have you ever been this north before?" I asked Emaline. "You seem to know the way pretty well."

"Once before. I visited Lilioira for the Queen's wedding when I was a young girl," she replied softly. "Everyone in Eldnol went."

I remember hearing about the ceremony back in Horith. The entire village was transfixed by the idea of such an event, for it was a rare occasion for royal weddings.

"What was it like?" I asked, generally intrigued by the idea of an Alorian ceremony.

Emaline's bright eyes lit up as she spoke of the day. "It was beautiful. One of the most elaborate and inclusive weddings in all of our history. The streets in Lilioira were full, and so was the lake that encapsulates the city. Music seeped from every building and food was everywhere you turned."

As she spoke, my mind conjured images as she described it. "The Queens felt it was only just that the celebration lasted for an entire week, although much of it is still hard to remember."

"Tell me about it," Hadrian said. "It was a fascinating week."

Emaline cracked a simple smile. "Yes, and it's thanks to your people why I cannot remember much of the final days."

Hadrian pulled a face, which Emaline found laughable. "I believe you named it Stinking Pig? I drank more than my body weight in that stuff. Niraen elves may not drink at a young age, but Alorian's do. Something about our blood diluting the effects of alcohol. It does not affect our bodies in the ways it does with... your kind. Unless you drink the amount I had. You'd feel it then."

I almost choked as I drank my water. Hadrian also found it entertaining, as he threw his head back and laughed. Just the mention of the ale made me feel warm inside.

"So, we have something in common," Hadrian said. "It was not long ago I introduced Zacriah to the drink. I will have some sent to you when I make it home."

Emaline busied herself with the crust of her bread, but I could see the offer touched her. "I don't need gifts." As quickly as a wave, her smile melted, and she closed off from us.

"I insist." Hadrian clapped and investigated the pot. "Now I hope you both are hungry because this is going to be a treat."

⌒

WE EACH LAY in silence after we devoured Hadrian's concoction. To my surprise, it was delicious and warmed me just enough. Emaline also had some after Hadrian went on and on about it. I could even see the pleasured shock on her face as she drained the wooden bowl.

The campfire was erected next to the riverbed. It was Emaline who chose the place to set up camp. She said if anyone was stupid enough to come for us, at least they would only have one direction they could attack us from.

With a full stomach and a foggy mind from the days travel, we each said our goodnights. Emaline turned her back on us. Hadrian took the chance and scooted over to me.

"This is the first time we are going to sleep together," he whispered in my ear. His warm arms were wrapped around me, and his Heartfire had dwindled to a slight hue, nothing more. But he was warm, which only made me melt into his embrace more.

"I didn't expect it to be like this," I replied, staring up at the bright sky. We were so far from home, yet the same stars smiled guarded the night above me. A view I couldn't complain about.

"You should know now never to expect anything." Hadrian's hot breath sent tingles from my back.

"I never do."

"To be frank, I could not think of a better place to share our first night. Where the stars can look down on us and the gentle hush of water is our songstress. It is perfect," Hadrian whispered. "Sleep well, Petal."

"Goodnight," I hushed, my eyes giving into the weight of sleep.

Hadrian, with his finger, pulled my collar down and kissed the base of my neck. "May you dream light."

I thought the scream was part of a mocking dream.

I ignored it at first until the one that followed sent a spark of panic to wake me.

CHAPTER
TEN

MY EYES SHOT open to see Emaline screaming as she was dragged through the air. The morning sky was overwhelmingly light as I looked up. It made the horror before me clear: we were under attack.

Emaline thrashed as the unknown being pulled her towards the lake. I stumbled up, fumbling blindly for a weapon, anything to use, but I couldn't see what it was that had a hold on her. The fire had died out, and dawn had brought a strange mist that seeped from the river and coated our camp.

Jerk's screech cut into my ears, deafening me. I clapped my hands to protect them from the cry. My ears rang, and the world sounded as if I was under water.

Whatever had a hold of Emaline was putting up resistance as she shouted for help. Driven by panic, I ran for Emaline empty-handed. I leapt over the makeshift campfire, which was nothing more than charred wood, and reached her before the river devoured her. Her eyes were awash with alarm.

She fumbled with the puckered tentacle wrapped around her waist. Grabbing hold of her upper arms, I tried to pull against it, but it was stronger and won. I slipped and almost tumbled to the ground, my legs still half asleep.

"Cut it!" Emaline screamed, slapping her palms on its slimy surface. "Quick!"

She forced water at the ground and created resistance. It gave me a moment to act before the creature pulled her into the river.

I had nothing to use. Looking around, there was no weapon, the griffins that held them circled in the air, out of reach. I spied Emaline's trident across our camp. But another absence distracted me.

"Hadrian…" I couldn't see him.

I didn't have a chance to look more. Emaline's scream reached new volumes as the tentacle pulled again. "Zacriah, QUICK!"

Her words pulled forth my shift, but the change was kept within my arm. I didn't have to look to know that my fingers had lengthened, and claws protruded from their tips. With a giant thrust, I raked them across the tentacle five times before they cut through the thick mound of muscle and fat. A strange sounded bubbled from the river, and the tentacle released her and retreated into the depths. As it disappeared, the mist intensified.

Emaline dropped to her knees, breathless and rubbing her stomach. A patch of green mucus clung to her clothing.

"What is that thing?" I asked, stumbling back from the riverside.

"Mer," Emaline answered.

On cue, the water exploded skyward from the river, and a towering figure burst forth. Its skin was grey and hung of its frame in massive clumps. Hairless, the creature's mouth opened and dripped with saliva. Exposed rows of sharp teeth and a snake-like tongue flicked towards us.

Its chest was open, revealing bones. They stood out like the legs of an insect, six on either side. Innumerable tentacles thrashed around its body, slamming into the riverbed and causing tidal waves of water to cascade over us.

I froze in disbelief. This was not how Mer were portrayed in stories and tales. Not horrifying beasts like what was before me.

Emaline moved first, snapping me back to reality. She ran, full force, towards it and stopped just shy of the drop into the river. Throwing out her hands, the water around the beast began to rise until it toward over it. I was sure the ground shuddered when she brought her hands down, and the water followed. It crashed on top of the Mer and thrust it back beneath the river.

It didn't stay down for long. Its many limbs burst towards us first, and the body soon followed. I threw myself to the side, narrowly missing one. My ribs screamed as I landed on the stump of a tree. In the rush, I didn't notice the smaller tentacle that wrapped around my ankle. My head snapped back and hit the ground as I was suddenly pulled forward. Dazed, I looked up and called on my air. I pushed as much of it towards the tentacle in hopes to loosen its grip. Water sprayed, and dirt shot in the direction of the river, disturbed by magick.

The grip slackened, and I pulled free. Relief flooded my body, and I had a moment to gain my bearings.

Emaline was occupied, throwing her own tentacles of water to combat the Mer's that came to attack her. And Hadrian was still missing. The Mer was focused on Emaline and only her.

I balled my hands, conjuring a force of wind, and sent it barreling towards the Mer, trying to catch its attention. I failed. The Mer didn't stop battling Emaline.

Water called to water; the beast wanted her.

I *had* to help.

The ripple of my shift came on fast, and with a large push, I was airborne.

I flew above the creature and hovered in the air. That got its attention. The long, pink tongue sailed for me. Up close, I could see the faint suckers that covered it entirely. They oozed a mucus that dripped from it as it swung for me. I slashed my air towards it, knocking it off course. The Mer's head was knocked to the side under the force, and the noise it cried was so loud, I was sure Thessolina could hear it.

A blur of white flew beside me, and I saw Emaline's swan-like wings flapping fiercely. Opal scales ringed her neck like a necklace, more than I remembered seeing when I first met her on King Dalior's ship.

"We need to buy some time for Hadrian to come back, confuse it," Emaline commanded, already dipping towards the Mer. With a giant rush, she pulled her hand and the water beneath it listened. A wave pushed against the Mer. It cried out again, stumbling awkwardly backwards.

"Tell me what to do," I screamed back.

We were just out of its reach, which only spurred on its hungered frustration.

"Fight it!" Emaline shouted back.

Emaline dropped like a stone. She pulled her wings tight to her body, and for a moment, I thought she was going to dive into the river. But the split second before she reached its icy touch, her wings opened, and she shot towards the Mer, a battle cry bursting past her lips.

I followed suit, flying towards it. We spun around the Mer, dodging its reaching limbs and flicking tongue. The rumbling noise it made intensified and with it, so did its movements. I twisted and turned, dancing within the air to keep a distance.

I picked up my speed just in time as one tentacle brushed so close to my face.

The Mer's breath was rancid. I tried to stay clear of its gaping jaw as the smell stung my eyes.

I could see Emaline's experience in her Dragori form. Her fast movements and trust in her beastly form showed in the way she flew. She slashed her clawed hands, and the water around the Mer began to spin, turning the creature in its cyclone hold.

I opened my awareness and willed my air to enter the Mer's sickly frame. I hoped to winnow the air from its lungs as I pulled on it. The Mer feigned to the side. I dropped my hold on its breath as a tentacle shot up beneath me.

"Keep it up!" Emaline shouted.

I focused on increasing my speed and sending volleys of air at its frame as Emaline locked it in her vortex that was building like walls around the creature.

There were shouts from the riverside. I risked a glance and saw Hadrian. He wasn't alone. Before I could work out who was with him, something collided with my neck. My wings ceased their beating, and my body froze solid.

I dropped into the river, unable to move. My mind was the only part of me with the ability to do anything; everything else was stuck. Broken.

I slammed into the water and was sucked beneath. The weight of my Dragori form only pulled me down further into the dark abyss of the icy river. I was paralyzed.

My lungs burned from the lack of air, and my head banged with pain as each moment passed. All I could do was watch the Mer thrash beneath the water as it carried its battle on above the surface.

As the water devoured me, scenes of a familiar fate flashed through my mind. Water, arrows, Browlin.

Bright blue flashed somewhere above me followed by a scream that sounded more like a song beneath the water.

My eyes closed as the burning in my body reached a new peak.

Then my face met air. I broke the surface, coughing and spluttering. Someone held me, but my body still didn't respond to my commands. I couldn't turn to see who it was.

Hadrian was shouting. Whoever held me breathed heavily into my ear as they swam us to the river edge. As we grew closer, I saw Hadrian leaning over the bank, arms outstretched for me.

"He is paralyzed," a deep voice panted in the water from behind me.

"Can you hear me?" Hadrian hoisted me from the water, carrying me in his glowing arms.

I tried to respond, but my tongue was swollen in my mouth, and my throat still ached from coughing.

Hadrian turned his attention back to the boy who saved me from the river. "Is there any more?"

"The Mer are solitary creatures, but it wouldn't surprise me if we've caught the attention of another."

Emaline shouted, "Then get out of the river!" She ambled over to us, and Hadrian passed me into her arms. She was unphased by my weight and paid me no attention as she held me in her grasp.

There were a splash and a huff of breath.

"Where in Volcras have you been?" Emaline bellowed. The way she held me meant my gaze was stuck to her face. And she was red with anger. I was glad she held me, so her arms were preoccupied, because I could feel her want to hit Hadrian.

"Scouting," Hadrian replied.

"What in this world for?!"

"Food, what else?"

Emaline growled.

"If I knew there was a such a creature, I would never have left. Cut me some slack." Hadrian's voice cracked as he finished he plea.

"I don't mean to be a pain, but if your friend doesn't get treatment, the Mer's poison will have permanent effects," the third voice interjected.

Although I couldn't move, his words caused enough panic for me to try and gargle my worry.

"And who are you?" Emaline asked.

I didn't care who he was; I just wanted whatever treatment he suggested.

"A friend. I can help," the third voice answered sternly.

He walked past us, and I caught a glimpse of curly brown hair, and a sharp face with a shadow of stubble.

"Come quick," he called as he ran off.

∽

FOR ME, THE walk went on for too long. The entire time Emaline carried me, her gaze shifted to mine and away again. From my vantage point, I could also see Jerk and the other two griffins gliding above us in the skies, following us.

We passed beneath a wooden frame, and I was dropped. There was movement in my peripheral, and a boy leaned over me. He couldn't have been younger than me, for his face was covered in a sooty beard. He studied me with his hazel eyes, then I felt my mouth being tugged open. I didn't catch what was in his hand, but whatever it was, he shoved it into the side of my cheek.

"He should start getting his feeling back in a few moments…" the boy said, holding my mouth closed with one hand and massaging my cheek with his other. A strong taste flooded my mouth and, against my will, began to drip down my throat. It wasn't such a bad taste, but it was not pleasurable either. "We got here just in time." He laughed. "Any longer and that would have been it."

I was glad he found it funny. Once he realized no one was laughing, he stopped and raised his brows. "Tough crowd."

"Or a bad joke," Emaline replied from somewhere within the room.

The boy looked over his shoulder at her. "Sorry, it's not every day we get a group passing by and battling the Mer."

"Trust us, it was not part of the plan." Hadrian strode forward and took the boy's place. "I can't leave you for a moment, can I?"

All I could do was open my eyes wider to respond.

Hadrian face had paled with worry, the corners of his mouth twitching as he ran a smooth hand across my cheek. "I do not mean to be brash, but how long will it be until he will be back to full strength?"

"Depends, could be minutes or days."

Hadrian gave Emaline a look. His lips pinched thin with worry.

"We don't have days," Emaline said.

"I get the impression you are in a rush," the boy said.

"Something like that." Emaline huffed.

The boy smiled, looking between them. "Well, how about I set up some food, and you can tell me what a dragon girl and boy and a boy with glowing skin are doing in Eldnol? Because I get the impression that this is a story I can't miss out on."

CHAPTER
ELEVEN

THE HUT TURNED out to be nothing more than a large room with a small side compartment. It was draped in plants and vials of mysterious liquids and had a strange smell. I caught onto it as my senses came back to me. Thick, dried mud mixed with an intrusive scent of warm straw. I recognized it from home when Fa would take me to the farms as the sun was at its strongest. It was an odd smell, but one that made me feel closer to comfort than I had in days.

The leaf had dissolved in my mouth and worked its magick. The boy, Jasrov, had me walk laps around the cluttered room to make sure all feeling came back to them. My legs moved as if they were stuck in frozen water, but with each footfall, I became steady and less like a new born fawn. His face lit up, pleased, as I managed another two rounds without his assistance.

Jasrov, although he asked, still knew nothing about why we were here. It was Emaline who took Hadrian beyond the hut to speak about whether we tell him or not. It wasn't that he gave off an untrustworthy aura, so I didn't see the problem in telling him. If only Nyah were here, she'd know the answer to their concerns.

"You're good with plants," I said, filling the silence.

There were plants of all shapes and colors in almost every available space. Hanging from pots and growing through walls; greens, pinks, purples and black, it was a maze of shrubbery.

"Yes, very good. Wait, does that make me sound narcissistic?" he replied, his smile overwhelming his small face.

There was no denying his beauty. His curls were kept close to his head, which framed his sculpted face. A single dimple cut into his left cheek, and his eyes burned hazel, such an intense color it reminded me of the strongest coco bean. His skin was rich brown, untouched by scars and marks. He reminded me of Gallion.

"Not at all. Do you live by yourself?" My guess was he was our age, eighteen moons.

"No way, couldn't hack living alone. Would end up talking the plants to death. It might not look like much, but it's home," Jasrov said.

It was clear from the moment Hadrian and Emaline left that he was a talker. At least he could admit it.

"Will they mind us staying?" I scanned the room again, trying to work out where we would sleep if Hadrian and Emaline decided to take him up on his offer to stay. There was not much room for the four of us, let alone where his mysterious companion slept.

"There isn't much room for the three of us to crash here tonight." I stumbled over my numb feet and almost went crashing, but Jasrov caught me.

His laugh sounded so much like Nyah's. "Don't worry about her, she doesn't take up much room and prefers sleeping where she can see the stars."

There was noise beyond the door, interrupting us. We both turned towards it when Emaline entered, face stern, with Hadrian behind, his eyes wide and unblinking. From the expressions on both their faces, it was clear the conversation must have been tense.

"We will stay," Emaline stated, "but only for one night. We must leave at first light. But I insist that I prepare supper for us all. It's my thanks for your help today. Also, by chance, do you have a map of Eldnol on hand?"

"I have no need for maps. Sorry!" Jasrov clapped his hands together. "Brilliant; I haven't had guests in, well, I can't remember how long."

"Then tonight shall be a good one," Hadrian said, not even trying to hide his sarcasm.

Jasrov seemed unbothered and didn't notice Hadrian's tone. Instead, he moved around the room, pulling weathered stools from hidden places and moving plant pots out of the way for us all to sit.

"I apologize for the mess; I've been experimenting with some new flowers recently. With the cold weather coming in from the north during this time of year, it's hard to keep certain species of plant alive."

"You're an Elementalist," Emaline said, fingering a hanging plant beside the door to the hut. Jasrov quickly came over and took her hand from it.

"Is it that obvious?" he said with a smile.

"Yes," we all said at the same time.

"Just try not to touch all the plants. Some are more dangerous than they look."

Emaline looked back to the one she had just touched with a sour expression.

"Where is your familiar then?" Emaline asked.

It all clicked. His companion must be the familiar. Why else would he mention her choosing to sleep outside? I felt excitement spark like a cinder at seeing what his familiar turned out to be. I could only imagine.

"Hunting, maybe. To be honest with you, she could be here with us now. I'm not the best at keeping track of her; that's her skill. I just stick with plants, she does the rest."

I'd heard of familiars before but never seen one. Back home, I had only ever heard of one Elementalist, known by the title Weather Witch. She lived somewhere between Horith and Olderim, and news of her traveled from the younglings who traded between towns. She must have been Alorian, for only a full high elf could master such abilities. Petrer once said he saw her on the way to Gilly May, a famous market beyond our town. He was convinced she walked around with a ferret wrapped around her neck like a breathing scarf.

"Speaking of hunting, I am going out." Emaline moved for the door again. "Our supplies are only packed for three, so I should find some food for tonight."

"Do you need company?" Hadrian stood up, but she waved him off.

"I said hunt, not frighten a possible catch. You have as much grace as an oversized bear. And with that blue gleam, we wouldn't get close."

"Point taken." Hadrian sat back down. "Are you sure it is safe to be alone?"

"You're worried about me? Sweet, but uncalled for. I will return soon enough and have more than you did this morning," she said to Hadrian then left abruptly.

Hadrian stared at the closing door, speechless. Jasrov was smiling, not sensing the tension.

"I should go. We shouldn't separate," I said. "I could do with a hunt. I haven't flexed my skill for weeks." I stumbled over my numb foot as I spoke. Jasrov helped me over to the bed and sat me down.

"You are not going anywhere," Jasrov said. His hands were speckled with callouses and his nails embedded with dirt. I noticed the rough brush as he sat me down.

"About my first question, what exactly are you doing in these parts? With griffins and full packs. More weapons than I have seen since Lilioira. It looks like you all mean business, whatever that is."

"Could you fix us a drink before we start?" Hadrian asked, shifting his cloak from his shoulders and placing it on the ground beside him. "My throat is as dry as your roof."

"I have just the thing." Jasrov smiled, scanning his eyes quickly over Hadrian's exposed glow.

He scrambled around in his side room, and Hadrian and I shared a raised brow.

"What happened out there?" I asked.

"I got a scolding, no more than I deserved."

I raised a single brow. "Why did you leave us? I didn't feel you go."

"I wanted to hunt," he lied.

His gaze shifted, and he thumbed the hairs growing on his chin. I could have pressed on, but I didn't. Hadrian would tell me when he is ready.

"She shouldn't have left by herself. Who knows what other beasts lurk beyond these walls? I have never seen anything like that Mer before. Eldnol is becoming more dangerous by the day," I said, turning the conversation on a different course.

"Emaline is the strongest person I have known since Fadine, and I still do not know her very well."

We hadn't known her for long, but in the past days alone it was clear just how strong both her mind and spirit were.

"Here you go," Jasrov said as he strolled back towards us. In his hands, he held three bone cups of some kind, the contents of each steaming. "I made it myself. Consider it a mixture of sorts."

"I don't mean to be rude, but what's in it?" I pulled a face as the sweet scent hit my nose.

"What isn't in it?" Jasrov laughed, which didn't help my wariness. "Just drink it and find out."

I looked at Hadrian, but he was already drinking. His face was screwed in anticipation, but it quickly relaxed, and he began to chug harder.

"This is incredible. It tastes like apple and pears but with something… something with a kick," Hadrian said.

"I am glad you like it. I'll fetch you another cup." Jasrov jumped up, snatching the cup.

Satisfied that Hadrian was still sitting up after finishing it, I took a sip.

It first tasted of nothing, but my mouth soon exploded with a song of many tastes.

Honey exploded with spice, and there was a hint of the mint that soon followed. My stomach rumbled as the liquid dripped down my throat and warmed my body.

"What is in this?" I asked, savoring the taste. I took another sip and wash it around my cheeks, allowing it to touch every inch of my month.

"You like it?" Jasrov skipped my question.

"Very much so."

Jasrov placed a finger to his lips and chuckled deeply. "It is a special drink made of boiled water and Marlow flower. It gives a different taste to each person that drinks it, or at least I hoped it did. No one else has tried it but you, so you have both confirmed that my concoction was successful."

"Well, it is incredible. This would sell well back in Olderim. I should speak to father—" Hadrian stopped.

This face drained instantly of the happiness and excitement that had just covered it. Even Jasrov seemed to frown as if it was his fault for Hadrian's change in mood.

"Did I say something wrong?" Jasrov questioned, his right brow raised above his burning eyes.

Hadrian seemed to be in a trance of sadness, so I answered for him.

"You wanted to know why we are here, so I will tell you."

And I did. From the beginning, I told him of the journey to Olderim, the feast, Nasamel, Elmirr and the Druid. Jasrov listened silently, pulling faces as I moved over our story. Not once did he stop me.

As I spoke, I felt a weight being lifted from my shoulders. It was good to talk about it, even if it was a stranger who saved me from a hungry Mer.

"I've heard of shadowbeings." It was the first thing Jasrov said. "It was only two days ago that Bell spotted them. I couldn't believe it when she showed me. Now it all makes sense."

"You saw them? Where?" I spat.

"Well, technically Bell saw them. She showed me. She was out doing whatever it is she does at night. It woke me. Images of the forest flooded my mind, showing me."

I didn't understand.

"An Elementalist can see through the eyes of their familiar, so I assume that Bell is the name of your missing friend?" Hadrian spoke up, his face straight.

Jasrov nodded, his curls falling into his eyes. "She pulled me into her mind the moment she spotted them. I sensed her distrust like a bad taste in my mouth."

"I need you to tell us everything." Hadrian sat forward, empty cup still in hand and knuckles white.

"It was difficult to see details. Looking through the eyes of a fox is like sticking your head beneath water and opening your eyes. But, I did see the shadows that seemed to seep from their skin. I remember that clearly. In truth, I played it off as nothing important at the time, maybe a trick of the night or my tiredness—"

"Where were they going?"

I could picture them clearly as Jasrov explained. "Somewhere north of here. Bell didn't follow them; I wouldn't let her. And I'm glad I didn't, not with a druid around. I still can't believe there is one still alive. I thought they all disappeared."

"We all did," I replied.

Hadrian stood up, sending the stool clattering to the ground. "We need to find Emaline now."

The possibility of her being caught sent knives of panic cutting into my mind. I too jumped up, and Jasrov joined.

"I'm sure she is fine," I said, trying to catch Hadrian before he reached the door.

He turned to me. "That is not a risk I am going to take. I know the pain that comes with being caught by the Druid. I can't let her experience it."

Hadrian pushed the door open and jogged into the evening. I turned to Jasrov, finger pointing towards him. "Stay here."

"No, these are my woods. I'm coming," he replied, standing straight as if that would help me believe him. "Plus, this is the most excitement I've had for a long time. I'm not missing out."

It didn't take long to track down Emaline.

Once I caught up with Hadrian, I brushed the cobwebs off my hunting skills and used them. It was clear she stepped carefully through the forest, so finding marks in the ground where she stood was nearly impossible. So, I relied on my magick. Raising a hand, I sent my awareness into the open air, searching the forest for a shift of breath. I caught something close, a slow, calm breathing hidden amongst the trees. I only hoped that was Emaline and not another beast waiting in the night.

Her face was a mixture of annoyance and surprise as I called up to her. She was perched in a tree, bow raised in the direction of the darkness.

Then a rush of hooves that pounded off into the night, and she turned our way with a thunderous expression.

"You scared it away!" she roared from the branch above us. I could see her lips move as she mumbled insults beneath her breath.

"We need to stick together. Jasrov told us of Druid sympathizers that have been spotted close by." Hadrian cupped his hands around his mouth and shouted back at her.

"Says the boy who disappeared this morning and left us as breakfast for the Mer," she replied.

"Save your energy," I interrupted before Hadrian could respond. "We should really go and rest. If there are sympathizers near, we should leave before they catch our scent."

"And I have some food back home you can have before *we* leave tomorrow," Jasrov said.

"You will not be coming tomorrow," Hadrian replied, shaking his head. "There is not a chance."

"I know the forests around here better than anyone, and with Bell, I could watch out for trouble. I'm surprised you're not jumping at the chance of having me along!" Jasrov stood proudly and even hit his foot on the ground in protest. "And shouldn't a Prince deserve as much protection from these beasts as possible?"

That took Hadrian by surprise; even Emaline's cheeks went red.

"I can assure you, forest boy, I am capable of protecting myself."

Jasrov shrugged. "Sure you can."

A low growl sounded behind us. We all turned around to locate its origins.

I scanned the darkness where the noise came from but saw nothing. Not even Hadrian's faint glow penetrated it. Emaline flinched and raised her bow, and I raised my hands, calling for the air.

"Looks like it," Jasrov jibbed. "Everyone, meet Bell. Bell, meet everyone," Jasrov said just as a red fox stepped into view. It was a stunning creature, as if the flames of the autumn sun created it. Bell's eyes were pure shadow, and her fur was the hues of autumn. She crept around the base of the tree, head held low as she snarled at Emaline, Hadrian, then me.

Jasrov moved for her, kneeled and ran his hand down her neck. "These are the visitors I told you about." There was a pause, and he seemed to respond to Bell again, although she made no sound. "Yes, you will get used to his smell."

Hadrian made a displeased noise as Jasrov looked up at him briefly.

"We should head back," I said. "It will be safer in Jasrov's hut than arguing out here."

"House," Jasrov interjected, not looking up from his familiar. "It's a house. Not a hut."

I blushed. "Yes, Sorry."

Emaline landed beside us. With a flip, she descended from the branch and hit the ground with force. "Shocking, but I am with Hadrian on this, he is not coming."

"*He* is standing right here…" Jasrov said.

Someone's stomach growled, which made Bell jump. Emaline held her hand to her waist and rubbed in circles.

"Come on. You should eat. It gives me more time to persuade you that I am coming along tomorrow," Jasrov said as he walked past us with Bell at his heel.

CHAPTER

TWELVE

IT TURNED OUT Jasrov, although used to being alone with his familiar, was exceptionally good at the art of persuasion. It was that, or Hadrian had had enough of listening to his pleas. By the time we drifted to sleep on the dusted floor of the hut and woke to the calls of birds in the surrounding forest, Jasrov was ready and waiting at the door with a sack hanging from his shoulder. I didn't mind new company on the flight to Thalas Temple. In fact, I almost enjoyed it. He was to help us get to the temple, and from there, we were alone. Since the map Penna had given us was destroyed during the struggle with the Mer, we were up a stream with no paddle.

We left at dawn when the mist of morning still clung to the forest bed. The skies were clear, the sun bright, but it still didn't take away from the brisk chill in the air. It was I who had to take Jasrov with me since I was the only one out of the three who welcomed Jasrov's company.

I worried about Jerk's reaction. It was hard enough flying alone on him, but now with Jasrov and his fox, it was almost intolerable. Jasrov quickly provoked conversation during the flight, which helped pass the time. With each conversation we had and memories we shared, he reminded me more and more of Nyah. It was comforting, but it also made me realize just how hard I missed her. It had only been a day or so, and already I was pining for her sarcastic company.

"Do you think he survived?" Jasrov asked, his breath forming a cloud of mist over my shoulder.

We had moved onto the subject of Petrer and the ship, and all I felt was empty.

"If he survived, then it's for a reason. But, for his sake, I hope we don't see him again." Even as I said it aloud, the wind around us seemed to plus in response to my emotion. I had tried not to think about Petrer and the evil sneer he gave me as Emaline swept me from the ship. I would see him again; I knew it.

Every slip of feeling I ever had for him had melted into the empty abyss within me. Now only hate bloomed when he was mentioned in conversation. After what he did to Browlin, his redemption was impossible.

"I bless the boy who is stupid enough to break your heart," Jasrov sang, his gaze shifting to Hadrian, who flew ahead of us.

"What about you? Is there anyone that holds your affection?" I thought it was best diverting the conversation from me to him for once.

"Just Bell." The fox around his neck quivered at her name. "There was one elfin girl in a town close to my house. She worked in the tavern, and she had a sweet smile. Bell nearly bit her hand off when she passed me my order. Bell is funny about who gets too close."

"I could tell…" Even now, she seemed to keep a narrow eye on me as we flew. "I know little about familiars. When did she come into your life?"

He smiled, his eyes locked on the horizon. "Just when I needed her the most. I've grown up without parents for as long as I can remember. Me and my sister were sent to an orphanage in a port town beyond the city Lilioira. After two years of surviving there, she became ill. The sickness attacked her lungs until she drowned in her own blood. We tried healers and magicks, but nothing seemed to fix her. When she died, I lost all motivation for life. That was when Bell found me. I left the orphanage and walked. I walked and walked until I no longer smelled the minty scent of the city, and all I could see was the forest. Just when I was ready to join my sister, I came across Bell when she was nothing more than a kit. I could hear her whelping and followed the sound until I found her. She was hurt. I stayed up for days, trying to help heal her. And I did. I saved her life, something I failed at with my sister. It was like a bond clicked into place, and she claimed me. Never left my side since."

I kept my face forward. Jasrov had lost a sister to sickness. I blinked and released a tear the wind quickly snatched from my cheek. I cleared my throat and replied, "I am sorry to hear of your loss. I couldn't imagine how hard that must have been."

"It was tough. But that is life. I've learned that it's what you do with a difficult situation that matters. It's down to you and only you to turn a shitty tale into one flourished with positivity."

"Wise words. I shall remember them." Jasrov's words sang to my very soul. "Can I ask what her name was, your sister?"

"Bell," Jasrov replied.

I almost choked on my own spit.

"Some believe that the soul of an Elementalist's familiar is a someone they once knew. Hence the name, familiar. I am certain that my sister never left me." He looked down to Bell and rubbed a hand on her head. "Isn't that right?"

She released a wild squeak in reply.

Somehow, I believed it. As the small autumn creature gazed up at her companion, they shared a silent moment. I didn't doubt his sister was forever with him.

～

DAY SLIPPED INTO night, signaling the end of our travelling for the second day.

Conversation flowed, and we only stopped once for a slight break to eat and let our griffins gain energy. By the time we reached Talliar, a small-town south of our destination, we were each exhausted and ready for sleep.

It was Jasrov's idea to stay at the Inn within the town, and Emaline was thrilled. So much so, she offered to take Jasrov on her griffin for the remainder of the day until we got there.

～

TALLIAR WAS A sweet town built around a small lake at its heart. It was not its aesthetic, but more the feeling of being in a town this size that reminded me of home: closely built buildings and the overwhelming smell of fresh, baked bread. The sounds of villagers reached the hill we landed upon, and I couldn't help but smile at the idea of a proper night's sleep.

Once we climbed off our griffins and unloaded our sacks from their saddles, they disappeared into the night. I kept my short sword with me this time. After the attack with the Mer, I wouldn't let myself be caught without the protection of steel again.

The griffins danced into the sky until they vanished into the thinning clouds that shrouded us. They would return tomorrow when we called. It was better this way; fewer wandering eyes would notice us without our great beasts.

Hadrian kept his hood up and face down, aware this blue glow stood out more when the night was upon us. None of the occupants of Talliar paid us any mind as we passed through their narrow streets. The streets were empty besides the odd Alorian who smiled at us when we walked by. Buildings oozed warmth from the fires lit inside, and laughter from families floated to greet us as we moved through open doors.

When Jasrov pointed out the building we were heading towards, I couldn't believe that it was known as an Inn. To me, the word symbolized warm hearth fires and rickety rooms with large brass keys. This building was more like a castle.

It was erected on the long jetty that extended into the lake. It towered high, lit by the many hanging orbs that reflected the orange firelight onto the Inn's brick walls. Even the water around it danced with the reflection of fire. Ivory pillars held up the curved roof that domed the entire building, highlighting the many balconies that jutted out of the roof's paneled design.

"I'm going to go in with Emaline," Jasrov announced as we began our walk across the jetty pathway. "It would be best if you both follow in after us and wait at a table. And Hadrian, keep your hood on. The moment someone sees your gleam, we will be the talk of the town."

"Let me give you some coin," Hadrian began, shifting his hand in the inner pocket of his cloak, but Jasrov raised a hand in decline.

"No need, they owe me a favor anyway, so I might as well call on it now."

"He has an answer for everything," Emaline said, walking next to Jasrov and into the Inn.

We followed Jasrov instructions, waiting for a moment before entering. Hadrian slipped his hand in mine. It was a nice to feel his heat. He didn't let go, not until we reached a small table in the corner of the main room as far through the bar as possible. Occupants of the bar nodded in our direction and smiled. This entire village seemed to be built on kindness.

"You are getting along with fox boy quite well," Hadrian whispered, his hand still holding mine beneath the table. He squeezed it for a moment but kept his gaze forward.

I turned to look at him and tilted my head in jest. "He is kind. We made the right decision letting him come along. I think he needed the company, and we needed some clear direction after the map was ruined."

"We still do not know a lot about him." Hadrian's hooded face was locked on Jasrov across the room.

"We don't need to," I said. "I have known you for a short time. Do you expect me not to trust you?" I winked.

Although the hood shadowed his face, when he turned his gaze to me, I could feel the smile plastered on his wicked face. "You will soon enough. I wish more than anything to take you away to a place where it is only us."

"One day," I replied, looking away from him. The promise of time alone was hard to imagine.

Hadrian leaned into my cheek and placed a heated kiss on it. I felt red bloom beneath his touch. "Yes, one day."

"Did we interrupt something?" Emaline asked through a yawn.

I shook my head. "No."

"Yes," Hadrian said.

"Lucky enough, I ordered two rooms," Jasrov said, throwing me a key across the table. "Get some rest. I've had food ordered to be brought up to you. Emaline, this is for you." He passed her the second key.

"Where will you stay?" Emaline asked, looking between him and the key.

"Don't worry about me, just get some good sleep. Thalas Temple is a short flight from here, so you should be well rested and ready for an audience with the Keeper."

Emaline shook her head. "Do not be silly. You will stay with me tonight. Take it as a thank you for your hospitality last night."

"Only if you are certain," he replied.

"I would not have offered if I was not. And I would rather keep my eye on you anyway."

Jasrov face warmed in color, and he ignored Emaline's final comment. "I shall meet you there later, thank you. But I'm going to stay down here and have a drink before I retire. Hadrian, Zacriah, your room is on the top floor. Easy enough to find because it is the only one on that level."

Hadrian stood. "Right, that is our cue." He extended a hand to me, and I took it. Hadrian pulled me up and guided me around the table. "See you at day break."

Jasrov nodded as he pulled a stool and sat down.

"Rest well," I said as Hadrian pulled me towards the stairs in the corner of the room.

We began to walk to the stairwell when we noticed Emaline had not followed. I turned back, but she waved me off. "I'm not tired in the slightest. I think I am going to stay up for a drink with Jasrov."

Emaline joined the table with Jasrov, and they instantly began talking. A warm sensation wrapped around my stomach, and I smiled. I was glad they were getting on so well. I could almost seem Emaline's walls were coming down. It seemed Jasrov could make each of us feel comfortable in his own way.

A hand raised before me. "Shall we?"

It only took us a moment to find the room. After walking up three flights of rickety stairs, we reached the top level of the Inn. It was silent up here; not a sound was heard from the lower floors. The stairs leveled off into a narrow hallway, and at the end, a single door stood waiting.

As soon as we reached the door and Hadrian slipped the key into the lock, he dropped the hood of his cloak, and we entered.

"Well, I didn't expect this…" Hadrian drawled beside me.

Beyond the door was a stunning, yet modest room. It was not a big room, but the high ceiling gave the impression of its grandeur. A large, four-poster bed almost took up an entire wall opposite us. Sheer curtains danced from the small breeze that blew in from the open balcony. It was the fresh smell I loved. Saltwater scents danced in with the breeze and coated the room.

Hadrian wandered over to the bed first, dropping the cloak from his shoulders and draping it over the nightstand. I followed and placed our two sacks on the floor beside the open door and began to remove the concealed weapons. I pulled my belt off and unclasped the dagger strapped around my ankle.

"Remind me to ask Jasrov what he did to get this room without the need of coin," Hadrian said as he peeled the weapons from his body as well.

I walked over to the balcony and looked over the never-ending water of the lake. The moon's reflection rippled slowly in the almost still water. The night sky had a blue undertone to it. Countless stars seemed to dance as they winked in and out of view.

"It's so peaceful here," I whispered, my attention captured by the stunning view beyond the balcony.

Hadrian was suddenly behind me, arms wrapped around my waist, and he perched his chin on my shoulder. I could feel the stubble from the material of my tunic. We didn't speak for a moment. I melted into his embrace and stared at the moon as it watched us.

"I wish the world would stop spinning, so I can live in this moment forever," I whispered, overwhelmed with the sense of home.

His hold tightened. "It still wouldn't be enough. I don't want to miss out on a single moment with you. Our story has just started; we have many more tales to experience together."

I turned around, my chest pressed against his. His heartbeat echoed mine as we held on to each other. "Tell me more…" I urged him to carry on.

"Even if I could steal the very stars in the sky for you, it would not be enough. If I could fly you to the Goddess herself and profess the feeling you give me, it would never be enough. You might be right; we still don't know each other. But the feeling I have here"—he picked my hand up and pressed it above his heart—"is all the proof I need I know that this is right. What we are doing is right."

With each word that dripped from his lips, I seemed to melt into him more. I leaned up on my toes and pressed a kiss to his lips. Hungered by my advance, he pressed his body into mine and guided me to our bed, lips still locked.

Our breathing synchronized, and our movements flowed. I knew at that moment, as my body touched the bed, I was ready to reach the ends of the world with him. To explore him for the first time.

I pulled back from him, breathless. "Are you ready for me?"

It was an innocent question, one that sent my heart racing.

Hadrian smiled and leaned in. "I have always been ready for you." He placed a kiss on my head. "But I want to savor it, to wait until I can have you day in and night out. I want to be selfish with you, not share you with anyone for hours upon end."

Tonight was not the night. I could see it in Hadrian's eyes as he leaned over me. No matter how strong the urge to pull him closer was, I resisted and smiled back up at him.

"I have a question for you, Zacriah, will you wait for me?" he asked.

I smiled and returned a kiss on his nose. "Until time itself dies out, and we return to the stars."

Tɦirteen

FOOD ARRIVED IN the hand of a shy young boy who knocked three times at the door. We untangled ourselves from our embrace, and Hadrian moved to get it. Watching the boy's face morph into shock as he stood before a man glowing blue was incredible. I stifled a laugh from the bed.

Hadrian paid him with extra coin, and the young boy left with a pleased face. He then brought the tray to the bed and began to feed me bread and cheese as we talked about Olderim and his past life. I repaid the favor by throwing small grapes into his waiting mouth. We both nearly choked with laughter as one hit his eye and rolled onto the floor.

Once the tray was empty of food and yawns interrupted our conversations, we prepared to sleep.

"This is better than the forest floor and a dwindling fire," Hadrian said.

I curled up towards Hadrian's bare chest, my back pressed into him. We fit perfectly together, even when he moved we seemed to do it in tandem. His arm always wrapped around me, his other propped beneath his head.

"You are warmer than any fire, Hadrian. Are you certain you are well?" I ran the back of my palm up and down his chest with concern.

He waved me off, smiling with his eyes closed. "Do not fuss, Petal. I am fine. I promise."

Somehow, I didn't believe it.

Hadrian didn't speak again. His breathing calmed and became a regular rise and fall. Satisfied he would not wake, I rolled over, gently moving his arm for a moment, so I could get closer to him. My face was inches from his, and his cool breath blew onto my hair.

There was something so peaceful about him when he slept, as if the worries he left behind didn't bother him in rest. His hair was growing back now. A dark shadow of hair. They covered the many scars and marks, giving an illusion of the boy he once was. Before the Druid, before this quest.

I ran a finger down his face, across his smooth skin and onto the coarse hairs of his growing beard. It covered his chin and down his neck, making him look years older than he was. His warmth did not waver, and the blue gleam pulsated with every breath he inhaled and exhaled.

I brought my fingers to my lips and pressed a kiss to them. Then I placed those same fingers to his lips.

"Night, my love."

Time melted, and I fell asleep with Hadrian being the last thing I saw.

∽

JASROV BURST THROUGH the bedroom door and woke us both. Urgency filled the room like burning fire.

"Get up!"

I shot up and reached for the dagger on the nightstand. My chest hurt from the sudden beat of my heart, and Hadrian burned hotter beside me.

"You both need to get up right now," he hissed, tugging at the sheet covering us. "Quickly!"

Hadrian growled, ignoring Jasrov. But Jasrov's panic cut into my consciousness, and I was fully awake in seconds.

Clinging to the sheets to cover myself I rubbed my eyes to see Jasrov picking up our belongings in a rush. "What's going on…?"

"Someone turned up asking after you. Bell heard them and showed me the cloaked figure at the bar."

I snatched my clothes from Jasrov outstretched hand and began pulling them on. "Do you remember what they asked?"

Jasrov nodded. "Whoever it is knows both of your names and asked for the glowing boy. I couldn't see their face, and voices always sound warped when it's Bell who hears it. We need to leave."

"You are right to wake us, where is Emaline?" Hadrian was up now; his dark lashes stuck together.

"She is already with the griffins beyond the town."

The urgency of Jasrov tone got us out of bed.

"And your familiar?" Hadrian was half dressed, stumbling as he put his boots on.

"She is still downstairs, stalling."

I clipped my cloak in place and picked up my sack. "Stalling, what does that mean?"

"Whoever it is may or may not be having a standoff with my Bell. Which means we have only seconds before our visitor finds us."

I looked to Hadrian. "We can't go down there."

Hadrian nodded, looking at the balcony for a moment. "We will not be."

We all heard the rip of Hadrian's clothes as his Dragori form came free. Shadow spilled from his back until his wings flexed free.

Jasrov's mouth dropped open as he scanned Hadrian horn to claw.

I followed suit, shifting into my Dragori form. My wings weighed my tired body down, and my scales itched. I looked down at my arm and saw more silver scales than before. It was clear from Hadrian's gaze beyond the balcony what means of exit we were going to take.

"Tell Bell to leave for Emaline." Hadrian's deep voice filled the room as he grabbed onto Jasrov who stood as still as stone. "If you can please be as still as you are now during the flight, I would appreciate it."

Someone shouted from the floors below. A commotion of bangs and noises sent my skin crawling.

I sprang forward, following Hadrian as he yanked Jasrov into his arms and leapt from the window. The moment the air touched my face, my wings spread wide, and I flew into the night. It was a bright sky, and the moon still hung in its proud place above us, which could only mean our sleep lasted a short time. Just for one night, I wanted normality. A break from this constant race that we'd been placed into. The moonlight shone through Hadrian's outstretched wings, highlighting their subtle red tones. I jumped around him, allowing the wind to lift me high into its embrace. While Hadrian carried Jasrov, I held our sacks in both hands.

From this height, the town looked no bigger than a wooden toy. Although the lake it was built around was vast, there were not many buildings as I'd first thought surrounding it. Seeing the world from this perspective made my stomach leap. That, and the fact Hadrian nose-dived beside me towards four dots in the distance.

I could see, even in the black of night, Emaline below with the three griffins and the shadow of Bell sprinting towards them. I also spotted another shadow far behind Bell trying to catch up.

Hadrian must have noticed too because he raised a free hand as an orb of blue flame grew within it. With an angered cry, he pushed the fire towards the ground, and it shot down to the shadow.

The fire burst in a line, causing whoever it was below to come to a tumbling stop. It would hold them for only a moment, but it was all we needed to reach the griffins, Emaline and Bell, and get back in the sky. Whoever chased us was persistent.

Once on the back of Jerk, I looked back towards the dwindling flames and saw no sign of the figure in the town below. There was only a bundle of clothing left on the street as if they had simple disappeared.

Townsfolk ran out of their homes, their screams reached us even from this distance.

News of blue fire would reach the Queen, and it would be yet another conversation we'd have with her regarding our delay in this quest. For there was only one being in all Eldnol with blue fire at the tips of his fingers.

As we flew off into the rising sun, I kept looking at Hadrian. There was a strange, pained expression on his face, and his eyes struggled to stay open. I called his name to get his attention, and he shook himself awake once more and mouthed that he was fine. I didn't believe it. I sensed his pain as if it were my own. He was told not to use his power, but he had, and it was taking a toll on him.

~

WE HAD REACHED the outskirts of Thalas by the time the sun had taken its place in the sky. It was a cloudless day, but the chill was still ripe in the air. It seemed Emaline and Jasrov had not slept at all, for their faces were flushed pale and eyes ringed with shadow. The silent flight gave my mind to time to dwell on whoever it was trailing us. Was it a Druid sympathizer? A shadowbeing? Even the idea of it being Nyah crossed my mind. The possibilities were endless.

Emaline led us with Jasrov on her griffin. She guided our convoy to the ground, and we landed on the wet, dewy grass. In the clearing, the ground was covered with tall grasses and yellow flowers Jasrov seemed familiar with. He picked at one and chewed on it.

"It's safe. Butter Mellow helps freshen a mouth. I consider the effects to be better than mint leaf," Jasrov explained.

"I could do with a handful of those," I said, mouth thick like cotton.

"Leave some for the rest of us," Emaline said, raising a hand to shield the bright sun and scan the surroundings.

Hadrian's and my clothes were in tatters from our shift, and the many hours of flying had driven the cold into my bones. I placed the Butter Mellow in my mouth and began chewing. Instantly the cotton taste was replaced with a buttery mint that freshened my breath.

"What ever happened back there could happen again," Emaline said. "How they found us is beyond me. It is not like Hadrian was walking around with his blue glow on show, and we haven't stayed anywhere long enough to be tracked."

My skin chilled, and I exchanged a knowing look with Hadrian. I scrambled around my sack for a spare set of clothes and began changing into them. I repacked the ripped shirt and trousers in case we needed it for fire.

"Someone did see him," I said, eyes still pinned to Hadrian. "A boy, he brought us up food and caught us... Hadrian did not hide the glow."

"I believed it to be safe," Hadrian admitted.

Emaline's rolled her eyes. "I should have guessed. Risking our mission *again*. You would think after everything we have been through you would be more cautious. Did the Druid drive all sense of sensibility from you?"

Hadrian growled, "I can show you what the Druid did to me."

His voice was deeper than normal, a strange shadow of anger passing over his eyes. Even Emaline caught it and raised her hands in defeat.

"Just think, Hadrian, this entire mission is to help you. Yet you are the only one putting it in jeopardy. If you do not care for the Staff, then we can turn around now and head back. I have more pressing matters in Kandilin than this."

Hadrian went to reply, but I stilled him.

"This is tiredness speaking. How about we regroup before we go to the temple? Hadrian, get changed into something not ripped. And Emaline, I should have gotten the door. If the boy did rat us out, it is my fault."

"I do not like mistakes," Emaline said bluntly.

"I understand," I replied, keeping my voice calm.

We took up camp out in the open. There was no forest to shield us, no lake to threaten us. Just the wide, rolling hills and cloudless sky. I could see Thalas Temple in the distance, nestled in the middle of the valley surrounding it. From this height, we could see the temple was awake, as smoke billowed from one of the buildings. I had questioned why we did not ask for sanctuary within the stone walls. The warmth of the fire would be better than camping in the open.

"Do you have anything in your sack for this bonecold I have obtained?" My teeth chattered as I asked Jasrov. Even with my new clothes on, I couldn't shake the chill.

"I might have something…" Jasrov dug in his sack, brows pinched in concentration. "Just give me a moment."

"Do you think they will have spare clothes?" I questioned, checking my cloak to make sure the shift had not ruined that. "Something more suitable for the chill of the north perhaps?"

It was clear the weather was getting colder the further north we traveled. Although the sky was void of clouds, the cold brisk of wind still bit into my exposed skin.

My spare set was a charcoal colored tunic and baggy slacks, mismatched and not thick enough to battle the cold air.

"You could do with a hot bath," Emaline said, fiddling with the saddle of her griffin. "That will burn away a bonecold better than any concoction *he* has hidden in that bag."

Jasrov pulled a face at the comment, then held out a small vial. "Here, this should help, or at least keep the symptoms at bay before we reach a proper healer... or a proper bath."

"What is it?" Hadrian asked, strolling forward and pinching the vial from my hands as if he didn't trust it.

"A mixture of all sorts. I originally came up with the concoction as a way of starting fires, but it turned out that pouring it on dry wood only made it wet and didn't cause the spark that I first thought it would."

"So, you decided to drink it instead…" Emaline laughed, munching on a dry slice of bread.

"Yes." Jasrov clapped his hands, innocent to the sarcasm of the question. "It warmed me up just right, so I've been using it during the winter months as a little extra warmth."

I raised a hand for Hadrian to give it back, but he didn't.

"How are you sure it won't set Zacriah's insides alight?"

Even that made me hesitant to want it back.

"Here." Jasrov plucked it from Hadrian's hand and popped the cork. "I'll prove it."

He took a small swig and stood there with a smile on his face. "See? I told you it wor—" Jasrov's faced dropped, and he raised his panicked hands to his throat. He began choking so violently that his face turned red.

Hadrian jumped forward but missed as Jasrov dropped to the floor.

Before I could intervene, Jasrov began laughing where he lay on the ground.

"What in this *world* are you playing at?" Hadrian shouted, his face still in shock. "I thought you were really hurt."

"Oh, you should have seen your faces." His laugh reached new volumes.

I kicked his shin and released my held breath. "Honestly, time and a place, Jasrov. Time and a place!"

"Well, next time, trust me when it comes to my concoctions. Stop questioning them. I am the expert and all." Jasrov raised a hand, and I pulled him up.

"Expert, of course." I winked.

Downing the vial of liquid, my body felt better the moment it went down my throat. The aching cold of my legs and arms disappeared. My throat even felt smooth, and my fingertips warmed.

"Now that Jasrov has stopped his little show, should we discuss what happened back there?" Emaline stepped forward, passing us each a slice of dried bread. "Can you ask Bell if she noticed any shadow or strange scent?"

There was a pause, and Jasrov eyes glazed white for a quick moment. I had not seen him fully share the link between his familiar. I even noticed Bell's dark eyes turn white just like Jasrov's. "She didn't see any shadow and mentioned how pleasant the smell was compared to what she normally puts up with."

Crumbs sprayed from Hadrian's mouth as he laughed. "You familiar is very honest."

Jasrov nodded. "Sometimes too honest."

"If we are lucky, whoever it was will not be bothering us again. If we keep moving quickly, we should stay ahead," Emaline said. "But I am less worried about that, and more concerned about who we bump into next. I would take a nice smelling stranger over a Druid sympathizer."

"Agreed," we all answered.

Jerk chirped from where he grazed on the grass. I walked to him, hand ready to scratch down his nose. "You've worked hard, Jerk. You deserve a long rest. I think we all do." I turned back to the crowd.

"The temple is not going anywhere, so whilst we have a moment, why don't we get some sleep? Who knows if we will get much once the Keeper guides us to the Staff?"

Hadrian straightened out the sleeves of his fresh tunic. "I must admit that sounds pleasing. But I would prefer to get this all over with; we will have plenty of time to relax once we find this Staff and deal with…me." He flashed the back of his glowing hand.

"I would prefer to meet the Goddess with a full belly, so eat up." Emaline threw us each another piece of bread and chowed down.

"I cannot argue with that," Hadrian replied.

I looked down the hill, contemplating for a silent moment what we would find in those stone walls. Finding the Staff of Light was the main priority, yet I couldn't see it through the haze of uncertainty that fogged my mind. Since we had landed, the dark shadows beneath Hadrian's eyes had only intensified. Cristilia's story of warning played in my mind as I saw just how drained Hadrian was. I just hoped we had enough time before we lost him to the Heartfire.

The billowing smoke still flowed proudly from the temple in the valley. Our next task was finding out who this Keeper was. Penna and his map did not indicate who it might be. I only hoped it would be an easy find once we entered the temple. As easy as asking one of the holy men or women. They ought to know.

I couldn't take this sitting around a moment longer. Jumping up, I hollered for Emaline and Jasrov while pulling at Hadrian's arm. "It's time we get down there."

It was agreed. The griffins took flight, probably to find food or a lake to bathe in, and we began our descent down the hill towards the stone temple. We stumbled down the slope like new fawns, feet awkwardly finding divots in the ground, so we didn't slip on the morning wet grass. Bell bounded down the hill, even being distracted enough to chase a small yellow bird that burst from a shrub. We all laughed as Bell made a leap and landed, empty-jawed, in a ball on the ground.

The closer we got, the more intense the smell of fire became. I shared a worried look with Hadrian. The smell brought back visions of the destruction in Nasamel.

Before I could complain, Emaline pointed towards the outer temple walls. "Look…"

We all followed her finger. What I thought from a distance was cracks in old stone were large vines that wrapped hungrily around the temple.

"I've never seen vines this big before," I said, turning to Jasrov for direction.

Jasrov pulled a face. "They were not here last time I visited."

"And when was that?" Hadrian looked as confused as I was.

"Two weeks ago…"

We all paused our descent and looked back at the temple. It seemed as if the all the pieces of the puzzle came together in that second. Then we began to run.

Hadrian had pulled the Alorian sword from its sheath on his back, and Emaline cocked an arrow in her bow. Jasrov was empty-handed, but Bell stayed close with her teeth bared.

"Stay together," Hadrian hushed, reaching the outer wall first. We could not see into the heart of the temple and its courtyard, but the last time I saw smoke like that that grew from the other side of the wall was in Nasamel. My heart sank, and my hand gripped tighter on the silvered dagger I had pulled free without realizing.

We huddled, Jasrov between us, as we walked around the corner of the wall.

This was no temple. Not anymore. Buried beneath earth and vines, it was in ruin.

Jasrov's angered shout lit up the sky, sending burning horror through my body.

CHAPTER

FOURTEEN

GREEDY JADE VINES the size of fully grown snakes looped around crumbled rock and stone. What once was a courtyard was now covered in soil and moss. Slabs of stone had been broken in half as weeds the height of Alorian elves grew through them.

"This is impossible," Jasrov whispered, his eyes wide as he looked at the damage before us. He stepped forward first, leaving the protection of our circle. "The temple, this… it has been destroyed."

It seemed like the temple had been in ruins for years. Every sense of mine became overrun with earth. As I stepped closer to the destruction, the strong taste of dirt coated my mouth.

"And you said you came here weeks ago?" Hadrian asked, hands gripped on the handle of his sword.

"Yes, and two weeks before that…" Jasrov said.

Emaline walked up to one of the remaining walls and tapped her bow on what seemed to be a bundle of foliage that bulged from the stone. She caught our attention when she began to pull the vines until they snapped loudly as they came apart. A hand, white in death, sagged from a hole in the cocoon of earth and vine. It hung free, its white skin a stark constant to the jade green around it. Emaline gasped, stepping away as the body tipped forward.

"No," Jasrov cried. He attempted to run for the body, but Hadrian pulled him back.

"Do not be a fool. It is too late," Hadrian said.

It was a man, clothed in a robe that was now flecked with dust and destruction. His eyes were wide and mouth open. Yet his chest did not move. The vines still claimed the lower half of his body, but that was not what killed him. An angered red mark looped around his neck. He'd been strangled.

"It's as if the earth had reclaimed them all," Emaline said, taking cautious steps back from the wall.

"What magick is capable of this…" I began. Even as I said it, a shiver ran up my spine. There was only one with magick dark enough to create such death.

I could see from Emaline and Hadrian's face that they knew as well.

"The Druid."

"This magick is unnatural." Jasrov stepped forward, arms wrapped around his waist. "We should leave."

"*We* are here for the Keeper. If there is even a chance the keeper is alive, we must go looking," I nodded my head to the central doorway to the temple, a dark hole less welcoming than I imagined.

"Zacriah is right," Emaline said. She wasn't about to give up now. "Be ready for anything."

Hadrian's blue flame seemed pulsed at the mention of the Druid. My wrist grew stiff.

"You can either stay out here all alone or stay close with us," Emaline said to Jasrov, moving towards the main entrance. "Your promise to get here is fulfilled; we no longer need you. So, go."

"You all have wings and weapons; all I have is a fox with pointy teeth. I don't see how that would help me if the Druid is in there." Jasrov tried to hide his shaking hands.

"Or if he comes for me out here. I am sticking with you, regardless of what my job was."

Emaline pulled a curved dagger from her belt and handed it to Jasrov. "If the Druid is in there, he will go for us first. It's our power he needs, not yours. At the first sign of danger, I want you to call for the griffins and get out of here. Return to Queen Kathine in Kandilin town and give her this dagger. She will know what it means."

"Do you think he knows about the Staff?" I asked. "If he gets it before us..." I couldn't fathom what that could mean.

"Yes, but not for the same reasons we are," Hadrian said, shrugging the cloak from his shoulders then dropping it to the mossy ground. "I will go in first, follow close behind." He held the long sword in both hands, flashing the Alorian steel in the direction of the temple door.

Before the griffins had left, Emaline had taken the trident and strapped it to her back. She pulled it free, swapping the forked weapon instead of her bow and arrow. The points of the four forks winked in the dull light, a warning to anyone watching from the shadows.

I had a sword at my waist and a bow strapped in my back. Even with the presence of my own weapons, I wished I had taken my metal claws with me. They were packed in my sack, which was high in the sky with Jerk.

Hadrian stepped over a pile of stone and into the darkness of the doorway. As he entered the dark temple, his gleam intensified and reflected off the walls. I stepped in first, Emaline following in after with Jasrov and Bell. Hadrian's Heartfire gave us enough light to see the damage to the temple. Once we entered, the walkway opened to stairs that disappeared down into the ground. With caution, we walked down, trying to keep as quiet as possible. All I could hear was the panting of Bell beside me and the occasional drip of water down the walls beside me.

The stone stairs went on for a while until we reached a level floor. Despite Hadrian's glow, it was hard to see more than three steps before us. What I could make out was that the vines had reached this far down and had overtaken the walls and floor. I even tripped, stumbling into Hadrian, who quickly stopped me from falling.

"Careful, Petal," Hadrian whispered.

I nodded, squeezing his upper arms before he turned back to carry on walking.

"Something doesn't smell right in here," Jasrov complained, placing a hand on a large vine that had overtaken the wall beside him. "The vines, they're dead. I can feel them, and they are empty of life. Whatever magick this is, it's more complicated than even I could understand."

My palm became cold when I proceeded to place it on a vine nearest to me. I raised my hand and brought it back down with vigor. The vine snapped and dropped to the stone floor where it crumbled into a dark green powder.

"If the Druid caused this, then he must be long gone. The magick is wearing off, killing the unnatural vines." Emaline said.

"Have you seen this magick before?" I asked.

"Never," she replied, shaking her head. "I have heard of it. This is not power the druids ever had. It's common knowledge to know they do not create life. Whoever did this is strong and can control earth in more ways than Jasrov or other earth Elementalists."

"Do you think it was the other Dragori?" Hadrian asked.

"For our sake, I hope not," Emaline replied, pushing past us. "Let's keep going and hope the Goddess sees us safely through this temple."

We walked further in, passing smashed stone walls and crumbled slab flooring. The room we entered was as tall as it was wide. Only the halo of blue light that Hadrian created meant we could see an arm's length in front of us.

"We should split up," Jasrov spat out.

We all turned to him, confused at his sudden confidence. His hands were shaking as he held onto the dagger Emaline had given him, but his eyes burned with an intense emotion that I could not place.

"Don't look at me like that." He frowned. "If we go in twos, then we might find the Keeper quicker. The temple is monstrous as it is. We will cover more ground if we separate. And I want to get out of here as soon as possible."

"Have you met this Keeper before?" Emaline questioned.

Jasrov looked at the floor. "No. In truth, I never knew one existed before you told me. But, since you don't know either, we all have the same chance of finding someone who claims to be the Keeper. Unless they are dead, of course."

Hadrian nodded. "Jasrov speaks sense, but you are going to need some light to navigate this place." He ripped a large part of the dry vine from the wall and placed his hand at one end. Blue fire burst forth and coated the top of the vine. "This will burn out quickly, so as long as you relight a new piece of vine, you will be fine."

Jasrov took it from Hadrian. "I was almost hoping you would come with me."

"I think it's best I stay with Zacriah," Hadrian replied.

Emaline patted Jasrov on the back. "I am more than capable of keeping you alive. Ask those two; I have a reputation for it."

A slight pop sounded from Emaline's waist. We watched the water skin open and a steam of blue seep into the air. Emaline controlled it with her hand until the steam formed an orb that spun inches from her open palm.

"Point taken," Jasrov said, awe fixed on Emaline's display.

Satisfied, Emaline clenched her fist, and the orb dispersed into a steam once more that retreated into her water skin.

"If we keep walking, we should come to a divide in the room. Two walkways…"

Just as Jasrov explained, the open space we stood within separated into two hallways. One to the right, the other to the left. Between both paths, a large statue stood untouched by the hungry vines. Dalibael. She stood proudly, her right arm extended out before her where the other was held behind her back. White stone veined with black like marble. She had been carved out like the many depictions of her showed. Flowing hair, tall body. Pure power.

"We are going this way," I said, pointing to the right corridor. "You take the other."

Hadrian just looked at me for a moment, but the look I gave him made him turn back and not ask any questions. I couldn't help but feel the Goddess was trying to direct me through her stance. If this was a sign, I was prepared to take it.

"There is nothing but an old library and eating hall down that way," Jasrov said. "A tree and benches."

"A tree?" I asked. "This far below ground?"

"You'll see," Jasrov said, turning to Emaline. "Then that leaves us with this pathway."

Bell was perched beside my leg. With her snout, she nudged my leg and directed my attention to her.

"Bell will go with you," Jasrov added. "That way she can alert me if you get into any trouble."

I looked down at the familiar and smiled. "Fine. Let's get going. We will alert you through Bell if we find anything, and you can do the same. I only want to meet back when we find the Keeper."

"If they are still alive," Jasrov said again.

With that, we departed from one another, Bell at my heel as I followed Hadrian with my hand in his.

I'd be lying to myself if I said I didn't acknowledge the twinge of fear in the pit of my stomach as we took our steps into the corridor. The dark had never bothered me before, but after seeing it spill from the beasts and creatures the Druid created, I was beginning to fear it.

Hadrian's gleam guided us through the narrow corridor, illuminating the many carvings that'd been etched into the stone walls beside us. They were incredible. Swirling sigils and marks of a language long lost. I ran my hand over one, my fingers dusting over a deep cut into the stone that up close looked like a star.

Empty bowls hung above us, starved of flame. Those would have lit the way for the many who travelled these passageways. Guiding them as Hadrian now did for us.

We reached yet another set of stairs, starting narrow at the top and leading down into another open space. Our footsteps echoed across the barren stone walls, blending into sounds that made me jump and twitch with nerves. The hairs on the back of my neck stood on end as we made it down into a room like no other.

Pillars of marble stood on each side of the room, acting as the ribcage for the many cases of books that lined the main floor. This space was lit by a single window high above. Streams of light brushed over the cases and filling the room with a fresh scent. We were so deep into the temple that the window providing daylight was far up. Unreachable.

"This place, it's untouched by the magick," I said, turning slowly to get the best look at every detail. I could see some vines leaking in from the ceiling far above, but none reached the many shelves that lined the room.

I walked over to the closest bookcase and picked a volume off the shelf. It was heavy in my hands, its face smooth and new.

"I have never seen so many books." My voice echoed, which prompted me to whisper.

"Whatever is held within these pages is important, not only to those who dwell in this temple but to the Druid himself. If it was he who was behind this, he must respect books more than life," Hadrian said.

I opened the book, and my eyes scanned over the many words that graced its yellowed page. "There are names and dates. Lots of them."

Hadrian leaned over my shoulder to get a look. "It seems that we have stumbled over archives of those who live in Eldnol and those who have passed on. It is not uncommon that the births and deaths are recorded. A census."

"So, these names are of Alorian elves?"

"Not necessarily. See here... *Malerious Jall* has been marked down as Morthi."

I read the name over and over, trying to figure out why a Morthi elf would be marked down here. "I don't understand."

"Because Malerious was born on Eldnol soil, he must be registered here," Hadrian replied, pointing to other names but not touching the page of the book.

As we flipped through the massive tome, we found other names of those born in Alorian who were of different descents. Now and then, there would be a name scratched out or a date not completed.

"Why are they kept here? Why not in the capitol where they are most protected?" I looked over the many books before me, at how innocent they seemed to be.

Hadrian whispered his answer into my ear, "This is a temple. There is nowhere believed to be more protected than the home of the Goddess. At least before the Druid."

Hadrian's comment highlighted just how dangerous our world was becoming. Even places of respect and worship where targets of the Druid's hate.

I placed the book back in its place. "We need to keep looking. What if Jasrov is right? Maybe the Keeper is dead... where is Bell?"

Hadrian shrugged and began to look around us. He raised his arms before him to spread his glowing light. "She was right with us the last time I checked."

"Bell," I hissed, picking my speed up with each bookcase I passed. Maybe she returned to Jasrov. But somehow, I didn't believe that.

I could hear Hadrian calling for her behind me, but I caught a blur of movement in my peripheral. I turned and saw Bell's bushy red tail moving behind another bookcase ahead of me.

"Bell!" I raised my whisper into a low shout.

As I rounded the corner, I spotted the familiar up ahead. She turned her head to look at me as if she waited for me, trying to show me something.

Away from the window's reach, this part of the library should have been bathed in darkness. But it was not. As I reached the other side past a few more bookcases, there was a pulsing white light that grew with each step. Bell screeched around the corner of the final bookcase, and as I rounded it, I saw what it was she reacted to.

A tree made entirely of white light stood in a courtyard of stone.

This far down into the earth, a tree of its size should never have been here, but it seemed the very temple had been built around it. The temple walls curved around the tree, opening into a circular space. As I looked up, all I could see was an open domed ceiling, which welcomed the view of clear sky far above.

Unlike the library, these walls were covered in vines and cracked stone. They looped in and out of the walls, devouring it within their earthy grip. But one thing was clear: the vines never reached the glowing tree. As if the very light acted as a shield, not a single sliver of earth reached the many white roots that spilled beneath the strange tree.

"Have you found—" Hadrian stuttered over his sentence as he joined me.

We both stood in pure silence, bathed by the impressive light.

From this distance, the trunk bowed to the right, giving the impression of a body in mid-dance. The foliage that graced its branches had a pale pink tint which matched the glow from the roots that flowed like water across the courtyard around it.

"Goddess above," Hadrian prayed.

Bell sat amongst the vines. She yelped and turned her head towards the tree.

Faint at first, a humming noise enveloped us both. It grew until its sweet sound made my feet move. As we stepped, against our own minds' command, into the shield of light which oozed from the tree, I felt my shift happen. I had no control over my body as the song controlled me. I could see Hadrian beside me stuck in the same trance.

I was not panicked. I was not worried. The light calmed me, and I gave into the pull.

The light called for my wings to burst free, and horns sprouted from my head. I couldn't move my neck, but out the corner of my eye, I saw shadow wash from Hadrian as he also shifted. The blue gleam faded until his skin pulsed with his golden hue before the Heartfire took over his body. No longer was he consumed by the lurking Heart Magick. He *looked* healed.

Welcome my children. The light voice filled my mind. It was both beautiful and powerful, causing a trickle to run down the back of my neck. I tried to locate the source but saw no one with us.

I have been waiting for your arrival.

I tried to open my mouth to respond but couldn't form words. We were still being pulled toward the tree, walking over its roots toward the gentle voice.

You are not the first to seek answers. A sister, not by blood, visited me, but her mind was not pure. I denied her, will I deny you? I sense a darkness lurking, following you like a shadow.

I came to a stop before the bark of the tree. The voice echoed in my mind each time it finished speaking. Finally, my body was back in my control. I turned to Hadrian who was already looking at me. His cheeks were red as he looked at his arms and hands then back up to me.

"No more fire..." he whispered.

"Did you hear that?" I asked.

He nodded, turning back to the tree.

"We come seeking the Keeper," Hadrian said, low and urgent.

That is the name given to me, although I have many names. As the voice spoke, an explosion of light burst above us. Pale birds flew from the branches, leaving them bare. They flew up, passing out of the temple from the open ceiling above. What I thought had been leaves turned out to be pale birds. As soon as they left, the tree looked different. Ominous.

I cleared the lump in my throat. "We are here to seek the location of the Staff of Light."

I know what you are here for, Zacriah Trovirin. It is your companion who is unsure what he seeks to find.

"We are here for the Staff's location, nothing more," I murmured.

It is not you to whom I speak. The Prince of Flames desires more, for it is I who can find that which is lost. Place your hand upon me, and I shall answer your desires.

Hadrian moved quickly and placed his hand upon the tree first. There was a loud crack, and the bark began to grow over his hand and crawl up his arm. His head was knocked back by an invisible force; his eyes glazed over.

"Hadrian," I shouted for him, trying to reach across the space between us.

Do not worry, my child, for I will not harm him.

"What are you doing to him?" I couldn't tear my eyes from Hadrian as the white bark engulfed his arm.

I will show him what he seeks most to find.

The bark morphed before my eyes into the silhouette of a face. The vision stole my breath.

Ask what you wish to find. I shall show you. Place your hand upon me before your chance is lost.

Reluctantly, I raised my hand and hovered above the bark. I trusted the voice, for it sang to me like the light ring of bells. Whatever magick this was, I knew it to be safe. I placed my palm upon the tree. The moment I touched it, the bark began to swallow my body.

As the tree faded from view, and I stepped into the white void beyond it; I stood before a woman with three faces.

CHAPTER
FIFTEEN

THE GODDESS WAS more than I ever imagined her to be. I knew it was Her as clear as I knew myself.

Pure light rippled from her tall frame. An aura of magick seeped from her very pores in waves of overwhelming splendor. Hues of red, gold and black danced amongst her veins, trailing up to the three heads that rested above her strong shoulders.

She stood before me, hands clasped gracefully in front of her. I raised a hand to my eyes, shielding them from the light that pulsed over me. Streams of tears cut down my cheeks and landed amongst the white floor.

With my gaze directed, I saw she wore a dress woven from beads, ivory and silk. It hung off her frame, constantly moving like water. The bodice was a mesh of silvered bark, and the glittering gems caught the light of the white space we stood within.

Look at me, my child.

Her voice rang out like the sweet chime of bells. The trickling of water. The high chirp of birds. As her command filled my mind, body and soul, the light dimmed. I looked up.

The first face was full of youth. A red mess of hair framed a freckled face with eyes of emerald. I knew that face. Nyah. I would recognize her cattish grin and laugh line creased eyes no matter what age she was. Why did the Goddess show me Nyah in youth?

The middle face had me gasping for breath as I looked upon my Mam. She smiled at me, crow's feet crowning her eyes and the corners of her mouth, her hair up in a bun of grey and silver. Her expression was placid and peaceful, the very same as it was when she waved me off all those weeks ago.

I wanted to reach out and touch her cheek to check if this was real, or no more than a horrifying illusion.

The final face was that of a crone.

She glared at me, her face gaunt and hollow. It took a moment for my brain to recognize who it belonged to, as it was not the same as I had seen before.

Browlin glared at me, aged by years from when she was killed. She opened her mouth to smile, showing off her toothless grin. I couldn't look at her. The memory hurt too much. A puckered red line shadowed her sagging neck—the mark Petrer gifted Browlin when he ran his dagger across her neck.

This version of the Goddess had never been drawn, painted or sculptured. Not once had I seen her depicted in such a way. With three heads, showing each stage of life.

You still have a lot to learn, my child, more than I fear you will get the chance to uncover.

She floated forward, two arms outstretched for me.

Her touch was ice and fire. It filled me with a cold breath that spread up my arms and into my chest. I found it confusing to pick which eyes to stare into until I settled on the middle face. I had longed to see Mam again. Now was my chance to drink in this vision of her, to see if it quenched my thirst for her company.

"Why them?" I asked, my hands passing through her hands like they were nothing more than a cloud.

You see what your heart wishes to see. I am youth, life and death.

I wanted to ask after them, to see if Nyah was safe. If my Mam was out of harms reach. And If Browlin finally lived with the Goddess herself in the land beyond our own.

The Prince who holds your heart has shown me his true desire. Now it is time for you to seek what you find. He was given a choice and followed his heart rather than his mind. What will you want to see? I see many questions in your mind. Do you want to find my Staff of Light? To see how your parents are faring? I will answer one, and only one.

The possibilities of seeing my parents again, to find out if they were still safe, was almost too much to pass up on. Even now, I could conjure an image of their kind, hardworking faces. But that was not what I needed most.

"I need to help Hadrian, to keep him safe from the Druid. I needed to know the Staff's location. Please, Goddess, show me where I can seek it."

All three faces shadowed with a pained expression. Although their gaze never faltered from me, they did darken.

With this knowledge, a lot shall change. For years the rise of the druids had been nothing more than a fading memory, but now I see its possibility. Are you certain you wish to find the Staff? Do you understand what it is?

"I fear if I ask, then I will not be shown the Staff's location."

You are smart and brave. I shall show you the location but heed my warning. Tell no one; I have kept the location bounded and safe for many years. In the wrong hands, I fear my reign will end.

I opened my mouth to question her more as an overwhelming sense of worry weighed me down. Her words gave no comfort.

She raised her iridescent hands and placed them on my chest where they hovered above my heart.

You are kind as you are fearful, Zacriah, my child. You must learn to see that sometimes the greatest strength comes from your reluctant mind.

Before I could speak, images flooded my mind as Dalibael shared the Staff of Light's location.

Like a bird, I flew over dark mountain ranges, over a castle nestled between snow and rock. I saw a room, a marble slab in its center. I smelled damp ash and heard the footsteps of a shadow figure. My bones chilled in the cold, vacant room. I tasted danger in the back of my throat. It is here. Slowly, the images flashed then built into a speed that my eyes could not keep up with. I lost my balance, stumbling back. My foot slipped, and I looked down as I began falling through the dark night.

When I opened my eyes, I was staring at the tree once more, Hadrian beside me and Bell nipping at my feet.

Frantically, I looked around for Her. Was it all a dream? A figment of my imagination? The images of the castle in the mountains was as clear as day. I was breathless, and my stomach flipped as if I had really fallen from a great height.

I tried to catch my breath and hold onto the images that lingered in the back of my mind. As I blinked, I could see them once more. I turned to Hadrian once my mind had stopped spinning only to see his expression empty, and the blue hue back in force. The light from the tree no longer spread over us.

"Did you see Her?" I asked Hadrian, stumbling over the dull vines to him. His face was pale, lips pulled thin.

He stood there, silent, a single tear rolling down his cheek. He nodded his head twice and dropped his gaze to the ground. The shake of Hadrian's hands and the fast rise and fall of his chest only added to my worry for him.

"What did you see? What did she show you?" I asked.

It took a moment for him to respond. His shoulders raised, and a cloud of air puffed from his mouth before he looked up.

"I'm sorry. I had to know." Hadrian eyes wet with more tears. He looked broken, youthful in his sadness.

I placed a hand on his shoulder and another beneath his chin. I lifted his face until our eyes held. Although taller than me, in sadness he was small, back hunched, arms hung weak by his side. "You asked after your father…"

He nodded. "I had to."

His sadness only meant one thing. The King's confirmed death.

"Don't be sorry, Hadrian; you did what you needed to do. Maybe now you know he had passed, you can move on from—"

"No, that is not what she showed me. He is still alive, Petal; my father is still alive. After all this time."

As Hadrian said it, his tears intensified, and his body folded into itself.

Bell screeched at our feet and a ruckus of noise grew from the direction of the library. Yet I couldn't tear my eyes from Hadrian.

"He's alive. My father, I cannot believe it… All this time I was certain my hope was wasted. But she showed me. It is what I have longed to know. There is a chance."

I clapped my hands, a small laugh bursting from my lips as I too began to share his emotion. "Where is he?"

He shook his head. "I am unsure where it is. I saw darkness, smelled dirt. I felt close to finding out, but then She pulled away…"

"Is that all you saw?"

Footsteps echoed beyond us.

"Zacriah! Hadrian! We got here as fast as we could!" Jasrov shouted. "Bell alerted us…"

I looked over Hadrian's shoulder to see Jasrov and Emaline. They were not alone, but the third person was hooded and held tight in Emaline's grasp. The third figure made no effort to struggle.

Emaline stern face stilled as she looked at the tree. "What is this place?"

Jasrov looked between her and us. "What is what?"

"The Keeper, Emaline, this is what we've been looking for," I called, pulling Hadrian with me towards them. We walked awkwardly over the vines, wings and horns still on display.

"Was this the tree you told us about?" I asked Jasrov, whose face was scrunched with confusion.

"Yes, it is. But what how is it the Keeper? It does not make sense," Jasrov said.

I looked back, the tree bright with life and its silvery glow.

"What do you see, Emaline?" I asked, unsure what Jasrov was talking about.

"It's beautiful. So bright, and that noise. Do you hear that noise?" she asked.

I tried to listen, but the hum that had been evident before we touched the tree had disappeared.

"There was a noise, but I can't hear it anymore. Can you?" I asked Hadrian.

"No." His reply was no more than a whisper.

We stepped off the vines and left the barrier of light. He lifted his arms, looking closely at the dancing flames.

"The light, it must have cleansed you while you stood within it," I said, taking Hadrian's hand to look myself.

"What light? And I don't hear a thing." Jasrov placed a hand on his hip.

"Only a Dragori can seek the Keeper. That is what Cristilia told us. Maybe you cannot see it because you are not like us." It was clear Hadrian, Emaline and I could still see it.

"There is nothing I seek to know," Jasrov puffed. "At least tell me we got what we came for?"

"Yes, I have seen its location... in sorts."

"STOP!" The hooded figure shouted, trying to break free from Emaline's grasp. "Do not speak another word."

The voice was muffled from the hood, but it was familiar.

"Be still!" Emaline growled, yanking on the arm of the figure.

"It is a trap," the figure said again. "Do not say another word."

"We found her. She was hiding amongst the ruins..." Jasrov shouted over the shouts.

The dagger was in my hand without much of a thought. Hadrian pulsed with light and stepped forward.

"Emaline, let her go," I said, eyes narrowed as the figure's voice filled my mind.

For a slight moment, Emaline faltered. But with a push, the hooded figure stumbled forward. A bruised hand reached up to grasp the hood and ripped it off.

As the light from the tree hit her face, I almost dropped to the ground.

"Illera?" I stepped forward then shouted, "Illera!"

Hadrian's hard hands grabbed a hold of me as I sprang forward, my feet lifting from the floor as he pulled me back.

Illera dropped to her knees and raised her bloodied palms in surrender. "You have to leave. He knew you were coming; it is a trap."

Her words didn't register quickly enough. Not when she looked so broken and defeated. Her violet eyes were shadowed by dark rings, her cheeks hollow and bones sharp. Blotches of dirt and bruises covered most of her exposed skin. Her blonde hair, once strands of sun and wheat, was now muted of color and knotted.

This was not the Illera I knew.

A high-pitched ringing filled my head as anger began to fill my chest. I reached for my power instinctively, wrapping it around her frame until I lifted her from the ground.

She dangled before me, feet kicking in protest, hands grasping for her neck and veins bulging against her skin.

"Why are you here?" I growled.

The last I had seen her was fighting on the ship.

"I… deserted…must…leave." My air wrapped around her throat; my vision turned red.

"Drop her." Emaline stepped forward. "Zacriah, if you do not let her go this second, I will be forced to make you."

"You don't know what she's done."

A warm hand gripped my shoulder and squeezed. "Let her go, Petal."

Hadrian's smooth voice unraveled my anger enough for me to release the wind that pinned Illera in the air. The sound of her knees hitting the stone ground made me cringe with discomfort. This was not me. I shouldn't act like this.

Emaline moved quickly, picking her up and pulling her arms behind her back again. I didn't miss the expression of sorrow she had as she held Illera close.

"We were right. The Druid has been here, and this woman says she stayed behind," Emaline said.

I burned holes through Illera with my gaze. I wanted her to look at me; I willed it. "I don't trust her or anything she says. She is on his side. From day one, she worked alongside his closest confidant. Do not think she has changed."

"You must leave. Please, you must. He knew you were coming. He knew you were looking for something. Leave me and go." Illera coughed, neck blotched red from her lack of breath.

The hairs on my arms and neck stood to attention, and I felt suddenly exposed in the open. "How do I know you are not lying?" I spat.

"I know what I have done to you, Zacriah. I am sorry, but you must believe me. You must Leave now."

Jasrov wrapped his arms around his chest and looked around with a face paled with fear.

"Something isn't right. Haven't you noticed the lack of bodies? These temples are known for being home to many worshipers, and yet we have seen only one. We *should* leave." Emaline looked behind her and took two steps back with Illera still in her hold.

"We leave her here," I said. I strolled past the group, biting down on my lip to stop me from lashing out.

Illera didn't respond or argue.

"No, Zacriah, stop and think. She comes with us; she may know more about the Druid, and we could do with all the information we can get. I would not feel right about leaving her alone here." Illera seemed just as confused as I was at Emaline's act of kindness.

"Stop and think? If we bring her, what is there to say she will not guide the Druid to us? What a coincidence you find her here. On Eldnol soil. Someone I know from home. The chances are slim. We leave her."

"No," Emaline snapped.

"I don't trust her."

"You don't need to, but I ask you to trust me," Emaline said. "She is no threat. I will be sure of that."

"Just go, leave me and go. I don't deserve your trust, Zacriah, but let me try and make things right. You must leave."

I walked before Illera, getting as close to her as I could. She held my stare this time, chin held high and muttered. "He will kill me either way."

Not dropping her pleading stare, I flexed my wings in threat, then I looked to Emaline who held her still. "She is your responsibility. Let her out of your sight, and I can't promise what will happen to her."

"Lower your tone when you speak to me, Zacriah. Do not forget whom you speak to." Emaline's face pinched in anger. Her brows turned down as her face morphed before my eyes. "I have given you my word, and my word is final. But never think you are above me. I do not take orders from you, ever. And I never will."

"Then it is settled." Jasrov stepped awkwardly between us. Bell's teeth were bared as she sensed the tension between us. "But can we go now? All this arguing is both loud and leaving us in the open."

"Stay alert," Emaline said, trident held before her.

We all moved, leaving the Keeper behind us without another glance. I didn't look back to see if Illera was left or Emaline still kept her. I walked ahead, almost hoping the Druid would surprise us. The anger inside me could do with an outlet, and the face of that smug demon was exactly what would help me exercise it.

Hadrian was quiet. He had hardly said a word after the vision with the Keeper. And even now, he walked ahead silently, lost in thought. I wanted to console him. To help him talk about what the Keeper showed him. Instead, I seethed in my own silence.

There was no sign of the Druid or an ambush the entire way out of the temple. Not a sound or movement that caught my attention. Even as I bounded up the final set of stairs, I reached out my air for others that could be waiting outside but felt nothing.

This fact only angered me more, proving that Illera was again not to be trusted.

When I burst out into the open air, I turned on the group. "She lied. I told you!"

Illera was breathless but shook her head, her violet eyes wide. "Please…"

Emaline held on tighter and showed her teeth as I stepped forward. "Zacriah..." she growled.

"I told you. Let her crawl back into the dark hole you found her in... have you even asked how she got here—"

A jarring crack stopped my screaming. I turned slowly to see where it came from and watched as the bundles of vines coating the ruins broke. All around us, the earth jolted as movement spurred beneath it.

I turned my head sharply to a noise closest to us. The body Emaline had found when we arrived started to move. To my horror, it lifted its lifeless face and reached beyond its prison of earth. Its bones creaked as it stepped free.

Opal smoke seeped from the empty sockets of the dead elfin's face. A golden patch stained the front of his tunic. A wound. He was dead but moving like the creatures that attacked us in the forest days earlier.

"Be still," Hadrian whispered beside me, heat flaring. He silently waved for everyone to step close until we were huddled together in the center of the courtyard surrounded by the waking dead.

The ground beneath us shook violently.

I tried to keep my balance as the many dirt-covered bodies crawled from the holes in the ground and joined the growing army. An army of countless dead.

An animalistic scream tore through the sky around us as a robed figure of the dead began to run forward. The ground shook again, sending me sprawling to the floor. Jasrov shouted; Emaline swore. In a blink, the running dead stopped. Emaline's trident no longer had a place in her hand. Now, it protruded from the dead's neck.

I risked a glance at her and watched Emaline pull a sword free. "Tridents are never the best choice of weapon anyway. Get up," Emaline commanded, pulling Illera up as she shouted at the rest of us. "Goddess bless us."

Not one other shadowbeing moved. They all stood still, black smoking seeping from their eyes like a burned candle.

Hadrian did not reach for a weapon. He raised both hands until flames laced across his palms. His eyes reflected the blue blaze and something darker.

One of the dead beings stumbled forward, raised its arm slowly and pointed right at us in threat.

"Hold your ground and fight like your life depends on it," Emaline called once more as she cocked her knees and readied her stance. "Because it does."

CHAPTER
SIXTEEN

THE THICK SCENT of earth filled my nose and mouth as flecks of it burst into the air. All around us grass and mud exploded, which blocked the view of our attackers for a moment. It was only a second, but it was all they needed to cause a distraction.

Surprised, I raised my arms and covered my face from being battered by stone and dirt. On cue, my wings wrapped around me, and the dull thud of mud hitting their leather surface was all I could hear.

I felt unprotected in those seconds, so I threw my wings wide. It was impossible to count the number of bodies that sprang free from the ground. The animated bodies of recently buried monks stood entirely around us, blocking us in a compact circle.

There were only four of us, excluding Illera, compared to the alarming size of the army of dead. We had weapons; they had the power of the Druid. Our chances were slim, but I was ready for a fight. I almost longed for it.

The Druid was not here. I scanned the faces, but only his army stood immobile before us. Skin flaked off their faces, exposing yellow bone and grey muscle.

Illera *had* spoken the truth.

"What do we do? What do we do?" Jasrov's panicked shout sounded from behind me as we stood in the eye of the dead's circle.

Hadrian raised a single finger to his lip. "Shh."

"Let me help," Illera whispered. "You are already outnumbered. Give me a weapon. I will fight with you."

"No," I hissed. "Emaline, keep her with you. If we don't leave, we are dead."

There was a loud crack as one of the bodies closest to me cocked his head. The sharp movement had snapped his neck and left it dangling awkwardly over his shoulder. Then smoke snaked out of his wide-open mouth, followed by a voice.

"Before I take what is mine, I must thank you. The Keeper was not as helpful when I asked for the Staff's location. I am glad you did not have that same problem."

As the Druid's voice billowed from the dead's mouth, I reached for my air as comfort, wrapping it around us in a turning cyclone to drown it out. But the voice only raised again.

"I wish I were here to welcome you home personally, but I must say I am rather occupied elsewhere. I hope you do not mind dealing with my soldiers instead. I can assure you they will not harm you if you just tell me what I need to know."

Hadrian released a growl so ferocious it even had me flinching. Sudden bursts of blue fire dripped from his skin onto the ground like lava, causing stone to hiss as it ate away at it.

Emaline dropped Illera to the ground and stalked forward, evolving into her Dragori form with each step. Bell sprang before Jasrov and screeched in the direction of the body. Jasrov held the dagger in both shaking hands.

"Are you prepared to play along? Or am I going to have to take you by force?"

"A weapon please," Illera pleaded as she stood behind Jasrov.

I recoiled from the glee in the voice. The black smoke that seeped from the dead's mouth was forming into the shape of a shadowed face. As the features became clear, so did the swaying runes that covered the face of shadow.

"Too scared to show yourself?" Emaline spat. "Are you so worried about what might happen to you that you send your creatures to do your bidding?"

"I think you may be my new favorite, Emaline Sowdin. Your spirit is strong, unlike your brothers."

"They are no brothers of mine," Emaline sneered.

"By blood, no. By spirit, yes," the booming voice replied.

Emaline was at the edge of my cyclone, screaming over the roaring wind. "I don't blame you for hiding; I would do the same after the last time we met!"

"I will give you the chance to step forward and come to me. If you do not, I *will* take you."

"I dare you to try." Hadrian's voice thundered towards the body. "I *beg* you to try."

The dead body of the Druid's mouthpiece moved towards the wall of my cyclone. It didn't stop until its face was plastered against the wall of air. My stomach turned as skin and bone were ripped from its face as he pushed it through my shield. It smiled, showing no sign of feeling and pain.

"You cannot hurt me." The exposed jaw moved as the Druid spoke. Teeth ripped from its mouth and joined my cyclone of wind. Around they spun in the holds of my power with skin and clumps of hair that were snatched from the shadowbeing's head.

The Druid's puppet stepped backwards, but the damage was done. Skin hung in flaps, and black smoke oozed from the destruction of its body. It was nothing more than a skeleton from the neck up.

"Now, you will come with—"

A dagger spun towards the dead, slicing the head from its body in one swift slice. The blade passed through bone until the skull crashed at the bodies feet. Silence followed.

We all turned to see who threw it. Cloaked in shadow and standing upon of a pile of stone, the figure reached for the bow strapped to its back and held it forward, cocked an arrow and let it fly. With vigor, it hit another of the bodies and pinned it to the crumbled wall behind it.

The elfin jumped down from the stone wall and landed beyond my cyclone. My wind caused the cloak to shift and the hood to fly from the figure's head, revealing a full frame of curly red hair and a stern freckled face.

"Nyah," I shouted, but she showed no sign she could hear me. She moved like swift water, slicing at the frozen bodies. That was their invitation. All at once, the dead moved. A wave of bodies joined the fight.

Magick slipped from my cyclone as I watched Nyah attack. The shield weakened as my concentration was diverted to her.

Her movements were fluid as she sprang up, twisting in mid-air and landing beyond two headless bodies. Sometime during her jump, she'd unsheathed two swords, which now hung beside her, dripping black smoke.

One attack after the other, she created a path towards my cyclone, slicing the heads of the bodies that reached her first. They fell like dead flies, littering the ground in her wake. Hadrian was shouting for me to drop my shield fully. Then we all watched from safety as a body stepped behind Nyah.

She did not notice, but I did.

I pulled on my magick, relaxing the cyclone. I threw my hands forward. Wind shot towards her, separating like a curtain around her body then closing once again around the dead that almost reached her. The shadowbeing lifted from the ground. With a heavy thud, I smashed it into the ground. Nyah caught on and swung her sword down, stabbing through its neck.

With my shield down, the many bodies that had waited around us moved for our group. The war had begun.

Nyah was a ball of fury, thrashing, slicing and serving all of those she could reach.

In my lapse of power, Emaline, Jasrov and Bell too left my protection and joined the fight.

Black smoke splattered across the ruins and dissipated into thin air. Growling, I sprang forward and reached a clawed hand. I grabbed onto the neck of a monk closest to me, and I squeezed. The cold flesh was weak, allowing my claws to pierce deep into it. No blood spilled, only shadow. I retracted them sharply until the head came away from the shoulders. I tossed it to the side and moved to the next, reaching for my sword.

It was not there.

Illera stood behind me, my sword in her hands. I watched my own reflection in the steel as she snarled and thrust the blade forward. I felt nothing, no pain, no kiss of steel. I looked down, expecting to see it buried in my stomach, but it was not.

She's missed me and stabbed into one of the shadowbeings behind me.

"Move," she shouted, pushing me to the side.

I ducked just as she pulled the sword up from navel to neck, ending the shadowbeing instantly.

"Remove the heads," Nyah commanded.

There was no time to thank Illera. She twisted and threw herself into the huddle of shadowbeings that surrounded Jasrov. He was fighting them off with the dagger, swinging it around with no direction. Bell bit onto ankles, only to be ignored by those she attacked.

One after the other, we took the Druid's soldiers down until it was hard to see each other through the clouds of smoke. Without weapons, the animated dead scratched and hit.

I could hear the song of blades cutting flesh, and the grunting screams as our group attacked.

Swordless, I pulled the bow from my back. Just running my hands over the familiar curve caused excitement to drown out the possible danger. With a shift of my wings, I was sent into the air and landed on a tall wall of the temple. From my vantage point, I rained arrows towards the shadowbeings. One after the other my attempts lodged in necks, heads and chests. I kept going, not sparing a breath until I reached back for another and came up empty-handed. Out of arrows, I dropped my bow and jumped back into the fight with only magick as my weapon.

Emaline worked with water and steel. She spun her sword, cutting, jabbing, stabbing. Around her water spun, leaking from the water sack at her belt. It lashed out like a snake, hitting faces and sending the shadowbeings tumbling.

If the Druid wanted us, his efforts were dwindling.

I waded through the smoke and crashed into Jasrov who held a short dagger in his hands.

"It's me!" I said as he almost stabbed me out of alarm.

Ahead of us, two shadowbeings ran forward. I pushed my palms towards them, sending a ball of air at their chests until they were sent flying backwards. I slashed and sliced whips of wind until the snap of bones became music to my ears. My wings acted alone, moving and stabbing their claws into chests and foreheads.

Jasrov panted heavily, but he did not fail in his efforts to keep the attackers at bay.

"Don't waste your magick." Emaline was suddenly beside me, stabbing a being with ease through its neck. "They will keep coming back unless you server the head."

How could I fight when my only sword was now in the hands of Illera?

Then the idea hit me. I scrambled through the action, trying to find the dagger that Nyah had thrown when she started this fight. As I searched, I kept the shadowbeings at bay by sending sharp bursts of air in their directions. I caught a glint out of the corner of my eye. There it was, resting on the ground only inches from where I stood.

I leaped forward, throwing myself to the ground and picked it up. I heard my name being called, and I turned to see Hadrian hovering in the air. Beneath him was a dozen or so of the shadowbeings, two of which held onto his leg.

They were unbothered by the volleys of blue flame he crashed down upon them. His wings faltered, and his eyes were blinking shut. Something was wrong. Very wrong. I snatched the dagger from the ground and lifted it up just as one shadowbeing reached me.

Serving its head, I ran for Hadrian, leaped over a pile of stone and sliced the dagger forward. It took three swings for me to make it to the two who held onto Hadrian. They dripped with fire, and I recoiled from the heat. Trying to stay out of the reaching flames, I kept my air at bay and sliced at one of the shadowbeings.

My arm muscles screamed as I cut over and over until the head came free. With Hadrian's free foot he kicked the other in the face, causing it to stagger back, and I lodged the blade into its neck and pulled.

Cold hands grasped a hold of me, pulling and digging nails into my flesh. I tried to batter them off me and lost the dagger in the struggle.

"You are mine."

The voice of the Druid seeped from one of the many mouths before me.

"Stop resisting."

"I will never stop," I screamed as nails raked down my arm.

I urged my wind forward until the howling of it calmed me. I closed my eyes briefly, reaching my wind within the shadowbeings' mouths like searching fingers. I didn't stop until I was aware of their entire empty bodies. I battled with the power within them. In my mind, silver wind clashed with black shadow. The many surrounding me stopped as I filled their bodies and pushed with all my might. My awareness grew, and so did the hunger within me. One by one, I expelled the dark from the shadowbeings bodies until not a sliver of smoke was felt within them.

When I opened my eyes, the ground was littered with the dead.

A sickly taste coated my tongue and inner cheeks. My stomach turned, and I gagged, bending over, hands on my knees, as my body expelled nothing but spit. My mind was light from the use of my magick.

There was no sound now, no noise of battle and screams of anguish.

Not only had my magick purged the Druid's power from the dead that had surrounded me, it had also affected the remaining shadowbeings. All around, the bodies lay motionless, scattered amongst the ruins of their home.

Illera and Emaline stood back to back, a look of surprise painted on their faces. Hadrian was the closest to me, standing amongst scorched earth. And Nyah kneeled on the ground, looking over Jasrov's body.

There was no time to celebrate our win.

Bell began to scream and yelp above her Jasrov. I moved for him, running until I hovered above his still body.

"They got him..." There was a lump in my throat as I shouted.

The side of his face purpled with bruises, his lips swollen and bloody. A deep cut separated his left eyebrow and ran down to his lip. Gold blood oozed onto his dark skin until all I saw was its shining liquid.

I concentrated on my body and shifted back into my elven form, not wanting my claws to catch him as I ran a hand over the large lump in the shadow of his hairline.

"He needs a healer." Nyah pressed her hands on his chest. I caught the faint rise and fall which gave me hope. "And fast."

Nyah looked up at her with a thunderous face, then looked back to Jasrov. She dipped her finger into the golden blood that flowed angrily from the cut. She pulled a cloth and held it on the gash to still the bleeding.

"I'm keeping him calm to prevent any damage." She scooped him into her arms, the muscles on her exposed, arms bulging.

Hadrian offered to take Jasrov, but she shook her head. "I will keep him stabilized, but we must leave. I have been trying to find you for a while, and I would have warned you if you didn't run from me this morning. A lot has happened in these past days, and I've been sent to end this mission."

Hadrian stepped forth, "End the quest? But—"

"We must leave for Lilioira at once. I'll explain everything on the way but it's not safe anymore, and if you want him to live, we can't waste another second." Nyah gave me a small smile that never reached her eyes.

Emaline whistled, and our griffins responded, landing amongst the battle remains. Jerk shifted his clawed feet, not wanting to touch the many bodies beneath him.

"Lilioira is a four-day journey from here, if that," Emaline said, snatching the sword from Illera's shaking grasp and handing it back to me. "And that is without stopping to rest."

Nyah nodded, eyes glazed with sadness that I had not seen her possess before. "We must return to the Inn you ran from this morning. We are not going anywhere until he is healed." She looked to Jasrov in her arms. They were the same age and equal height, but she showed no concern at holding him.

"That was you. The person who found us at the Inn," I said.

"Who else would it be?" Nyah replied. "Come, there is not time for it."

We separated into partners on the griffins and left the remnants of battle behind.

Our team of three was now a seven. Emaline flew with Illera, who was no longer our prisoner of sorts, not after she risked her life fighting alongside us. It was not that I trusted her, but she had the chance to end me, and she didn't. I wouldn't forget that. But the bubbling distrust I had against her still echoed inside of me.

Hadrian gave up his griffin to Nyah who flew with Jasrov. Nyah wrapped her hands around Jasrov waist to keep him steady.

Hadrian rode with me.

"Can you take the reins?" he asked, eyes ringed in black.

"Are you hurt?" I asked, concerned.

I placed a hand on his forehead and came back quick. He was so hot and his skin clammy.

"I just need to rest," he replied weakly. "I will be fine. Just…"

His eyes rolled back slightly. I helped him up and took the reins. Jerk following my command as he followed the group into the skies.

We did not talk about it the entire flight back to the Inn. Our clothes were once again in tatters from shifting before the Keeper, so Emaline gave us a large blanket to cover ourselves in until we got to the village.

With each beat of Jerk's wings, I worried for Jasrov. I knew he had no practice in combat, yet I had left him when I went searching for the dagger. If only I had stayed, he may not have gotten hurt.

This was my fault.

Hadrian's wellbeing also prickled in my mind. He laid his head on me, body limp. I couldn't see if he was still awake or sleeping, but his body was too warm, even this high up as the cold wind battered us.

My mind spun with guilt, and the haunting words of the Druid joined that vortex. He knew we were looking for the Staff.

But what could he possibly need with it?

CHAPTER
SEVENTEEN

NYAH SPOKE IN hushed tones to the barman, who nodded and left the Inn without another word. There was urgency in the way he walked for the door and how it slammed closed after him.

"Take him to the top room." That was all I caught the barman say before he left.

Nyah didn't waste a second before carrying Jasrov's limp body towards the stairs and disappearing up into the waiting dark. Bell pounced up behind her.

I jumped when the door to the Inn opened and the barman returned. Behind him, a beautiful elfin woman followed. Her face flushed red with worry. A healer. They reached the stairs before the door closed behind them.

We were a cluster of intense worry. Emaline chewed her nails and Hadrian slumped on a chair completely exhausted. The dark circles under his eyes had intensified since we arrived, and his breathing had shallowed. I wanted to ask the Healer to check him, it might still my worrying. Illera was quiet as well, her eyes jumping at every sound and movement as if she was constantly in danger.

No one spoke until Nyah returned. Her face was pale as she came down, her hands coated in gold. Jasrov's blood.

The barman then offered us free ale by the jug load. Nyah carried two over to the table where Hadrian, Emaline, Illera and I sat, dirt covered and sticky with sweat.

"How is he?" I shouted across to her.

Nyah swiped a hand across her forehead and nodded breathlessly. "He will be okay."

"I must admit, it is good to see you, Nyah." Hadrian extended a hand and shook hers.

"Can someone write that down for me?" she replied. "I don't want to forget that princey said something nice for once."

He sniffed and nodded. "So, it was you who came searching for us in the early hours of the morning?"

"And I would have reached you if you didn't go running. I mean I at least thought you would be happy to see me. Except I get a blast of your strange fire as a welcome."

"Yes, I must apologize for that."

"How did you find us?" I asked, pulling her in for a hug. She returned it, crushing me within her hold.

"With difficulty. I have been following a day behind you. Your emotions left imprints during your travel. I just had to work out which was the right ones and where they led to. That is how I got here."

Nyah kept looking at where Illera sat with her head down. "I see you've picked up some new and *old* friends on the way."

"You could say that," I said. "I'm just glad you finally caught up. You told me you would follow straight away, what kept you a full day behind us?"

"Oh, I knew you had something planned," Hadrian interjected.

Nyah winked. "I tried to, but"—her expression darkened—"there was trouble in Kandilin."

My mouth dropped open, mirroring Emaline who sat forward and slammed her hands on the table.

"What do you mean trouble? When?" Emaline was red with rage.

"After you left. I guess the Druid caught word of Queen Kathine's visit and decided it was the best time for him to attack. I couldn't follow straight away, and I am glad that was the case. I stayed back with the Queen and Nesta when we were ambushed."

Something the Druid said flashed back to me. *I am occupied elsewhere.*

"Kandilin is now in his control and the people with it," Nyah said. "I was planning on leaving a few hours after you. I could still feel you and thought I'd catch up. It was during a feast that night, everything turned sour." Nyah didn't look up as she spoke. Her gaze was pinned to her hands, which fiddled before her.

"Kandilin is as protected as Lilioira; how could the Druid get past the guards and wards?" Emaline asked, eyes wide, her chest heaving with each labored breath.

Nyah shrugged. "They walked right through the main gate in the north of the town. It was a big surprise to us all. It was horrific. By the time I knew what was happening, there was gold everywhere. Someone must have betrayed us. A sympathizer of the Druid, or someone in league with him. We were unprepared, that was the greatest downfall."

"No," Emaline shouted, standing from the table. "Who? Tell me who it is. I vow I will end them for betraying my people."

Nyah reached across the table and placed a hand on Emaline's arm. "We don't know, but I promise I will help you find out. I will not stop until those innocent lives lost are repaid."

"Avenged," Emaline seethed.

Emaline began to relax, her face losing its redness. I knew what Nyah was doing. She held onto Emaline's hand as she spoke.

"Not many of us managed to escape, but I did help secure the Queen. She is the one who has commanded me to retrieve you and bring you to the capital. The war has now begun. That is why she has called off the quest. It is no longer the matter of importance."

Faces of those I'd seen in Kandilin passed through my mind. "Who else survived, Nyah?"

Nyah audibly swallowed before answering, "Queen Kathine and a handful of the locals..."

No one spoke. There must have been thousands of elves living in Kandilin.

Nyah choked on her words as a cry overcame her. She shook her head and coughed, tears pooling her emerald eyes. "I've never seen anything like it before. So much blood and destruction. By the time I got free, the riverways were stained gold—"

"And Nesta?" Emaline whispered, eyes red-rimmed.

Nyah shook her head. "The council was attacked. I was right there with Nesta when it happened. She gave her life to save Cristilia."

My heart sank into my stomach. Hadrian released a labored breath.

We drowned in moments of silence. Nesta was the first to show me great kindness in Kandilin. She'd died saving the council she mistrusted. Fate was unfair.

Emaline's lips quivered as she inhaled sharply.

Nyah reached for her again, but Emaline pulled her hand away. She looked up, anger rippled from her in waves. I felt her building pressure as if the moisture in the air quivered with her.

The squeak of the chair caused the hairs on my arms to stand.

"Emaline?" Hadrian said as she stood abruptly.

"Leave me," she growled. "Like you should have done in Kandilin. I could have been there." She was shouting now. "I could have been there to help her, *save* her."

I flinched under her cry.

"I will not forget this," Emaline said, eyes burning across the group.

We watched her walk for the stairs; even Illera stood as she if call out for her, but she promptly slumped back down.

"What on this earth was that about?" Hadrian said, face paled.

"They are—were very close. The reason why Emaline didn't want to leave Kandilin for this quest in the first place. Nesta told me all of this after you left," Nyah said. By the look on our faces, she guessed we had not been told. "You didn't know?" she asked.

"It was not for us to know," Hadrian responded. "Emaline was not ready to tell us."

It made sense as to why Emaline had been so reluctant to come.

"We need to give her some time," Hadrian said, his gaze stuck to a spot on the table. "Grief can't be rushed or ignored."

Nyah cleared her throat. "I will visit her shortly as I have something to give her." She pulled out a silver chain from her pocket that I recognized instantly as Nesta's necklace. The same silver acorn hung on the chain. "Nesta would want her to have this."

Overwhelmed with Emaline's sadness, I grabbed for Nyah. "I am so glad you are safe. I don't know what I would have done if you were hurt."

Nyah shared a look with me, one that spoke many words. "The Druid is not ready for me. When he is, I will show him what a mistake that would be."

"Tell us everything," I said. "His soldiers. Anything you might remember that could help us."

Nyah placed the necklace down and turned to Illera. "Why don't we ask one of his soldiers since we are so lucky to be graced in one's presence?"

Illera looked up for a beat but quickly retreated into her shell. This was not the girl I had known from Horith. Quiet and unkept. This girl was broken, lost, disturbed.

"Nothing?" Nyah hissed.

"Zacriah asked you, Nyah. Leave Illera alone... for now." Hadrian stood, standing in the way of Illera.

"But—" Nyah started.

"I said for now," Hadrian finished.

Nyah looked at me for confirmation, and I nodded. Then she began to tell us all she knew.

"But before I left Queen Kathine, we created a mental tether, something Gallion taught me. It allows me to communicate with her. From the last bit of information she gave me, it would seem that the Druid and his army of shadowbeings have disappeared from Kandilin. Griffin riders have scouted the town from the skies and report it to be empty. All sign of life has left with him. No word has been mentioned of him until today."

"And the civilians of Kandilin? The dead?" I asked.

"Are no more. They rose during the fight, filled with whatever power the Druid has."

"This tether, can you communicate with her even now?" Hadrian interjected.

"She is sleeping. Why? What is on your mind?"

"Are you certain Kandilin has been abandoned?" Hadrian ignored her question.

She nodded. "I believe in what my Queen tells me."

I didn't miss how she referred to Kathine, nor did Hadrian, but Nyah's plain expression suggested she had not realized she said it. Her Queen. Hadrian looked away, leaving that comment untouched.

Nyah turned her face back to Illera. "You know, one touch and I will see just how trustworthy this elk-murdering demon is."

Hadrian knocked twice on the table, distracting Nyah from Illera. "No matter what has happened before today, Illera fought by our side and will thus be treated with respect. She could have turned on us during the fight, yet she did not."

Nyah turned sharp to him. "Have you forgotten what she's done? What part she has played in this?"

Hadrian closed his eyes. "I have not forgotten, but I have forgiven. I trust that once she has rested, she will gladly tell us what she knows. Is that correct, Illera?"

She nodded. "I know you do not trust me, and I do not blame you for feeling that way. All I ask is for you to give me the chance to make things right. I will tell you all I know. There is not much to tell, but I vow not to hold anything from you."

"Maybe you can start off by explaining why you've decided to go against him." I could see Nyah struggling to keep the rage from her voice. "Just a suggestion."

"I don't believe in killing." Her statement was honest and matter of fact. "One moment we were in hiding and the next I stood in the middle of hell. All around me, his power devoured the holy men and woman of the temple. Destroying, killing, murdering. I couldn't watch. He wanted me to do it, to help his efforts, but I couldn't. He was too busy to notice when I slipped into the temple and hid. That's all I did. While those above me screamed and begged for their lives, I hid in the heart of the temple. When you found me, I thought they were still part of his army. I thought he was coming to punish me, do to me what he's done to so many."

Illera shook as she spoke, her eyes muted and a light sheen of sweat coated her pale forehead. Her disheveled appearance only intensified as she went over the events at the temple. She looked up at Hadrian, eyes burning with a strange emotion. "I was wrong. I felt powerful and lacked any sense of what was right. There is no excuse for why I did it—"

Hadrian raised a hand to silence her and placed it on hers. "Do not explain yourself, Illera. Many actions are made in fear; I do not blame you for doing what you had to do."

"You are wrong. I did not act out of fear. I did it because of my status. Finally, I was being treated with respect. I wanted to prove to the King, to Alina, that I was worthy of the way they treated me. I did it because I thought it was right."

"You see where you went wrong. That is an important step," Hadrian said.

I bit down on my tongue. "You saved my life back at the temple, consider whatever was between us resolved."

Pure relief coated her face. "I will do anything to help you."

"I believe it," Hadrian said, smiling through his blue gleam.

"I have heard something that might help," she said. "The Druid has found something. Something that is keeping him distracted. I have seen the power *it* has, what it did to the temple. You saw it."

Hadrian shared a look with me, his forehead creased. "Do you know more? Have you seen it?"

She shook her head, her hair falling over her shoulders. "No, whatever it is, he is keeping it close to him."

"How big is his army, Illera?" I asked.

"A small group of shifters from Olderim," she replied. "And the rest—the dead—he uses them as his army just as you've witnessed. If it's his power that slays them, he can use them to do his bidding."

It would make him unstoppable. For we are the few, and he is many. Whatever the dark, unexplainable power the druids had over death could overwhelm us. Our cities and towns had been built on the bones of our ancestors. If the Druid could use them, only destruction would follow.

I leaned forward, my elbow resting in a puddle of Nyah's ale. "Where is he hiding?"

Illera's ocean eyes glazed over and she seemed to stare off into another world. "I do not remember. He doesn't trust anyone. Perhaps he knew I would rebel against him. After the battle on the ship, those who survived were taken to a place with no name or light. Just the dark."

"You remember nothing?" Hadrian questioned. "Nothing at all?"

She shook her head again. "Just that it was cold. Very cold."

EIGHTEEN

ILLERA WAS EXHAUSTED. Days of hiding within the temple ruins had taken its toll on her. She took a spare room with Nyah, leaving Emaline to have time alone in the third bedroom. With the healer still with Jasrov in the room we occupied earlier, it left us to sleep on benches by the bar. I didn't mind.

If Hadrian was close, I wouldn't care where we slept.

Hadrian had quickly fallen asleep on the bench we previously sat at, warmed by the open fire the Innkeeper kept alight for us. No one asked questions about Hadrian's gleam, but it didn't stop the looks every now and then.

I stayed awake until those eating and drinking left for their dwellings and the Innkeeper locked the door. Only then did I feel comfortable enough to lower my guard and rest.

But no matter how hard I tried, I couldn't sleep. The fire died to a faint glow, and the only noises from within the Inn were the creaking of its walls. I gave up on the idea of sleep and opted for a walk. Anything to shake the unease from my body.

The Inn was small and narrow, and I had soon explored every inch of it. I gazed out the window and looked upon the open lake. My body craved space and fresh air. I unbolted the door and left, sparing a glance back at

Hadrian, who slept without stirring. I went out in the night's embrace and headed down the long wooden jetty that reached out the back of the Inn. My bare feet hit the damp wooden panels and creaked with each step. Once I reached the end, I perched down. My nose filled with the bursts of salt and the slow lull of the singing ripples. I dipped my feet into the lake, my toes only just reaching the cold water. Then I closed my eyes and gave into the nightly breeze. Giving into my magick was warm and familiar. I held onto the silvery strings of breeze that wrapped around me as I spun them, twisting and turning until the water splashed with my disturbance.

I was transfixed by the reflection of the night sky that bounced from the lake's glassy surface. Losing myself in the view, it was hard to distinguish where the night met the water. Clouds floated softly across the lake, covering the bright disc moon and distorting its reflection.

"That fox hasn't left his side the entire time." Nyah walked up behind me, encased in a large cloak. "She almost nipped the tips of the healer's fingers when she got too close."

She sat beside me, wrapping half of the cloak over my shoulder, so we were both protected from the subtle chill.

"Bell didn't try that with you when you touched Jasrov at the temple," I replied, resting my head on her strong shoulder. "She must like you."

"Clearly, she has good taste in people." Nyah's presence was just what I needed, even if I didn't know it.

A messily excuse of a laugh burst from my lips but died once it reached the cold night air. I could have sat with Nyah in silence, enjoying her familiar warmth all evening. I had not realized just how much I had missed her in the past days, not until the empty part of me filled when I saw her on the ruins of the temple.

"How did you know I was out here?" I asked.

Nyah pulled a face with one brow raised. "Oh, I don't know. Might have something to do with my empathic abilities."

She knocked my shoulder and smiled, but I found it hard to respond with one.

"So much has changed in such little time," I said, trying to hide the shake in my voice. "I can't help but feel so defeated."

Nyah held her legs close to her chest and released a heavy sigh. "I know the feeling."

"We finally find the Keeper and get insight to the location of the Staff, but then Queen Kathine calls off the quest without another thought. We can't just give up. I must find it."

Cristilia's story had not left the back of my mind. All that power. All that destruction.

"We have to go to Lilioira. I know you believe this Staff will help Hadrian, and I am sure you are right, but we must return to the Queen. It is not worth the risk to find it."

"It is a risk I would take." I chewed on my finger to still my worry. "Have you seen Emaline?"

Nyah shook her head. "I was going to visit her, but she didn't answer me. She will need time to come to terms with what has happened, so I didn't want to push it. I am a stranger to her."

"She hates us now. Although, I get it. Without us turning up, maybe Nesta would still be alive."

"What Emaline and Nesta shared was special. This will be hard on her. Let her take it out on you if that makes her feel even the slightest bit better. That is what friends are for."

I sighed. "She never told us about Nesta. I didn't even know they knew each other."

"And it is not my story to tell, but the relationship they had was special, beautiful. Something not even I could ever hope to experience."

Some unknown feeling tugged at my heart at the mention of Emaline. I looked back to the Inn to a window where Emaline's room would be. There was no light inside.

"She is going to need time," Nyah whispered.

"It seems time is the one thing we do not have to spare."

I had so much I wanted to tell Nyah. So many words to spill.

"Hadrian knows his father is alive," I said, and a weight lifted from my chest. "He asked the Keeper, and she confirmed it."

"You think he is going to try and find him?" Nyah asked, resting a hand on mine.

"I know he will. That is what I would do, would you?"

"Hadrian, in a sense, has not seen his father since his mother passed all those years ago. Now we know the man he has lived with, ruled beside was not his true father at all, he will want to find him. But that is his choice, not one you can influence."

She spoke the truth, something I'd imagined many times in the past hours.

"I would never stop him from searching," I said. "If that is what he needs to do, then I will never stand in his way."

"That is why he holds such love for you; he knows you support him through thick and thin," Nyah replied.

I just hope we have enough time to find the Staff first.

Hadrian had not mentioned it, but I could see his struggle. His burning skin and tired eyes told a tale of a boy in pain. Whatever the Heartfire was doing to him, it must be bad. I wanted to ask Nyah but couldn't bring myself to admit it aloud.

We sat like that for a long while, exchanging stories of the past days. I told her of the Mer creature that attacked us and how we stumbled across Jasrov. I told her of the Keeper and the Goddess, leaving out the mention of her face being on one of the Goddess's three heads.

"We will need to seek someone who knows Eldnol like the creases in their hands."

"But why the need for secrets and cryptic images; what is the Goddess hiding from me?" I asked. She'd shown me brief images and feelings when I asked for the Staff's location. It was dark, the air was hard, and snow-shrouded my vision. But the castle, like the points of two swords reaching for the sky and made of black stone; that image was clear. The Staff was there.

Nyah knocked my shoulder in comfort. "The city of Lilioira is large and filled with many who could help. When we leave tomorrow, if weather permits, we will arrive in three days. I will help you find someone in the city who will help make sense of the images the Goddess shared with you. Until then, you really should get some rest."

I looked at her through my pale lashes. "Will you do your thing and help me sleep?"

She stood and raised a hand to me. "Happily."

After we entered the Inn and Nyah helped ready my mind for sleep, my final thought faded to the Druid.

His face morphed in the dark of my closed eyes and smiled as I fell into sleep.

CHAPTER

NINETEEN

THE FEW HOURS I slept made me feel worse off than I had before them. I woke, body stiff, on the bench opposite Hadrian, whose back was facing me. Nyah towered above me, nudging me with her freckled hand. A jaw breaking yawn didn't help me stir, but when Nyah nudged me harder, I managed to open my resisting eyes.

"Whaaah," I grumbled, rolling onto my side.

"The Queen's promise of travel has arrived." Her ginger hair was pulled back into a bun on the top of her head. A single curl escaped and rested across her cheek.

I mumbled a response even I couldn't understand.

"Get up and be quick about it. We should leave as soon as possible."

My voice was rough and strained. "Have you even slept?"

Nyah smiled and knocked a gentle punch on my arm. "We will have plenty of time to catch up on sleep on the way. I will meet you outside. The sailor whose boat we are borrowing needs payment. I better go before he thinks we have tricked him out of it." She sauntered off, the door to the Inn slamming closed behind her.

My mind wanted to ask after Jasrov and Emaline, but Nyah was gone before I could open my mouth.

My body was tense from the hard night's sleep. I stretched out; my bones clicked and groaned in protest. Hadrian also stirred to life, turning towards me with a smile.

"Bright morning, Petal," Hadrian said. A crust of dry saliva was stuck to the side of his mouth, and his short hair was a tangle of messy clumps. I couldn't take my morning eyes of the muscle in his arms as he stretched. "How did you sleep?"

"It could've been worse," I replied, my mouth cotton. I could've used some Butter Mellow from yesterday to help battle the morning breath.

He reached a hand over the small gap between us, and I grasped a hold of it. His blue hue was still warm, but not as overwhelming as yesterday. That was the first sign that Hadrian looked refreshed. The dark circles seemed to have receded.

"You look well rested." I squeezed his hand and smiled.

He huffed and ran a tongue across his teeth. "As if this bench was a cloud. I do not remember when I fell asleep, but I know I did not wake for anything. It has been a long time since I have slept through the night like that."

"You clearly needed it. You look… refreshed," I added, giving him another look up and down. He knew what I meant. It was hard for him to hide how exhausted he was after yesterday's battle.

We had a few moments of silence as the Inn was still quiet. His golden eyes pressed upon me, lighting me up from the inside out.

"I could get used to this view." His voice was deep and rough as stone.

"Even with my knotted hair and morning breath?" I joked.

"Even with your knotted hair and morning breath," he agreed.

He squeezed my hand a final time and released, swinging his legs over the side of the bench and stretching. His yawn made me yawn like a contagious sickness.

"How about I fetch us some warm apple ale before we go and assess our home for the next few days?" Hadrian stood and walked to the barman. As he passed me, he ruffled a hand through my hair. "Now, that is better."

Yesterday's tension in Hadrian's face had melted away, as if the events never occurred. We had not talked about his father since the temple, but I knew it would not have left his mind. I promised myself the conversation would be brought up later, and whatever Hadrian said, I would support. It was the least I could do for him.

Hadrian came back and placed a wooden mug on the table before me. The sweet of the juice pleasantly dripped down my mouth, making my stomach growl. I needed a meal. My stomach screamed for one.

"The barmaid told me Jasrov is up and walking; I am going to go and see him. Will you be fine for a moment?" Hadrian asked.

"He is?" Whatever the Healer had done to him must have worked quickly.

"She told me he is still sensitive, but aware. I will not be long," Hadrian stroked his hand across my cheek with a smile.

"I should go and help Nyah," I said. "I am just as worried about Emaline as I am Jasrov. We should speak to her."

"There was no mention of Emaline or Illera. Nyah stayed with Illera last night. If there was any issue, she would have told you already." I must have pulled a face at the mention of Illera's name, for Hadrian's brows furrowed. "You still do not trust her, do you?"

"It is that obvious?" I ditched the empty mug on the table and stretched the sleep away.

"Do me a favor, Petal, and try with her. Until she gives us a reason not to trust her, she is one of us now."

I raised my hands in defeat. "I am not distrusting but more cautious. It would be foolish to forget the past and move on without more than a thought."

"Foolish?" Hadrian scoffed. "Who knew that trusting someone was foolish? Were you foolish when you trusted me when we first met?"

"Hadrian, I am always a fool when it comes down to you."

"A handsome fool," Hadrian said as he leaned forward and placed a light kiss on my lips. I held my breath as he came in close, conscious of the unpleasant morning breath.

"I shall see you on the ship."

I couldn't hold off any longer. I hobbled to the bar, gave the mug back, thanking the barmaid and the Innkeeper for their hospitality.

When I made it outside, I was surprised at the view before me. Where I sat with Nyah the night before was now the resting place for a boat, not a ship.

It was the color of moss, shaped like a curled leaf. The main mast bowed slightly with what seemed to be a folded cream material cocooned around it. On deck, I spotted Nyah's halo of red curls, talking to a sailor. The sailor was an old elfin man with a hunched back and eyes full of adventure. His skin was weathered and mapped with wrinkles. Each one told a story, I was certain.

I also spotted Illera, her face laced with sweat as she carried folds of material and wooden crates from one place to another. She must have felt my stare because she looked up, smiled weakly, then got back to her task. Even she looked better than she had the night before.

Tearing my eyes away from the working Illera, I looked for Emaline, who was nowhere to be seen. The boat was not big, so I could scan it quickly. I was certain she was not on it. I looked back to her room and still saw no life within the window.

"Zac!"

Nyah caught me standing on the jetty and waved me forward, meeting me on the ramp up to the boat.

"Wonderful, isn't it?" she proclaimed, turning arms full as if to show it off.

"It is… not what I expected," I replied. "What type of boat is this?"

Her brows furrowed. "It is a cargo boat, used for transporting goods from town to village along the river. Queen Kathine informed me it's the fastest mode of travel, especially with three Dragori on board."

"Shouldn't that slow us down?" I questioned trying to spot what powered the boat. All I could see were oars leaning up against the boat's sides. "I expected a ship."

"A ship would be too obvious if anyone is looking for us. I thought better we stay as unnoticeable as possible."

She linked her arm in mine and walked me on board. "I wasn't going to mention this last night, but you each have a job to do over the next few days. Not that you would mind, would you?"

"What do you mean, a job?" I couldn't tear my eyes of the minimalistic design. It was clear the lack of material used would help it move across the waters. With less weight, it would reach its destination faster than a bulking ship. It was inconspicuous also. The Druid would not expect us to be stowed away on a cargo boat.

"I just mean we are all going to have to pull our weight for a few days. Some more than others." Nyah rolled her eyes at the last comment and clapped a hand on my back. "It will mainly be you and Emaline doing the work since your abilities are more favorable on a wooden boat."

"Why can't we get there with our griffins?" I asked. It made more sense to fly.

"The griffins should only carry one rider. With the added bags and the seven of us, including Bell, I think it's best we don't do that to them."

"How about I tell you when Emaline is here, killing two birds with one stone and all that?"

I nodded in agreement. "Have you heard from her? I haven't seen her since…"

Nyah looked over my shoulders and her face morphed from concern into a smile that didn't quite reach her eyes. She shook her head and waved an arm. I turned to see what changed her tune so quickly and was greeted by Emaline walking up the jetty towards us.

It didn't look like she got much sleep. She walked with a hunch and heavy step. Her arms clenched tight by her sides.

"Did you manage any sleep?" I asked as Emaline joined us.

"Sleep? I do not know what that is." Her reply was firm. I noticed her long dark lashes seemed to be clumped together and the tip of her nose was red.

I reached a hand for the bag Emaline carried. Reluctantly, she gave it over.

"Listen, I do not want to spend the next however long stuck on a boat with constant stares my way. Can we just move on? It is hard enough without the reminders you all are giving me with your pitiful eyes."

Emaline wrung her hands, her gaze stuck to her feet. "Put me to work. I would rather keep busy if you do not mind."

"There is one job you could do," Nyah began. "The griffins, we no longer need them. Could you go and release them from their duties? And Zacriah, if you both go, you can carry the supplies back here."

Nyah slipped something cold into my palm.

"I—" I tried to give an excuse, to say I was too busy to go with Emaline, but Nyah stopped me with a sharp look.

"When do we leave?" Emaline asked.

"The sooner the better."

Emaline nodded and turned. "Noted."

She walked off first, and I hesitated to follow, until Nyah pushed my back.

"Talk to her," Nyah whispered as we both watched her walk off.

"What do I say? I'm not an empath; I might bring up the wrong thing... make it worse."

"You don't need my magick to make someone feel better," Nyah said. I looked in my palm and saw the acorn necklace. "Be yourself. Speak your truth. You will be surprised just how much listening can help those who don't think they need to talk."

I fisted the necklace and held it tight the entire walk to the hilltop beyond the village. The morning was bright and warm despite the coming chill of winter. The sun hung in the sky, unbothered by clouds. All I could see was blue and the occasional bird that danced above. I caught up to Emaline when she stopped in an open expanse of grass. A perfect space for three beasts to land.

It was Emaline who called for the griffins, all three arrived only moments after she whistled for them.

Jerk landed first, his amber feathered coat glistened in the sun. Like a pup, he bounded across the grass for me; his head twitched with excitement. I raised a hand to stop him, so I could stroke him a final time. I couldn't predict how difficult this was going to be.

"Calm yourself," I muttered, scratching beneath his beak.

Emaline was steps ahead of me, fussing over her griffin while Hadrian's chewed on a bush to our side, unfazed. If I had the power to read its mind, I would probably hear his relief when we said we would be leaving them. He was always the one who seemed to hate flying with us. Wild spirited, just like the boy who rode him. Did they even understand us? I never had thought about it.

I began to unclip the saddle from Jerk's back, pulling the empty pouches from his side until he was free. It was strange; I could almost see the confusion in his glassy eyes. Jerk turned his head like an intrigued pup and made a deep throat noise of displeasure.

"It's time for you to be free," I said, running a hand down his folded wing.

I leaned into his pointed ear. "Don't tell anyone, but I've rather enjoyed having you around. I hope our paths cross again."

Jerk raised his neck and sang into the sky. A flock of birds burst from the bush Hadrian's griffin ate from, startling it.

"Shh," I whispered, placing my forehead on Jerk's. "You are free now. Fly, swim, annoy your siblings. I had the pleasure of riding with you. Even if you threatened to dismount me midair almost every day."

Jerk chirped again. I looked into his dark, orb-like eyes, and he blinked, then turned and moved away.

I was about to go and unpack Hadrian's griffin when Emaline got there first. I helped her, working silently by her side. Every now and then I would look up, something to say on the tip of my tongue, but I didn't build the courage to say anything.

By the time all three were free of their saddles and bags, I stood beside Emaline, and we watched them. All three were perched, staring at us as if waiting for a command that they had gotten accustomed to.

"Go," Emaline whispered. I turned and could see her eyes were wet. "Go."

Hadrian's was the first to leave, followed swiftly by Emaline's. Jerk sat there, unmoving.

I stepped forward and tried to shoo him away with my arms, but he didn't listen.

"Come on, Jerk. Explore, live, fall in love," I said. "Do whatever it is you do, we no longer need you."

I raised my air, guiding the wind beneath him ever so gently. It urged him to stand.

"Goodbye, my friend."

He sprang into the air and began chasing the others.

"Saying goodbye is harder each time it happens," Emaline whispered. "I wonder if it will ever get easier."

"I don't think it will ever become easier," I answered, watching our griffins become no more than dots.

Emaline expelled a tempered breath. "It is still strange. I keep thinking *she* will be there when I return. But then it hits me. It does not feel real."

"I am sorry for your loss," I replied, pulling the necklace from my breast pocket and passed it to her. "Nesta gave this to Nyah. She wanted you to have it. Nyah looked after it until now."

She was speechless for a moment as she stared down into her open palm. Then she fisted it and placed her hand over her heart. "It was the promise I gave her years ago. A promise I have failed in keeping."

"She meant a lot to you..." I remembered the promise Queen Kathine gave Hadrian before we left Kandilin.

"More than words could ever explain."

"Nyah told me that you were like sisters, close from childhood. I can't imagine what you are going through." I turned to look at her, but her face was kept forward. A single tear rolled down her dark cheek until the collar of her tunic absorbed it.

"She was everything to me in so many ways. For me, the way I love is different to most. My relationship with Nesta was beyond sexual, for those are feelings I do not experience. But I still love. My heart is hers; my soul will always be hers. It has been many years since we were in a relationship. After she left for Lilioira to train, we parted ways as friends. Nesta was my sister, my friend, and now, she will be my guardian." Emaline cried fearlessly, tears rolling down her grief-stricken face.

I felt the lump in my throat grow and my vision blur as I shared in her emotion.

I wrapped my arm around her. She rested her head on my shoulder and let her tears flow. We stood like that a while, unmoving.

"You loved her?" I asked.

I felt her nod her head, my shoulder damp.

"In ways I never knew possible," she said.

I knew someone in Horith who shared the same feelings as Emaline. He once explained to me how he did not feel sexual attraction, but that was it. He was still valid. His feelings, love and emotions. All valid. He still loved, and even when I left my home, he had been in partnership with the baker's daughter for countless years.

"You are valid," I said.

"Nesta accepted me. She respected the way I loved. When I broke off the relationship, it was because I simply did not love her like that anymore. I realized when she left for the city to train that it was better as sisters, as friends."

"No matter what Nesta was, it will be hard. I want you to know we are all here for you. Let us share in this with you, to help take the pressure of this grief off your shoulders."

"Thank you." She lifted her hand and looked at me. Her ocean eyes wet, lashes clumped together.

"What are friends for?" I said, smiling.

I felt more connected to Emaline.

"We should head back." Emaline pocketed the necklace and picked up four sacks. Two on each arm.

"Are you ready? Because they can wait if you are not," I whispered.

She nodded. "I feel better than I did. Thank you for listening to me."

"Always."

The walk back to the boat was full of memories and moments Emaline shared with me. She told me of a time when she and Nesta worked in a bakery in Kandilin over the winter periods, rolling dough until they were dusted in flour. She told me about Nesta's partner. Nesta had met him in Lilioira during her training and had since shared a long-distance relationship. Emaline explained she had met him once and believed he was perfect for Nesta. She worried that he had not heard news about Nesta's death. She would have to tell him.

We laughed when we spoke of the childish games they played with peaches and bats and cried when she told me of her heartache the first time Nesta left home alone to join the Queen's faction of soldiers. Emaline told me about the beautiful way she loved and the open mind she had for others. If everyone was more like her in even the smallest of ways, the world would be a much better place.

By the time we reached the boat, I felt like I knew Nesta on a whole other level than I had before. Emaline planted a kiss on my cheek and left me on the jetty. I watched her go, my heart full after our encounter.

Nyah smiled at me from the stern of the boat, a knowing expression crossing over her heart-shaped face. It was Illera who greeted Emaline when she walked on the boat. There was something in Illera's eyes that had me questioning her. She faltered in her jobs as Emaline passed her and almost forgot what she was doing. It was only when Emaline moved off did Illera regain her composure and carry on.

CHAPTER

TWENTY

MY HEART LEAPED when I caught eyes with Jasrov. He was sitting on a bench beside Nyah, who was busy chatting with him. From this distance, I heard his laugh as he threw his head back at something she said. Typical Nyah. Making someone laugh only hours after their health was in dire need.

I wanted to speak to him the moment I saw him, but I was with Emaline, helping her get settled for her first shift.

Nyah had explained that Emaline and I would take turns guiding the boat. With our magick combined, we would reach the bay closest to Lilioira faster than if we each had to row. Emaline offered to go first, using her connection with water to guide the boat from the jetty, through the lake and onto the river that led north. I promised I would take over at sunset, but by midday, Emaline was exhausted. Using that much power for a prolonged time drained her. I took over until my own body refused to listen before sundown.

"…and Bell, I found her when I needed her most—" Jasrov stopped his conversation with Nyah the moment I walked up to him. He stood up, a slight twinge of pain crossing his face, and enveloped me in a hug.

"Can you believe I helped fight?" he said, joy plastered across his face. "I managed to slice the heads off four of them. I counted! Four! I mean, it was easy, of course, but still I can't believe I managed it."

I helped him sit, the bruise on the side of his head a patchwork of faded yellows and browns. "You did well. But you still need to relax."

I sat him back down. "I see you have met Nyah."

He blushed. "I have."

"You spoke about me before?" Nyah asked, biting her bottom lip as she got lost in the view.

"Nothing but good things, I can assure you," Jasrov said quickly.

"Well, regardless, Zac is right. You have not healed fully yet. You heard what the healer said about letting your body rest. I should let you—"

Jasrov hand shot across the space between them and touched her arm before Nyah turned away. "Please stay. Your conversation is taking my mind off the pain."

He turned his lips down and opened his eyes wide in pleading.

"I'll stay."

"Whatever the healer did to you, it seems to have worked," I said, getting a good look at the damage on his face. The purples had faded, and his cut had scabbed. His dark curls blew in the wind as the boat moved, showing the place where the bump had been. Now it was no more than a slightly darker shade than the rest of his skin.

"It was amazing," Jasrov replied. "What I can remember about it anyway."

"At least *you* enjoyed yourself," I said, voice laced with sarcasm. For his age, Jasrov oozed the innocence of a youngling. It seemed to please Nyah, who did not stop smiling at him before shyly looking away as if I caught her doing something bad.

Bell snapped, involving herself in the conversation.

"Jasrov was just telling me about Bell. Such an interesting story. I've never met a familiar before."

Jasrov seemed pleased with Nyah's explanation. "Well, yes. I mean, it is pretty fun having one around."

Was that a blush I could see spreading on his cheeks?

"I must admit I feel bad for not helping. There must be something I can do on board, anything at all. Just say, and I will do it." Jasrov's injuries spoke for themselves. "If you put me in charge of the food, I can make sure everyone is well fed with the supplies we have?"

"If you are feeling up to it…" Nyah said. "But you must promise me you will not push yourself."

Nyah reminded me of how Mam would speak to me back home. Jasrov seemed to love it, as he smiled at the attention Nyah gave him.

"Could you do me a favor first?" I asked Jasrov, looking over my shoulder at Emaline. "Go and ask if Emaline needs some company."

She had only just taken over from my second shift as the night twinkled with starlight. Before she even started, her face was pale and eyes heavy. I needed a short sleep. Something, anything, to get some energy back.

"How is she?" Jasrov asked, a shadow of concern clouding his face.

"Strong. Very strong."

∽

THE THREE DAYS journey passed in a blur of exhaustion.

It took a day for Emaline and me to figure out our levels of energy that were required to keep the boat moving. Emaline lasted longer than I; after two hours, I was falling asleep on the spot. Our overenthusiastic start came to a halt when we all realized resting was necessary to keep going. On the first night, we stopped in a passing cluster of homes beside the river to rest. Hadrian spent most of the day leaning over the side of the boat and emptying his stomach. He was relieved when we stopped, and he got to stand on ground that was not constantly swaying.

Reaching the limit of my magick felt wrong. First, I was watching the mast billowing under the force of my air, which screamed in pleasure from my use. But that soon would cease, leaving me with sharp pains in my head and heavy limbs.

Everyone was silent and tired on the last day. No one spoke a word. The only noise was the rushing water and the overplayed voice of the sailor who occupied us. His singing was as choppy as the waters we glided across.

Once we reached the port, I was thankful to see the back of the river and promised myself I would leave my magick alone for a few days. It was the least it deserved.

Illera had been quiet most of the journey, not entering conversations by keeping busy. If she was not sleeping, she was rushing around the boat, re-tying the mast ropes and scooping overflowing water back into the river.

It was the final morning, the gates of Lilioira visible in the distance like an illusion conjured by exhaustion, that Illera finally spoke.

She walked up behind me, hands red and cracked.

"They are going to hate me," Illera grumbled. "Once they find out what I have done, who I was with, they will exile me or worse."

That was the most I had heard of Illera over the past days. Her anxiety was palpable as she wrung her hands together.

Emaline was sat on the bench beside me as we both use our magick together for the final push to the city. She replied before I could form the words.

"No one is going to hate you because they will not know." Emaline's expression was void of emotion and voice matter of fact. She only turned to me for a moment. "Are they?"

"We have no reason to distrust you Illera," I said, trying to keep my focus on channeling the air into our mast. "You are nothing more than a companion of ours."

Illera sat down between us, her blond hair dirtied and matted in its ponytail. "What will you say?"

I felt the boat slow as Emaline disconnected from the water and looked at Illera. "You will be my guest. No one will question your presence, not if I can help it. Word of your connection with the Druid will not pass into the city. We will leave it on this boat."

Illera smiled, something that before today would have me questioning her sincerity.

"They will notice my heritage. Why would a Niraen elf be on Eldnol soil, especially during times like these?" Illera questioned.

"Leave the explanation to me," Emaline said, resting a hand on Illera's shoulder. "You saved my life back at the temple; I will not forget that."

Illera knew little about Nyah's abilities, which had come in handy over this trip. I almost felt sorry thinking about it, but I had asked Nyah to check if Illera could be trusted. Nyah found no reason as to distrust Illera's intent, something I had to keep telling myself over the many hours we were in such proximity to one another. I may still have been wary of her, but I trusted in Nyah's power.

Illera placed a gentle hand on Emaline's shoulder, which Emaline looked down at it with a hint of a smile.

"You do not even know me, yet you show me kindness," Illera breathed. "Thank you."

Emaline nodded and focused back on the port ahead. Illera took that as her cue to leave. There was something in the lingering look Illera gave back before she busied herself again. I didn't have long to dwell on it as Emaline pushed her final energies into the water, guiding me to do the same with my air.

∾

WE DOCKED THE boat when we reached the bank. Nyah thanked the sailor who joined our journey, not that he did much to help. Between his singing and constant storytelling, he almost drove me mad.

The port was empty. As we guided the vessel slowly around the many jetties and extended walkways, we expected to see someone, anyone, amongst the buildings and posts. This was a place for ghosts now. No guards or soldiers. Not even the trill sound of birds clung to this place.

"Where is everyone?" Jasrov asked, climbing from the boat first. His bruising had faded over the three-day journey with the help of the salve that the Healer provided. Nyah had helped Jasrov apply it nightly in thick layers. I had not seen her with such gentle hands before.

The only sound I could hear was the gentle crash of water against the wooden poles propping up the jetty.

"No one is allowed in or out of Lilioira, not with the threat of another attack," Nyah said, pressing her fingers to her temple. She was still for a moment; her brow pinched in concentration. "Queen Kathine knows we have arrived. She's told me that we are to wait here for our escort. It will arrive shortly."

Jasrov turned his head dramatically from Nyah to me, as if he couldn't believe what Nyah was saying.

"You still have a lot to learn about me, fox boy," Nyah said to him with a sheepish smile.

"I can't wait!" Jasrov replied over-enthusiastically before looking away from our amused faces.

Nyah didn't register it as she closed her eyes and shared a silent word with the Queen.

We stood around, waiting for a sign of an escort when Bell began screeching and pouncing. We looked up to see a small cloud of dust framing four riders who rode towards us.

The guards reached us with the speed of lightning. Each horse was monstrous in size, a multitude of colors and builds. The closest stallion was midnight black, with a thick mane of shining hair. The soldier atop was equally as large, a trait for most Alorian elves.

"The Queen requests your presence immediately." The soldier atop the black stallion dismounted and strode towards us. His rich brown skin almost glowed in contrast to his uniform of ivory and whites. They were all dressed the same; the Queen's emblem pinned to their cloaks: a beveled feather of silver and white captured on steel midfall.

Hadrian stood forward, his glowing blue hand outstretched in greeting.

"Your Highness," the soldier greeted.

"If Queen Kathine needs us, let us return to her with haste," Hadrian said, his regal aura returning after so many days. "You can see we are all in no fit state to have an audience with Kathine. May I request a bath before?"

"Certainly, your Highness. Queen Kathine has ensured rooms are prepared. You will be taken to them the moment we arrive," the soldier responded

The soldier looked over the all six of us, then to Bell, who ran rings around his legs.

"We will need to enter in two groups," he said. "Prince Hadrian, I have been asked to ensure you are in the first group. Is there a preference to who joins you?"

Hadrian turned to face us, the days' worth of travel had made the whites of his eyes yellow. "Emaline, would you stay back with Illera for the time being? I am sure these fine soldiers will return to you both as soon as they can."

I didn't miss the unspoken word passed from Hadrian and Emaline. Emaline nodded, taking her place beside Illera who was visibly nervous by the soldier's presence.

"We will see you soon," I mumbled to Emaline and Illera. "Be safe."

Emaline raised a hand and the water behind her rose. "We are very safe. Do not worry about us."

Hadrian, Nyah, Jasrov and I were pulled up onto the back of a horse. Bell wrapped herself around Jasrov neck, her ears raised as we moved to the city.

We left our two companions in the dust of our horses. I didn't stop looking their way until the billowing cloud blurred their forms. Then my attention was solely glued to the looming gates ahead.

Lilioira was hidden within the valley of mountains. The only way in or out was through the gates nestled in the rock face. Compared to the greens, greys and earthy tones of the surrounding view, the gates stood out like a sore thumb. Made from folded bronze and other strong metals, they decorated the rock face surrounding it with its grandeur. If Queen Kathine wanted to be inconspicuous, she failed. But somehow, I knew that was not what she was going for. She wanted those stupid enough to be enemies to see her power and strength before they got close to the city. The gates were no more than a message. A symbol.

The last time I had seen gates such as those before me was in Olderim. Much like Olderim, Lilioira's gates had depictions carved into the metal surface. These were not as high and ominous. Instead, as we watched them open before us, I felt a rush of safety—a feeling I had forgotten existed during the past week.

From books and Fa's tales, I knew Lilioira to be a kingdom rich in both coin and magick. A hub of life for many, some of which never leave the constraints of the cities walls. There was no need to leave when everything they possibly needed was inside. Besides adventure.

As the gates closed behind us, it shut out all light. For a moment nothing happened, but then bowls of fire burst into life, illuminating the long walkway before us in ruby flames. The passageway was carved in the belly of the mountain and led until it reached the valley beyond it. Where the city was found.

All around, I could smell earth. The bowls of flames gave enough light for me to see the steep walls of rock on either side of us. The passageway was carved though a mountain of sorts. I could not see where the ceiling was, as darkness lingered amongst the highest points.

The horses began to move once more, their hooves echoing around us.

No one spoke a word, making the smaller sounds even more obvious. The dripping of water and the clatter of reins. The puff of the horses as our soldier escorts guided them through the way.

Soon, a sliver of light could be seen ahead, which grew the closer we got to it. As we passed the bowls of fire, they extinguished in a hissing puff, leaving the passageway behind us dark once again.

Whatever magick laced this passageway was as mysterious as the city's location.

A cold chill rushed to greet us. It howled through the narrow space, carrying a light scent of cherry blossom and orange. The closer we got, the narrower the passage became. We ended by walking in single file. Horses behind horse.

I was the last to leave the passageway. My head rang from the sudden white light beyond. I rubbed my eyes, wobbling in the saddle. Once my eyes adjusted to the light, I opened them, taking in my glance of the glory below.

Hadrian made no reaction and nor did Jasrov. He had seen it before. But I shared a look with Nyah, one that mirrored what we were both thinking.

A city of dreams. A place two common born elves from Thessolina would never dream of visiting.

"Welcome to Lilioira, city of light and life."

CHAPTER
TWENTY ONE

NESTLED WITHIN THE craggy hillside below us, the city glowed with life. I looked down from a great height, seeing both its splendor and power. Constructed in a valley, Lilioira was protected on all sides by mountain faces. As if the Goddess herself punched down from the sky, creating a space between mountains for this very city.

Ivory colored buildings with pointed roofs and arched windows sat between large trees, waterfalls and crags. From where we looked, I could see the city was connected by walkways of tile and sandstone. Trees covered in pink blossom speckled the spaces between buildings. Countless bridges connected small streets to one another. There were so many small ravines cutting throughout the large city. I saw its source. A large waterfall misted the side of a mountain to the north of the city and ran throughout. That was what gave the air a fresh taste.

"I ask that you each dismount and walk the remainder of the way," one of the soldiers said. "We will return for your friends and have them brought to your rooms before you are taken to see Queen Kathine."

"Thank you," Hadrian said, pushing himself from the horse and landing beside it. He patted the dark stallion's behind.

In a trance, I climbed from the back of my chestnut colored horse and helped Jasrov from the back of his. Nyah jumped down effortlessly and walked to the edge of the path to look down.

"That is a very steep drop," she mumbled, her legs shaking as she glared over.

"Rowan will guide you to the city." He turned back to Hadrian and bowed his head. "Do not stray from her. With the current events, tensions are high in the city and newcomers are not as welcome as they once were."

Rowan, the female soldier, stepped forward after clapping her horse on its behind. She removed her helmet and smiled, holding it beneath her arm. "Stick with me and you shall be fine."

She was classic Alorian: beautiful, tall and her presence was strong. Her thick black hair was collected into a braid and hung over her shoulder. A long sword was strapped around her waist, its hilt wrapped in dark leather.

"Good to meet you all. Queen Kathine has waited patiently for your arrival. Let us not keep her waiting much longer shall we," Rowan said.

As she stood, she rested on the Staff in her left hand. It was not until she began to walk ahead of us that I noticed her subtle limp. Her milky cloak trailed on the dirt path, which soon evened over to slabbed stone. Her Staff struck the stone path in a steady rhythm, echoing up the sharp mountain face beside us.

The farther we descended the narrow pathway, the more foliage and green we saw. Even the wall beside us was draped in bluebell creepers and thick emerald vines. We had to walk in twos, or else there would not have been room for us on the path. Hadrian stayed up ahead talking to Rowan as we closed in on the city.

To enter Lilioira, we passed over a bridge so long it almost seemed to float over the rushing river beneath. Soldiers were stationed on each side of the bridge, spears held still beside them. I felt self-conscious under their gaze, but Rowan walked past them without a crease of concern on her face.

I had to stunt a laugh when Bell leaped from Jasrov shoulders and began to explore. A few times Jasrov had to call for her when she got too close to a soldier and began nipping at his steel boots.

The presence of the countless soldiers beyond Lilioira second gates told me all I needed to know. Queen Kathine believed an attack by the Druid was imminent.

"Open up," Rowan called as she stopped before a set of gates. She raised her hands to the two gate guards who stood overlooking us from either side of the gate's walls. "Come on, boys."

After moving her hands in three specific signs, the gates rose. First, they just seemed like slabs of metal, but as they lifted higher, I saw sharp spear-like protrusions beneath which had been hidden in carved holes on the ground. If they fell upon the enemy, they would pierce straight through them.

Once the vibration of the gate signaled its stop, Rowan moved forward, tapping her Staff on the ground as she walked.

Hadrian slowed to walk beside me.

"How are you feeling?" he asked, head kept forward.

"Frustrated," I admitted.

"It is because of the Staff?"

"I don't think we should have given up. We are finally close, and you are..." I looked to him. "Well, are you feeling better?"

"Do not worry about me, Petal. It will be good to be in one place again. Maybe there is healer here who know more about Heart Magick. Gallion maybe. I am certain we will find another way to help me. Nothing bad will happen, I promise."

With the warning of Cristilia's story still floating in my subconscious, I could only worry about what it meant— leaving the Staff.

Domed pavilions linked with walkways and taller buildings all around us. The grey stone streets were wide and full of life. The farther we walked into Lilioira, the more elves we saw. For every three elves we saw, a soldier stood by, statuesque and watching.

We moved through the interlocking buildings, passed by pillars and walked beside water features. Cool sprays of mist coated our faces, tempting us to catch the droplets in our mouths. I was thirsty and hungry and in dire need of a wash.

The palace came into view as we rounded a street lined with shops and hanging signs.

The Queen's living space was erected at the highest point of the city. To reach it, we had to walk up many steps. No matter how high up we climbed the steps, the presence of soldiers did not waver. Once we reached the top, we were each lost for breath. All except Nyah, who stood tall with not a single drop of sweat on her forehead.

"Welcome to the grand city of stairs, as I call it," Rowan said, with a hint of a smile. "Your friends will arrive shortly. Until then, please wash, dress. You each have been supplied with fresh clothes for your stay."

"Do you know when there will be food?"

Everyone looked to Jasrov, who had asked the question we had all been thinking about.

Rowan smiled, gripping her Staff with both hands and leaning her weight onto it. "A feast is being prepared. Once your audience with Queen Kathine has concluded, I can assure that you will have your bellies full before sundown. How does that sound?"

"Perfect," Hadrian interjected. "Shall we?"

Rowan nodded. "Follow me."

We were let inside the palace quickly, where we followed Rowan through a winding corridor and up yet another set of stairs towards our rooms. The T-shaped floor we entered was magnificent. Full of fresh air, due to the open arched windows and the sweet scent of roses and lilies that spilled from large vases.

"You will find everything you need on this floor," Rowan said. "I will return for you shortly. Is there anything else I can get for you?" she asked, twisting the head of the walking Staff in her hands. Up close, I noticed the many rivets in the wood and the metal clasp at the end. It was not a flat base, but a sharp spike.

"There is one thing." Hadrian spoke up. "Can you provide me with a long sleeved and hooded cloak?"

"I will speak to our tailors immediately. I am certain they can accommodate."

"Are you aware if an empath by the name Gallion knows we have arrived?" I questioned, half for Nyah.

Rowan's face twanged with confusion at the name, but Nyah responded for me. "Gallion knows."

As Rowan bowed and left, I caught her before she got away. Away from the crowd, no one could hear my question. "Is council member Cristilia here? In the city?"

"Cristilia arrived with Queen Kathine, yes."

"I must speak with her," I said. "Please, can you pass on a message. I would appreciate if you could keep this between us, for now?"

Rowan nodded "I will pass a message if I can find her. I know Queen Kathine has kept her busy in the past days. I am not sure I have seen her since she arrived."

"Well, if you do…"

"Yes, I will tell her you are looking for her."

⁓

WE WASTED NO time in rushing for a wash.

Nyah went first, followed by her new roommate Jasrov, leaving Hadrian and me to explore our room.

"I finally feel comfortable, Petal," Hadrian said, looking over at the view of Lilioira from our balcony. "I am overcome with a sense of nostalgia. Last time I visited was with mother and father. When times were…different. And the city has stayed the same when everything around it has changed so dramatically."

"I still wish we were looking for the Staff," I replied, standing beside him. The view was beautiful. Even from there, I could see many Alorian elves mixing with soldiers in the streets below. Music floated up to greet us, the light tune of string instruments from an unknown location within the city.

"All those lives down there in the streets. They rely on the Queen for safety from this unknown threat. We cannot leave now." Hadrian's knuckles were white as he gripped the windowsill.

I rested a hand on top of his and ran my thumb in circles. I wanted to agree, to say I understand, but I didn't. Surely, if the Queen knew the threat Hadrian could be to the very people he just spoke of, then maybe she would send us back for the Staff.

"Do you feel safe?" he asked, turning his golden eyes towards me. His face was thinner than usual, his beard now thick and as dark as his brows.

I didn't know how to answer. For once, I did feel safe, surrounded by so many armed with steel and silver. But I would trade that safety for the Staff. And how safe was I really with the looming possibility of Hadrian causing more destruction?

"I do."

"I am unsure how long we will be here for, but I need to find some answers whilst we are here," Hadrian said, turning back to the view as if searching for something within it.

"Your father, you want to find him?" I asked, although I knew the answer.

Hadrian didn't reply straight away. He seemed to shake himself, replacing the stern expression with his heart-stopping smile once again.

"My father is out there. When the Druid is distracted, I will find him. And this city might hold the answers for me to locate him."

"Do you think the Druid still has him?" I probed. It was possible. What the Goddess had shown Hadrian sounded much like what Illera had explained she felt before she escaped.

Hadrian shrugged his shoulders, brushing off the possibility, and kissed my head. "For the Druid's sake, I would hope not. Lilioira is filled with many who have magick even I will never understand. I need time to find answers, and I know I can get them here."

"If there is any way I can help..."

Hadrian placed a finger on my lips and a warm kiss on my forehead. "I will call on you, I promise."

"Please do." I tried to make my smile genuine. "How about you go and clean-up first? You do not smell like a prince."

Hadrian laughed, leaning his face in close. "And how do princes smell?"

"Go and have a wash," I whispered, pushing him towards the door, "then I will answer that."

Hadrian stole a kiss before he left me lost in my thoughts. I pressed my back against the door and let my smile fade.

There would soon come a time when Hadrian would leave. I knew it in my heart.

I had to ask myself. Would I stop him?

$\backsim$

THE SOUND OF running water was a song to my ears.

Closing myself in the washroom, I faced what was in store for me. The wall farthest from me was not made of the same light wood and stone as the rest. Open rock covered in moss and small green leaves took up the entire space. Running down the rock face was a fast stream of water that splashed on the floor, dripping through it. There were no windows; the only light came from the dripping wax candles in the far corners of the room.

I stripped off my tunic and slacks, chucking them into a pile. Days' worth of sweat, salt and dirt had dried onto them. I didn't notice just how bad they smelled until I had washed in the natural waterfall. A dried piece of coral was waiting for me to rub my body raw. It felt incredible as I scratched at the dirt. I didn't stop until my arms and legs were red. The water was neither cold or hot, a perfect temperature to wake me up and prepare me for the rest of the day. I could have stayed beneath the stream for hours.

Once dried, I pulled on the clothes left for me. The ivory shirt was too big for me. The material swallowed me whole. The trousers fit better, held up with a leather belt that was left for me.

I found a small mirror hanging on the wall and moved to it. My hair was still wet, giving its silver-tone a darker illusion. I pulled the long strands from my face and twisted it into a bun. My braids had come undone long ago, and I had no skill in redoing them. That was what Mam did for me. I had grown used to the plain bun.

In the reflection, I saw movement behind me. My breath caught as I turned around to see the visitor.

Gallion stood, hands on hips, with a smile and bright eyes; it made my heart leap.

"You, my boy, need a haircut."

CHAPTER

TWENTY TWO

GALLION SEEMED DIFFERENT. His frame was not as full; his skin had taken on a pale undertone. Dark circles framed his wise eyes, and his cheeks were so gaunt in the low light, it gave the illusion of a bone skull.

But as he waded over and threw his arms around me, his familiar warmth had not wavered since our last encounter. I melted into his fatherly hold. Allowing myself, for just a moment, to think of nothing but the feeling of familiarity.

"I have heard your adventures have been testing." He held me at arm's reach, eyes scanning over me from head to toe. He then pulled me into yet another hug.

"My adventures are incomplete," I grumbled, straightening the new shirt I wore. "Although I am sure you have worked that out by our early arrival."

Each passing minute in Lilioira only made me feel more aware that the Staff was being forgotten. It was no longer the main priority. Would it take another blue fire to prove Hadrian's need for healing?

"Indeed, but I have a feeling it is not over yet. Let us walk and talk. Queen Kathine and her wife are waiting for you, and I don't want to be the one to keep you any longer than you already have been."

Side by side, we left the bathing room. I followed Gallion's directions without question.

"How have you been?" I asked. Did I bring up his physical change? How the weeks had aged him years.

"I have been better. I am not as young as I used to be. All this fun is taking its toll on me more than I like to admit." I'd noticed the slight hobble in his walk, which I added to the list of worries for him. "Queen Kathine has been very welcoming, but in return, I have kept myself busy. I feel better knowing I am earning my keep and helping her efforts in locating the Druid."

"That doesn't surprise me. You have talents that would help in such a time of unrest. But even Queen Kathine would allow you to rest."

"Lilioira is a hub for many with gifts and powers. I am just one extra old man who sleeps more and eats less," Gallion muttered. "Do not worry about me. You have enough in that mind of yours already."

I tried to keep my gaze on the passing corridors and open pavilions, but my curiosity took over. Glancing at Gallion, I noticed the pinch of his face and the way he rubbed his hands together. In the natural light, I could see just how much he had changed. He had aged considerably in the past few weeks. His already grey hair was almost entirely white. His scars stood out more than before; even his eyes were rimmed with red.

"Stop looking at me like that, my boy," he said, catching my glace. "Haven't I told you not to worry?"

"Not everyone is as skilled at forgetting as you," I replied.

"Now." Gallion stopped me. "I had to leave you in Kandilin, you know this. You were supposed to be safe. If I had known what was to come, I would never have gone. It has all been necessary. The libraries in this city are far greater than any other, twice the size of the library in Olderim and holds more. I must admit, I was rather surprised to see the volume of tomes containing histories and information on not only Eldnol, but Mortagis and Thessolina as well. I never took Queen Kathine as a collector."

As he spoke, I remembered the library in the temple. I couldn't imagine another being as impressive as that.

Curious, I pushed on. "What does Kathine believe you will find in these books?"

"Queen." Gallion pulled on my arm. "Don't let anyone hear you dropping her title. She has earned it, and we must use it."

I nodded, cheeks red. "Sorry. I didn't mean any offense."

"My son, you have not offended me, but this palace is crawling with the Queen's people. They hold great admiration and love for Queen Kathine and her wife and would not treat you with kindness if they had the slightest whiff that you do not respect her. Of course, I know you do, but strangers make rash decisions from the smallest of proof."

"I understand." I smiled at two elfin women we passed. They were dressed in aprons and had hands full of glass bowls dripping with a multitude of flowers. "What does Queen Kathine believe you will find in the libraries?"

"Mystery shrouds the Druid. She hopes we can find something within the books and histories to suggest his story. A name, anything. In war, mystery and secrecy is a great weapon."

"And you think you will find something?" I had believed all histories of the Druid's and their history had been destroyed once their reign had ended.

Gallion gave me a look, his bright eyes alight with mischief. "Everyone has a story, dear boy. It is just a case of uncovering it."

"And you are going to be the one to do it?"

"Who knows? There is a lot this old man can do that might surprise you."

I raised a brow and scoffed on a laugh. "I don't doubt that for a moment."

The hallways of the palace were wide and open. I drank as much detail as I could see. From the arched ceilings coated in twisted vines to the large bots that bloomed with bright flowers. The farther we walked, the more the calm atmosphere seemed to dissipate. The presence of soldiers standing guard increased and with it a sense of urgency. It meant one thing. We were close to Queen Kathine.

"If you need any company, call on me. I have a feeling Queen Kathine will not want us leaving for a while."

"Zacriah, if you think the Queen does not have a role for you, you are very wrong. Niraen elves may have forgotten about the Dragori, but, in Eldnol, you are referred to as royalty. Gods. You have a lot to learn about your position in this story." He nodded to the soldiers who stood before a large door. We came to a stop, and he turned to me.

"Have you heard from Nyah?" I asked.

"Of course." Gallion clapped his hands. "She is a strong empath. I am impressed with the growth of her power with so little training. All she needed was direction, and she has improved with incredible leaps."

Pride flushed Gallion's face with a new life of color.

"Did she tell you about Illera?" As I said her name, I whispered, Emaline's stern face flashing behind my eyes.

Gallion nodded. "She did."

"Well, what do you think about it?"

Gallion crossed his arms over his chest. "My opinion does not matter. In fact, I think you should drop this curiosity with Illera's loyalty. Don't you think she has risked enough? If she were going to betray you, she would have before she entered the most guarded city in this world."

"But—"

Gallion placed a hand over my heart.

"You are trying to convince yourself to distrust her, my boy," he whispered, face close to mine. "I feel it here. You've already made your mind up, haven't you?"

I dropped my gaze to my feet.

"See?" He lowered his hand. "Now, let us go in. I must say you have gathered yourself an unlikely team. I look forward to being introduced."

Gallion raised a hand to the soldiers, and the doors opened soundlessly.

∽

QUEEN KATHINE AND her wife, Sallie, sat at the head of the room with two thrones of ice and thorn. Queen Sallie held a baby to each of her breasts, feeding them while they gave commands to a line of soldiers before them. Rowan was amongst them.

Gallion directed me to the side of the moderate room where Hadrian stood with Nyah, Jasrov, Emaline and Illera. As I joined them, they smiled in welcome. Jasrov face was burning red, his gaze stuck to the other side of the room. I followed it to see the cause of his embarrassment. Bell lurked amongst the many potted plants, pouncing and screeching while she played. I even caught the subtle smile Queen Sallie gave as she looked up at the little familiar.

Nyah nibbled her lip, her shoulders shaking as she watched. That seemed to calm Jasrov a bit. They shared a silent smile and looked down at their clasped hands. My heart leaped with excitement for her.

Hadrian greeted Gallion, placing two kisses on each of his hollow cheeks. If he noticed Gallion's frail body, Hadrian did not say anything.

"Petal." Hadrian took my hand.

"My prince."

"About that answer…"

I leaned in and took a smell. He was cloaked in fresh scents that were pleasant to be around.

"You smell delectable," I whispered, hiding my smile.

Hadrian made a low hum, between a laugh and a growl. "Do not say such things."

"And why is that?"

"How do you expect me to behave when you throw comments like that at me?" He squeezed my hand.

"I don't expect you to do anything." I squeezed back.

We faced the room together and waited.

"… return by sundown tomorrow with news and make sure you have something to tell. I want the surrounding land to be scouted. Any sign or suspicious activity must be reported immediately. Am I clear?"

The line of soldiers stomped their right foot in agreement.

"We will be expecting refugees to arrive today and over the following week. I want you to send a team of soldiers to patrol the roads and keep our people safe. If the Druid chooses to attack them, I need you to be there ready for that possibility." Queen Kathine literally glowed as she spoke. The large stained-glass window behind haloed both Queens where they sat. Queen Kathine wore a frosty crown of silver and crystal. It caught the light from the window and created dancing orbs on the floor.

"Update me on plans regarding the housing for my people," Queen Kathine commanded. "There will be countless Alorian's flooding to this city, and I want them to feel comfortable and safe."

Rowan stepped forward, her Staff colliding with the floor. "Each family in this city has offered their spare rooms to the those seeking asylum. Children will be kept with mothers and those willing to help fight will be welcomed into the ranks."

Queen Kathine smiled on as her wife gave the final command. "This truly is a city to be proud of. Please ensure this transition for our new arrivals is smooth. They deserve some peace after their journeys. Rowan, you are the strongest of my commanders. I trust you will keep an eye and make sure we are without problems in the coming days?"

Rowan bowed. "I will do as I must."

With that, Queen Kathine blessed them, and the soldiers left the room without another word.

Gallion ushered us forward before slinking back into the shadows of the room.

Both Queens stood to welcome us.

"I must say, I am relieved to see you. When Nyah informed me of the attack at the temple, I was worried," Queen Kathine announced. "When she informed me that you helped in the fight, I was thankful. Welcome Jasrov and Illera."

Jasrov and Illera bowed as Queen Kathine referred to them.

"I should bow to you both for helping fight alongside the Dragori. I am sure you have worked out just how dangerous being around them can be. I admire your strength and will to stay beside them during these times."

Jasrov beamed. As if Bell knew she was being referred to, she raised her pointed snout and bared her teeth in a grin. Illera also smiled, her hands clasped firmly behind her back.

"Now." Queen Kathine sat first followed by her wife. In tandem, their children cooed in satisfaction. Queen Kathine reached across to her wife and plucked a child bundled in cloth and held her to her gown. "I believe it would be best we get the full rundown of the events that took place during your journey to the temple. Nyah has shared insight, but I would like to hear it again."

Hadrian stepped forward. He was not wearing the same clothes that I or the others were given. Instead, he was dressed in similar garb to the Queen's. Silver cloak pinned around him, covering the white and brown uniform beneath. Rowan had provided him with the cloak he requested. It covered his arms like a jacket and trailed behind were he stood.

"I must first share my congratulations to your little princesses." Hadrian bowed, waving a hand to the babies. Queen Kathine was cleaning spittle from the child's mouth. "May their lives be long and full of the Goddess's light."

"Prince Hadrian, thank you." Sallie's voice was lighter than her wife's. Compared to Queen Kathine, she had a short hairstyle, which framed her full face. Her hair was straight and as red as fire. Her full cheeks were pink, matching the cloth that wrapped around the child's small body in her arms. "It is an honor to have you in our home. It has been many years since I last saw you, and, my how much you have grown."

Hadrian tipped his head. "The years have been kind to you too, Queen Sallie."

She shared a grand smile and tipped her head in thanks.

"I will start from the beginning, please do stop me if you have questions," Hadrian said.

We all stood as he recounted the events since we left Kandilin. Hadrian told our story with emotion and gestures, speaking the truth and only concealing the part where we found Illera. Where she was concerned, we picked her up at the Inn.

"…it was Zacriah who found the Keeper first."

Hadrian turned back, reaching a hand for me to step forward. I followed, taking his hand in mine as he gave me the space to speak.

"The Keeper, who was it?"

"More like what was it…" I started.

I told them about the tree, and how the roots and vines of the Druid's power could not touch it. I described the feeling when we touched its bark and the experience beyond it. Speaking aloud about what I saw was freeing. I didn't look to Nyah or Gallion when I mentioned the faces of the Goddess, but I could feel their gaze on the back of my neck. I did not mention what Hadrian had told me. That was not for me to tell. All the Queens needed to know was I found the Staff's location. Not that it mattered anymore…

Queen Kathine asked no questions as she listened to me recount the events that lead to us abandoning the Staff of Light. She sat forward on her throne, almost on edge with the baby swaddled in her arms. Once I finished, she cleared her throat, raised her head slowly and held onto her child tight.

"My heart aches with pain for the many lives lost at the temple. I only hope we can avenge them all, but I must admit, I am worried about the future. Little is known about the Druid and his power. Even Cristilia is lost for knowledge. We have been searching for anything that might help us pinpoint who the Druid is, and how he survived."

The mention of the last remaining council member reminded me of the others that had been killed in the past days.

"I will call for Cristilia," Queen Kathine said. "She has been busy searching with Gallion for any information that may help us understand who the Druid is. With each day they spend within the books, I worry we are too late, and the knowledge is forever lost."

"Pardon my forwardness, but the Staff… I still feel that it is important we find it." I didn't want to speak on Hadrian's growing weakness, not in front of so many.

"I am sorry, but we need you here." Queen Kathine's tone dropped. "I cannot risk sending our only three Dragori away again. Not after what happened last time. This city is full of innocent lives and will soon be bursting with more. I need you all here to help me protect them. That is the Dragori's duty."

Emaline looked at the floor. The unspoken mention of Nesta's death weighed upon the room.

Gallion stepped forward. "May I suggest we allow these brave adventurers to eat and rest? I am sure we can spare the remainder of the day and allow them to regain some strength before tomorrow. What good are three Dragori riddled with exhaustion?"

I was thankful for Gallion's suggestion. After relaying the events of our previous days, I did feel exhausted. At the mention of food, my empty stomach turned in anticipation.

Queen Kathine smiled, raising a spare hand for the soldiers standing at the doors. "Yes, that is the least I can do to show my appreciation for what you have all done. Take the rest of the day. With tomorrow, comes a new day. And with it, new responsibilities. I have prepared a feast.

Please, enjoy it. If there is anything you need, and I mean anything, do not hesitate to ask."

"I request an escort," Hadrian said.

I shot him a look.

Queen Kathine looked through her long lashes at the prince. "I shall have one sent to you. When is it you need on by, and do I dare ask what for?"

"Sunrise," was all Hadrian said.

"So be it. Rowan will be sent to collect you in the morning. She will take you were you need to go without question."

Hadrian tipped his head in thanks.

"If that is all, I must ask you to leave. My children need to sleep. Enjoy the feast, we will speak tomorrow."

We were dismissed. As we each followed Gallion and the soldiers from the room, Queen Kathine called for Emaline to stay back.

"Emaline Sowdin, my dear girl, may I borrow a few more moments of your time?"

We each turned to watch her raise a hand for Emaline.

"If that pleases my Queen." Emaline bowed.

As the doors shut them into the room, I heard the mention of a name.

Nesta.

TWENTY THREE

"FETCH ME THAT book, would you?" Gallion asked as he took seat at one of the many oval tables in the vast library room. The room was a maze of shelves, lit by candles and faint sunlight from the narrow windows that lined the many walls. As we entered, I was hit with the thick scent of old pages and ink. It took a moment to still the dizziness and appreciate the strong smell.

"Could you be more specific?"

Gallion's request confused me because many books surrounded us.

Noticing my hesitation, Gallion pointed to a tome resting on the shelf framed with dripping rose-scented candles. "I want to show you something I came across before you arrived."

Following his instruction, I fetched the book. My arms ached, its size deceiving. The cover was made from black leather, even touching it made the hair on the back of my neck stand to attention. A strange smell seeped from the cover, intoxicating my senses. I held my breath the remainder of the walk to the table, happily ditching it before Gallion. I rubbed my hands on my slacks to rid them of the lingering touch.

"I was surprised to find such a novel in Lilioira, but I can't say I am not glad. It's been brilliant bedtime reading material." He flipped open the book, turning pages as he looked for a location. "But the side effects seem to be disturbing dreams and early mornings."

"What could possibly be inside the pages to cause such reactions?" I questioned, peering over his shoulder at the yellow stained pages.

"Well that answer is dependent upon the reader," he began. "To some, it is a history. To most, it is a myth. Falsities lined on a page in the form of writing and depictions." He came to a stop on a page that was covered in writing I'd never seen before. Thick black marks and lines overlap each other in harsh designs. "These pages hold the accounts of the Druid's final reign. Their rise and fall. I have been hoping to find something that gives us insight into whom our tormenter is. But I have yet to find anything to quench my thirst. At least this is better than nothing."

"I can't read it." I scrutinized the page, trying to make sense of the jumble of marks. I pressed my finger above one part that caught my eye. It was more shape than a word: a three-pointed mark like a pyramid made from black ink.

"Like calls to like," Gallion said, looking up at me. "I have not grasped the dead language of the druids, but their symbols are similar to what we have used over the years. It just so happens that your finger is covering their sigil for air. A universal sigil that is the same for both the elves and the druids."

The candle flames flickered as a breeze filled the library. It had connected to my power at the mention of the mark.

I closed my eyes and felt its presence. It comforted me like the rocking of a baby in its mother's arms.

"What does it read?" Curious, I pushed on.

Gallion cleared his throat and read.

"… one for air, fire, water and earth. The conjoining of four elements creates the fifth. The element that rules over them all… at least that is what I can translate from these five symbols. The rest is difficult. I would usually rely on images to work out what the text is trying to say," Gallion said.

Enthralled by the Druid words, I was almost lost for words. What did it mean by a fifth element? I had not heard of this before, nor did the book Hadrian had given me mention a fifth.

Taking a seat beside Gallion, my arm pressed to his side and tried to make sense of it.

"The book Hadrian gave me on the Dragori only spoke of four. What does it mean by a fifth?" I asked.

Gallion shook his head. "For me to answer that I would need to be fluent in this language, but unfortunately, I am not. But I have been wondering the same."

"Is there not anyone left who can read this?" I pointed to the book. There must have been someone.

"If there is, they would not step forward willingly. These texts were banished and destroyed. Hence why I am so surprised to find it."

"I can't help but feel sad," I admitted. Gallion gave me a look, one that screamed understanding. "I hate to say it, but how could we do this to an entire history? I don't think we should celebrate the hate and death the druids brought with them, but we, as a world, need to look back at those times and learn from them. Not push them under a vase and forget they ever happened."

"You're very wise for someone who only weeks ago jumped out of windows and ran away in forests unattended," Gallion mocked, a kind smile on his face.

I knocked his shoulder with mine.

"You are right, my boy. Suppose we did respect the Druid's history, we may already know the answer to who the Druid is. And maybe we would not be in times of such tension in the first place."

I rested my hand on the pages of the book and closed my eyes. "How can one person cause such panic in three kingdoms? It should be easy to find one person when the entire world is looking for them."

Gallion released a slow, tempered breath.

"Perhaps that is the problem. Maybe we are wasting time looking, and not putting enough effort into thinking about what exactly we are searching for."

Those words stayed with me the rest of the day. They hummed in my mind as we searched countless books and found no more information that could help us.

I returned to my room by the time the city of Lilioira was fast asleep. Taking my time, I mulled over the conversation Gallion and I had. I would've been lying if I didn't admit I had hoped Gallion had figured something more out. A new lead of information on the Druid or his location. But, that had turned out to be wasted wishful thinking.

The corridors of the palace were mostly empty of life. All except the few soldiers who, every so often, walked past me. I passed through an open walkway with no walls or ceiling. It gave a view of the night sky, which was covered by thick clouds. I could see no stars amongst the stormy sky. The moon glowed behind a veil of clouds, its shape no more than a blur.

A chill filled the air, warning the arrival of snow. I could feel its building tension all around me. By morning, the city would be bathed in white.

I expected Hadrian to be asleep, but when I pushed the door open to our room, I saw him sitting on the bed, topless, back facing me. I closed the door quietly. I had not seen him since he left that morning with Rowan at sunrise. Between searching the library and finding more questions for Gallion, I had not thought of Hadrian much that day.

He didn't acknowledge me straight away. He was bent over something, his shoulders moving up and down slowly. I caught the sound of a sniffle as I waded over to him, kicking the boots from my feet.

Climbing on the bed, I scrambled over the sheets and wrapped my arms around him. Despite the cold night, he was still warm.

"Talk to me," I whispered into his pointed ear.

He was crying, streams of tears wetting his cheeks and some clinging to his thick lashes.

Hadrian took a deep breath. He raised his hands, lifting a piece of parchment into my view. It was faded and ripped, its edges frayed and worn. But the image on it was untouched.

"Fadine gave this to me as a gift the night we first met," he said, his voice strained and low.

On the parchment was a painting of a woman. I recognized the figure even though I'd never met her.

"Your mother…" I muttered, hugging him tighter. "It's beautiful. She's beautiful."

The painting was simple, a mix of a few colors. This close I could see just how similar she was to her son.

Despite her golden hair and ocean eyes, the shape of her face was familiar. Thick, dark brows and a sculpted jaw. She was no doubt Hadrian's mother.

"I am punishing myself by looking at this painting?" Hadrian shook his head with vigor, wiping the tears that glistened down his cheeks and onto his neck. "Sometimes my grief creeps up on me when I least expect it. I am sorry you have seen me like this."

I climbed from the bed and kneeled on the floor before him. He was still looking down, so I peered under his gaze.

"I want to make this clear; I will always celebrate your ability to show emotion. It is one trait that only makes me fall more in love with you."

Hadrian looked up, his blue fire blaring and his golden eyes shining. "You love me?"

"I do, more and more with each passing day." Saying it aloud made my heart leap. The last time I had spoken those words was to Petrer, but the thought didn't sour this moment. No, this was different. The way I felt for Hadrian was different. He could never be like Petrer.

Hadrian leaned down and pressed a kiss to my forehead, my cheeks one each, and then my lips. We held each other for a moment until my face was wet from his shared tears.

"I cannot express to you just how lucky I feel." Emotion rolled off him. He pulled me up from the floor and placed me on his lap. I wrapped my arms around his neck, and he held me to his chest. "I have realized something..."

"Tell me," I said, leaning my head on his.

"I realized just how much my mother would have loved you." He folded the parchment and slipped it into my hand. "I'm certain of it. As a child, she would also talk to me about love, and what it felt like. I would see it glow behind her eyes when she danced with father. I would spend nights trying to imagine the feeling. And now I know that what she was talking about is this feeling, this moment."

"I know I will never get to meet her," I said, cradling his face in my hands, "but being with you makes me feel close to her soul. You share it."

Hadrian raised his glassy eyes and placed the painting in my hand. "I want you to look after this for me."

I was stunned, "But it was a gift for you."

"One day I am going to wed you, and what's mine will be yours. What is the difference between you sharing what is mine now?" He pressed another kiss to my face. "I mean, only if you want to marry me. I do not want to sound like I am sure it will happen..."

Hadrian was endearing and thoughtful. Always worrying about his words and the way he speaks them.

"You will have to wait and see," I muttered, my lips hovering above his. "Let us get some sleep. I promised to meet Gallion in the morning before we see Queen Kathine again and worry that with a foggy mind, I will be of no help."

We crawled beneath the light sheets on the feather-stuffed bed. I told him about what I had found with Gallion, which wasn't much. Then I asked him about his day. He told me of his trip into town, and his search amongst the city for someone who could help him locate his father.

"Any luck?" I whispered, tracing my finger across his face.

"I will soon see," Hadrian replied through a yawn.

"Go to sleep. We will talk more tomorrow." I rolled over, so Hadrian could not see my worry. His reply had been short, too short.

As we lay there, Hadrian hugging me from behind, I closed my eyes and took slow, deep breaths.

I traced my fingers over the dancing blue flames beneath the skin on his arm that was draped over me until his breathing evened out.

What was he hiding? I willed for sleep to take me away, but now uncertainty embedded itself in my stomach. I trusted Hadrian and only hoped he would tell me in his own time.

CHAPTER

TWENTY FOUR

I WOKE ALONE. I was certain of it the moment my
consciousness took over when my eyes were still laced with
sleep dust and my cheek sticky on the feather pillow.
Hadrian must have left when I was deep in sleep. I rolled
over, aware of the empty space beside me. It was still warm
when I placed my hand on creases from Hadrian's body.
Something rustled beneath my stretched fingers. I squinted
through tired eyes and raised the parchment above me. It
was the picture Hadrian gave me last night. He must have
been looking at it again before he left.

A knock at the door distracted me.

"Come in," I called, sitting up. I brought the bed sheets
up to cover my modesty. Despite the open window and the
fat flakes of snow blurring the views beyond, the room was
warm. I put it down to magick as my visitor entered.

A head framed in silver locks poked around the corner
of the door. "I've bring'd ya breakfast." The small boy
strolled into the room. He stopped at the end of the bed
and placed the tray down. "I hope ya like steamed plums
and oats. It's Tiv's favorite."

I leaned forward, peering into to the wooden bowl
centered on the tray. Faint steam floated into the air. It
looked like a slop, speckled with purple chunks. Looking at

it, I wanted nothing more than to throw the strange gruel away, but the smell made my mouth water.

As if reading my mind, which wouldn't be hard to imagine in this city, the boy leaned forward. "Best not to look at it for long. It tastes much nicer."

I took the bowl, surprised by the warmth as I cupped it. "I am sure it will be fine. Thank you," I said, hoping he would leave me, but he didn't catch my hint.

"The cook laughed at the name Tiv give it. He said porridge makes it sound not tasty!"

"What's your name?" I asked porridge Boy.

"Tiv." He tipped his head. "You are one of the Dragori, aren't ya?" He looked at me, unblinking, with large eyes of white. His skin was milky as well as his hair and lashes.

I blinked the sleep dust from my eyes. "News travels fast here…"

Tiv chuckled like a small bird. "You've reminded Tiv." He shuffled in his aprons pocket. "Tiv meant to give you this, everyone in the kingdom gets one every morning. Here you go…"

I placed the painting of Hadrian's mother down on the bed beside me and took the rolled parchment from Tiv's small hand. Unrolling it, I read the neat writing upon it.

"What is this for?" I asked, scanning the page over again.

"News. Every morning Tiv sees the Queen's birds deliver them all around the big city. Didn't you hear them? Even from home, Tiv can hear them. So, so loud." He placed his small hands to his pointed ears and shook his head.

Maybe that was what woke Hadrian so early?

"Mother sleeps heavy too. She does not hear the birds like you." He must've been no older than six; so young to be working in a palace, too small to be away from his parents.

"Tiv better get back to the kitchens before cook comes looking. He doesn't like playing games of chase." He bobbed towards the door, a smile plastered across his thin, snowy complexion.

"Nice meeting you," I called over to him. "Thank you for the..."

"Porridge!" he said with a smile. "If you like it, Tiv bring you some tomorrow?"

"I would like that," I replied.

He left me to my food, which turned out to be full of flavor. Both a perfect blend of sweet and savory, it filled me up and warmed my stomach. I emptied the bowl and changed for the day. Looking beyond the window, I saw snow now covered every inch of the city below. The sun hung high, but that didn't stop the sharp breeze. I pulled a fur-lined cloak and wrapped it around me, ready for another day of searching through endless tomes for a scrap of insight into the Druid. I only hoped Hadrian's day was better than mine.

⌒

AS I LEFT my room, I saw the back of Jasrov. He was moving slowly, hand on the door as he closed it. His back was hunched, and he stepped back on his tiptoes carefully, making no sound at all.

"Morning," I called.

Jasrov jumped, causing the door to make a loud noise as it closed. "You scared the life out of me."

"How was I supposed to know that you were sneaking out?" I asked, tugging my cloak. The hallway was colder than my room, acting as a wind tunnel through its design.

"Nyah is sleeping, and I didn't want to wake her. We only got to bed a few hours ago; I thought she would appreciate some extra time to rest." Jasrov face was still flushed with red. Bell was running circles around my feet.

"Why the late night?" I smiled knowingly.

"We were talking. Lost track of time." Jasrov yawned, a tear escaping his dewy eyes. "Innocent chatter."

Putting the two most talkative people I knew together was not the best idea.

"I get the impression that you have taken a fancy to her," I said as we walked away from the rooms and towards the bustle of the palace.

Out the corner of my eye I caught Jasrov raise a hand and rub it down the back of his neck. "Why do you think that? I mean, she is lovely, yes. But... urm... is it that obvious? I mean, does she know?"

"Deep breaths." I laughed. "Call it intuition."

Jasrov nodded, spouting an awkward laugh. "Of course, intuition."

"I trust I don't need to give you the big brother talk?" I said.

"What, you're her brother?" Jasrov raised a brow.

"No, Jasrov, it's a figure of speech."

"Of course, it is. No, no speech needed. We are just friends."

I knocked into his shoulder. "Somehow, I don't believe that."

Bell screeched up in agreement.

Jasrov changed the subject quicker than I could blink. We brushed over the audience with the Queens yesterday, and I brought up the parchment of news I was given that morning. It turned out Jasrov had gotten one as well, but his was delivered by the birds Tiv mentioned.

"One quite literally flew into the room and dropped it on my face. The blasted thing was incredibly loud. Bell was not happy by the wake-up call; she chased the bird from the room. For a moment, I thought I was going to have to apologize to the Queen for shortening her flock…"

Jasrov was waving his hands as he explained his ordeal. I was thankful mine hadn't brought it me. By the sounds of it, a visit from these birds didn't sound pleasant.

"Queen Kathine is incredibly open to her people about the Druid. I gather she has been sending updates daily to the city," I replied.

"It is custom for daily news to be shared with the city. When I stayed in the city for a short time, we would receive news. Back then, it was about the next festival or musical event. It keeps everyone connected, especially in a city as big as this," Jasrov explained. "You can imagine. Being kept in the dark only creates mass panic. By the Queen keeping her people up to date on the latest news, it will give them a sense of control over the situation at hand."

We walked by an elfin man and woman standing by a pillar. It was hard not to notice the shock on the man's face as we passed. He began to point our way and whisper beneath his breath. My guess was they also received the same note as I had this morning.

I heard one word whispered above the rest.

"Dragori."

I picked up my pace and dragged Jasrov with me.

The entire page gave the description of our arrival to the city. It depicted us to be royal guests. As I read it earlier, I remembered what Gallion said about the Alorian people holding the Dragori in high esteem. I could see what he meant now as the throng of people grew, and they each stopped and stared as I walked past.

Jasrov wrapped a hand around my shoulders and leaned in close. "Keep smiling and talking to me. You won't notice..."

Suddenly aware of my expression, I smiled and looked to Jasrov. We talked about random topics, raising the volume of our conversation when someone stepped forward to stop us. Once we reached the private rooms of the palace, away from prying eyes, we stopped.

"By tonight, the entire city will see you," Jasrov said.

And he seemed to be right. The entire morning, while I searched the many parts of the palace for Gallion; I noticed more stares and whispers. By the time I found him, I wished I could fade into the shadows and hide away from the constant stares.

∽

"**DESCRIBE WHAT YOU** saw," Gallion said. "Don't miss out on any details. Smells, sounds, sights. It can all help locate the Staff."

I closed my eyes, conjuring the image of the Goddess and what she showed me. Gallion had agreed to help me work out the location even though Queen Kathine was confident the search for it had finished.

"It was cold and dark. Tall walls of obsidian. Snow-covered floors." When I spoke the words, the image came clearly to me again. "There was no smell. As if the place had been empty of life for a long time. I saw mountains. At first, I couldn't tell the difference between the walls of the dark castle and the mountainside. It seemed to blend into one."

The hairs on my arms stood on end. As I closed my eyes, I was standing amongst the snowy tops of the mountains. The entire time Gallion kept his hand hovering above mine as I shared the images with him. His touch was warm; his presence heavy. He anchored me to the library while my mind explored an otherworldly memory.

"Did you see the Staff?" Gallion's voice whispered through the haze.

I shook my head. "No." The memories kept flashing towards the marble slab the Goddess had shown me.

Gallion pulled back. With it, the visions stopped, and I was back standing in the middle of the library. Many Alorian elves bustled from shelf to shelf, some in deep conversation, others watching us with wary eyes.

"Wait here," Gallion muttered as he rubbed his scarred fingers on his chin.

I sat down on the stool tucked beneath the large, thick oaken table. Piles of books sat beside me, some as tall if not taller than I. I followed Gallion with my eyes as he fumbled for a hefty tome on a shelf to our left. He wrestled it out of its slot and brought it back to me. It still surprised me how Gallion made sense of the books, telling them apart from one another. To me, they each looked like dusty, leather-bound, tomes with faded spines and crusted pages.

Gallion would stop before the shelves and share silent words with the books, as if they told him which to pick. Again, this city was full of magick I did not understand. It was entirely possible I supposed.

"During my searches, I came across a mention of a Druid safe hold high up in the mountains north of Eldnol... just over the reach of this very city." I leaned over the large book as Gallion searched for the right page. "It was something you showed me. It reminded me of a depiction I came across. I am sure it is the... ah, here."

On the page, in greys and blacks, was a drawing of the very image the Goddess showed me. Nestled in the face of the mountain was a castle of sorts, towering black spires reach into the sky glowing with fire and dusted in snow.

"When the druids shared our world, they dwelled in all corners of it. Living in shadows, they survived in the very places we elves would not dare go to. Once they were defeated, most were destroyed, razed to the ground in hopes to wipe the memory of their existence from our lands. But, if what the Goddess showed you is correct, we may have missed one. Or left it for a reason."

I was lost in the image. I tried to read the writing beside it, but I couldn't make it out.

"What does this say?" I pointed to a word that was darker than the rest, as if the writer had copied it over and over in the same spot.

"It's the name of the Druid lord that resided in the halls of this place. Gordex. But my question is why the Staff would be left within a Druid's dwelling?" Gallion's tone changed.

"Maybe it was hidden in plain sight? Kept in the place where our kind would not search, and the druids had no need for?" I asked, not believing my own words.

"Until now," he said. "A Druid has returned, one we do not know the name of. We must see Queen Kathine immediately and open the quest to the reclaim of the Staff. We might have found the lead we have been looking for."

"She will never let us leave," I said.

I stood up abruptly and caused the stool to screech across the floor. That got the attention of the many who used the library around us.

"We must try, my boy. Let us not waste the Goddess's efforts. It is imperative the right hands find Staff of Light. Its power is as mysterious as the Druid we seek. And I have already told you what mystery can mean…"

I let the words linger before I responded. I looked up into Gallion's hollow eyes and separated my lips to speak the answer.

"Weapon."

TWENTY FIVE

GALLION UPDATED THE Queen on our findings in the library, even showing her glimpses into my thoughts. I stood in utter silence as Queen Kathine's eyes fluttered when Gallion pushed my memories into her mind. Even after seeing what the Goddess showed me and the strange map Gallion had found, Queen Kathine views did not budge.

"Absolutely not." Queen Kathine's shout drained the color from my face. "In a time like this, you must stay close. I will not risk your lives again in a chase for a phantom promise. Did my words before not remind you just how important it is that you stay and help protect my people?"

The snowy weather had coated the throne room in a chill.

In the light of the early afternoon, the stained-glass windows reflected colors onto the slab stone floor. A dance of red, blues and greens. I had not noticed the hearth during my last visit, but today, it spilled flames to warm the cold room. Although, I was certain Queen Kathine's angered attitude would warm the room without the need for a fire.

"What about Prince Hadrian?" Gallion stomped his foot, keeping his tone level with the Queen's. The old man held no emotion back as he argued with his Queen. "No one knows the toll of Heart Magick and the damage it is having on him. We may have three of the Dragori, but, in reality, we only have two. Hadrian is in no state to protect himself, let alone your people. I can sense his failing health just as clear as you can see it."

"Our people, Gallion, our. Do not forget it. Prince Hadrian has not expressed his ailments with me, and until he does, I will not allow this wishful quest to continue. That is final. I respect that you will not bring this matter up again. Not when my mind should be preoccupied with the hundreds of Alorian's heading for this city for shelter."

I stepped forward and bowed my head, although my want to scream with frustration was bubbling deep inside of me. "With all due respect, Queen Kathine, Hadrian is stubborn. He would never be the one to admit his suffering. It was how he was brought up, pushing his own problems to the pits, sacrificing them for his kingdom. It is no different."

Queen Kathine stopped before her reply. She rested back in her throne, ocean blue dress beneath plated armor that accentuated her muscular frame. Her painted nails grasped the edges of her throne, scratching at its surface.

"You hold high love for the Prince?" Her question almost knocked me to the floor. "Why else would you spend so much effort into arguing his wellbeing to me? I should not admit this, but Hadrian is a prince, is he not? Nothing is stopping him from leaving Lilioira but my word. Not even I can command him to stay."

"Hadrian, Prince Hadrian, deserves somebody to love him. It has been many years since he has been shown love of any kind." My reply was quiet. I was suddenly aware of the painting he gave me folded in my breast pocket.

"Indeed, his mother's untimely passing affected us all. Even across the seas, we mourned for her. She was a friend of mine. It is thanks to her that I was introduced to my wife. Believe me, I understand Hadrian and the way his mind works."

I was sensitive to the Queen's story as she talked about their friendship and the many years they knew each other.

"Hadrian is not my blood son, but I have watched him grow up. From when he was born to when his mother passed, I saw him countless times. I assure you, I care for him. But I love my people. I have a promise I must keep for them all. They rely on me for protection, and for the first time, they feel safe. Do you know why?"

I cleared my throat and looked up. "Because we are here."

Queen Kathine closed her eyes and released a sigh. "Your presence within the city means more to the people living within it than even you could begin to believe. That is why I cannot allow you to leave again. It is up to you whether you listen to my command or not. I am not your Queen. But I beg you to consider."

Even if I could leave, I knew nothing about the location of the Druid safe hold. It could take days to locate it in the books and tomes that Gallion went through. But, to keep the peace, I bowed to Queen and smiled.

"I will consider it," I agreed.

She gave me a look. It was brief enough that I could've passed it off as nothing, but there was something about the way she stared at me in that moment that made me feel like she already knew what I would do.

"Before you leave, I would like to tell you about the evening's event." Queen Kathine stood up and waved for the guard closest to her. He walked over, armor glinting in the light, and passed her a rolled parchment.

She walked down the steps from his dais and stood before me where she towered more than a foot above me. After handing me the parchment, she looked at Gallion. "Tonight, I will be hosting a festival of sorts in the main city. For one night, I need you, Emaline and Prince Hadrian to put on a brave face and walk beside me. It will not only calm the cities excitement for having you here, but it will also help instill some calm back into their lives."

"Of course," I replied, unrolling the parchment to see a note to follow. I scanned the details as Queen Kathine explained them.

"We will begin our procession at the palace gates and end in the main square in the lower city. The parchment explains everything. If you have any questions, please feel free to ask your tailors. They will be meeting you in your room when the midafternoon sun turns amber."

I considered Gallion, whose posture was stooped as he stood. Did he know about this already? His gaze suggested so.

"I shall see you this eve." Queen Kathine took my hand in hers. "And please think about what I have told you. Think of the lives beyond this palace who rely on you to stay."

She squeezed my hand for a moment then turned back to her throne, leaving Gallion and me to exit the room with more questions than we arrived with.

"I said she would not listen," I whispered to Gallion.

It took him a beat to respond.

"And when have you started to listen to instructions and commands? Last time I checked, you had instincts far powerful than mere words a foreign Queen tells you."

I halted, but Gallion kept walking. I needed to speak with Cristilia. Only she had the power to help, and I needed to do it before Hadrian's time had run out.

NYAH SCOLDED ME for sneaking up on her. It was never my intention. As I walked through the many themed gardens behind the palace, I was deep in thought. So much so I didn't notice Nyah and Jasrov ahead until she called my name.

Bell barked, and I looked up. I caught Jasrov's lightning movement of his hand as he dropped it from Nyah's. He busied himself with straightening the golden jacket and matching slacks while Nyah's cheeks bloomed the same color as her hair.

We shared awkward words of welcome, and Nyah grasped a hold of the conversation and steered it away from the possibility of me asking what they were doing lost in the gardens. She was draped in a long, emerald cloak that covered the elaborate dress beneath. Her wild hair was pinned from her face with a silver circlet, highlighting her map of freckles across her face. Despite the stunning gown, I noticed a lump on her leg, which flashed iron as her skirt shifted. She would never be caught without a weapon.

"I thought you were with Gallion all day?" Nyah chirped, sparing Jasrov a glance.

"I have been," I replied, "but wanted some fresh air. My nose is clogged with the smells of mildew from the books. I thought I would clear my nose *and* mind with a walk."

"Well you have come to the right place," Jasrov added. "We have been through many, and they each are better than the other. See the rose bushes? One whiff of those and you will rid the smell of books as you wish."

"Yes, thanks." I pined my next comment to Nyah. "I heard you didn't get much sleep last night. I trust you are well rested now?"

I had never seen her so skittish before.

"Well, yes... where is Hadrian?" She thrusted her question at me, giving me an eye to stop. One of her brows twitched, which warned me to stop my teasing. It was clear Jasrov and Nyah were getting along just as I thought they would.

"No clue. It's not the first disappearing act since we arrived. Have you seen him today?" I asked, wringing my hands around the parchment Queen Kathine gave me.

Both Jasrov and Nyah shook their heads. They had not seen him since yesterday.

"Could you see if you can sense him?" I asked Nyah, who gladly agreed. Anything to take the attention of her and Jasrov.

Nyah's forehead creased as she focused her concentration.

"He is in the city. Because I haven't been there myself, I can't tell you exactly where he is. But I am sure he will be back soon," she said.

What could he need there? I pushed the tingle of worry to the back of my mind and moved on.

"And, is he okay?"

"He is warm. Very warm. But unless I can touch him, I won't be able to check just what that means. And I have a feeling he doesn't want me prying anyway," Nyah said.

"You're right." Hadrian was private. If he knew I had asked Nyah to go poking around, he would not be happy.

"Did you hear Emaline was promoted to Nesta's position?" Nyah added. I had also not seen Emaline since Queen Kathine asked her to remain after our audience, but it made sense. She was a born warrior. There was no one better for the position.

"I wondered what was keeping her occupied," I replied. "Emaline is a leader; it makes sense for Queen Kathine to promote her position. I still remember the soldier's admiration for her when you fought on the ship. Nesta would be proud."

"She left with some scouts this morning. Said she was looking for any sign of the Druid or his shadowbeings in the surrounding mountain range. With all the new refugees coming, she is worried it leaves them open to being attacked," Jasrov said. "Knowing there are others to protect beyond the city fuels her need to help."

"Emaline is a protector above anything else. Having such an important role will help her deal with her grief, carrying on Nesta's legacy," Nyah continued.

"What about Illera?" I asked.

"She is with Emaline. Her choice. Did you not hear? She took it upon herself to tell the Queen the truth and offered her services to help. It turns out Queen Kathine was excited about having a shifter as part of the scouting team." As Nyah explained what happened, we walked beneath a row of arched trees. They grew on either side of the path and towered above us, branches and twigs locked together in a reaching embrace.

"She really wants to prove herself," Jasrov said. "To prove to us that she can be trusted."

"I would tell you if she couldn't be trusted," Nyah stated.

"I don't doubt it," I added, staring ahead at the cascading waterfall which dusts mist of water across the lush bed of grass.

"She seems to be more comfortable staying close to Emaline. And we will seem them during the festival tonight, hence the dress code." Nyah signaled to what she wore, picking the skirt from the grass bed and twisting it around.

"You have reminded me. I have been told to meet the tailors back in my room. I just hope Hadrian returns in time for his fitting. I haven't spoken to him for a while, and I don't even know if news has reached him about tonight's festivities."

Jasrov scooped Bell into her arms. "I can send Bell to find him?"

I shake my head. "It's fine. It might teach Hadrian to stop running off if he finds out he is late for something. Plus, do you think he would turn down the opportunity to get dressed up and parade around the city?"

Nyah laughed. "Well said. He will not miss that for anything."

"Is it just me or does this celebration seem strange? With the Druid still out on the loose..." Jasrov face clouded with concern.

Nyah pulled at the long sleeves of her dress and held the cloak tighter. Although the snow had melted to a point, the sky still throbbed above, threatening more. "The entire reason behind tonight is to remind the city and its people that they are safe no matter what happens in the coming days, weeks or hours. The Dragori's presence is going to help return some normality to the people of Lilioira."

If it helped instill calm for some, it was worth it. It was more the request that was written on the parchment Queen Kathine gave me that made me uneasy.

∽

I WAS MORE than surprised to see Cristilia pacing before my bedroom door when I arrived. Her hands were clasped before her, and her usual neat façade was no longer present. Her hair frayed out of its rushed bun; her clothes seemed disheveled and unkempt.

When she spotted me, she ran over, encasing me in a hug that lasted longer than it should have. Her thin frame felt as if it would snap in my arms.

"My dear, I am so relieved to see you back," she panted, holding close to her wiry frame. "I am sorry I have been absent since you arrived, but I have been overwhelmed with the task of preparing for tonight's festivities and other tasks. Being the last remaining council member, all tasks have been placed in my arms. Rowan did pass on your message, and I came as soon as I could."

"I'm just glad to see you," I said, pulling away from her. "I was beginning to worry you would not find me."

Her dull eyes looked me up and down. "I hear you have been through a lot."

"You could say that," I replied. "And you too."

I could not imagine how the attack at Kandilin affected her.

Cristilia dropped my gaze for a moment. "Many have been sacrificed, spoils of a war to come. It will not be the first nor last. I am certain of it."

"We failed," I muttered, unable to keep up the small talk any more. "The Staff, it's still out there. So many have died while we, the supposed protectors, have wasted time."

Cristilia took my hand and pulled me to the end of the corridor. Ahead of us was a bench, the back made from knotted slates of wood that threaded over each other. We sat down beside each other, Cristilia's hand still in mine.

"You must not allow yourself to believe in those poisonous thoughts," she replied. "You found the Keeper, didn't you?"

"Yes, but—"

Cristilia raised a hand, stifling my reply. "And you were shown the location of the Staff?"

I nodded.

"Then why have you given up?" she questioned.

I placed my head in my hands, frustration boiling my blood.

"Do not give up. You know what will happen if you do not find the Staff." There was serious panic in Cristilia's voice. It spiked my own worry.

"Queen Kathine has made it clear that she does not want us to leave. And maybe she is right. What if the Druid attacks again and we are not here to protect the city?"

Queen Kathine's comments about the protection of her people had taken root deep in my consciousness. Even if I wanted to leave, the weight of the many that relied on us was heavy on my heart and mind.

"You must ask yourself what you find most important," Cristilia mumbled, her lips stained purple from the cold. "Prince Hadrian has been different, has he not?"

"Yes," I agreed. "He has not told me, but I have felt it. Seen the pain cross his face when he uses his magick. And he has been absent since we arrived here. Something is brewing within him. It scares me."

"You hold great love for the Prince. So much so that you are consumed with the thoughts of leaving yourself, even if you have not truly decided. You know as well as I that the longer the Prince is consumed by his Heartfire, the weaker he will become. Even if he does not admit it." Cristilia shifted in her seat until she faced me. "There will come a time when you will decide what you are going to do. Stay in Lilioira or leave for the Staff. Only you can decide what is most important."

"You think I should go and retrieve it myself?" I picked up on what she was suggesting.

"What I think you should do is follow your own instincts, not those of others." She leaned in, echoing what Gallion had suggested earlier. "Do not let Queen Kathine hear what I tell you. She would not be happy her only remaining council member is going against the direct orders she has bestowed upon you."

A gentle hand rested on my shoulder. "Take time to truly think about what it is you feel is most relevant. Staying in Lilioira and waiting for the Druid to come, or going after the Staff before it is too late for Hadrian? How will the Dragori protect the people in this city if one is soul lost?"

"Even if I leave, I have no idea where the remaining dwelling is," I admitted.

"Do not give up." Cristilia's smile faded. "If it was the other way around, would Hadrian give up on you? I must leave. I still have many tasks to complete before this evening. Perhaps I will see you during the procession…" She bowed her head and showed her teeth through a smile.

"I hope our talk has helped you somewhat."

In part, it had helped, but I also felt more conflicted with my choices than I had before.

"But…"

Cristilia didn't let me finish. She bowed and slipped around the corner in a rush.

I was left alone for a moment before the sound of footsteps pounded in the distance. I thought it was Cristilia returning until I looked up to see Nyah. Her face was ruby, and a dagger was held out to her side. I raised my hands as I walked to her. "Nyah, what's with the silverware…"

"Are you okay? I thought someone was trying to hurt you—I came as soon as I could!" Nyah replied, her voice rough and words frantic.

She lowered the dagger when she saw I was alone.

"What do you mean?" I asked.

"I don't know, but something was off. I couldn't work it out; I thought it was one of those creatures the Druid makes, a void of thoughts and emotions. Who was with you, Zac?"

"Cristilia. That was it!"

Nyah looked stunned. She pushed the cloak out of the way and slipped the dagger back into its holder around her thigh "Odd. I haven't felt anything like that before. I know I can't read her, maybe that is what it was."

In the commotion, someone opened my door.

"Tiv heard shouting." Tiv poked his round, milky face around the door. "You're late. Quick, quick, come inside."

He soon ushered me into my room, but Nyah didn't leave my side, not until she was satisfied the two tailors and little Tiv were not a threat.

Something was off about her reaction. I tasted her anxiety; it coated the back of my throat. But soon the thoughts of Soul Lost overwhelmed any other thought, and I was a prisoner to my own worries.

TWENTY SIX

THE LONGER I held my arms up, the more they ached. Now and then, the more nervous tailor of the two would push a needle too far into the material wrapped around my arm, and it would prick into my skin. My bottom lip was a mess of rips as I bit into them to stifle my cries. I felt the most uncomfortable I had been in a long time, and I made sure the tailors knew it.

The first was short for an Alorian elf. He had a crown of chestnut curls and a thick body. He huffed and puffed as his scrutinizing eye looked me up and down, deciding which materials were best matched together. Whilst the other tailor, a kind-faced girl with equally curly hair that trailed down her back, stood in the distance hardly looking at me.

I couldn't blame her for having such nerves, not when I stood before them with my wings open behind me and my horns protruding from my head. It made sense why they asked me to shift. It allowed them to create clothes that would not rip when I needed to shift. They would come in useful during the coming weeks. But with each prick of the needle and pull of my arm, I became more irritated.

Tiv sat, legs crossed, on my bed. If he wasn't here, taking my mind off the uncomfortable fitting, I might have roared in frustration by now.

"…and mumma says there will be music and food. Tiv can't wait. Mumma also told me Janila Barnhem is singing this eve, and she is Tiv's favorite singer of all." Tiv spoke fast through a mouthful of bread. "Do you like Janila's singing?" he asked.

I turned my head to look at him but quickly had it pulled back by the male tailor's small hand.

"I've never heard of her," I replied. "The last person I heard singing was a smelly sailor, which lasted for three whole days. As long as she sounds nothing like him, then I am sure she will be fabulous. *Anything* would be better than him."

Tiv laughed so hard he almost toppled from the bed, his pale eyes creased as he pinched them closed. "Tiv loves her songs. You will see. You will see."

"If you like her, I am sure I will too," I replied, trying to ignore another pin that poked into my thigh. "Where do you and your family live? Is it in the palace?"

"No, no." Tiv shook his head. "Tiv lives in the city, near the pretty fountain. It has a pretty lady made of stone. Tiv likes the water that pours from her eyes and mouth. When winter comes, Tiv watches as it turns to ice. Pretty ice. Sometimes mother will let me dance on the ice, but she is scared I will break it and fall in. I tell her that won't happen, but she still worries."

What I had learned about Tiv was he loved to talk. If I asked a simple question, I was sure to get a long-winded answer. Not that I minded; his innocence was sweet.

"And do your parents work in the palace with you?"

"No, just Tiv. Mumma is a weaver and helps sell pretty clothes in the market. And my father is a soldier, just like his father and his father before that. He is away now. Tiv hasn't seen him for days and days." His voice softened as he spoke of his father. "I want to be like my papa, I want to be a strong soldier and stop the scary monsters outside the city."

The male tailor pulled back, telling me to lower my arms at last. I took the opportunity to stretch and look at Tiv. His silver hair matched my own, it was like looking at my younger self. "I reckon you will be a gallant fighter."

Tiv sat up straighter and smiled. "Tiv thinks you are right."

I was surprised to see just how much time has passed. The sky had taken on a deep purple tint with the arrival of night. "It is getting pretty late. When do you finish working?"

For such a young boy, I worried about him. The heart of the city was a couple of miles walk from the bottom of the palace steps.

"Tiv finished a long time ago." He laughed, eyes closed in glee.

"Have you been keeping me company when you should be home preparing for tonight?"

"Maybe," Tiv cooed. "Tiv should go. I want to look handsome for Janila. Mumma always says I look handsome once I bathe and comb my hair."

He sprung from the bed, his little feet clapping against the floor. "Will you wave later?"

I nodded. "You can be sure I will. If I see you, I want to come and meet your mumma. She sounds wonderful."

I was taken aback when Tiv wrapped his arms around my legs and hugged me. I was still for a moment but then returned the embrace. He was so cold, even in the warmth of the hearth lit room. His white skin was almost see-through, and I could catch a hint of golden streams beneath it.

"You are cold," I said.

"Just how I like it," he muttered into my new trousers then pulled away. "Tiv sees you soon."

I ruffled my hand through his hair. "You will."

Before he disappeared from the door, I called for him. "Get home safe!"

Tiv stopped and smiled. "Tiv is a gallant soldier. Tiv will be very safe."

With Tiv's absence, I was left with the tailors who seemed to speed up their process of creating my new outfit. By the time they were finished, Hadrian had arrived, and I couldn't hide my annoyance. Leaving me all day without much of a word. He was late, so much so that the shy tailor stood forward and rushed him back out the room into another to get ready. He barely spared me a glance as he left again.

Everything happened so quickly. Once the two tailors left me, another three elves strolled into the room and guided me to sit in a chair. They all must've been sisters because they shared the same dark hair and deep-sky eyes.

Just when I thought the prodding and poking had ended, I was wrong. They began messing with my hair and adding powders to my cheeks and neck. Unlike the tailors, I soon found this process more relaxing. Even more so when they began running their hands down my wings. I couldn't see what it was they were doing, but it lulled me into sleep.

⌒

"RISE AND SHINE," Hadrian muttered, his breath brushing across my face. I opened my eyes and saw him standing inches from me. I was half-hanging from the chair, and the three sisters no longer filled the room.

I cleared the dribble from my chin with the back of my hand, then stood up and walked past Hadrian.

"Do not let the sisters see you rubbing off their powders," Hadrian said behind me.

"Where have you been all day?" I turned on him. I could hear my sharp tone and didn't relax it. "You leave without a word. Do you know that if you simply tell me when you disappear it might save me from worrying all day?"

"Exploring," he said, then changed the subject promptly. "It is exhausting keeping this form for a long time. I am not surprised you had slept. This must be the longest you have kept it up before."

"Don't change the subject, Hadrian. I am worried about you enough."

He turned away from me, his reddish wings held tight to his back. "I did not ask for you to worry."

"You don't need to." My breath came out labored. "I am not your keeper, but I sense you are hiding something from me. The last time someone did that—"

"If you are referring to the insidious Petrer, do not bother. I understand your past may create distrust, but my absence is innocent." Hadrian turned back around and faced me. His curled horns were coated with red sparkles of some kind, which stood out against his blue glow.

"Then tell me what is happening in that mind of yours." I took hold of his warm hands. "I do trust you, Hadrian. But I will not play silly games and pretend this is all fine, and I have no problem with you disappearing. Tell me; let me help you with whatever it is you are doing in the city."

Hadrian released a slow sigh and looked down at me. Although, in my Dragori form, I was taller. He still had added height.

"If you are looking for someone to help locate your father, then tell me. Two of us could make light work..."

Hadrian leaned in and placed a kiss on my lips to silence me. I felt just how dry his lips were as they danced with my own.

"I am not well, Petal." It was the first time he admitted it. "I do not know what is happening to me, but I am not myself. I feel like I am battling a darkness that is fighting to reach me." Hadrian took my hand and placed it over his heart. "I have kept it from you because I worried if I said it out loud, it would only make it more real."

I wrapped my arms around him. "Tell me what I can do to help you."

"You do help. Being with you takes my mind off it. Gives me a small release. Listen." He pulled me back and held me at arm's reach. "I want to enjoy tonight. Please, just for tonight can we forget about it? I promise no more disappearing. I will take you with me tomorrow into the city. But for tonight, let us just enjoy ourselves. I need some time away from my thoughts and you are the only person I know with the ability to do that."

"If that is how I can help, I will do that." I raised his warm hand to my mouth and kissed it. "How about we go and find the rest of the group? The procession will begin soon I am sure."

Hadrian placed a kiss on my head in thanks. "Have you seen what you look like yet?" he asked. "I am not leaving until I get a good look at you."

I shook my head. "Not at all."

"Let me tell you. They have created a masterpiece." His eyes ran up and down me, undressing me. "Here…"

With his hand still holding mine, he guided me to a gilded mirror that rested up on the wall. We stood before it, Hadrian behind me so I could get a good look.

I was dressed in silver and ivory with threads of purple that coiled up my tunics sleeves and trousers. The jacket was tight fitting, showing off my frame. My boots had been polished and reflected the candlelight in the room. But it was the smaller details that took my breath away. I leaned into the mirror and took a better look at the powder that covered my curved, pointed horns. The dust caught the light and glistened as I moved. My wings were the same. When the sisters were running their hands across them, they must have been spreading this strange coating of glitter. My hair had been cut once again, the sides shaved back down and my bun neat. I even caught the three braids they had plaited, just like my Mam would have done.

I was the embodiment of my element.

"Not that I have not recognized it before, but you are the most beautiful creature I have ever seen," Hadrian slurred behind me. His purr caused the hairs on my neck to rise. He leaned in and placed a lingering kiss on my neck. I melted into his embrace.

I turned around to him and moved him before the mirror.

He truly was the Prince of flames. He was dressed in deep reds and blood orange tones. From his trousers to his jacket, he was fire. The moving blue glow beneath his skin was not as apparent in his uniform, overshadowed by the bright, loud colors he wore. On his head, a crown rested. It was bronze with etched swirls wrapping all around it. The points had been made to look like dancing flames.

"You look wonderful," I whispered, taking him all in. I almost wished the night would be cancelled. "They did a pretty good job on you as well."

"Fire and Air," he said. "Do you remember what I told you back in Kandilin all those days ago?"

"That fire is nothing without the air that fuels it," I echoed the words that had stayed with me during the days when we first arrived in the town.

His smile reached his golden eyes that pierced the darkening room. "Just as air keeps a fire roaring, you keep me going. That will never change."

TWENTY SEVEN

WE ALL MET in the Queen's throne room. Hadrian and I walked in, hand in hand, interrupting the huddle of our group who stood waiting.

Illera turned our way first, leaving Jasrov and Nyah deep in conversation. They were laughing about something I couldn't quite make out. I noticed Emaline where she sat on the steps beneath the throne scratching Bell behind her ear, a lost expression cut across her painted face.

She, like Hadrian and I, had been dressed around her Dragori form. Her white feathered wings hung limp behind her. Her gown seemed to be made from the ocean itself. Blues and purples were washed together, giving the long, lace skirt a faded illusion. Her sleeves covered the majority of scales that overlapped the skin on her arms, but the cluster on her chin was left out and proud. Opal flecks of glitter dusted her brown skin. As her hand moved to rub Bell, they captured the light in dancing winks.

"Look who has decided to turn up," Nyah called, waving us over. "We were about to send out a search party for you both. You especially, Hadrian..."

"Patience, Nyah, we would not be late to our *own* party." Hadrian laughed, taking her hand and shaking.

"You both look amazing," Jasrov commented, straightening his gold-colored jacket and matching slacks. "Truly. I don't think I have ever worn anything so nice."

Hadrian bowed, dropping my hand and shaking Jasrov's as if they hadn't seen each other for a long while. Nyah no longer wore the emerald cloak. To show off her dress, she spun until two wing-liked flaps of jade material lifted from the back of her gown.

"I could get used to this." Nyah picked up her dress.

"When they suggested accessories, I have a feeling the tailors were not talking about weapons, Nyah," Hadrian said, spying the dagger around her thigh.

"It's shiny and sparkles, what more could you ask for from an accessory?" She winked.

Illera's dress was ivory, reminding me of the gown Hadrian's mother wore in the painting I left back in our room. It was simple, yet stunning. It pooled around her feet. Lines of black material cut across the bodice. Her hair had been gathered into a long braid that swung behind her.

"When will the festivities start?" I asked, stretching my wings in hopes it helped relax my muscles.

"Can't wait?" Nyah said.

"Something like that."

"Emaline, come join us." Jasrov waved her over.

"Hopefully soon," Nyah answered my initial question.

"Blue suits you," I said as Emaline walked our way. I noticed the swing of the acorn necklace that sat proudly above her dress. She caught me looking at it and fiddled with the chain.

"It was always Nesta's favorite color. She would be glad to see me in it tonight."

A nervous-looking maid walked over with a tray in hand. We each plucked a thin glass from it. The liquid was the color of diluted sunrays. I raised it to my ear and listened to the symphony of fizzes and pops within the glass.

Jasrov sniffed it cautiously, and Nyah raised it to her eyes, which made them look large as I peered through the glass at her.

"What is this?" she asked, turning her head. "It sings."

Hadrian raised it within the small circle we created.

"To Nesta," he toasted. "We drink this in her honor and name."

I raised my glass, and Illera, Jasrov and Nyah followed. We all looked to Emaline, whose eyes shone for a moment, then she slowly raised her arm.

"To Nesta."

We each lifted to our mouths and sipped, solidifying our toast.

The liquid sun fizzed across my tongue, making my cheeks clamp and salivate. It was a sweet drink. A waltz of honey, grapes and pear. I recognized each taste clearly.

"Illera, I hear you are helping scout," I said over the lip of my glass.

She looked to Emaline. "I have been lucky enough to be given a chance to help, yes."

"Your shift has come in handy. Frightening to some Alorian elves at first. It is not every day they see a beast amongst them," Emaline added, smiling Illera's way. "She does not give herself credit."

The doors opened behind us, and we all turned to see the Queen and her family walk into the room. They were both dressed in midnight gowns with pearl beading and silver thread. On their heads were crowns of ice and leaf. Both looked powerful, ethereal and poised, like the powerful enchantresses I had read about in stories.

"I hope you are prepared," Queen Kathine said, sweeping across the floor to us and shaking each of our hands. "My, haven't my tailors worked hard on you all? Truly stunning."

"They have." Hadrian stepped forward and kissed the back of her waiting hand.

"Now, Prince, enough of the formalities. How about we get going? If you listen carefully you can practically hear the excitement of the city. Let us not keep them waiting a moment later, shall we?"

"Can I ask what it is you need from us? What is in store when we head into town?" I asked.

Queen Kathine regarded me with a smile and proceeded to explain the nights events. She talked with the procession from the palace to the main city square. Once we reached the square, she would address the crowd.

"...then, as detailed in the parchment you all received, I will ask you each to display your magick. Illera and Nyah, you will go first, followed by the three Dragori. A grand finale."

I glanced at Hadrian, who watched and nodded in agreement.

Something about that didn't sit right with me, especially with Hadrian's pulsing blue gleam beside me. I had seen what happened to him when he used his abilities. He knew the risks. Before I could argue my point, Queen Kathine moved to leave the throne room and beckoned for us all to follow.

"No rest for the wicked," Nyah whispered behind me.

"You would know." I winked back at her, trying to hide my worry. I was certain she could sense it regardless.

As we stepped towards the top of the stairs, I could see just how many came out to see us. The streets bustled with cheers and screams. The sea of watching elves exploded as they caught their first glimpse of us. Then we began the two-mile procession. Hadrian didn't move from my side the entire time, his warm presence a constant as thousands of eyes bore down on us.

My feet burned, and my body ached with each footfall towards the city center. I kept my smile wide and head held high. The entire city smiled back, waved and clapped as we passed. As well as soaking in the love that surrounded me, I absorbed every detail of the city I could catch. From buildings to streets lined with shops and taverns. In truth, Lilioira was no different to Olderim. The same smells, tastes and visions. The only difference being the blood of those that dwelled within these impressive buildings.

Lilioira was large and impressive, but when I had to walk the main streets, I realized just how big it truly was. From the main doors of the palace, all the way to the main courtyard of the city, elves stood to watch as we walked by. Soldiers stood between them and the procession, although it was clear no one was a threat. Their beaming smiles and frantic calls made that clear.

My head spun with each face I passed.

Queen Kathine showed no sign of discomfort as she led the way, surrounded by a cohort of guards that circled her. She would occasionally move to the edge of the path and touched the hands of her people and accepted bunches of flowers.

Hadrian would do the same, as if it was as easy as breathing. He would let younglings reach and stroke hands down his wings and skin. He even held one child, who cooed and reached for his face to the parents' glee.

I pushed Cristilia's story into the dark pits within my mind and forced a smile.

Nyah, Jasrov and Illera hung back, smiling and waving but never going so far as to visit the crowd. Nyah did not enjoy this type of attention. She hardly looked up from the floor and stuck to Jasrov side. Jasrov didn't notice her discomfort, as he was too busy worrying for Bell.

I gave up trying to follow Bell's movements as she dove into the crowds and demanded attention. I might not have been able to see her, but I could hear where she had gone. The elves with her would laugh and cry with pleasure as the familiar meddled with them.

Emaline stuck close to the Queen, but she did greet the many elves who begged for her attention. A bright smile lit up her face.

The sky had melted from the dusk hue to pitch black of night. The many lit lanterns lining the pathway pooled enough light to create the illusion of late afternoon. There was a crisp chill in the air thanks to the lingering snow that clung to the path and building rooftops. Now and then my boots would squelch within puddles of slush that everyone else seemed to skirt around. I was too busy taking in every single detail I possibly could to notice where I stood.

Once we reached the heart of the city, I noticed the water fountain straight away. As Tiv had explained, it was of an elven woman. She carried two jugs of water and was caught mid-movement. Leaks of water poured from her eyes, but her expression was not a sad one. She had a serene look about her.

"Take a seat," Queen Kathine hushed, gesturing to six oaken chairs that were in a line beneath the fountain. "Only when I call your names should you come up."

I scanned the surrounding crowds and looked for Tiv. I didn't spot him until I was guided to my seat. I caught his moonlight hair as he waved, jumping up and down for my attention. I lifted a hand back, and he began tugging on the woman beside him. I had no doubt she was his mother. She was very much like him, short and silver. Beautiful. White hair spilled over her narrow shoulders, the same light color of her eyes. I smiled and raised a hand. I would be sure to visit him once I was free.

"Welcome all," Queen Kathine called, her voice loud. It washed over the crowd, stilling them into silence. "My heart warms tremendously to see my people here to share in this celebration. Thank you all for helping me show our guests just how kind and welcoming we are."

There was not a sound from the watching elves as their Queen spoke. I looked at them as they were in awe at the woman they loved. No one looked anywhere but at her as she stood on the lip of the fountain and spoke.

"We, as a collective, are going through a time of uncertainty and worry. I pleaded with the Goddess to show us strength, and she listened. Lilioira is a safe hold for her children, a place where lurking evils will not penetrate. Now with the arrival of our guests, the three Dragori and their aids, we have added protection. I am lucky to be Queen of such loving elves as all of you. With the growing number of refugees, you have opened your hearts and homes, sharing bread and comfort with those who are displaced. I wanted to give you all a night where you can be free from your worries and hardship; a night where we can all celebrate under the watchful eye of the Goddess. Let us dance, drink and eat together like we have done all our lives. We will not let such worry ruin our way of life."

Queen Kathine stood back and raised her hand to the side. "It is not a festival without a ballad from our favorite songbird."

I watched a woman glide through the crowd and up the steps of the fountain to stand beside her. She was tall and elegant. Her dark hair was gathered behind her, apart from two slips that trailed down the front of her bodice to her hips. The dress that flowed around her body was a light pink covered with chains of gold that looped around her.

Even the tiara on her head was gold; it wrapped around her hair as if it was a fitted hat. A hexagonal necklace shielded her delicate throat, each part holding a gem of striking colors.

"Thank you, Queen Kathine," the singer said, cheeks flushed with color.

I was enough distance away that the gold did not affect me, but I could feel it as a tingle in the back of my mind. My grip tightened on the chair's arms until my knuckles turned white. It will not harm me, I repeated in my mind.

Out of the corner of my eye, I saw Emaline turn her head to look at me, and I nodded, letting her know I felt it too. Hadrian glowed brighter; in defence or stress, I could not tell. His face may have remained calm, but his tense posture screamed otherwise.

The woman bowed to Queen Kathine then stood tall as she faced the crowd.

Hadrian placed a firm hand on my thigh.

Queen Kathine floated from the fountain and took a seat at the end of our line.

Once she sat, the song began. All eyes were on Janila as her voice spilled into the air.

Tiv was right. Her voice was the most enchanting I had ever heard.

By the third note, I forgot about the gold and allowed her tune to pull me down its lazy river. Her voice dipped and changed as she told her story through her song. I closed my eyes and allowed her to take control. I felt the tension building in her voice as the story ebbed and flowed.

It must've been magick. The ability to calm a body and mind with no more than a voice. A siren. Her eyes never closed as she sang, not as she moved elegantly from song to song. By the time she reached the final note, I was in tears.

They cut down my cheeks, and I didn't care if it turned the many powders that cover them.

As Janila took a breath, I was on my feet. My hands clapped, adding to the thunderous noise of the crowd around me. The only one left sitting was Queen Kathine, but her smile reflected her pride for the performance.

Janila took a slow bow, her hair falling before. When she straightened, she swept her hair back into place and walked away from the fountain with a head held high with pride. The crowd engulfed her in their embrace until she disappeared from view.

The crowd was chanting Janila's name over and over, begging for her to come back. I wanted to join them, but Queen Kathine raised a hand and everyone stopped.

"What a beautiful song choice, fitting for such a celebration." Queen Kathine gestured for us to sit once again. I spared a glance behind me and watched the crowd calm and listen to the Queen again.

"Before we proceed with the feast, I have a final performance as such. I would now like to invite our guests up for you all to meet. They have their own talents they would like to share with you."

The crowd murmured in wonder at what Queen Kathine meant by her words. But I knew.

We were to display our powers. For myself and Emaline, this was fine. But Hadrian? I wondered how much of his soul would be affected by using his magick to please the crowd rather than to protect.

CHAPTER
TWENTY-EIGHT

ANTICIPATION WAS PALPABLE in the air around us.

"Each of our six guests have unique magicks and strengths that they have offered up to the protection of this city and its people. It is time for them each to show you just how safe you all are."

We each stood and waited for our names to be called as Queen Kathine had explained before we left the palace. The only member of our group who had not been asked to stand was Jasrov. He didn't seem to mind as his studied stare was lost in Nyah, who stood beside him. A look of pure admiration painted across his relaxed face.

"I would first like to ask for Nyah Kane and Illera Daeris of Thessolina to join me before the people." She raised a hand for them. "We are lucky that the Goddess has sent more than just the Dragori to our city. Their trusted allies have helped them in their journey and have pledged to help protect our city from those who wish to risk our safety."

Nyah and Illera walked in tandem up to the fountain and stood on either side of the Queen. Illera held her violet stare above the crowd and her quaking hands pinned behind her. I followed Nyah's stare to Jasrov who was watching her with intent.

"Behold, power from the shores of Thessolina. We have heard of their unique, rare ability to shapeshift. Our guests both are blessed with such a magick that the Goddess herself has given them." Queen Kathine nodded in command, and in seconds, both Nyah and Illera exploded into black shadow.

It was for a split moment that I was reminded of the shadowbeings. How had I never noticed the similarities before? The shadow; the seeping hands of it were the very same as the creatures resurrected by the Druid.

Within moments, they were no longer standing beside the Queen, not in their elven forms at least. Now a white lion sat still, and an emerald moth, the size of my hand, rested on Illera's pointed ear, which twitched beneath the moth's delicate touch.

"Shapeshifters, a power only unlocked by Niraen blood." Queen Kathine turned to the lion and moth and bowed. "Illera Daeris has agreed to help scout the surrounding mountains of Lilioira to ensure the many seeking refuge within our city make it here safely."

Illera opened her saber-toothed jaw and purred for the crowd.

"Do not be fooled by Nyah Kane's small appearance. Not only has she been blessed with this ability, but gold blood dilutes her Niraen blood. Nyah has been gifted the ability of an empath. She has already proven her true nature to me tenfold. Without her, I would never have made it out of Kandilin alive."

The crowd gasped as Queen Kathine told her truth. Someone clapped, and my head snapped toward the origin of the sound. It was Jasrov, clapping alone with not a care in his world.

Both creatures moved for the steps, and by the time they reached the level ground, they were back in their elven forms once again. Both Nyah and Illera bowed for the crowd then took their seats. Jasrov stood as Nyah joined our group again then sat with her. His whisper caused her to blush and hide her face.

"Wonderful, just wonderful," Queen Kathine called. "Now I ask for the guests of honor to join me before the watching gaze of my people. Let them see just what the Dragori will do to keep our enemy at bay."

Queen Kathine talked about the Goddess and the story of the Dragori as we took to the steps and joined her. She spoke of the druids' creations, how the Goddess claimed them for her own and used them against the druids to help end their destructive reign. The events she told where the same as I had read in the book Hadrian had given me weeks ago.

"…You must be asking yourselves where the fourth is?" Queen Kathine asked. "We have scouts and the very best of my close ranks out searching for news on the fourth Dragori's location. Fear not, the Goddess will guide her to us just as she had with our guests. Air, Fire and Water. Three of the four elements that created life. Magicks that once only belonged to the Goddess. She has looked down upon these three elves and chosen them to fulfil her bidding. We trust in her knowledge and trust in her choice. Let them show you why they were picked."

Queen Kathine gestured for Emaline first, who stepped forward.

"Show your people why they should no longer be afraid."

Emaline followed her command, and all eyes landed on her.

There was a pause as she inhaled.

A loud groaning noise filled the uneasy silence. I didn't know what she was doing at first, not until a shadow passed above me. I looked up and watched the water from the fountain lift into the air and spin in an orb of blue. As Emaline's hands moved quicker, so did the sphere of water. Not a single elf in the crowd diverted their stare from the water and its commander as she displayed her gift.

Emaline's white-feathered wings spread wide and the sphere of water vibrated. With a large thrust of her arms, the orb exploded into mist, layering the surrounding crowd in glistening flecks. Once it settled, everyone began shouting for more. Their infectious excitement made my heart pound in my chest.

"Emaline Sowdin of Kandilin, what an incredible display." Queen Kathine moved over to her, shaking her hand then turned back to the crowd. "Emaline has joined my service as an elite soldier. A guard to this city and its people. You all were told of the news of my second commanders passing in the battle of Kandilin. Emaline has filled that opening and now works with guiding our soldiers. Let us show her our thanks once more."

She began to clap, and the crowd echoed it. Queen Kathine shared a quiet word with Emaline, who nodded and moved back to her seat.

How could I follow such a powerful display as Emaline's? I had not spared a single thought to my performance. But as Queen Kathine called me to step forward, I was as lost as I was before.

"Zacriah Trovirin of Olderim, please take your place and show my people why they should no longer hold onto fear."

I turned to the waiting eyes, each full of anticipation and wonder. Tiv had squeezed through the crowd and stood before the many tall elves around him. His face was awash with excitement.

There was no time to plan or think. I trusted my instincts and gave the waiting power.

I closed my eyes, welcoming my wind. Only weeks ago, I was lost to it, and now I felt its presence like an extra limb. It was mine to call on, mine to control.

It started as a whistle, faint but there. Then, as I called for more, the noise turned into a roar, and I was everywhere.

My wind raced through the crowds. It lifted hair and clothes in a flurry of gusts. My reach moved like a snake, slipping around the many bodies as I touched them all with my element. It was not as visually pleasing as Emaline's display. But I wanted to let everyone feel the brush of my magick, to know that I would keep them safe.

I pushed more energy, willing the wind to move faster and faster.

Satisfied, and slightly exhausted, I dropped my connection to my wind and opened my eyes.

Once the roar of air died, the sound of excited screams reached me. I bowed and stepped back. Dizzied for a moment, I only hoped no one noticed my slight stumble before Hadrian's strong hand stilled me.

"Incredible." Even Queen Kathine's flattened her hair with eyes wide. I waited for her to speak, but she seemed lost for words for a moment. It was the first time I had seen her in such a state of awe.

"I felt the Goddess's presence, like a cold touch to my heart. Thank you." Queen Kathine grasped my forearm and shook it.

I tipped my head to her and moved down the steps to my seat, leaving Hadrian with the Queen. Emaline greeted me at my seat and patted my back, then we both sat down to watch the final performance.

"Prince Hadrian Vulmar of Thessolina." Queen Kathine voice silenced the excited crowd again. "We are blessed to be graced by the presence of royalty from our sister continent. It has been many years since the Vulmar family have set foot on Eldnol soil. Never did I think we would see him again under these circumstances. But our Goddess works in mysterious ways."

Hadrian smiled at her, his blue flame flaring as he opened his mouth to speak.

"Kind people of Lilioira and Eldnol, my heart is full. I have spent little time amongst you, but I have seen love here, which reminds me of home. I thank Queen Kathine and her family for her hospitality. In return, I extend a promise to you all. My promise is to look over you as I would with my own, to treat you like family and ensure you are kept safe from harm."

My heart warmed as Hadrian spoke.

"The Druid has thrown Eldnol into chaos, but I vow never to leave until he is stopped. For he is only one, and we are the many."

Never to leave. His promise echoed across my body and mind. Hearing those words finally helped the seed of worry within me. I'd believed he would leave. Maybe he found nothing to help him during his days in the city.

With his final statement, he closed his eyes. I felt the heat of his power before it happened. All the lanterns around the crowd and the many candles that lined the courtyard burst with light. Their red flames replaced with deep blue and reached high into the night sky. Everyone shied away from the sudden bright light, raising hands over eyes to shield themselves from Hadrian's blaze.

I couldn't take my eyes off him.

Haloed in light, Hadrian looked powerful. Beastly. His hands stayed by his side, but his forehead creased with concentration as he displayed his magick. Up and up the flames snaked into the air and began reaching for one another. Hadrian pushed and pushed, and the flames grew stronger and hotter.

I turned to the crowd whose faces were slack in wonder. Blue fire reflected in their eyes as they watched the Prince's display. Even Tiv's excited expression had melted into one of shock. He shied away from it like ice to a flame.

Suddenly, the flames died, and the crowd reacted audibly. I looked back to Hadrian, and my heart sank.

Something was wrong. I could feel it within me.

Red blood ran from his nose. It dripped, splashing against the white stone of the fountain. Tears of red then seeped from the corners of his eyes, standing out against this blue fire. Slowly, he opened his eyes and looked directly into mine. His body began to shake, his hands clenched to his sides. Then his golden eyes rolled into the back of his head, only showing the dull white in the reflection of the still burning flames.

I was frozen in shock as Hadrian, my Hadrian, began to tilt.

Illera ran up the steps, despite the burning heat that rolled from his body. Guards moved Queen Kathine out of the way, and the crowd began to scream in panic behind me. Hadrian flared brighter, and Illera scowled away, but then she dove forward once again.

Every flame in the city died out, and the ground shook as Hadrian collided with it. Swallowed in darkness, it was the feared screams of the city that lit up the night now.

I stumbled for my Hadrian until my palms were wet and warm as I fell beside him.

His skin no longer glowed blue. I rested my hand on his arm and felt cold.

Ice cold.

TWENTY-NINE

IT TOOK FOUR of us to carry Hadrian back to the palace.

Emaline and I picked him up from his sides, and Illera kept a hold of his head while Nyah lifted his feet. In his Dragori form, his body was heavy and limp. His wings trailed the path until Jasrov joined and lifted them up.

All around us, the crowds were alight with terror, screaming and running amidst the confusion of what they had just witnessed.

I could hardly see Queen Kathine, nor did I care to look where she had been taken to. Hadrian was all I cared about.

"What happened to him?" Jasrov called above the screaming city. "The blood. He was crying blood."

"Stop the bleeding." Nyah's voice joined the frantic call of questions.

"Illera, you're hurt," Emaline shouted.

I didn't answer any of them. I couldn't. Not as my bloodstained palms held Hadrian up. Words were lost to me.

I couldn't see much of what was going on as we stumbled in the dark towards the direction of the palace. Not once did I look up to bother checking. I just pushed my feet faster and willed more strength to hold him up.

I only knew we'd reached the bottom of the steps beneath the palace when we almost stumbled up the first part. Even then, I didn't tear my eyes from my sleeping prince.

"Jasrov, run ahead; prepare a healer," Emaline commanded.

"I have already told Gallion; he is preparing a room now."

Nyah must've connected with him through their empathic link.

We were being knocked from all directions as the crowds no longer stayed in neat groups. They ran around the dark streets, racing for home. We had failed them. Our one job was to make them feel safe, and now they ran in fear. But worst of all, I had failed Hadrian. I knew he was not well. He had told me that every time he used his power, a darkness would build within him. Even with that knowledge, I hadn't stopped him. I should've stopped him.

"Zacriah?" Illera's voice hushed beside me.

I shook myself from my lost state and looked at her, trying to figure out what I had missed.

"What?" I whispered.

"Do not worry. We are going to your room. That is where Gallion is waiting for us," Illera answered. "He will be fine."

Will he? His body was cold to the touch. The Prince of Flames with no warmth or fire in his blood. I didn't want to imagine what that could mean. The blue gleam had disappeared, which made me worry more. At least its presence told me he had time.

"Illera, let go of his head for a moment and give me your hands," Emaline said.

"I'm fine," Illera replied.

"Give them to me. You burned yourself before the fire left his skin. I need to cool them down before…"

Jasrov took Illera's place for a moment while we made up for her lack of strength.

"The burns are bad," Emaline muttered. "Nyah, warn them that Illera will need help as well."

"Honestly, Emaline, please do not fuss." Illera's voice was stern. She retook her place, moving Jasrov out of the way.

I glanced up at the noise that greeted us. I watched a handful of soldiers racing down to intercept our climb. I let them take *him* from my arms. I did nothing but listen to Nyah tell the soldiers where to take him. Then I watched, dumbfounded and frozen, as they took him away.

Emaline and Nyah guided me the remainder of the walk to the palace. Once we reached the top, I called out for our group to stop. I knew what I needed to do.

"The Staff of Light. It is the only hope we have in helping him," I called breathlessly. Back in my elven form, I felt weak from the prolonged use of my shift. Once we reached the newly lit lanterns at the palace gates, I could see that Emaline had also shifted back, and her eyes were ringed with shadow.

"Queen Kathine will never let us leave," Emaline panted, resting her hands on her thighs as she caught her breath.

I glanced to Nyah whose expression seemed to scream in agreement with Emaline.

"Even if we went, we still could waste days trying to find its resting place," Nyah replied.

Jasrov was sitting on the steps, Bell up close to him. "We can't just leave Hadrian."

They still thought we had no lead. I had not mentioned what Gallion had told me and what we had found within the books.

"Speak up." Nyah stared at me. "Tell us what Gallion knows!"

I should have known not to dwell when Nyah was near. Her hand still held mine, allowing her to read my emotions.

"I can't say it now, not with our audience." Many soldiers stood around us. Hadrian's flare had put the entire city on high alert. "I need to go and see Hadrian, then I need you all to meet me at the Queen's library."

A plan brewed in my mind, but for it to work, I would need everyone's cooperation.

"Illera, a word…"

She halted back, giving me a moment to tell her what I needed from her. It had to be her. She was the only one who could help me.

She agreed to my whispers before promising to meet me in the Library.

The foundation of the plan that brewed in my mind was now out in the open. I would leave with or without the Queen's agreement, and I would need the help of each skill our group had to offer.

⌒

I WATCHED THE slow rise and fall of Hadrian's chest, mentally counting each one. I wouldn't take my eyes off him, not wanting to miss any sign that he was getting better. But for the time I stared at him, nothing miraculous happened.

Two healers floated around him, placing a hand on his head, chest and stomach, which seemed to restart his breathing if it ever faulted. Gallion stuck by me, overseeing the healers' dance and made comments, which brought me out of my frozen state.

When I first made it to the room, I lost my breath when I saw Hadrian's appearance. He was laid in our bed, white sheets scrunched around his body. His face was peaceful. Not a single crease or wrinkle across his placid expression. All blood had been cleaned from his face, leaving him with a light sheen of moisture across his skin.

"His consciousness has separated due to the trauma of the Heartfire. I cannot quite reach him, and I worry that my prodding will hinder his healing rather than help. I am impressed he has held the Heartfire at bay for so long. The prince is stubborn," Gallion said.

"He warned me, Gallion," I said, trying to make sense of what had happened. "Before the procession, he told me of the darkness he was battling. Every time he used his magick, it seemed to chip away at him. Yet, I did nothing. I should have stopped him. I knew it was bad, but I didn't stop him. This is my fault."

"It was the final straw that broke the elk's back," Gallion muttered. "You should not waste energy stuck in the worries of the past. I think it is clear there is only one way to help Hadrian now. And I sense you have already made your mind up."

"The Staff."

Gallion tipped his head in agreement.

"Hadrian mentioned something to me." I looked back to his body. "Have you ever heard being Soul Lost before?

Gallion's face paled. "Unfortunately, I have. It was as much of a myth as Heartfire..."

"Someone told Hadrian that. He wouldn't let me question him more on it. Now I worry that is what has happened to him... whatever it means."

"It would explain why I can't sense his awareness." Gallion leaned forward and placed a hand on Hadrian's barefoot. "He seems to be no more than a shell. Wherever his soul has gone to, I think we can both guess."

"The Druid."

Gallion's sad expression answered for him.

"I'm going." I stood up, unable to look at Hadrian any more.

"I know," Gallion replied. "I should not aid you, not when I work for the Queen now. But Hadrian is as much a son to me as you are. You *must* risk searching for it."

Gallion stood up and moved to the cabinet in the corner of the room. I heard the rustle of paper and watched him pull out a rolled parchment from a sack.

The parchment was yellowed and stained.

"Where did you find this?" I asked, running my finger along the lines of ink on the old map.

"I believe it found me. I was searching in the books and this was fitted in a shelf that I'd not gone through yet." Gallion leaned over me and pointed to an image I recognized. "This is Lilioira. And this"—he ran his finger up north of the map—"is the Druid Keep. If what we found is true, this is where I believe it is. The dwelling that was left untouched. It would be a risk going, but if this is what the Goddess showed you, then I wholeheartedly believe the Staff will be found there."

I squinted and looked closer. If what Gallion said was true, the Keep was closer than I had first thought. I'd seen enough maps to understand their scaling and knew that the journey would take a day at most.

"I could reach it and be back before the Queen notices," I said, scrutinizing the page for as much detail as I can.

"Don't underestimate her, Zacriah, she is the spearhead of Eldnol. She will have eyes in more places than you would realize. You won't be able to just walk beyond the gates, not with the city's current climate of panic."

Gallion was right, but it didn't matter what obviousness he pointed out. Sitting before the person I cared for the most whilst he was lost, I would do anything to help him. Anything.

"Then I won't leave through the gates," I whispered, possibilities flooding me.

"Would you do something for me?" I turned to Gallion, resting the map on my lap.

"For you, my boy, I would do anything."

"Stay with Hadrian. I'd hate for him to wake and be surrounded by strangers. Promise me."

"I will not leave his side, no matter what."

I wrapped my arms around Gallion and held on. "What if the Staff is not there...?"

"Do not allow your worry to deviate your mind from the task at hand. Go, look. You will know if the keep is the home to the Staff." Gallion pulled back and tapped his finger on my temple. "You will know," he repeated.

Each step I took away from Hadrian was as painful as the last. I wanted to turn around, to spare him a glance, but I didn't. I would not say goodbye today. No. Not today.

I repeated that over and over as I leave the room. I didn't look back until I reached the Queen's library.

Only then did I allow myself a moment to breathe and imagine the boy I would return to.

∽

EVERYONE WAS WAITING for me when I entered the library. The moment I walked into the room they all stood with faces of pure anticipation. Nyah raced over, holding her dress from the floor.

She encased me in a hug. "How is he?"

"Not good," I replied. "Gallion is certain his consciousness has separated from his body. The Heartfire has done its damage."

"I'm sorry," Nyah whispered.

"What can we do?" Emaline stood forward. "There must be something..."

"There is, I hope."

Nyah guided me over to the rest of our crew. "Hadrian is lost unless we get the Staff, but we know Queen Kathine thinks about that." I pulled the map from my belt and unraveled it. "Gallion found this, and if what I believe is true, the Staff is being kept here..." I pointed to the labelled drawing of the Druid Keep.

"Impossible, all the Druid's dwellings were destroyed years ago." Emaline walked around a table and stood with her hands on Illera's shoulders. Illera looked up at Emaline, sharing an unspoken word. "This map should not be followed."

"That's what Gallion believed, but what a coincidence that the one remaining Keep is the home of the Staff. And it is where I need to go."

Jasrov took the map and opened it on the table. He placed stacks of books at each corner to keep it from folding in. Then we each stood around to see it fully open before us.

"I've seen many maps of Eldnol, but never one like this." Jasrov looked over the map and pointed to a different depiction. "It shows all the old dwellings that were destroyed in the great purge once the druids passed. I know this one." He put his finger on a rushed sketch at the bottom of the map. "It is rubble now, but that didn't stop my sister and I from playing amongst the ruins of that Keep. This map is from the time of the druids, maybe even made by them. If it says there is a Keep over Lilioira mountain range, then I would believe it."

"Even if it still stands, what makes you think the Druid is not there now?" Emaline asked.

"I am with Emaline," Nyah said. "It all seems too obvious. Illera, when you remember parts of where the Druid kept you, do you remember it being near mountains?"

Illera's eyes shone as she relayed what she had told us numerous times. "All I remember is the dark. Nothing but the dark."

"It is impossible for the Druid to be there." A shadow detached from the wall behind Illera. Emaline and Nyah reach for concealed knives but faltered when they saw who it was.

Cristilia materialized from nothing. "I do not mean to impose, but I thought it best I lead you into the light. I have seen a lot in my life. My ancestors were part of the few who cursed the Keep you seek..."

"A curse?" Nyah interrupted, moving her hand away from the hilt of her dagger.

"Indeed. During the great purge, the majority was certain that removing all traces of the Druid's existence was the only way to heal and move forward from their hate and destruction. But, there was a handful of elves across the three continents who knew that was a mistake. It is why Lilioira holds such extensive documents and books that once belonged to the druids. It was Queen Kathine's grandmother who helped store the documents and protect the remaining Keep from being purged as the others. In fact, she worked alongside the four Dragori of their time, using their blood to create a protective circle around it. They did this to ensure that only one with Dragori blood would be free to pass into the Keep once more."

"Wait." I turned on Cristilia. "You knew all along, didn't you? You knew the Staff was being kept there?"

Cristilia's face morphed before my eyes. Her delicate hand covered her mouth as if my accusation pained her. "No, only the Keeper knew of its location. What you have found makes sense. You could speak to the Queen, even she knows of this curse. Has the old empath Gallion not mentioned it during your findings?"

Emaline's distrust for Cristilia was clear in her knotted brows and squinted gaze. Her knuckles were white as she held onto the edge of the table.

"The Keep's location is—was common knowledge amongst the council. But the Staff was shrouded in mystery."

"As you are…" Nyah stepped forward. "Why can't I read you, Cristilia?"

"I am Morthi…"

Nyah shook her head. "As you have said before. Let me touch you, let me read you…"

"Enough!" I reached out to stop her.

Nyah backed down, but not without a final sneer.

"Cristilia has helped us more than any other in this city. Show her respect," I shouted.

"It is fine. Nyah is right. You should not trust anyone. But I assure you, I want nothing more than to help. Let us waste no more time. The Queen is being kept in her quarters. But by sunrise, she will be back out, and the first place she will go to is to Hadrian. If you are going to leave, you must do it before then."

"We haven't decided if we are going yet," Emaline replied. "I have a duty to the Queen. As much as I want to help Hadrian, the people of this city come first. I'm sorry, Zacriah, but I am staying."

"I understand. That is why I am going with Illera."

The entire crew was stunned into silence. Illera just closed her eyes and nodded.

"I will go," Nyah announced. "Illera has been with the Druid enough. You can't just tell her to go somewhere without asking."

"I have already agreed to it." Illera stepped forward. "I will go; it is my choice."

"You don't have to prove yourself," Emaline replied, panic coating her voice.

"That has nothing to do with it."

"Why?" Emaline breathed. "Haven't I lost enough?"

Her plea took me by surprise.

"Nothing will happen, Emaline. I'm coming back. You heard what Cristilia said. The Druid will not be there, the curse prevents that. We will go in, get the Staff, and come back. I have Zacriah's back and he has mine; don't you?" She turned to me.

It was the first time since we found Illera that a speck of the old self came through. She had something to fight for now.

"I do."

"What do you need us to do?" Emaline asked, gripping onto Illera's hand.

We took our seats around the table, and I spilled the secrets of my plan, giving everyone a task.

Nyah was to stay and keep Queen Kathine from noticing our departure. With their link, she could influence Queen Kathine's mind and still any wandering thoughts.

Emaline would stay to protect the people just as she had asked for. With Hadrian lost to us, that would leave the city without a Dragori for protection if the Druid came.

Jasrov would work with Gallion. His abilities may help find remedies for Hadrian. At least that was what I hoped...

Cristilia tried to argue against Emaline staying. But no matter her pleading words, Emaline put her foot down and refused. Before Emaline and Cristilia came to blows, I sent Cristilia to prepare a pack for the journey. We would need supplies to see us through to the Keep: weapons, food and clothes.

It was simple enough. A seamless plan that we checked for problems.

"For Hadrian," I said.

We each looked at one another, nodding in agreement.

This *was* for him.

TĐIRTY

"NYAH, I NEED one final thing from you," I called across the room to her. Everyone had busied themselves talking in whispered tones, as if the library would turn against us and tell the Queen of our plans. Even if she did have eyes and ears in this place, I would not stop from going. It had to happen.

"You don't ask for much." Nyah winked. "Tell me what you need."

I guided her around the table and away from the group who fussed over the packs. Once I was certain we were out of earshot, I unveiled the last part of my plan that needed to be in place.

"The link you created between the Queen, so you could communicate. Do you think you could create one between us?" I asked.

"Are you sure?" Nyah looked unsure. "It is not as simple as you might believe. I will have access to all your thoughts and emotions."

"Was that the same with Queen Kathine?"

"She had time for me to show her how to build a wall. It meant I would only have access when she allowed it, or when I asked."

"Asked?"

Nyah took my hand as she explained.

"By creating a link, we are essentially opening the locked doors of our minds. When they are open, I can come and go when I please, not that I particularly care for what goes on in that head of yours. It is very similar to accessing your emotions through touch. When I touch you, I'm able to unlock the door and peer inside. It limits what I can see. But these connections are more intrusive. I don't know it feels for the other person, but my consciousness will knock against yours when I am wanting to connect. But to protect what you hold dear, you must mentally close that door. Otherwise, it will be open to me always."

"I can do it. Tell me how to make the wall," I said.

Nyah shrugged her shoulders. "It is different for everyone. You will only understand once we make the connection. Are you certain you want it?"

In truth, I wasn't sure. I had things locked in my mind that I wouldn't share with Hadrian. But I trusted Nyah's abilities, so I nodded.

"I'm willing to risk the secrets to ensure I have connection to someone near Hadrian. Something could go wrong. I will want to know."

"We can break it when you get back," Nyah reassured, reaching for my hands. "It makes me feel better knowing I am still with you in a way. It doesn't feel right, you going with Illera and not me."

"This is coming from the girl who told me to trust Illera."

Nyah tipped her head to the side. "It is not you I'm worrying about in this partnership."

"Then there is no need to worry." I grabbed ahold of her. "I'm ready, and it must be Illera. She has skills that we will need to navigate. And I trust you to stay back and keep everything in order as you always do."

Her hands glowed with a ruby light that snaked up my arms in a twisting dance. With its light touch came a shiver that crawled across my body and into my mind. Nyah's awareness filled me entirely.

"Close your eyes and open your mind." Nyah's voice was no more than a siren call. I listened and followed her instruction, imagining a door in my mind.

Open up.

Nyah spoke again. But this was different than before. New. It was an echo in my mind, bouncing across my consciousness.

I heard a knocking, and I reached an invisible hand to the handle. I pushed it open. As it swung open, fresh light burst through.

My eyes shot open, and Nyah held onto me, smiling. I swayed from the dizziness that over took my body.

I wish I had something witty and clever to say as the first thing you hear, but alas, I am stumped.

Nyah spoke, but her mouth did not move.

If only you could see your face right now.

"What?" I asked aloud.

Nyah tapped her head.

If you want to talk to me, think it. Don't say it.

Even in my mind, she was assertive.

I don't know what to say, I thought.

That will do.

Nyah reached forward and knocked a fist onto my shoulder. "You are too good at that. Now, before I say the wrong thing and you start thinking about princey in ways that I don't care to know, try and build a wall."

Even as she said it, she dragged some memories to the surface.

"Imagine the door and block the open entrance. Do it in whatever way works best for you, then when you are ready, tell me, and I will try and enter."

I closed my eyes again and imagined the door to my home. It materialized quickly, the door still wide open to the waiting light. I tried to reach for it and closed it with the handle, but it didn't move. When that didn't work, I tried willing it to shut, but it stayed open.

It's not working, I thought.

Build a wall, don't close it. Only I can close it for good. The wall will just keep me at bay.

I pictured it again, placing brick by brick before the door. I reinforced it with pillars of wood until a structure blocked the open door and waiting light.

Did it work?

I waited for her to respond, but she said nothing.

Nyah?

Still, she didn't respond.

I felt a cold trickle, as if a droplet of water ran down the other side of the wall. Over and over it kept poking its presence into my mind until I gave in and had a look at what it was.

The block is strong, maybe a little too strong. Nyah's awareness filled my mind again. *You're going to have to feel out for me when I want to contact you.*

Was that you? The cold presence I felt on the other side?

Yes, it was. That was my consciousness trying to reconnect with yours. Think of it as me walking through the first door to your home but coming across another. Your wall will stop me seeing into your mind, but you will feel when I am trying to connect with you.

I mentally bricked up my wall once more. Satisfied it was strong, I opened my eyes and welcomed the sight of the dark library once again.

"You must remember to feel out for me. I will be expecting you to give me updates with how you get on." Nyah closed the gap between us and wrapped her arms around me. My face pressed into her hair, smothering me whilst we said our goodbyes.

"Are you both ready?" Cristilia asked. "If you want to make it out, we must leave quickly."

"Yes," we answered together. Illera left Emaline with eyes rimmed with tears. Nyah sauntered over to Jasrov who wrapped an arm around her shoulder protectively. I stepped forward, beckoning Illera to join.

"Take my hands and stay quiet. Keep to the shadows, and we will stay unnoticed." Cristilia reached out for us.

"You think this will work?" Nyah couldn't help but double check.

"Each step into this quest is a risk that must be taken. I promise to get them from this city. I understand the importance," Cristilia said.

When I grasped her in one hand and Illera in the other, a rush of white noise wrapped around us like it had that night in Kandilin. I could see Emaline, Nyah and Jasrov still, but their expressions had changed, and their eyes searched the space where we stood, as if they couldn't see us.

"Stay close," Cristilia whispered again, moving towards the door. "Let us go whilst the night is still upon us."

We moved throughout the palace unseen. Everything distorted around us as we passed buildings and patrolling soldiers. No one spared us a look or thought. We first walked in the direction of the palace gardens. I recognized them from when I had found Nyah with Jasrov earlier that day. Cristilia stayed ahead, moving her arms around in circles, keeping the bubble of darkness around us.

Illera looked my way every now and then, yet we shared no words. In the grasp of the shadows, I was building into a bundle of worry until a cold trickle ran down my mental wall, and I knew Nyah was with me.

Once we were away from firelight, we stopped. Looking around, we were surrounded by trees and tall walls of foliage. My legs ached from the slight incline as we walked from the city. I knew Cristilia had dropped her shadows because our surroundings became clear and lost the wavering illusion that had followed us since we left the Queen's library.

"Fly from here. Stay close to the rock face until you are out of sight. It is a long flight up, but do not give in. It is important you make it out before the scouts see you," Cristilia said, her dark gaze looking upon us both.

"Here, give me your sack," Illera said as she slipped it from my back. "I will hold onto it while you carry me. I have a feeling the design was not made for wings."

Was it the cold chill that made me shake, or the nerves that raced alongside my blood? Looking up. I couldn't see where the rock face stopped. I just hoped, with the lack of sleep and food, I would make it far enough.

"Keep our friends safe," Illera said, her tone cold and untrusting. What was with everyone treating Cristilia with such disrespect? "If any of them are hurt whilst we are gone, I will hold you responsible."

"Your distrust concerns me, Illera, is there something I have personally done to offend you? To make you feel like *I* am not to be trusted because it was you who worked alongside the Druid, not I," Cristilia replied, matter-of-factly.

Illera didn't respond to Cristilia, instead she turned to me. "We should get going. Dawn's breeze is close."

I turned and mouthed thank you to Cristilia who nodded, still shaken by Illera's comments.

Then the beast was free. With a thought, I allowed my wings to grow through the slits in my uniform. It had been less than an hour since they last been free, and I could feel their reluctance to be out again. I willed them to calm and promised a rest soon.

"May the Goddess watch over you," Cristilia called as I rose into the air with Illera in my arms. She held her arms around her waist, hugging herself. Even she looked worried or sad in the minimal light. I knew that expression. Regret.

She said something else that I couldn't catch as my winds battered down, and we flew straight into the night. When I looked down, she was no longer beneath us, and the clearing of the gardens was empty once again.

CHAPTER
THIRTY ONE

ICY WINDS ATTACKED my face, wings and exposed skin.

The higher I flew into the night, the colder it became. Even Illera was shivering in my arms. I bit down on my lip and carried on, trying not to give into the exhaustion that flooded me. Away from the city light, it was hard to see my surroundings. I tried to stick as close to the rock face as possible, hoping to stay concealed amongst the thin clouds.

With each beat of my wings, we got closer to the tip of the wall of rock. I dared to glance down and regretted it. Illera hated this too. Not once did she stop pressing her face into my chest. I had to be careful I didn't hold onto her too hard. My claws were free and a hair's width from digging into her skin.

By the time we passed over the lip of the mountain wall, I had to stop and rest.

"You managed to fly for longer than I thought you would," Illera said, pulling an extra cloak from her pack and wrapping it around her shoulders, then giving the next to me.

"I've surprised myself," I said, shifting back into my elven form. I felt the relief of my wings that folded back into my skin.

"I'm going to scout," Illera announced, dropping her sack before me and pulling a gleaming blade free from its holder. "Do you want to set up camp here? I don't mind carrying on if you are feeling up to it. But we—you should rest."

I admired Illera's strength. After the flight, I wanted to curl in a ball and sleep, but Illera was making an effort to keep me focused and on track.

"I just need to gather some energy and then we will carry on." I looked around, trying to gather my surroundings. The sky was still dark, dawn no more than a distant thought.

Illera nodded, her violet gaze intense. "Then I will be back soon."

As she sauntered off into the night, I opened my mind to Nyah's. Letting the wall in my mind down, I connected with her.

We are over the lip of the surrounding mountain.

And you felt the need to wake me to tell me?

We are friends. You sleep when I sleep. I tried to keep my inner voice light.

Is Illera not good company? Or is your missing for me too much to bear?

My laugh rang out in my mind. *Illera is scouting whilst I gather some more energy. We aren't going to stop for a while. Maybe until the sun is up.*

Maybe I will wake you when you stop to sleep...

I don't think so. I slammed my brick wall up, which drowned out Nyah's sinister laugh.

I rummaged through my pack and pulled out some dried loaf. My stomach gave me a short pain as I chewed on the food. It had been many hours since I last put anything into my mouth, and this was not enough to fulfill my energy supply. But it was better than a slap on the belly with a cold fish.

"Zacriah, come look at this…" Illera's voice sounded distant.

I jumped from the rocky ground and picked the two packs up. Running to where she stood, I saw what had caught her attention.

We looked out over the sea of mountain peaks. An orange glow seemed to halo the farthest mountains, morphing into red as the sun rose from behind them. As the morning rays broke over the view, my skin warmed. It was beautiful, a field of snow and rock.

"I guess it is time to go," I said as we watched dawn creep over the countless peaks before us.

"Can we just watch it for a moment longer?" Illera was lost to the view, the glow of the sun reflected in her wide eyes.

It was clear to see what we were about to deal with. In all directions, mountains stood tall, tipped with white and gray. Clouds moved slowly above, thick and full. Their color suggested more snow was close, and so did the harsh nip in the air.

"Before we go, I want to get something out in the open." Illera's voice was soft.

"What's that?"

"To apologize."

"If it means you would never feel the need to put yourself through it again, then go ahead. Although you do know there is no need?"

"What I have to say goes far beyond what happened in Olderim. We both know it sparked back home. I've had a lot of time to think about how I treated you, how I treated everyone really. Over and over I would replay conversations I've had with others, and it only makes my stomach turn. I really regret it. I should never have treated people the way I have. For that, I apologize."

I turned to her, wondering why even after her apology, her face was pinched with sadness.

"Can I ask you one question?" I said.

"Yes."

"I just wonder what triggered the great dislike you had for me. I'm not saying I ever tried with you, but I just wondered since we are rehashing the past."

Illera sighed. "There is never excuse for bullying, and what I am about to say is far from an excuse. But in truth, I was jealous. Like most of those who live in Horith, I was a rage of jealousy."

"But you were the wealthiest of us all? You have a life of privilege and comfort. How could you be feeling that way towards the rest who don't have anything?" It didn't make sense. I wanted to tell her about the many times I wished for her life. I'd never need to hunt or go hungry again with her mounds of coin.

"I was rich with coin, but not with love. That was one thing I never had in abundance. Not like you. My parents blame me for the way their lives turned out. I am—was nothing of importance to them." Illera's head dropped. "Before I came along, they lived with triple the coin and a life of pure luxury. Because of me, we had to move to Horith and start a new life. They blame me for it."

I wrapped my arm around her shoulder. "Your parents are fools."

Illera laughed through a blocked nose. "The acorn doesn't fall far from the tree."

"Enough of that talk. You are no fool. What fool would risk their life and turn against a powerful being like the Druid? What fool would face their past and grow from it? We have all made mistakes and acted in ways that we dwell on and wish we had been different. But what is the fun in being perfect? Perfect is boring."

Illera dried her wet checks with her sleeve.

"Emaline was right about you," Illera said, picking both of our packs from the ground then handing mine to me.

"Do I even want to know what she thinks of me?" I replied.

"She said you had a kind heart, one that is open to forgiving."

"Well, Emaline is wise." I laughed.

Illera paused for a moment, a new expression covering her face. Her cheeks bloomed red and a smile pulled at the corners of her lips.

"Yes, she is, isn't she?" she said with a lost smile.

I looked back to the breathtaking view and shivered with anticipation.

"Finding the Keep in this maze of peaks and snow could take days," I mumbled.

"Do you have the map?" she asked.

I stuck my hand in my belt and pulled Gallion's map from it. My cold fingers where numb and stiff as I bent down and unrolled it across the ground.

Illera gave me a look. "If this is the Keep, and it's north, then we should follow the sun since it rises in the north. As long as we keep that way, we should find it..."

"Okay." I picked it up, looking out towards our destination. "Then what are we waiting for?"

❧

ILLERA WAS SURE footed and fast in her lioness form. I gripped tightly onto her fur, which had taken me a while to get used to. Unlike my flight from Lilioira, Illera showed no sign of slowing or fatigue. She powered on, leaping from rock to rock, boulder to boulder until we stopped for a rest. Even then she shifted effortlessly and made camp before I even had a clue how to help.

The weather had changed dramatically in the hours we travelled. The deeper we lost ourselves in the maze of mountains, the thicker the air became, and snow covered most of the ground. I had to pull my fur-lined cloak around my face to help protect myself from the chill. I even gave into using my magick to divert the air from us as we moved, but when we stopped, I regretted that instantly. I had gotten so used to the bubble of warm air I had kept around us that when I dropped it, I almost fell over as the true temperature slammed into me.

Shivering, I surveyed the small space we made camp within. I first thought it was the mouth of a cave, but as I explored I realized the cave only went so far until I reached a dead end. When I got it to the camp Illera already had placed our wood in a pyramid ready for the fire.

"I need some help," she said, gesturing to the pile before her. "I am going to create some sparks with this." Illera lifted a piece of flint and a bundle of dried straw Cristilia had packed for us. "When I tell you, I want you to direct a small stream of that magick you have into the straw. Once we get smoke, I will transfer it onto the pile of wood. When I do that, pump more air into it until we have ourselves an inferno."

I was stunned. "You know so much about making a fire, I would have thought you had people to make them for you back home."

"I did but that did not mean I never watched and listened."

"Good point," I replied, kneeling before the pile and readying myself.

She stuck the flint until small sparks came into life. We huddled close to keep the cold air from beyond the cave to hinder our attempts. Once she got enough spark onto the bundle of straw, she gave me my cue and I raised a finger, directing air into the bundle for smoke to billowing. Fire soon followed. Before long, we sat before the flames. Feeling coming back to our feet and faces.

"What is it about Cristilia you don't trust?" I questioned, feeding more air into the fire.

Illera broke some dried bread and passed me half. It was soaked in honey and wine, which gave it an incredible aroma. My mouth watered before I put the piece into it.

"I can't put my finger on it. That and Emaline doesn't trust her. I find that Emaline has good instincts."

I shook my head, mouth full. "All she has done is help, not hinder. She is no different to Gallion."

"Can I ask you a question then?"

"Do I have a choice?" I winked.

"Why do you trust her…?"

I sat back, bread forgotten. "I—I can't put my finger on that either. I just do."

She scrunched her lips and hummed. "Somehow I don't think that is an answer."

"Illera, I'm certain we can trust her. Without her, I'd never have found the Keeper. Perhaps we would never have been told about Heart Magick if she didn't bring it up. You weren't in Kandilin when this all kicked off, but Queen Kathine would never have brought up Heart Magick."

"Once we retrieve this Staff and return, then she will have earned my trust."

I raised my hands in defeat. "If that makes you feel better."

She nodded with a sly smile. "It does."

"I am going to get some shut eye for a few hours. Then we can get back out there." Illera pulled the cloak around her and shuffled to the wall of the cave.

"I'll join you. And when we head out, can I fly for a while? You have done your fair share of carrying me."

"I thought you'd never offer." Illera smiled through her cascading blond hair.

TฦIRTY-TWO

ZACRIAH, WAKE UP.

A voice rang out in my mind, blending with the dream I was stuck in. I brushed it off as I ran through the dense jungle as the cloud of darkness swallowed the world behind me. My heart pounded in my chest, my legs burned. I needed to survive. Hadrian was running ahead of me; I needed to reach him.

The roaring of the darkness grew louder the closer it got. My arms and legs grew heavy, as if I was running through wet sand. I couldn't speed up. Hadrian was getting away.

Wake up!

I look up, but I can't find the voice. Is it coming from the darkness?

The world around me melted away, and in the bright light stood Nyah. Her arms were crossed over her chest and her face reflected her displeased stance.

Now.

I bolted up, the dreamland melting away from the realization it was not real. I look around the cave for a sign of the dark cloud, but all I see was Illera snoring with her mouth wide and the flurry of snow as it covered the land beyond the cave.

Nyah? I questioned in my mind.

Your dreams are distracting, you should see someone about them. I should have warned you about sleeping during the day. It is impossible to keep your mind's protection up when you sleep.

She had been there. It was as clear as the day outside that Nyah was within my dream, trying to coax me out of it.

You saw it all?

Unfortunately, yes. It is just your worry for Hadrian?

I think my worries are justified. How is everything back in the palace? I sent my question out to her.

If you mean Hadrian when you say everything, then no improvement. Jasrov has been trialing an abundance of potions and concoctions, but Gallion senses no change.

Disappointment rang threw me.

How is it where you are? I hope you and Illera are getting along.

We are. We just had a rest but will be going off soon. The map suggests we are close. I hope it is right.

Talking about rest, I need to go and take over from Gallion. He has not slept yet. Stay safe and get back as soon as you can. I worry about Hadrian's soul the longer it is lost.

I will try. Please promise me you will do everything you can possibly think of to help Hadrian. If there is even a chance he—

Zac, we are taking care of it. Don't let your mind be clouded. Find the Staff and get back to us. Promise me?

Promise.

I felt Nyah's cold presence vanish. I sagged back to the floor, my back screaming from the discomfort. All I could think about was Hadrian. Even if I found the Staff, how would we use it to help him? I knew my worry would only conceal the desire to find the Keep.

"Illera…" I called over to her.

She shot up. "I'm awake." She wiped something from the corner of her mouth and straightened the piece of hair that was stuck at an angle. "I'm awake!"

"We should get going," I told her but kept the conversation with Nyah to myself. Out of sight, out of mind. I needed to focus fully on the Keep.

Packing camp did not take long. The fire had gone out whilst we slept, so we left. Illera covered the cold wood with a spare cloak from her pack in case we needed to stop here on the way back. This helped lighten the load for the next flight.

When we stepped out of the cave, I realized just how much time we had lost to sleep. What felt like minutes must have been hours, for dusk was upon us. Silently panicking from the loss of time, I shifted and picked Illera up.

I didn't know if it was the sleep that helped my energy or the missing hours, but I reveled in the speed I kept up as I reached new heights and flew ahead. I used new levels of magick to keep the snow from blurring the directions ahead and to keep the cold away. It worked well enough.

CHAPTER
Thirty Three

IT WAS ILLERA who spotted the Keep first.

I was too busy focusing on keeping us from freezing that I only saw the pointed black towers ahead. They blended into the mountain side, but the closer we got, the clearer it became. It was just like the vision the Goddess showed me. Black points like swords cutting into the snow-coated mountains.

Illera pointed vigorously, her mouth moving, but the winds snatching any possibility of me hearing her.

My response was in the change of my flight.

A heavy storm of snow had settled upon us during the flight, which made navigating close to impossible. But a strange tugging in my gut brewed moments before Illera saw the Keep.

Nestled in the mountain face, the Keep was a creature of obsidian towers and sharp points. How this place was ever made this far from paths and so high from the ground was beyond me. The Druid's power was greater than I could imagine.

The Keep was an elegant yet intimidating building. Its sheer size was unprecedented, especially when I landed on the stone walkway beyond its main gates. My feet hit the crumbled stone ground just beyond a sheer drop. Looking down, it seemed that something used to be here. Maybe a bridge, but now, it was split stone covered in snow.

Illera was quiet, her eyes wide and breathing slow.

We both took in the vision before us.

Ahead of us, the midnight gates towered high above, closed. A littering of snow covered the ground before the Keep and the tall spires around us. As the rush of nightly wind burst around, it carried flurries of snow from the ground, twisting into a small cyclone before stilling.

"I cannot believe it," Illera mumbled, taking a step forward. "This is the right place?"

"It is." The same black towers. The very same gates. We had made it.

"It looks empty and forgotten, but it feels alive," Illera said, moving towards it.

A strange emotion vibrated from the walls around us, yet there was no sign of fire light or life. Illera walked for the gates, leaving me to catch up. When she reached them, she pushed, but they did not budge.

"It's locked." Illera punched the door in annoyance. "All this way and we can't even get in."

"Is there not a key hole?" I asked, moving close.

I couldn't see anything that would suggest it was locked. The only mark on their surface was the two brass door rings covered in rust and dust.

Illera stepped backwards. "Not that I can see." She was shouting now over the scream of wind. "You try."

Back in my elven form, I took Illera's place and leaned into the cold metal door. Pushing it, there was no sign of movement. After years of being closed, they seemed to have been sealed from the world.

"I didn't see this coming," Illera said, kicking a pile of snow on the ground. "How hard is it to open a door?"

"Maybe this is part of the curse that was placed on the Keep? The one Cristilia told us about."

Illera shrugged her shoulders. "Last time I checked, you had wings, horns and freckled scales. But I don't see the door opening for you. She did say only a Dragori could open it, but clearly she lied."

The answer smashed into me.

"Illera, you are incredible!" I clapped, placing my hands on the door again and letting my Dragori form come through. My hands morphed before my eyes, stretching into claws and knuckles dusted in scales.

The moment my wings burst through skin and the wind brushed against my curled horn, the doors released a large creak and opened. A burst of wind exploded from the slip in the door and cascaded over us both.

"What is the smell?" Illera complained behind me, covering her face as the air washed over her.

It was stale. It gripped the back of my throat and made me gag. I let go of the door, giving it a final push, and it slammed against a wall inside. The sound vibrated like the deep beat of a drum.

"Shall we go and find out?" I replied, holding my hand to my nose.

"We should stay close. Who knows what has been locked in here this whole time?"

"Illera, the only thing that will harm us is the cold, so let's go in before it claims us."

We passed into the waiting space, Illera close behind. My bravery was an act. Inside, I was aching to turn and run. It was Illera's presence that kept my feet moving forward. The further we walked in, the lesser the light from outside became. Soon we stood in pitch darkness. I felt disorientated, lost in the Keep like a youngling in an unknown world.

"I can't see my own hand before my face," Illera whispered, but the Keep caused her voice to echo louder and louder. "I left the flint back in the cave…"

"We have been in the dark since we found out about the Staff, what difference does this make?" I replied, trying to keep our moral high with some light sarcasm.

"Lead the way then." Illera's hand slipped into mine and we kept moving blindly through the dark.

I kept my spare hand out before me, trailing it against walls and trying to use my sense of touch to guide us. I found closing my eyes helped me concentrate on directing us through touch. Although it was already dark, there was something in the act of giving up that sense that helped us forward.

I only stopped when the smooth stone that grazed beneath out finger tips changed to rough wood. A door.

"Stay close," I muttered as I pushed this new door open. With it, we welcomed the faint night light that illuminated the room beyond. I didn't want to speak, not when our words echoed across the tall walls and increased in volume.

The room beyond had no ceiling, which allowed the view of night to be seen from above. In the faint moonlight, we dropped our hands and moved around the large space, getting used to the oval design.

"This place is too big to stumble around together." Illera's voice carried from the opposite side of the baron room. "We should split up, cover more ground."

Already, we had lost time navigating the dark just to find this room.

"Wait," I said. "We should wait out for morning and hope the sun reaches into every dark corner of this place. Then we split up."

"Even you don't want to do that, and we need to find it. Zacriah, we are close."

"Fine," I replied. "Just be careful, okay? I have a feeling Emaline would not want to hear that anything happened to you."

Illera didn't hide the smile at Emaline's mention. "I appreciate your warnings, but I will be fine." She flashed the sword as she pulled it from the scabbard. "If you find anything, shout."

"Is now a bad time to announce that I have a fear of dark places?" I added as she almost left. My hands shook at my sides.

"The dark can't hurt you, Zacriah," she said with a smile, slipping from the room.

"It's what is hiding in the dark that can…" Illera was no longer near to hear my reply.

∽

TIME SLIPPED AWAY with each footfall in the waiting dark before me. My eyes had adjusted slightly to the dark, which helped make out some shapes as I lost myself in the Keep. I walked through the maze of corridors, tripped up stairs and walked into furnishings. My nose was full of dust, and my body was numb from the cold that rushed from the many glassless windows.

I could only imagine how warm this Keep would've been when it was full of life and flame. How the many druids would not feel the cold of the surrounding mountains as they were busy plotting against the elves.

Just thinking about those evil beings and the unearthly powers they once possessed sent a shiver crawling up my spine. I pulled my fur-lined cloak closer and pushed on.

It was the sixth room I ventured into that gave me hope.

As I pushed the oaken door wide, the room burst into light, stealing a gasp from my lungs. In utter surprise, I stumbled in, taking in the rush of light that sprang on each hanging bowl of flame. Magick. I knew it. I could feel it in the air that whispered around me. I was close; It told me so.

I closed the door behind me, wondering if I should call for Illera. But I didn't. I wanted to be sure this was it.

Unlike most of the oval rooms I had entered, this was created in the shape of a horse shoe. It's dark, towering walls raised far up. So much so I couldn't see the ceiling in the shadows of the walls. Curved stone arches opened on one side of the room. The view was of rolling mountains and night; it made me dizzy on my feet.

On the other side was a stone podium of some kind, tall enough to be the same size as me. As I got closer to it, I could see the marble's textured white veins running through black stone. The same slab of marble the Goddess showed me.

It was cold to the touch. I half expected an opening to be on the side I couldn't see. But as I walked around it, there was nothing. It was just a large slab of stone. I knocked on it thrice. It was hollow.

I knew in my heart and mind the Staff was resting inside its prison of marble. I could feel its hum singing to me. Taunting me.

Trying to move the marble slab was impossible. I lifted, pushed, kicked, but nothing happened. It didn't budge an inch.

"Illera." My shout got louder and louder as it echoed up the walls. "Illera!"

I would need her mind and muscle to help work out this puzzle.

Silently, I waited for her response. I even tried to quiet my breathing to really listen out if she heard me. I was about to shout again when I heard footsteps. Good. The Staff was so close.

"I think I have found it," I said, sparing a glance behind me as Illera walked in.

As she stepped into the light, I saw her stark white face and the shine of firelight against a blade pressed to her neck.

Fear collided with my blood. I brought my arms up, calling for my air as the face of her attacker came into the light.

"Cristilia?" I gasped.

Her laugh was deep and earthy. Her smile pointed and eyes piercing green. She looked like Cristilia but was slightly shorter than I remembered. She lacked Cristilia's poise.

"Zacriah, don't—" Illera was cut off by the blade that pressed farther into her throat.

Not wasting a moment longer, I punched a fist towards Cristilia. The roar of my air as it shot forwards deafened the room. Cristilia raised her spare hand high and the stone ground raised to meet it. My wind slammed into the stone barrier.

The floor shook. I stumbled into the marble slab, hitting it so hard I saw stars. The entire room groaned as it moved, dust and rubble exploding into the air. Then a voice caused my blood to turn to ice.

"I do love a reunion." The Druid moved into the room and stood beside Cristilia and Illera. Red blood ran down Illera's neck and stained her cloak. "I would have preferred all three of you to have been here as planned, but I'll settle for one."

His milky skin was covered in sigils and marks, highlighting his hollow cheeks and narrow face. His round ears were stained with ink, his eyes seeping shadows of black. Seeing the Druid in this true form horrified my senses.

I pushed myself from the floor, reaching for the hilt of my sword.

"Cristilia, why?" I shouted, preparing for another volley of wind to send her way. I wanted answers first.

Everyone distrusted her but me.

The Druid raised a hand before she could answer. "I too have asked Cristilia why. Why fail me? In truth, I blame her skittishness for ruining my plan. It was simple, tell them about the Staff, have them walk into my web together like the worthless creatures they are. And I can have all three. Killing three birds with one stone."

I looked to Illera, whose eyes were pinned wide, then to Cristilia, who didn't flinch as the Druid insulted her.

"How rude of me. Let me introduce you to your sister of sorts." The Druid wrapped a short arm around Cristilia. "And between you and me, don't call her by that name again. She doesn't like her blood sister very much, isn't that right?"

The girl nodded. The girl who was not Cristilia.

"I will kill you for what you have done." My voice deepened, the tone even surprising me. I let the shift happen right before the Druid's eyes. Let him see what will tear him apart.

"I am sure you want to, but then how will you ever help your Prince retrieve his soul?"

His words stopped me from pouncing.

"I have the Staff. I do *not* need you," I growled.

"You are empty handed, dear boy." He raised a marked hand towards the slab of marble. "Threaten my life again…" The Druid's hand disappeared into the folds of his black cloak and soon pulled out an orb of glass. Within it, blue fire danced and spun. "And I might just drop this. Then your Prince's soul will be lost forever."

"You wouldn't dare. You need the Dragori."

"Calling my bluff. I must admit you have grown in confidence since our last encounter." He put the orb back into his cloak. "I am impressed. Very impressed."

"Marthil, release the deserter and go and introduce yourself."

The girl, Marthil, pushed Illera to the ground without more than a second glance. Illera scrambled across the floor, away from her, as Marthil walked over to me. With each footstep, the ground shook. The halo of dark curls that crowned her head caused her green eyes to stand out. Her ears held two points each. She was Morthi, just like Cristilia.

"Stay back," I threatened, opening my wings wide in warning. Another step and I would end her.

Marthil just smiled, displaying her yellow stained teeth. A muddy smell pouring from her mouth. She raised a hand across the space between us and I noticed the heaps of dirt embedded beneath her nails.

"Master has told me many stories about you." She even sounded like Cristilia. "I don't like stories very much."

Her hand hung in the air. I refused to take it.

She dropped it and turned back to the Druid, slamming one foot on the ground in protest. "He shows me no respect. You told me they would!"

He raised his hands and tilted his head to the side. "Now, now, Marthil. They will learn to love you. You will see."

This interaction between them both was strange. Like a father to his daughter, calming her amidst a tantrum. But Marthil was no younger than I. Her weathered face aged her, but her dark skin still glowed with youth.

"If not, you uphold your promise and let me grind them. That is what you said!"

"No, no grinding, my girl." He walked over to her and ran a hand down her cheek. She gave into it like a cat. "We need him… for now."

She opened her piercing eyes slowly and smiled my way.

The Druid looked over Marthil's hulking shoulder to me. He looked at me like he owned me, a possessive glare that cut deep into me.

I held my ground, risking a glance at Illera, who was moving for the door. She was trying to escape.

"What do you want?" I kept my voice as calm as I could against the anger. Anything to help Illera escape.

"What I have wanted from the start. Respect. Revenge. Call me greedy, for my list goes on. Now, shall we retrieve the Staff, so I can get into my new home?" The Druid clapped his hands. "It takes more than one Dragori to break the curse of those vile elves put on my parents' home. If Hadrian and Emaline would have made it here with you, it would have been much easier to retrieve it, but we have Marthil, so it should work."

I looked to the girl again. Marthil, the final Dragori. Cristilia's sister. All this time, Cristilia had been getting us here because she knew. She knew what was at stake.

A knowing smile passed on his lips. "Marthil. Remember what I told you to do?"

"How could I not? You drone on about it enough." She held no fear of the Druid.

"Good girl." Her response thrilled him.

"I will not help you," I said.

"Oh, you will." The Druid laughed. He turned to Illera, who was close to leaving the room, and raised his hands. Black smoke seeped from his palm and encased Illera. It lifted her from the ground. She floated over to him, squirming and turning within his dark cocoon. "I have wondered how long it would take for someone to die through strangulation. Let us see if this gives you the motivation you need."

Before my eyes, the smoke hold around Illera settled and her body dropped. Before she hit the ground, she came to a stop as the black smoke gathered around her neck.

My panic set in as her face turned blue and the whites of her eyes red.

"Quick now, Zacriah."

TĐIRTY FOUR

"TELL ME WHAT to do!" I screamed as Illera's legs kicked out in the air. Her hands tried to grapple with the smoke that held her in the air. As I choked out my words, Illera lost consciousness. "Tell me!"

"I knew I could show you the importance of following my orders," the Druid said.

"Please," I pleaded.

"Marthil, you know what to do."

The girl pulled my arm with strength that ripped me from the ground. I almost fell as she dragged me to the marble slab. When we both stood before it, her hand morphed into sharp claws and scaled skin. Before I could react, she raked her claw down my palm until my blood spilled across the stone floor. As the sting made my head spin, she cut her own palm until black blood joined with my red. Then, with brute force, she slammed my palm and hers onto the slab's surface.

"Your blood is as important as your soul," the Druid said. "Very important indeed."

A hiss of air sounded beneath us, brushing against our feet. The marble slab rose, lifting from the ground until it hovered high above us both.

"Give it to me," the Druid shouted, pointing to the object that spun slowly in midair before us. The Staff of

Light, a knot of dark wood with an obsidian stone rested neatly like a crown.

There, right before me, was the key to healing Hadrian. But to take it for myself would mean sacrificing Illera's life. I didn't waste another moment. Sticking my hand into the open prison and taking the Staff, I threw it with the biggest force towards the Druid. No longer in need of Illera, he flicked his hand, and she dropped to the ground. The sound of her body as it collided with the stone ground made me shout in discomfort.

The Druid effortlessly plucked the Staff from the air and smiled, releasing a pleasured breath. "After all these years, you have returned to me."

He spoke to the Staff like it understood him.

In the distraction, I took my only chance. I spun around, widening my wings so they slammed into Marthil. She stumbled back, the ground rumbling, but I moved quicker. I clapped my hands together, sending a blast of wind her way. It collided with her until she flew across the room and slammed into the stone wall.

With a breath, I called for my wind and reached for the Druid whose attention was on the Staff. With speed of lightning, he raised the Staff before him and slammed it into the ground. It made no noise, but its effect was obvious. The breath in my lungs was snatched from my body, and I toppled over. I clawed at my throat, trying to retrieve my breath, but I couldn't find it.

"Try a move like that again, and I will let Marthil show you how she treats *bad* people."

My breath came rushing back to me as the Druid pulled the Staff towards him.

"She seems to get along with you just fine," I shouted, slicing a hand towards the floor in another rushed attempt at hurting him. My body jerked backwards, and I flew off my feet. Stars burst behind my head as it connected with the floor.

I looked up and saw two of Marthil standing above me, fists clicking together. Her devilish grin spurred me on. I kicked up, using my winds to push myself from the floor. I felt my foot connect with her stomach and watched as she stumbled back.

"Enough!" Marthil screamed, and the ground copied. Rage plastered her face red as she raised her hands and the ground raised with them. I watched the snaking crack spread from beneath her feet towards me and the rubble that raised from the gap. The pelts of dirt and stone hovered around her as her hands shook with anticipation. I knew what was coming next.

Her hands burst forward, and with it, the earth followed. My wings wrapped themselves around me, cocooning me in leather protection. But it didn't stop the pain. As the pelts rained down on me, I felt them rip into my wings, cutting and slashing.

"Marthil, you have made your point," the Druid said, voice calm and unbothered, as if he didn't want her to stop at all.

The attack of stone ceased at his words.

"We have the Staff and Zacriah. I think it's time we pay our home a visit."

Marthil's voice was still speckled with anger. "I want to be the one to kill him when the time comes."

"Where are you taking me?" I coughed.

"Since Olderim was taken from me, I think it's time I take Lilioira from those who spoiled my plans."

Lilioira. No.

"They will kill you the minute you step foot through the city gates," I shouted, my wings stinging.

The Druid shook his head, twisting the knotted wood Staff in his hands. The black crystal embedded at the crest a piece of sharp obsidian caught the moonlight across its dull surface. "They can try. They will fail. If you think I am walking in without insurance of some kind, you are mistaken, my boy. Marthil, prepare our guests for the journey."

Marthil shot forward and pulled me from the ground. She yanked my arms behind my back and something tight wrapped around my two wrists. Whatever it was squeezed and hardened. It felt like a bracelet of stone. There was no point in fighting it, my wings were useless, and whatever power the Staff held also made my magick weak. I gave into my elven form and sagged in Marthil's hold.

Illera was still unconscious on the ground. When Marthil walked over to her, I willed her to stay down. Please be alive, I pleaded.

Marthil checked on Illera.

It all happened so quickly. Illera burst into black shadow, disorienting Marthil. In the time it took me to gasp, Illera was her white lion again, and she pounced through dissipating shadow and sunk her jaw into Marthil's arm. Marthil scream was so loud I shied away. Black blood stained Illera's snowy face as it poured from the wound and covered the floor. Marthil fell back in time for the Druid to slam the end of the Staff into Illera's temple. She crumpled once again.

"I never liked cats," he spat. "Marthil, get up. Now!"

Marthil's face was paled as she clung onto her arm. I gagged on the floor as I took in the extent of damage. Muscle and ripped flesh hung in chunks, dripping black blood. Her entire body was shaking. I tried to wriggle free from my constraints, but I couldn't break them.

I needed to get out. I needed to get Illera and leave. But my wings were in tatters and the pain was almost unbearable.

In my peripheral, movement caught my attention. The Druid raised the Staff and the black stone seemed to pulse. I felt it in my bones as it expanded and contracted. The power was strong; my eyes became heavy.

Marthil howled as the Druid placed the crystal into her wound, and her entire arm turned black. Steam hissed at the touch and the wounds slowed their bleeding. Her breathing shallowed, and her eyes rolled back in her head as the Druid mumbled into her ear. The marks on his body seeped darkness as he placed whatever spell he spilled from his wretched mouth.

In moments, the bleeding had stopped completely, and Marthil was standing, flexing her healed arm. Skin had knitted together, covering the bite completely.

"Let me grind her," Marthil sang, stepping toward the lion that caused her pain. "We don't need her. Let me kill her. Someone. Something."

Marthil was childish when she spoke.

"Take my word, as soon as we reach our home, she is all yours. I gift her as your play thing, do as you will with her. But first, we must get there."

"Don't touch her!" I shouted, my attempt at keeping my voice serious failed me.

"Oh, my boy, has the severity of our situation finally sunk in? Have you just realized the truth of what is about to happen?" He walked over to me slowly, the Staff hitting the ground with each step. "I am going to take the city as my own. In truth, I am glad my attempts at controlling Olderim have failed. It was a weak city with equally weak inhabitants. Niraen elves were a bad choice even after I gifted *them* with a unique skill. But Lilioira is the home of the most powerful

Alorian elves and the strongest soldiers in this world. All of which will belong to me, thanks to you." He stopped before me, a tall shadow of dread. "We leave now."

I needed to warn Nyah and give her time to get as many people out of Lilioira as she could.

Nyah, leave the city. The Druid has the Staff. He is coming. I sent my awareness out, crashing into her mind.

As if the Druid sensed it, he turned back on me like a snake, whipping his head around and with it, his hand. My cheek stung as he back handed me.

"Do that again and I will let Marthil have her way with my traitor right now," the Druid shouted. I looked to Illera and Marthil, who toyed with three rugged stones, which spun above her hand. "Do I make myself clear?"

I nodded slowly. I only hoped Nyah heard me. I could feel her cold presence requesting entry in my mind, but I kept my mental wall strong.

"Now we wait for our informant to open our means of travel," the Druid mused, staring at the dark wall to our left. He closed his eyes briefly and his marks flashed with darkness. Then a rush of wind coughed into existence and a jeweled hand paused through the shadows of the wall.

"Marthil, I trust you can take your play thing. Leave your brother to me." He grabbed my shoulder with a vise like grip, then we moved towards the shadow and reaching hand.

His touch pained me. I looked toward his hand as he yanked me forward and spied four rings, each made of gold. They drained me, pulling my magick into his shadow.

My eyes grew heavy, but I tried to fight the urge to give in. I needed to stay awake.

We passed into the shadow. The floor dropped from beneath me and the cold of the Druid keep was replaced for the fire warmth of Queen Kathine's throne room.

CHAPTER

TDIRTY FIVE

FOR ONE WEIGHTLESS moment, all I saw was darkness. It lasted for no longer than a blink of my eye. With a great tug from the Druid, I stepped through the circlet of shadow into a familiar room.

The first person I saw as we stepped into the throne room was Jasrov. He stood beyond Cristilia, who was guiding the Druid through the portal. It was her hand the Druid had a hold of. Jasrov was shouting, but all I could hear was white noise. My vision kept blurring. Jasrov pulled something from the wall beside him and rushed forward, his mouth open in a silent scream.

He passed Cristilia and reached the Druid. The steel blade crumbled at impact, folding in on itself as it came into contact with the Druid's stomach. I tried to shout for Jasrov to run, but my voice would not work. I watched Jasrov's face morph into confusion and look up into the Druid's dark gaze.

The world seemed to slow. The Druid dropped me, and all sound came rushing back at the lack of the gold's touch. I slumped to the ground as the Druid wrapped his large hand around Jasrov throat and lifted him into the air. Jasrov dangled, hand clenched around his throat. The sword he had picked up clattered to the floor.

Marthil clapped from somewhere behind me.

The Druid did not speak. The only noise shared between them was the deafening snap of Jasrov's neck as the Druid violently twisted. All the life in Jasrov's eyes blinked out of existence, and his mouth drooped open before he was discarded to the floor. Dead weight, he was thrown carelessly across the room where he landed in a heap.

My eyes filled with tears, and my breath was snatched from my lungs. I stared helplessly at Jasrov's lifeless body where he lay, his face looking directly at me. I tried to form his name on my lips, but it died alongside him. He did not blink; he did not move.

He was no more.

A piercing cry lit the room, and I dragged my gaze away from Jasrov to see Bell. She stepped out from beside one of the large vases where she had hidden.

"A familiar, what a waste."

Bell's head turned from side to side as she looked upon her elf. I could see the confusion painted on her small red face. She ran over to him and stopped beside his head.

In that moment, I cared no mind for the Druid and what he did. Not in that moment. My heart shattered into a million pieces as Bell began licking the leaking tears from Jasrov's face. She lapped them up, cleaning his paling face. Then she lay down beside him, curling up into a ball in the crock of Jasrov's broken neck. I watched her small chest rise and fall. Then after a final shuddering breath, it ceased. Her final breath was peaceful as she joined her master.

"I am sorry," I heard someone cry.

I snapped my head towards it.

Cristilia was kneeling beneath the Druid, her usual calm exterior shattered. Her hands clasped together, begging, fear evident as her façade shattered.

"Stand," the Druid commanded.

"You promised. You said no one would die," Cristilia cried. "I just want my sister."

Marthil stepped forward, dragging Illera by her legs. Cristilia looked up at her mirror image and stopped her begging. She clutched at her chest.

"Sister." The word was no more than a whispered breath. "Marthil, it's me. We are together, finally."

"Would you just look at me, bringing family together," the Druid said.

Marthil regarded Cristilia like a stranger. Her gaze spoke a million words. That was a look of someone who had no idea who the person that stood before her was. They were sisters, that was clear. A spitting image. But Marthil looked beyond Cristilia with no more thought.

"Who is this who claims to be my sister?" Marthil asked to the Druid. "The woman who left me alone, allowed my own people exile me?"

"The very one."

Marthil cut her gaze back to Cristilia, who was shaking with sobs.

"I just wanted to help you, everything I have done was to finally help you," Cristilia cried out.

"Let me kill her." Marthil scaled face twisted in anger as she shouted. The room shook under her anger.

"No, sister. I never... whatever he told you is a lie—" Cristilia ran forward. "I helped you. I did everything he said to help you, to get the Staff. It will fix you."

The moment she got close to Marthil, she was backhanded across the room. Her body slumped into the wall. When she looked up, a trickle of black blood ran down from the corner of her lip.

The Druid, visually pleased with this altercation, reached for Marthil to stop her from attacking. "We have time for this la—"

The doors to the throne room burst open. Frothing water greeted us, knocking Cristilia, Marthil and the Druid to the ground. It did not touch Jasrov or me, nor did it reach Illera where she was dropped.

Gushing azure waves spun like a vortex around them, keeping them to the ground.

"Emaline!" I muttered. I took the moment to try and get up, but my body did not respond.

"And here I was thinking our last encounter put you off, Druid." Emaline spat his title.

He had no chance to respond as he spun over and over in the prison of water.

"End this," Queen Kathine said. I had not noticed as she stood in silver armor, two curved swords raised in her hands behind Emaline.

"How dare you step foot in my kingdom without invitation, Druid," the Queen screamed. "Prepare to meet your end."

I tried to locate the Druid in the rush of water. I finally spotted his dark, wet hair. He raised the Staff and brought it down into the water. I watched in horror as the water split like a curtain, moving away from him.

Free of Emaline's grasp, he stood tall and confronted the Queen.

"Why would I need an invitation into my own home?"

Emaline's face was pure shock as her water receded from the room. I could see her concentration as she tried to regain control, but the power of the Staff was stronger than her magick. It pulsed with dark light, emanating from the stone that crowned it.

As Cristilia stood from the water and helped Marthil up, Queen Kathine's voice filled with rage. They both dripped with water, hair in wet clumps and face streaked with it.

"I trusted you, witch." Queen Kathine's voice was pinned for Cristilia. Kathine pointed one sword at the Druid and the other to Cristilia, who pinched her eyes closed.

"Family comes first, Kathine, you should know that more than anyone."

"It would seem I do not know what you mean by family, Cristilia. Not the type you have at least." Queen Kathine raised the curved blade up higher in threat. "What I do know is you will look beautiful with my blade pierced through your neck. I always admired your appearance when dressed in silver."

Cristilia dropped her arms to her side, and two dark axes burst from her shadow. She sprang up, legs apart, but her attempt was weak. Queen Kathine growled and moved to swing the sword, but the Druid called out.

"I am afraid, Queen Kathine, I cannot let you kill Cristilia. As much of a pain as she is, that was a gift only her sister can have." He stepped forward, dragging the Staff across the ground. With each step, the floor dried of water in steams of hissing puffs.

"Another step and your head will be mine," Queen Kathine sneered.

This was her home, the birthplace of her people and children. I could see the territorial nature burning off her.

The Druid tutted, causing the skin on my arms to prickle.

"I have waited in the shadows for a long time, Kathine. My time has kept a fire burning within me, a passion for control. If you think I will let you stop me, then you are wrong. Now, I think it is time you show your new King some respect." He raised the Staff with both hands and brought it down to the ground. As it touched the marble floor of the throne room, he spoke a final word.

"Bow."

The throbbing of the Staff's power pushed me down until my forehead touched the cold marble. Both Emaline and Queen Kathine dropped to the floor as well. Discomfort spread along their face as their knees collided with ground.

"That is much better. Marthil…" The Druid turned his hand behind him and Marth stepped away from her sister, who was also forced beneath the Staff's power. "Bring down the gates. I do not want anyone leaving or coming without me knowing from now on."

"Please?" Mathril's voice crackled.

I didn't miss the slight squint of the Druid's eyes as he looked at Marthil. Then, to my surprise, he replied.

"Please."

Marthil nodded and moved for the door, flexing the wings on her back. In the light of the throne room, I got a better look at her. The surface of her wings was grey, like the face of a mountain, curtains of leather and spikes. Her horns reminded me of antlers, tall and imposing with many protrusions. Marthil embodied her element.

"And if they put up a fight?" Marthil called over her shoulder.

"If they try and stop you, grind them all."

Marthil cracked a smile. "Oh, I will." The floor groaned with her excitement.

Emaline cried in discomfort, clearly wanting to stop her, but the power of the Staff kept her down.

Marthil's large wings began to pump, and she lifted into the air. Raising a clawed hand, the throne was ripped from the ground until it hovered at Marthil's side. She threw it effortlessly towards the window until it shattered and rained glass over the room. Then she flew into the night, disappearing to complete the Druid's deed.

"Please…" Queen Kathine pleaded, her body shaking as she held her bow. "Do not harm my people."

"Kathine, enlighten me as to why would I bring harm to those who now belong to me? You are mistaken. I will treat them in ways you have never dreamed. They will help me take this world back and reclaim the legacy that their ancestors worked hard to eradicate."

"Druid," I shouted, trying to wiggle into a sitting position. "As long as we are alive we will work against you, do you understand?"

"Oh, be quiet, boy. Your voice is grating on my nerves." He moved the Staff in my direction and flicked it down. Instantly, my voice was pulled from my body, rendering me speechless.

"And you will now refer to me as King. King Gordex. Is that clear? It goes for you all."

Gordex. A name that registered in the back of my mind.

Like the chime of a bell, realization of where I had heard it slammed into me.

Gallion's mentioned the Druid Gordex who was the leader of the keep in the mountains. But it was not possible, he should have died. Even after years, the Druid before me looked no older than me. A child.

"You hide behind a name that is not yours," Queen Kathine said.

"Not hide, no. Thrive. My father's name is mine to claim since your grandmother was the one who drove him to his death. Isn't that right, Kathine?" Gordex sang. He walked to where she kneeled and bent down. Pressing the knotted crown of the Staff on the Queen's shoulder. "Now, call me King and I will spare you."

"Only in death will I refer to you in such a way," Queen Kathine seethed.

Gordex's face morphed into pleasure as the lob of phlegm splashed against his dark robes.

"Act like the woman you are, not a common slob," he jibbed.

"I am no woman; I am a Queen."

On cue, a blade flew from behind the Queen and aimed straight for Gordex. A blur of silver embedded up to the hilt in the Druid's chest.

The next moments happened in slow motion.

Nyah flipped over the kneeling Queen and landed in the room. Gordex glanced down at the dagger then up at the girl who threw it. His lips curled and turned white. Spit linked his lips as his mouth opened in a pained shout.

Nyah took three bounding leaps toward the Druid and slammed her hand onto his head.

Her eyes rolled into her hair line and the Druid's turned coal black. His body seized, and hands tensed as they battled mentally.

The Staff clattered to the floor, releasing us from its hold. Queen Kathine sprang from the ground and ran for Cristilia, who was cowering in the corner of the room. Before she reached her, Cristilia faded into the shadow of the room, practically rolling into a portal she opened to escape. A string of curses slipped from the Queen's lips.

Emaline reached Illera and stood above her, readying to fight anyone that came close.

"Slam your hands on the ground as hard as you can." Queen Kathine stood above me. "Break the stone that binds them."

Her face was blotched red, but her crown had stayed in place.

I tried breaking the stone bindings Marthil had encased my wrists with, but I couldn't. Over and over I slammed them down against the marble floor, and with each hit, pain shot up my arms.

Nyah made a noise; her face showed pain. Whatever was happening between her and the Druid Gordex was coming to an end. I could taste it in the back of my throat, copper like blood.

A noise in their direction started as a purr and built into a deafening roar. The entire room shook. I lost my balance and spilled to the floor, landing inches from Jasrov and Bell's lifeless forms. My head rang, and my vision blurred. As I came to, I saw the Druid standing above Nyah who was on the floor beneath him, Staff pinned down on her chest.

Red blood leaked from her nose and ears. Dust covered us all as the earthquake settled. Once the noise dulled, I could hear the screams of the city. Panicked cries that sang across the world.

Gordex was breathless from Nyah's mental attack but showed no signs of physical damage besides the blade embedded in his chest. He paid it no mind, not until he pulled it free and threw it to the ground. I expected to see blood, but only black shadow spilled from the gash until it closed entirely.

"Your resistance is wasted; the city is mine."

CHAPTER

TDIRTY SIX

I DIDN'T QUESTION Gordex when a group of shadowbeings strolled into the throne room. Covered in golden blood, their vacant eyes were dazed as their puppeteer gave them orders.

We were kneeled in a line and bound in ties and chains. It was pointless to fight against their strength. Illera was awake, a trail of red blood dampened her hair line and tinged her blond hair ruby. She was disoriented and panicked when she shifted back into her elven form and a shadowbeing waited above her. She tried to kick out, but he lifted her effortlessly from the ground and brought her into line.

Emaline tried to comfort her, but her tied arms made it difficult. I could see her burning desire to reach out and console Illera.

Queen Kathine had been gagged, stopping her relentless attempts at conversation with the Druid. Although, I wouldn't have called her screaming and slurs conversation.

Gordex did not speak to us. He only spoke to his shadowbeings, then to Marthil, who walked through the broken doors of the throne room like it was her own.

"The gates are down. The city is trapped," Marthil said, wings held close into her strong back.

"From the sounds of the city, you had some fun." Gordex laughed, echoing the screams beyond the windows.

"They tried to stop me, so I ground them all." Marthil smiled, clicking her knuckles together.

It made sense as to who these shadowbeings had been. I looked at them again, noticing their Alorian uniforms, which were mangled and covered in dirt. Guards of the gate who Marthil had killed and allowed Gordex to raise as his own. Then my eyes landed on one guard, Rowan. Her eyes seeped shadows, as if her body was hollow. A cavern of empty darkness. Her mouth was slack, and her skin held a pale hue. She had guided us into this city she once protected. Now, she is the very thing she fought so gallantly to stop.

If only my hands were free, I could have used my magick to expel the shadow from their bodies like I had in the temple.

"Fetch me the Prince of Flames. I think it is time you meet your other sibling." Gordex waved a hand.

"I do not like fire, Druid. Send someone else." Marthil disregarded his command.

There was something about her willingness to refuse him that gave me hope.

"No, my dear, he will no longer be a problem. Bring him to me," Gordex commanded again.

Marthil bowed her head and left. As she walked away, she passed two shadowbeings who pulled Jasrov's and Bell's bodies and discarded them to the corner of the room. I could hear Nyah's heavy snivels as she watched on.

As if her reaction annoyed Gordex, he turned on her sharply.

"Enough of that! If I sense any of you talking again, I will rip your throats out," he growled.

But Nyah had not spoken? I glanced up and noticed Queen Kathine look away. They must have shared a silent word through their link.

Knowing Marthil had gone for Hadrian, my heart picked up its speed. I held out hope Gallion would be with him, ready to protect him as he promised. But I had seen Marthil's magick and knew Gallion would fail under her power. And what of the Queen's wife and children? Where were they? If only I could communicate with Nyah, she would have an idea how to get out of this. At least I hoped.

"Why…" Queen Kathine muttered, spitting out the cloth that gagged her.

Gordex released a sigh. "I have been waiting for someone to ask me that. For years, I have played the answer over in my mind, rehearsing it so it's perfect. Why you ask? Why not? Was it not your people who band together to destroy mine? Killing the history and memory of the druids, as if it a just act. I have one word that captures all of my emotions. Revenge. I have waited in the shadows of this vile world for years, waiting for the time when I can avenge my people. My family. And finally, the birth of the Dragori signaled the start of my own quest."

He paced before our line, hands twirling as he told his tale.

The treatment of his people was unkind. Even I could see that. This was our punishment for our ancestors' actions.

"Is there not a way we can live in harmony? Bring forth a new time of druids and elves?" Queen Kathine pleaded.

"Oh, Kathine, we are beyond that. I am truly the last left. In an ideal world, I may have accepted, but you are years too late."

"Then why all of this?" I spoke up, trying to make sense.

"It is time I bring the druids back into this world. My people have learned from their past mistakes. Giving life to the Dragori, their creation, allowed the Goddess to take them from us. So, I will not give them life, I will raise them in death. A council of five; and I think I may have found my first member." Gordex gazed towards Jasrov's body.

"No," Nyah screamed, trying to stand.

"Quiet!" Gordex shouted louder and raised the Staff.

"One vital part of history your people removed was the mention of the element spirit. With the combined powers of the four Dragori, this Staff will hold their powers and allow me to work against your precious Goddess. I already have two souls, all I need is the final two."

He looked to Emaline and me.

"With your Heart Magick, I will finally restore the trapped souls of my ancestors and give them new bodies. Powerful bodies."

"Impossible," Queen Kathine muttered.

"Not entirely." Cristilia faded through shadow back into the room. Her courage refreshed as she saw us all bound.

"You…" Illera growled.

"Yes, me." Cristilia bowed. "Zacriah, being untouched by Heart Magick, you were able to bring down the cursed barrier of the Keep."

"Thus, allowing myself and Marthil inside," Gordex added.

"The Staff of Light is no tool for the elves, no. It was a prison our ancestors created to keep the souls of the druids they slew trapped inside."

"And now you have it…" Queen Kathine whispered, eyes wide in defeat.

"We have the power to raise them once more." Gordex words were final.

The entire room chilled as the Druid's plans were revealed. After the weeks of guessing his motivation, I would never have thought of this.

"When evening greets us tomorrow, I will raise my brothers and sisters and create a new world where the scales of power finally tip toward the druids. And the best part is that you have no way of stopping me."

Thunder clashed outside the smashed wall. A burst of light that illuminated the horror of the world beyond. A world that was going to change. Forever.

∽

AS WE WERE dragged through the torn halls of the palace, I could see the blush pinks of dawn. We were pulled in a line, each with two shadowbeings holding us to stop our attempts to escape. We passed through an open pavilion that gave way to the view of a city in smoke. Queen Kathine was in front of me, and her shoulders shook as she took in the destruction of the city. The air was tainted with blood and destruction.

At first, I didn't know where we were being taken to. Cristilia was guiding us, her white skirt stained as she floated over rubble. We didn't stop moving until we took steps down into the belly of the palace. It was dark and smelled rank. I knew the atmosphere of a prison even without visiting one before. The smooth stone walls were replaced with rough brick and the floor became uneven and damp.

"One in a cell." Cristilia turned for us, gesturing to the line of rusted cages that nestled in a row at the side of the dark room.

"For you," Cristilia said as Emaline passed. In a flash movement something was wrapped around her wrist. No. My mind grew cold with panic. No.

The gold band clipped easily around her thick wrist, stilling any chance of her using her magick. "That will keep you quiet. I even have one for you, Zacriah. I have heard you are well versed with these accessories."

"Why would you do this?"

I tried to pull away, but Cristilia spun me around, so my back faced her. I felt her touch on my arm, then the heavy weight of the gold band as she clipped it around my wrist.

"The Druid promised safety for my sister. I would do anything for her. Know that I believed he would not harm anyone. But, as long as she is safe, he can have his way with the rest of you. Part of me feels sorry, but then again, why would I? Only you should me kindness, Zacriah. The rest of you can burn."

I was pushed forward and stumbled toward an open cell. As I passed through, the gate slammed shut behind me, and Cristilia had her face pressed between two bars. Her eyes were wild.

"Once the gold has time to work away at you, your Heart Magick will be free. Soon, the Druid will raise his army, and the need for you and your Dragori siblings will be no more," she sneered.

She turned away, but I fought out my words through the draining of my strength.

"And your twin? Will you allow the Gordex to dispose of her when he no longer has need for her?"

Cristilia stopped walking away. In that moment, I could sense the weak chain in her armor.

She didn't respond. Instead, she waved to the shadowbeings and said, "If they talk, cause them pain."

Then she swept up the dark stairs and left us each locked in our own prison of silence.

CHAPTER

Tђirty Seven

WE KEPT QUIET for a grand total of a few seconds. Emaline began screaming, and Queen Kathine's fist connected with the stone wall at the back of her cell. Over and over she punched until her knuckles shredded. But she didn't stop. Nyah was silent with her eyes closed, and Illera was trying to still Emaline's angered shouts. If Emaline was feeling the same as I, then the tingling discomfort in her wrist was growing. I could feel the energy and magick being drained from me once again.

I saw the guarding shadowbeings move and tried to warn the group, but I was too late. They faded through the bars of our cell like ghosts. The noises silenced as they grew close, and I shied away as one raised an Alorian steel dagger to my arm.

Once the cell blocks were silent again, they turned and left.

I closed my eyes and risked my next move. If Gordex was close, he would sense it. But what more could he do to me? He already expressed his need for the Dragori for the evening. He wouldn't kill me before then, I knew it.

Tell me Gallion made it out.

He has.

Thank the Goddess, I thought. *And he took Hadrian with him?*

He did. Her answers were short. I could feel the sadness in her voice.

I wanted to scream with pleasure. I could only imagine how Gordex and Marthil would react when they found Hadrian missing.

I hate to burst your bubble, but Gordex has Hadrian's soul. I have seen his plans. With Hadrian's vacant body here or not, it will still happen.

My mood dampened. Nyah was right; Gordex had shown me the orb concealed in his robes. If that truly was Hadrian's soul, we were in more trouble than I realized.

I am sorry.

Don't be.

Jasrov sacrificed himself, Nyah. He was so brave. You would have been proud.

I am—will always be proud of him. He was not a fighter, but his strength came from something much more than using a sword or fighting.

I could feel her presence as it shied away from mine.

You really cared for him, didn't you?

I do.

She shut off from me, her awareness severed mine so hard I stumbled back into myself. Her refusal to regard in him in past tense broke my heart.

Without light, it was difficult to keep track of time. It felt like I'd been in this cell for hours by the time I heard steps coming down the stairs. The gold band had driven me to exhaustion, and my throat felt as if I'd swallowed a handful of glass. I barely had enough energy to look up to see the small figure that slipped into the cell room unnoticed by the guards.

I rolled over on the floor, looking to the rest of our group, and no one else seemed to notice our guest.

Crawling on all fours, I dragged myself towards the bars of my cell, trying to get a better look. Nyah noticed me and whispered to catch my attention, but I was too caught up in the small shadow behind the guards to look back.

Tiv. Flame light from a hanging lantern close to him reflected off his impish face for a moment, then he disappeared in the dark again. I heard the rattle of metal, then watched the two guards drop to the ground.

I watched the two bodies struggle to stand. The floor beneath them was covered in ice. It glistened like flecks of glitter beneath the hanging flames. Pure, silver ice coated the floor.

"Tiv," I said as he jumped over the shadowbeing's reaching hands.

"Tiv is here to rescue you."

I released a breath of relief.

Tiv ran for the Queen's cell first, bowing as he unlocked the door. He had taken keys from the guards as they fell. The shadowbeings struggled to stand, over and over, falling back down.

Tiv had moments before the shadowbeings regained their composure and caught him. Their animated, lifeless bodies could not work out the puzzle that had become of them, but they would in time.

"You are a good boy," Queen Kathine said, turning so the chains faced him. As if it was rehearsed, he raised a hand and touched the chains. A cold whisper spread beneath his fingers, turning the grey chain white. Then with a giant tug they snapped beneath the Queen's strength.

She moved quickly, running towards the fallen guards and pulling a sword from one of their scarabs.

"May the Goddess accept you," she said before bringing the sword in an arch from the dark room. The thud of their two heads hitting the ground was heavy. Tiv did not watch.

"Open the cells; freeze their chains," Queen Kathine commanded.

"Tiv will."

Illera was let out, then Nyah. Illera ran for Emaline who was slumped on the ground, and Nyah came to help me. I tried to push the pain and weakness into the pits of my body. She fumbled to help me up. The pain didn't hinder my want to escape. Knowing Hadrian was out there, I needed to return to him.

"Tiv, do you remember the route?" Queen Kathine questioned.

He nodded. "Tiv never forgets a good hiding place."

"Then take them. Get them out of the city. Go, go."

Nyah began to move me towards the stairs, but Tiv stopped her with a hand.

"This way. Follow Tiv."

We stumbled through the dark prison, leaving Queen Kathine in the dark behind us. No one complained or urged her to follow. I knew she'd rather die than leave her city.

My feet half dragged on the floor, but Nyah kept me upright as we moved ahead. When we reached the end, Tiv moved a large rug that hung on the wall to the side, revealing a small, narrow tunnel in the wall.

"We must hurry," Tiv said, his voice light and filled with innocence. "Long tunnel till we see light. Let Tiv guide the way."

Tiv climbed into the tunnel first. On his hands and knees, he shuffled into the dark hole.

Illera went next, she pushed Emaline in first and went in after. Nyah helped me towards it.

"You go first. I will slow us down," I said, pushing at her arm with as much force as I could muster.

Nyah nodded.

She climbed into the tunnel and followed after the group. I turned for the room. I didn't know what it was that caught my attention. There was no noise, only a rush of wind. It was faint at first, but it was growing. The gold distorted my reality. I could not tell if the sound was phantom or not. If I had access to my magick, I would have sensed what it meant.

"Stop!" Marthil screamed. She sped through the air, flying towards me.

I barely had time to gasp as she slammed into my body and my back connected with the wall. My breath rushed from me, and my awareness faded.

In the movement, I used the little strength I could muster and grabbed a hold of her pointed horns. With a yank I pulled them down, and her face connected with my waiting knee.

Nyah tried to yank my foot through the tunnel, but Marthil's hold was superior.

"Get out of here!" I coughed as Marthil raked a talon into my shoulder. Warmth spread down my arm and across my dirtied tunic.

Go. I pushed the word into her mind.

I felt her hand let go of my ankle. Marthil dropped me to the ground, ready to stop their escape.

As she reached through the tunnel with a snarl, I reached for her.

My arm strained as I pressed the gold band into the exposed skin of Marthil's back and held it there. She fell instantly, her Dragori form melting away before my very eyes.

Keep your eyes open, I told myself. The want to give into the waiting darkness was unbearable, but I needed to give Nyah a chance to escape. They had to leave.

"Let go of me," Marthil cried, her voice sounded different as she pleaded. "Please, stop."

Her begging was wasted on me. I kept the gold band pressed into her as she tried to pull it away with fumbling hands. For the life of me, I would never let go.

CHAPTER
Thirty Eight

I CAME TO on a bed of cloud.

Rolling to my side, I extended a hand towards Hadrian, ready to wrap my arms around him. In the bliss of sleep, I was not aware of the time and events that had happened, but when my hand reached an empty space, everything came flooding back.

I bolted up right and looked around the room, for I was not alone.

Four shadowbeings stood guard in each corner of my room. Black shadow seeped from their eyes, mouths and ears. I scrambled to the head board and curled my naked body into a ball. It was day now. A full sun hung in the sky beyond my room, giving the city a sense of calm, but I could still see pillars of smoke rising from the streets in the valley below.

"Finally, you are awake," Gordex muttered. He was perched on the end of my bed, his back towards me. "I was very close to killing you, Zacriah. I lost a sense of what I needed you for and only wanted to punish you for trying to escape. But then I remembered."

He turned slowly to face me, his inked face and dark eyes youthful for such an old being.

"Thank you for your Heart Magick. I must say your soul is a powerful one. I suppose you had a lot to fight for. I had the gold band removed. There is no need for it now that I have what I wanted. Your magick. But I have decided to leave your soul intact, not like your precious love who still rests in the orb within my robe. I believed it would be nice for Marthil to have someone similar until, well... until you both help me get the final piece to this puzzle."

I looked down to my wrist, not that I needed to. I could sense the lack of gold wrapped around it.

My words were lost to me. As I investigated the eyes of the man before me, I wondered if my friends had escaped. The sense of loneliness that encased me was enough of an answer.

"Your chance at raising the druids has failed," I spat, pulling the white sheet to cover my chest.

"For now, yes. But I have spent many years admiring failure. If you think this minor hiccup in my plans means the end to them, then you are wrong." He leaned in close, so his hot breath caused my throat to tighten in disgust. "They will come back for you, and when they do, I will get what I want most. The final Heart Magick of the Dragori."

His open threat to my friends caused anger to burst through me. He may have a link to my power, but I felt connected to the air once again, this time in a much stronger way.

I raised a hand, calling for the air to wrap around Gordex. It roared and screamed as it moved around the room, ripping his dark power from the four shadowbeings bodies until they crumpled to the ground. This magick was more powerful than ever before. Like Cristilia's story, I was the monster now.

Gordex's gaze did not waver for a single moment. He showed no signs of pain or discomfort as I lifted him from the bed where he sat and into the air. My air. He only smiled, and his laugh melded with the song of my wind.

"I admire your attempt, but as good as I am at failure, so are you." Gordex opened his arms and my magick drained from me. I watched it gather around his hand, in a ball of silver streams. He slowly relaxed to the floor and lifted his other hand. A ball of red flame encased it, crawling up his fingers and arm.

His tongue clicked in slow tuts, and the floor shook.

"As you can see, I may have left your magick within you, but I too have control of it. And when Emaline returns, I will have the final piece. Then this world will see just how powerful the new age of druids will be."

"I will kill you," I promised.

"Riddle me this." Gordex smiled. "How do you kill someone who is already in the grasps of death?"

Before I could conjure my answer, Gordex opened his arms wide. Fire and earth exploded from his palms and blinded me. The ground shook a final time in warning.

"Time to get up, for I have someone I would like you to meet," Gordex said as he walked for the door. "The man who was once King is anxious to meet you."

❈ The End ❈

ACKNOWLEDGEMENTS

Jill, for helping me bring this book to life. For sculpting it from stone into the statue we are both proud to share.

Gwenn, for the art once again. Your skill, talent and friendship truly inspire me. There is a part of me who writes the books just so I can work with you again.

Claire and Chris, for this amazing formatting. Thank you for helping bring this to life. Without you it literally would be words on a page. Also, being my support through everything, and I mean everything. I know I have you in my life forever. Thank you.

Emily, for being such a good friend over these years.

The Quinns, thank you for embracing me with open arms. I am blessed to have met you and will always love you.

Harry, for being Harry. I love you.

Readers, for keeping this dream of mine alive. Publishing without the support of a traditional publisher is hard. But you all make it easier. Thank you for being such an open-hearted team.

Book 3

Poisoned In Light

Coming Soon…

COMING SOON

THE OFTOMES 2018 DEBUTS

EMPRESS UNVEILED BY JENNA MORLAND

"A fast-paced, mystical adventure mixed with heartbreak and hope that will keep you turning the page well into the night." **Brenda Drake**, New York Times bestselling author.

COMING AUGUST 2018

SAVING DEATH BY R. L. ENDEAN

"A heart-pounding romance you'll love curling up with on a dark, chilly night!" **Lorie Langdon**, author of the Doon Series and Olivia Twist.

COMING OCTOBER 2018